W9-ATR-031

A Winter by the Sea

Books by Julie Klassen

ON DEVONSHIRE
SHORES ✦ 2

*A Winter
by the Sea*

JULIE
KLASSEN

BETHANYHOUSE
a division of Baker Publishing Group
Minneapolis, Minnesota

Published by Bethany House Publishers
Minneapolis, Minnesota
www.bethanyhouse.com

Bethany House Publishers is a division of
Baker Publishing Group, Grand Rapids, Michigan

Printed in the United States of America

Library of Congress Cataloging-in-Publication Data
Names: Klassen, Julie, author.
Title: A winter by the sea / Julie Klassen.
Description: Minneapolis, Minnesota : Bethany House, 2023. | Series: On Devonshire shores ; 2
Identifiers: LCCN 2023030984 | ISBN 9780764234286 (paper) | ISBN 9780764234293 (cloth) | ISBN 9780764236235 (large print) | ISBN 9781493443628 (ebook)
Subjects: LCGFT: Christian fiction. | Romance fiction. | Novels.
Classification: LCC PS3611.L37 W56 2023 | DDC 813/.6—dc23/eng/20230711
LC record available at https://lccn.loc.gov/2023030984

Scripture quotations are from the King James Version of the Bible.

This is a work of historical reconstruction; the appearances of certain historical figures are therefore inevitable. All other characters, however, are products of the author's imagination, and any resemblance to actual persons, living or dead, is coincidental.

Map illustration by Bek Cruddace Cartography & Illustration

Published in association with Books & Such Literary Management,
52 Mission Circle, Suite 122
PMB 170, Santa Rosa, CA 95409-5370
www.booksandsuch.com

Baker Publishing Group publications use paper produced from sustainable forestry practices and post-consumer waste whenever possible.

23 24 25 26 27 28 29   7 6 5 4 3 2 1

To Nigel Hyman
and the staff and volunteers
of the Sidmouth Museum,
who have been so generous
and helpful in researching
and reviewing the books
in this series.

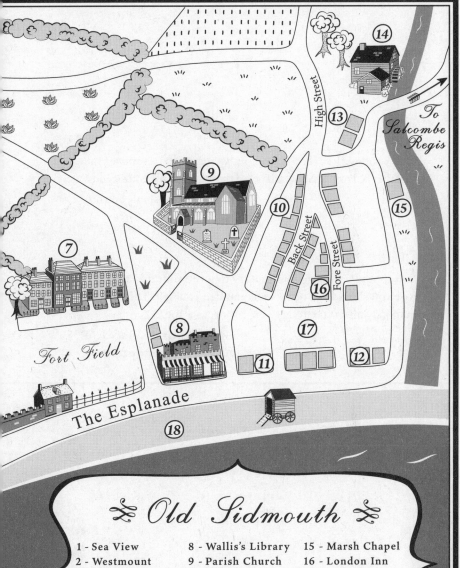

High Street

To
Salcombe
Regis

Back Street

Fore Street

Fort Field

The Esplanade

⇜ Old Sidmouth ⇝

1 - Sea View

2 - Westmount

3 - Woolbrook

4 - Peak House

5 - Heffer's Row

6 - Old Fort

7 - Fortfield Terr.

8 - Wallis's Library

9 - Parish Church

10 - Old Ship Inn

11 - Baths

12 - York Hotel

13 - Poor House

14 - Water Mill

15 - Marsh Chapel

16 - London Inn

17 - Marketplace

18 - Beach

19 - Chit Rock

20 - Lime Kiln

21 - Western Beach

I still continue [sea] bathing notwithstanding the severity of the Weather & Frost & Snow which is I think somewhat courageous.

—Eliza de Feuillide (Jane Austen's cousin)

You should have a clever secretary to write your dispatches in case you should not be so well qualified yourself. This gentleman may also serve to get you out of a scrape.

—Francis Grose, *Advice to the Officers of the British Army*

Go on doing with your pen what in other times was done with the sword.

—Thomas Jefferson, letter to Thomas Paine

1

Many wearing rapiers are afraid of goose-quills.
—William Shakespeare, *Hamlet*

OCTOBER 1819

I f a quill pen was truly more powerful than a rapier, as Shakespeare suggested, then a pen must also be more powerful than a needle.

Emily Summers mused on this as she sat in the parlour, writing in a notebook. Around her, her mother and sisters sewed together over tea and pleasant conversation. Even Viola, her recently married twin, had come over from Westmount with her needlework bag to join them. Only their oldest sister, Claire, was absent.

Emily was not fond of sewing and, except for one childish sampler completed years before, avoided the task. The only one of her family less skilled with a needle was the youngest, sixteen-year-old Georgiana, who sat bent over a wad of fabric and knotted embroidery floss that was supposed to become her sampler. Mamma required each of her girls to finish one, insisting all young ladies should be skilled in needlework.

Glancing at Georgie's bird's nest of tangled thread, Emily

doubted her mother's aspirations would come to fruition. Emily's own sampler had not been much better. Mamma had not even bothered to frame it as she had the others. Viola's and Sarah's hung in Mamma's room even now. She had no idea where Claire's had ended up.

Despite the warm chatter around her and the warm tea inside her, Emily felt a cold knot of emptiness in her chest. An awareness that something or someone was missing—or more accurately, two someones.

She paused to consider the feeling. She had long desired three things in life: to be reunited with her eldest sister, to return to May Hill and marry Charles Parker, and to become a published author. She had little confidence any of these would ever happen. Claire was living in exile in Scotland after a failed elopement, and Charles, the neighbor Emily had always loved, had broken her heart by cutting ties with their family at that threat of scandal.

Despite all that, however, her last goal seemed the most unlikely.

With a sigh, Emily scratched out a few more lines in the novel she was attempting to write. It felt as tangled and patternless as Georgiana's sampler.

Giving up, she placed the quill back in its holder, set the notebook aside, and picked up a book instead. She had begun reading a new work Mr. Wallis had lately published called *Scenery on the Southern Coast of Devonshire; Comprising Picturesque Views, at or near the Fashionable Watering Places: Sidmouth, Budleigh Salterton, Exmouth, Dawlish, Teignmouth, and Torquay*. Why authors insisted on such long titles, she did not know.

Emily had not been to all the featured towns. Her interest was piqued by their descriptions, and she hoped she might one day visit them.

At the thought of travel, she caught her twin sister's eye. "Any progress in convincing the major to take a wedding trip?"

Viola lifted one shoulder in an unconcerned shrug, her focus returning to the new shirt she was stitching for her husband. "Jack is not keen to travel. Not yet, at any rate. Had his fill sailing to and from India." She turned toward their older sister. "Would you please pass the scissors?"

Sarah paused in her embroidery to oblige her.

Viola snipped a thread, then shifted her gaze to the volume in Emily's lap. "How is Mr. Wallis's new book?"

"Interesting. Although it would have been improved by skillful editing. I have noticed several repetitions and missing words."

Viola nodded. "I know I've said it before, but you should offer to edit for him."

"I doubt he would appreciate my interference," Emily replied. "Not everyone admires my ability to point out the mistakes of others." She winked at Viola, who had been a regular recipient of Emily's criticisms in the past. Thankfully their relationship had improved over the last year.

"Perhaps if he learns of your talents, he would also be willing to publish your novel—that is, if you ever finish it."

Emily tilted her head to study her sister's face. "Why are you so eager to find employment for me? I am hardly idle."

Georgiana spoke up. "It's only fair. After all, you found employment for Vi, placing that advertisement without her knowledge."

"It worked out rather well, you must admit," Emily defended.

Her twin looked up from her needle with a barely suppressed smile and a hint of a blush. "It certainly did."

Viola had been born with a cleft lip. Although it had been repaired after several surgeries, she still bore a vertical scar from nostril to mouth and a shortening of her upper lip, both of which were barely noticeable. Even so, Viola had always avoided people outside the family, living like a recluse. Begrudgingly, she had begun reading to invalids after that advertisement appeared in print. Through it, she met her future husband, along with a dear friend who lived in the poor house, and Viola's life had changed for the better.

Might Emily's own life be changed by taking on some new employment as well?

"I can talk to him for you, if you'd like," Viola said. "Just to return the favor."

"No, thank you. I can talk to Mr. Wallis myself . . . should I decide to. I don't know that I'd have time to edit for him with my responsibilities here."

Nearby, Mamma grumbled as she struggled to rethread the small eye of her needle, then glanced up over her half-moon spectacles. "Actually, this might be a good time. Things are quieter now that autumn has arrived. Some people overwinter here, but it's unlikely we shall be busy during the colder months, especially over Christmas."

"I shall think about it," Emily said and returned to her book.

After a few minutes of comfortable silence, the front-door knocker sounded. Georgiana eagerly tossed aside her needlework to answer it, even though their housemaid, Jessie, would have done so, given the chance.

A moment later, their friend and former lady's maid bustled in, all aflutter, Georgiana on her heels.

"Astounding news, ladies!" Fran Stirling proclaimed. "I could not wait to tell you. You will never guess. You are to have royal neighbors!"

"Royal neighbors? Besides Viola, do you mean?" Emily teased.

"Yes, even more royal, if you can imagine."

Mamma sat forward. "Not the Prince Regent—not when he has the Brighton Pavilion?"

"No." Fran's cheeks rounded with an eager, pursed-lip smile. "One of his brothers. The Duke of Kent, his wife, and their baby daughter. Not to mention a whole suite of servants."

"Where are they to stay?" Sarah asked. She patted a nearby chair, and Fran sat.

"Woolbrook Cottage."

"No!" Viola exclaimed. "That's just beyond our house."

Fran nodded, eyes alight. "General Baynes has leased it to them for the winter, although the arrangement is supposed to be a secret."

"Then how did you learn of it?" Sarah asked, not truly surprised, for Miss Stirling seemed to be acquainted with everyone in town and heard the latest news well before they did.

"The general hired Mr. Farrant to carry out a few repairs on the place before Their Royal Highnesses' arrival."

"Ah." Sarah smiled. "Leave it to you to know the very person."

Mamma thoughtfully shook her head. "And here we anticipated an uneventful winter."

The following day, as Sarah and Emily tidied the dining room after luncheon, a sharp triple knock rattled the front door.

Sarah and her sister shared a look and then made their way into the drawing room to receive the unexpected callers. Mamma and Georgiana joined them as Jessie led two tall strangers into the room.

13

The young maid, her eyes wide and fearful, squeaked, "Captain something and . . . oh, I forget." She turned and fled the room.

The older of the pair, who looked to be in his midthirties, frowned after her. "Is the girl feebleminded?"

Sarah's face heated in both embarrassment and indignation, yet she managed a calm reply. "Not at all. Only easily intimidated."

"Ah." The older man seemed to take the words as a compliment, his broad shoulders straightening yet more. He wore civilian dress but possessed an officious military bearing and a severe expression.

He looked to his companion, who was nearly as tall, although younger.

The younger man obeyed the silent command and completed the introductions in a low, eloquent voice. "This is Captain John Conroy, equerry to the Duke of Kent and Strathearn. And I am James Thomson, private secretary."

Both men bowed smartly.

Mamma nodded, while Emily curtsied, her gaze fixed on the younger man's handsome face. Belatedly, Georgiana lumbered to her feet and followed Emily's example, although with far less grace.

Sarah clasped her hands to conceal their nervous tremble. "I am Miss Sarah Summers. This is my mother, Mrs. Summers, and these are my sisters. How may we help you, gentlemen?"

With a brisk nod, the captain replied, "The Duchess of Kent requires a milder climate for her health. Therefore, His Royal Highness and I have selected Sidmouth as an ideal winter residence."

Georgie blurted, "We know."

The man scowled, leveling a suspicious glare at her. "Who told you? The news is not yet public."

"I . . . That is, our . . ."

Sarah squeezed Georgie's hand to forestall her, not wanting to cause any trouble for Miss Stirling.

"It is only natural that such good news should travel quickly through town," the secretary said, clearly trying to smooth things over. "General Baynes, or the property agent, or the tradespeople we've contacted might have mentioned it."

"Very true," Sarah said. "It is an exciting prospect."

Mamma added, "An honor for us all."

The captain huffed before continuing. "Their Royal Highnesses shall reside in Woolbrook Cottage with as many attendants as the house can accommodate, which unfortunately is not all. The duke travels with a large suite of servants, advisers, et cetera. We have also rented a house in Fortfield Terrace for the upper staff, but we need accommodation for a few others. We understand you run a sort of boarding house here."

"Yes," Mamma agreed. "Although we prefer the term *guest house*."

He ignored that. "How many rooms have you available?"

They all looked to Sarah.

"We have six guest rooms," she said. "Seven if we include a small adjoining chamber. Three rooms are now occupied, but all save one shall be available come the end of the month."

Their current guests included a Mr. and Mrs. Johnson, who shared one room, while their twin sons slept in the adjoining chamber. The family planned to stay with them through October. Mr. Hornbeam was their other guest, and as far as Sarah knew, he had no plans to leave.

"How soon would you need accommodation?" she asked the men.

"Not until December."

"Would you like to see the rooms?"

Captain Conroy waved a dismissive hand. "No need. I am

sure they will suffice for lower staff. Proximity to Woolbrook is key. I estimate we shall need an additional three or four rooms."

"And the specific dates?"

"Yet to be determined. Mr. Thomson here will write and apprise you of all pertinent details once arrangements are finalized."

Sarah hesitated. They were to hold in reserve four rooms with no specified arrival date? She was tempted to protest, to say they could not promise to keep rooms available without guaranteed dates, but Captain Conroy's fierce expression dampened her courage.

Besides, as Mamma had said, things had been quiet and guests few. The prospect of three or four rooms occupied for the entire winter was an opportunity they could ill afford to jeopardize.

"Very well," Sarah said. "We shall await your instructions."

2

John Wallis, proprietor of the Marine Library,
was not one to miss a chance to be able to add
the prefix 'Royal' to his establishment.

—Nigel Hyman,
Sidmouth's Royal Connections

With Viola's exhortation echoing in her mind, Emily
walked to the Marine Library to speak to Mr. Wallis, respected local publisher and bookseller.
The slight, bespectacled widower in his forties possessed a
thin, intelligent face. Single females flocked to his circulating
library, but Emily had never seen him show romantic interest
in any of them. His attention seemed firmly fixed on his two
sons and his many publishing ventures.

While other women cooed over his tales of famous visitors,
Emily had always been more interested in the authors he'd
met over the years. During the twelvemonth the Summerses
had lived in Sidmouth, Emily and Mr. Wallis had enjoyed
many conversations about books and authors. Surely the man
realized how well-read she was. Was Viola right? Might he
be willing to allow her to edit future works for him, perhaps

correcting galley proofs when they arrived from the printer? If so, she would enjoy earning a little money of her own while learning all she could about publishing.

Reaching Wallis's establishment, Emily tentatively entered. The jingle of the library door usually gave her a thrill of pleasure. Not today, however. She was too nervous.

Inside, she looked at the desk and among the shelves of games, maps, and periodicals. She saw neither Mr. Wallis nor his usual clerk. Instead, she saw only the older of his two adolescent sons, sitting on a stool, idly swinging his feet.

Perhaps Mr. Wallis had gone upstairs for something and would return any moment.

Approaching the boy, she said, "Good day. Is your father available?"

"No, miss. Gone to meet someone at the York Hotel. I'm to stay here and watch the till."

"I see. Will he be back soon?"

"Don't know."

"Very well. Keep up the good work."

She gave the boy a smile and left the establishment. She wondered who Mr. Wallis might be meeting—another famous author, perhaps? Emily's spirits lifted at the thought.

She continued east along the esplanade toward the large seafront hotel. Not far past it stood Sidmouth's other library, which Emily had never entered. Her family's coffers did not extend to subscriptions at two circulating libraries.

Entering the York Hotel vestibule, she saw no one about but followed the sound of voices to an open door opposite the reception desk. This room appeared to be a private parlour, with blue-and-cream-papered walls, fine upholstered furniture, and a long case clock. Mr. Wallis stood within, talking with three other men. On a table before them were spread two long prints of some kind.

Compared with Mr. Wallis's slender frame and scholarly appearance, the three other gentlemen boasted tall, straight-backed, masculine bearings. She recognized the tallest two from their visit to Sea View—the imposing Captain Conroy and the duke's handsome private secretary. She eyed the third man, on whom everyone's attention seemed to rest. This older man struck her as vaguely familiar, with his broad figure, bald pate, and thick L-shaped side-whiskers. Not a famous author, then. This, she realized, was Prince Edward himself, the Duke of Kent.

She had seen drawings of the former military man in the newspapers—although they were most often unflattering caricatures.

Mr. Wallis said, "Your Royal Highness, please allow me to present to you this engraving of a much-admired panorama of Sidmouth, which I commissioned by the well-known artist Hubert Cornish."

The prince expressed his decided approbation and graciously replied, "It will afford me much pleasure to show it to Her Royal Highness."

They continued their conversation, and a few minutes later the meeting concluded. Captain Conroy was the first to turn toward the door. Emily quickly stepped back, but not before his black-eyed gaze flicked over her with decided *dis*approbation.

As the visiting men exited the parlour and proceeded out of the hotel, the duke's private secretary glanced back at her with a brief nod of recognition.

Mr. Wallis was the last to emerge, looking both exultant and exhausted.

He paused upon seeing her. "Ah, Miss Summers."

"Quite august company you keep," she said.

"Do you know who that was?"

"I believe so, yes."

"I should not say anything. Not yet."

She confided, "If it concerns the royal guests visiting Sidmouth, I already know. At least in part."

"Do you indeed?" He blinked at her from behind his small rectangular spectacles. "And how are you privy to such information?"

"Some of his staff are to stay at Sea View."

"Ah, I see."

She gestured toward the recently vacated room. "And how did you manage to arrange such a meeting?"

He stepped closer and lowered his voice, expression animated. "I am glad you know who has come, for I may burst if I can't tell someone. When General Baynes mentioned in confidence that a certain personage would be visiting Sidmouth to consider properties, I made so bold as to write to invite His Royal Highness to meet me here so I might present him with an engraving of the long print of Sidmouth. I was never so stunned as when his secretary wrote back to accept. What a privilege!"

"Well done," Emily praised. She quickly decided that this was not the best time to mention the errors she had found in his latest publication.

Instead, she walked quietly out of the hotel with him. As they reached the esplanade, Emily glanced toward the beach and saw a man at the water's edge wearing only a towel wrapped around his waist. She barely stifled a gasp.

The man picked up a long floral dressing gown from a rock and pushed his arms into the sleeves, adjusting each velvet-trimmed cuff.

He sauntered toward them, robe open, belt hanging loose, center of his chest bared.

Mr. Wallis turned to see what had drawn her attention and frowned. "Popinjay," he muttered.

The man's curly dark hair fell over his forehead. Long, sharply angled side-whiskers framed a face that—while not handsome—was interesting, with a nose that seemed almost Mediterranean, its center portion dipping nearer his lips.

As he neared, he gave her companion a sardonic smile. "Ah. Wallis. You should have joined me. Nothing so refreshing as a bracing dip in the sea. The shock of the cold water drives the blood from the skin, and immediately brings it back to the surface." He pounded a fist to his chest. "Now my entire body glows with warmth and vitality. Whereas you . . ." His gaze flickered over Wallis's rather spindly form with meaning, but he let the sentence go unfinished.

Without apparent self-consciousness over his state of undress, he dipped his head to Emily and passed by with a polite "Miss."

She turned and watched him continue on, following the esplanade to its end.

"Who is that?" she asked uneasily.

Again Mr. Wallis frowned. "My competition."

When Emily returned to Sea View a few minutes later, she heard Mr. Gwilt's singsong voice in the parlour and realized he was probably entertaining the twin sons of Mr. and Mrs. Johnson again.

Whenever Emily saw the ten-year-old boys, she was reminded of her own twin sister, although the boys looked far more alike than she and Viola ever had. Her sister had reddish-brown hair and hazel eyes, while Emily's hair and eyes were dark brown. Viola was also smaller, though she occupied a large part of Emily's heart. Emily missed Viola's daily presence now that she was married and living with her husband. Thankfully, Westmount was only a short walk up the lane, and the two visited each other often.

Mr. Gwilt had been a guest himself last summer and had stayed on as part-time accounts clerk and odd-job man, assisting their increasingly frail manservant, Lowen.

A widower of about fifty, Mr. Gwilt was a small Welshman with an amiable disposition, unfailingly kind to all. Yet he possessed one peculiarity. He'd arrived at Sea View with an eyebrow-raising companion—a parrot in a cage, kept lifelike thanks to the efforts of a friend who dabbled in taxidermy. Moreover, Mr. Gwilt had the unsettling habit of speaking about and to his feathered companion as though he were still alive.

While at first wary of the man, Emily had come to like him. Especially after she'd learned he had long devoted himself to caring for a wife who had lost her memory and ability to speak. During those years of silent isolation, he'd talked to Parry to assuage the loneliness. And even after the parrot died, the habit lingered.

That tendency had diminished in recent months as Mr. Gwilt found his place in Sea View, becoming one of their retainers and nearly one of the family. He still mentioned Parry often but acknowledged the bird was no longer alive.

Once Mr. Gwilt transitioned from guest to staff, Sarah had insisted that he keep the parrot in the room they had given him belowstairs near Lowen and their cook.

But Sarah had made an exception when Mrs. Johnson told her how much their sons enjoyed the tales of Parry's adventures Mr. Gwilt made up to entertain the boys on rainy days. When the boys begged to see the parrot, Sarah had relented, but only while the boys were in residence, she reminded him.

Now Emily paused in the parlour doorway to listen. The parrot was perched in his cage on the side table, while Mr. Gwilt perched in the armchair nearby. The boys knelt before the cage, gazing in wonder at the colorful creature.

"As a young bird, Parry longed to see more of the world," Mr. Gwilt told them. "Wanted to be famous, he did. So he bid farewell to his island home and flew off in search of his destiny. Parry flew and flew, but no matter how far he went, he could not find land. He grew exhausted and finally had to return home.

"Then one day, a ship dropped anchor in the bay. Sailors rowed to the island in small boats to gather fresh fruit and water. The leader of these men lured Parry with a bet o' mango, captured him, and put him in a cage. Parry was sure his life was over. He would soon disappear and the world would remember him no more!"

Emily listened with interest until Mrs. Johnson appeared to tell the boys it was time to dress for dinner. The two groaned, but Mr. Gwilt assured them he would continue the tale another time.

He and Emily watched the trio depart, then Emily asked, "Have you ever thought of writing down Parry's adventures? They would make a wonderful children's book if the Johnson boys are any indication."

"No, lass. I just make it up as I go, I do. Couldn't write it down. I am a man of numbers, not letters."

"I could help you."

"Oh, now. You have too much to do as it is."

"Not at all. I would enjoy it. You might as well."

"I suppose we could give it a go, when I am not needed elsewhere."

"Excellent!" Emily replied. She had not succeeded in furthering her own aspirations that day, but the thought of helping someone else lifted her spirits.

They began that very evening.

3

Oh, that joy so soon should waste!
Or so sweet a bliss
As a kiss
Might not for ever last!
—Ben Jonson, "The Kiss"

A few weeks later, Emily sat alone in the bedroom she shared with Sarah, trying to compose a new scene in her novel.

After a time, she paused to reread the last line she had written, groaned in disgust, and scratched it out. She was attempting to write a romantic scene between hero and heroine, and to describe their first kiss. She felt ill-qualified. How was she to describe experiences and sensations foreign to her?

For the truth was, Emily had never been kissed. Not romantically. And a kiss from one's mamma did not count.

Charles Parker had almost kissed her once—at least she had thought he'd been about to before they were interrupted. Yet Emily wasn't sure she ought to try to recall that occasion in much detail, when doing so would be painful, considering how he had distanced himself soon afterward.

Instead, hoping for inspiration, she pulled out a special notebook where she'd jotted down romantic lines from novels and poetry.

She flipped a few pages and read part of a Ben Jonson poem she'd copied.

> *So sugared, so melting, so soft, so delicious. . . .*
> *O, rather than it would I smother,*
> *Were I to taste such another;*
> *It should be my wishing*
> *That I might die kissing.*

Sugared, melting, soft, and delicious sounded good. But to die kissing? That seemed a bit extreme.

Emily sighed and shut the notebook.

Perhaps she ought to visit the circulating library and find a new romance or book of poetry to read as "research." She loved to read, and sadly for her, reading was far easier and pleasanter than the arduous work of writing.

So that afternoon, Emily again walked down the esplanade toward Mr. Wallis's establishment. Ahead of her, two women stepped from the circulating library onto its awning-covered veranda, pausing to talk.

"He was in a strange mood today."

"I agree—not nearly as amiable as he usually is."

"And here I wore my new hat." The woman sniffed. "Ah well. Oh! You are coming to my party tonight, I trust? I've hired a fortune-teller to entertain us—a frightful old crone. It should be excessively diverting."

To Emily, the prospect sounded more horrid than entertaining, but as the women walked away, concern for Mr. Wallis overrode other thoughts. Had something bad happened to cause his strange mood? Was he unwell?

She pushed through the library door and saw him slouched in a chair at his desk.

"Good day, Mr. Wallis."

Despite his usually impeccable manners, the proprietor failed to rise in a woman's presence, and the fair eyes behind his spectacles seemed oddly dazed.

He blinked up at her. "Ah. Miss Summers. You will never guess what has happened."

"Nothing bad, I hope?"

"Quite the opposite. It's too good for words."

"Do tell me!"

Leaning forward across the desk, he began, "Do you remember when His Royal Highness, the Duke of Kent, came to town last month looking for a suitable property? And I presented him with the panorama of Sidmouth?"

She nodded. "Of course."

"I have just received a letter. From Kensington Palace of all places! I have the amazing honor of being appointed 'Bookseller to Their Royal Highnesses.' My dear Miss Summers . . ." His voice shook. "This is my proudest moment." He gazed in awe somewhere over her shoulder. "You know what this means, do you not? Prince Edward extended his royal patronage. My establishment can now rightly be called the *Royal Marine Library.* Is that not astounding?"

"Oh, Mr. Wallis! I am so happy for you."

He nodded, and his vague gaze suddenly sharpened.

"Let's see that young upstart top that."

A short while later, Emily emerged from Wallis's Library, a newly borrowed book cradled in her arms.

Lost in thought, she did not see the man approach until he was almost upon her. Looking up, she jerked in surprise, dropping the book with a gasp.

Here was the man she had last seen clad in nothing but a towel and dressing gown. The "upstart" himself—Mr. Wallis's younger, flamboyant competitor.

He was now fully dressed in gentlemen's attire, albeit far more colorful than most—burgundy frock coat over floral waistcoat.

"Allow me." He bent to retrieve the book from the rolled earth of the esplanade.

Straightening, he wiped the dust from the cover and read the title on the spine. "Excellent choice. I admire your taste in poetry." He glanced at the door she had just exited through before returning his gaze to her. "If not your choice of library."

She gaped at him, feeling unaccountably self-conscious. Even embarrassed.

"Then again"—the corner of his narrow mouth quirked—"if this is how you treat books, perhaps I should be relieved you frequent Wallis's."

She swallowed a guilty lump. "I . . . I am usually more careful."

His blue-green eyes sparkled with humor, and she realized he was teasing her. "I am relieved to hear it."

He bowed. "Good day, Miss Summers."

With that he turned and swept away.

She watched him saunter down the esplanade, tipping his hat to ladies as he went. Emily supposed they must have seen each other from a distance around town in the past, but she was sure they had never been introduced. Mr. Wallis had certainly not deigned to do so.

Then how did he know her name?

Sarah sat at her worktable in the parlour, embroidering small flowers onto a needle case. The worktable contained compartments for needlework supplies, and the silk bag suspended beneath held fabric.

As she stitched, thoughts of Callum Henshall revisited her, unbidden. The musical Scotsman and his stepdaughter had been their very first guests last spring. When they departed, he left her with a small memento—and a heart torn between duty and longing.

Sarah laid her embroidery in her lap and opened one of the table's compartments. From it she carefully withdrew the spiky thistle—spiny bulb, dried-flower crown—the symbol of Scotland. Mr. Henshall's handsome face shimmered in her mind's eye, looking at her with warm admiration and a hint of sadness. For a long moment Sarah stilled, staring off into her memories and feeling wistful.

Georgiana came into the parlour, letter in hand. "Effie has written again. Remember Effie?"

Sarah looked up with a start, neck heating, as if caught doing something wrong. She was glad her little sister could not read her thoughts.

Sliding the thistle back into the compartment, Sarah replied, "Of course I remember Effie."

Georgiana had befriended the younger girl during their stay, and Sarah had grown fond of both Effie and Mr. Henshall. In fact, she thought of the kind, attractive widower far more often than she ought.

"She mentions you in it," Georgie said, tossing the letter onto the table before her.

Georgiana turned to go, and Sarah noticed she was dressed for the outdoors in cap, spencer, and half boots.

"Where are you off to?"

"Cricket on Fort Field."

"Who else is playing?"

Georgiana shrugged. "That apprentice Billy Hook will be there. Hopefully several other lads as well."

"Any other girls?"

Another shrug. "Hannah promised to come. Though I doubt she shall play. She mostly comes to ogle the boys."

"Well, I am glad your friend will be with you. Have a good time."

When they'd first come to Sidmouth, Mamma had insisted her daughters accompany each other on walks and errands into the eastern town. But they had been there for a year now, and Mamma had relaxed her rules. The Summerses trusted their neighbors and felt safe in the area. Besides, the playing field was only a short walk from Sea View.

When Georgie had gone, Sarah skimmed Effie's girlish, chatty letter until she came to the lines directed to her.

"Please do greet Sarah for me and tell her I think of her at least once a month. She'll know what that means!"

A smile tickled Sarah's mouth as she recalled having to explain some feminine facts of life to the girl, but her smile quickly faded when she realized that was the extent of the message addressed to her.

In past letters, Effie had usually written something about her stepfather sending along his greetings, but not this time. Perhaps Mr. Henshall had forgotten her. Or met someone new. And why should he not? After all, she had discouraged his overtures, even his request that he might write to her directly.

This is for the best, she told herself.

Her heart did not agree.

Dinner that evening was a refreshingly casual affair, Sarah decided, gazing around the table at her family. Mr. and Mrs.

Johnson and their sons had departed, and their only remaining guest was Simon Hornbeam.

Mr. Hornbeam had been with them for several months now. He was a dear man of about sixty who had become one of the family, almost like a kindly grandfather. He had remained on as guest—his finances being more robust than Mr. Gwilt's—after his grown son had failed to join him in Sidmouth. He had also met a former acquaintance in town, a Miss Reed, which probably helped explain why he'd stayed on so long.

As they began the meal, Emily asked, "I wonder why the Duke of Kent would come to Sidmouth . . . especially at this time of year. Surely Woolbrook Cottage cannot compare to Kensington Palace?"

Sarah said, "The captain mentioned wanting a milder climate for the duchess's health, remember?"

"That may be the officially stated reason," Mr. Hornbeam said. "But not the only one."

They all turned toward him. The older man had been clerk assistant of the House of Commons until his eyesight failed him. He still had many acquaintances in Parliament and knew a great deal more than the rest of them about government and the royal family.

As if aware of their scrutiny, he tilted his head in thought and adjusted his dark glasses. "I don't think it such a secret that I should not mention it. In fact, it is well-known in political circles that Prince Edward is in debt. From my limited experience, I believe he is a clever, well-read man but has a lifelong habit of spending well above his means. A London committee, which included his comptroller, advised him to economize. He is coming here primarily to retrench."

"So," Mamma said, "we are not alone in having to change our mode of living due to financial constraints."

"No indeed. You are in good company. Quite august company, as a matter of fact."

"I know I should recall this," Emily said, "but where is he in the line of succession?"

"Fourth," Mr. Hornbeam replied. "But he has long been considered the strongest and healthiest of his brothers. There is every reason to believe that he might one day be king, and if so, his baby daughter would be next in line."

"What about his older brothers?"

He shook his head. "No legitimate heirs. Ever since the death of the Prince Regent's daughter, the king's other sons have been vying to produce a legitimate heir to secure the succession. Prince Edward was the first to achieve this. There is a chance his older brother, the Duke of Clarence, may yet have a family, but if not, your new little neighbor might very well be the future Queen of England."

"Heavens," Sarah breathed. "In that case, we had all better be on our best behavior when they arrive."

4

The [Duke's party] reached Woolbrook Cottage on Christmas Eve. The weather on their arrival was bitterly cold.
—Deirdre Murphy, *The Young Victoria*

DECEMBER 1819

With guests from the duke's household expected to arrive at Sea View any day, the Summers family decided to keep their own Christmas celebrations simple that year.

Their finances were still tight, so they also limited themselves to handmade gifts—things they could sew or make themselves. This left Emily and Georgiana at a distinct disadvantage.

Emily decided to write poems for each family member and inscribe these onto cards, bringing out her languishing watercolors for the purpose.

Georgiana, however, had no idea what she might make.

Sarah said, "You need not make anything, Georgie. Presents are not required."

"I can't be the only one not giving gifts!"

"You will think of something," Mamma assured her. "Something small."

They observed St. Nicholas' Day on December sixth and afterward exchanged their modest gifts: embroidered needle cases, handkerchiefs, fragrant potpourri Sarah had made from dried flowers, and Emily's lighthearted poems, with lines like *To Sarah, our anchor. She works hard and we thank her. . . .*

Presents opened, Mamma began to rise, saying, "Thank you, everyone."

"Don't forget me!" Georgie jumped to her feet and handed around quarto-sized sheets of paper with crooked hand-drawn borders and the word *Certificate* across the top.

"I've made each of you a certificate, redeemable for a service from me."

"Excellent idea," Sarah said.

Mamma read hers and looked up with a smile. "'Good for a long walk, followed by a foot rub.' Perfect."

Sarah read hers next. "'Help in sifting flour, grating sugar, and washing up after baking.'" She nodded. "I shall gladly accept that offer."

"Mine is the best," Emily said, waving hers in the air. "'Good for one turn cleaning the water closet.'" She turned to her twin. "What does yours say, Vi?"

"She promises one hour of reading to Mrs. Denby in my place."

Emily huffed in mock offense. "That's a privilege, not a favor!"

Georgie giggled. "Well I know it!"

Viola looked at their youngest sister with approval. "Even so, nothing would make me happier than to see you spend time with Mrs. Denby. Thank you, Georgiana."

The next day, as Emily helped Jessie clear the breakfast table, she noticed a pendant at the housemaid's neck—a small wooden cross on a simple chain. The cross had been richly carved and polished. Emily could guess which handsome fisherman had made it, as she had often seen Tom Cordey carving after a day's fishing. She had also seen Jessie's blushing smiles whenever he was near.

"That's new, is it not?" Emily asked. "A gift from Tom?"

"Yes, miss." Jessie dipped her head as a blush rose to her cheeks.

"It's lovely."

"I think so too."

Snow was a rare occurrence in Sidmouth, but that year the snow fell fast and thick, transforming the esplanade into a crunchy white walkway, framing shop windows, glazing tree branches in icing sugar, and shrouding each headstone in the churchyard. Even the slopes of Peak Hill and Salcombe Hill were dusted in white.

The major's father and brother came to Westmount for the holidays, and the Huttons invited the Summerses to an early dinner on Christmas Eve. So the ladies donned their warmest cloaks and walked up the snow-covered lane to join them for the evening. The major's friend, Mr. Sagar, joined the party as well.

Later, when the ladies returned to Sea View, they found Mr. Gwilt and Lowen decorating the front door with pine boughs, holly, and ivy.

Sarah beamed. "What a lovely surprise!"

The others agreed and praised the men for their efforts.

"Were Gwilt's idea," Lowen said, with a nod to the younger man.

Mr. Gwilt laid a hand on his elder's stooped shoulder. "And I could not have done it without you." He turned back to them and added, "We want the place to look nice for our important visitors, now, don't we?"

"Indeed we do."

At that moment, the sound of hooves and the jingle of tack drew their attention as several horse-drawn vehicles turned up Glen Lane, carriage lamps blazing.

Emily breathed, "And just in time."

Emily and the others hurried inside, where it was warmer. They gathered at the library windows to watch the caravan pass by, the carriage wheels coated in snow: two traveling chaises, a larger coach, and a phaeton, pulled by a mismatched assortment of horses.

"How dreadful, having to travel on such a cold night, in the midst of a snowstorm," Sarah said.

Emily nodded. "And at Christmas."

"Look! There's a birdcage in that carriage!" Georgie pointed. "Poor things must be freezing."

"Do you see the duchess?" Emily asked, craning her neck.

Mamma squinted. "Difficult to tell."

"No time to stand here gawking," Sarah admonished. "Our new guests could arrive any minute. Quick, put away your outer things. Oh! And I'll need to mop the wet floor from all our boots."

"I'll see to it, Miss Sarah," Mr. Gwilt reassured her. "You prepare yourself."

"Yes, my dear. Tidy your hair," Mamma said. "The wind has blown it from its pins."

"Why am I so nervous?" Georgie asked.

"So am I," Emily agreed, setting aside her fur muff and unclasping her mantle.

"Come, everyone," Sarah urged. "It won't do to have us all fluttering about like startled pigeons when they arrive. Go. Go."

They dispersed, hurrying to stow their things, refresh their appearances, and prepare to receive their official guests.

When the door knocker sounded a short while later, Emily whirled to answer it, but Sarah grabbed her arm and whispered, "Let Jessie go. Let's at least pretend to be dignified."

Georgiana smirked. "Then I had better make myself scarce."

"No need for all of us to overwhelm them," Mamma said. "I will wait in the parlour. Call if there is anything I can do to help."

Emily followed Sarah into the library-turned-office and stood nearby as Sarah sat at the desk, lamp burning bright and registration book at the ready.

Jessie showed in three men, their hat brims and shoulders dusted with snow.

The first in line was Mr. Thomson, the private secretary who had accompanied Captain Conroy on his initial visit to Sea View.

As Emily remembered, he was tall, dark-haired and dark-eyed, with a thin, aristocratic nose and a slender, athletic build. He appeared to be in his mid to late twenties and was in need of a shave—the beard stubble darkening his fair face made him look perhaps a little older than he was.

"Mr. Thomson, a pleasure to see you again," Sarah said.

He bowed. "Miss Summers." He turned to Emily and nodded to her as well, his gaze lingering on her a moment before abruptly shifting away again.

Sarah placed the register on the high top of the library desk and turned it to face him.

Setting down his valise and a long, narrow case, he signed *James Thomson, Esq.* in an elegant hand.

"We are giving you a room with a view of the sea." She handed him the key to the room named Maple, which had been Emily's own room before they started the guest house.

"A view sounds excellent. Thank you."

"If you will wait while I hand round the other keys, I might explain mealtimes, et cetera, at one time."

"Of course." He stepped to the side.

Emily spoke up. "That's all right, Sarah. No need to make Mr. Thomson wait. I can show him to his room and explain the mealtimes and all that. I can recite your speech word for word after hearing it so often." She smiled winsomely at the man and then back at her sister.

Sarah managed a tight smile in return. "Very well, Emily."

Ignoring her sister's annoyance, Emily looked again at the tall, striking man, picked up an extra candle lamp, and gestured toward the door. "Shall we?"

"Yes, please."

She glanced swiftly at him, fearing to see a hint of innuendo, but his expression remained serious and inscrutable.

Mr. Gwilt offered to carry the man's valise.

"Thank you." Mr. Thomson handed it over with a polite nod.

Emily led the way upstairs. "I hope you will enjoy your time in Sidmouth, although I doubt it can compare to London. How long were you there?"

"About eight months. Before that we were in Germany, where the duke lived before his return to England."

"Germany? How fascinating."

"Yes, Bavaria is beautiful."

"Do you speak German?"

"Enough to get by."

"Impressive."

At the top of the stairs, she turned left and felt an odd hitch in her chest as they approached the first room. It had been Mr. Stanley's room during his stay. That young man had seemed to admire her, but later she'd learned he was engaged to marry another. She pushed thoughts of him from her mind as she opened the bedchamber door and led the way inside.

The room had large windows overlooking the sea, as well as a convenient dressing room.

He glanced around the interior. "Very nice."

Then he offered Mr. Gwilt a coin for carrying his bag.

Mr. Gwilt hesitated and glanced at her in question. He was still growing accustomed to some aspects of his job.

She nodded encouragingly, and he accepted the coin.

"Thank you, sir." With that, Mr. Gwilt hurried away to help the other guests.

Emily tarried. "May I ask, what does a private secretary do?"

"Take dictation, answer letters, sort through correspondence. I also have oversight of charities, reviewing the many requests for His Royal Highness's patronage. That part interests me the most."

"That does sound interesting," Emily said, thinking Viola would find it *very* interesting indeed.

She added, "I hope you are not sorry to be consigned to Sea View. I suppose you would have preferred to stay in Woolbrook or even Fortfield Terrace with the other upper staff."

"Not at all," he replied. "In fact, I volunteered to lodge here."

"Did you? Why?"

He glanced at her, then away again. "I had my reasons."

She wondered what they were and told herself not to be flattered. She had been taken in by flattering words before.

The impulse to flirt with an attractive man was still there, Emily realized, but with effort, she quashed it. This time she would be more careful. She was not eager to be hurt again.

In the office, Sarah smiled in welcome as another dark-haired man stepped forward. This one had a broad nose, olive skin, and hazel eyes. He was a bit older than Mr. Thomson, perhaps in his early thirties.

He introduced himself as Antoine Bernardi, assistant cook and pastry chef, and wrote his name in the register with a loopy flourish.

Sarah's attention was piqued by the mention of his profession. She was not certain, however, how her mother would react to hosting a cook as a guest in Sea View. She decided she would refer to him as the duke's pastry chef, which sounded grander.

"And would you like a view of the sea as well?" she asked.

"A room near the kitchens would be most convenient."

Sarah looked up with a start. "Mr. Bernardi, you are here as our guest. We do not expect you to help in the kitchen."

He shrugged. "Force of habit."

Did he mean he was accustomed to sleeping near the kitchen, or that helping in the kitchen was a habit he meant to continue while residing at Sea View? Surely he would leave early every morning to assist the head cook at Woolbrook and remain there through dinnertime. At least Sarah hoped so. She decided to let the comment pass and handed over keys to the Willow room.

He stepped aside, revealing a third man, who held a wooden chest about three-and-a-half feet long with iron bands and lock. Another case and a smaller valise sat atop it. Based on his hunched posture and the neck muscles straining above his cravat, the load must be terribly heavy.

"Oh!" Sarah exclaimed. "Do set that down. It looks heavy."

"It is." He set his burden on the desk with a clank, breathing rather hard.

This man had faded ginger hair and signed his name in a hurried scrawl.

Sarah tried to make out his signature. "Mr. . . . Deering?"

"During. Selwyn During."

"Ah. Welcome, Mr. During."

He asked in a rush, "Do all the rooms have sturdy locks? I trust you will assign me a room with the securest of locks?"

Sarah blinked, somewhat taken aback, and then hurried to reassure him. "All our guest rooms are equipped with new locks." She quickly decided against giving him the chamber with the smaller adjoining room, as there was only a traditional latch between them.

"Any other preferences I should know about? A view of the sea or countryside, or a quieter room at the back of the house?"

"I would prefer a quiet room, set apart from the others," he replied. "And with no access from any ground-floor windows."

Mr. Bernardi, she noticed, rolled his eyes.

"Very well. The Oak room is upstairs at the back corner of the house. It is one of our largest." She thought about handing the man his key but realized he did not need anything more to carry.

After Sarah had explained the mealtimes and quiet hours, she rose to lead the men to their rooms.

Mr. Gwilt waited in the hall. He glanced at Mr. During's burden and offered in his cheerful Welsh accent, "May I carry that for you, sir? Looks heavy, that does."

During hesitated, studying him with wary eyes. "Who are you?"

"Robert Gwilt, sir."

"Mr. Gwilt assists us around the house," Sarah explained, surprised by his wariness. Was it not usual practice at inns and hotels to help guests with their baggage? Just what was in that chest?

Mr. During straightened his narrow shoulders and puffed out his skinny chest. "Ah. I appreciate the offer, my good man, but it is my personal responsibility to keep this chest safe."

"You may assist *me*," Mr. Bernardi said, handing over his valise with a friendly smile.

"With pleasure, sir." Mr. Gwilt took the valise, then extended his free hand toward the large satchel in the cook's other hand. "And that one as well?"

"No, thank you." Bernardi lifted the bag with a long wooden pestle and several other handles protruding. "I prefer to keep the tools of my trade close at all times."

"Right you are, sir."

"Very well. This way, gentlemen." Sarah led the way up the long flight of stairs to the bedroom level.

Reaching the landing, she turned left, pointing out the water closet before passing Mr. Thomson's room.

As she reached the next room, Sarah barely resisted the urge to run her fingers over the door. This had been Mr. Henshall's bedchamber, and she could not pass by without thinking of him. In his honor, they had named the room Scots Pine.

She installed Mr. Bernardi in Willow, a corner room with only a partial view of the sea, but closer to the back stairs in case he was serious about wanting to be near the kitchen.

And finally, she showed Mr. During to the room in the far corner, on the other side of the linen closet and back stairs. It had once been her father's room and was also the most set apart.

She opened the door for him and led the way inside. "Will this suit?"

He glanced around and set down the chest on a dresser with another clank. Sarah flinched, guessing he had scratched the polished wood surface.

He turned back toward the door. "Pardon me. May I . . . ?"

She handed him the key and stepped aside so he could test the lock. Then, without meeting her gaze, he nodded. "Yes, this will suffice. Who all has keys to this room?"

"We have one other key that allows us to enter for cleaning when a guest is absent."

"And where is that key kept?"

"In a desk drawer in the office."

"Hmm . . . I shall need to think about that."

Sarah watched him in some concern. "Well, do let me know if there is anything else you need."

He nodded, his expression remaining serious. He was probably only thirty, but he looked older as well as somber and distracted, and Sarah wondered if he ever enjoyed himself.

She had barely stepped out of the room when she heard the key turn in the lock. She looked back in surprise before continuing.

Mr. Bernardi stood in the passage, leaning casually against his doorframe, arms crossed.

"Don't mind During. He has a bloated view of his own importance."

"Why? What duty does he perform for the duke and duchess?"

"Table-decker and keeper of the plate."

Sarah looked at him in mild alarm. "That was the royal plate chest? Tell me that poor man is not lugging around tableware for fifty."

Bernardi shook his head. "Woolbrook is fully furnished with its own. That particular chest contains items of a more ceremonial nature: silver candlesticks and awards for valor during the duke's military career. That sort of thing."

Sarah glanced back toward the locked door. "He takes his responsibility seriously, then."

Bernardi shrugged. "I suppose so. An insufferable bore, though."

Sarah was curious but decided not to encourage more gossip about one of their guests. "Unless there is anything else you need, I shall see you at breakfast in the morning. Oh, and as tomorrow is Christmas Day, we shall be attending church if you would like to join us."

"No, thank you," he answered bluntly.

"Oh. Well. As you like."

Sarah walked away, feeling ill at ease as she considered their new lodgers. Why did they always seem to receive more than their fair share of male guests? She wondered if the men were married or single, then put the question from her mind, telling herself it did not matter in the least.

The next morning, Mamma, Sarah, and her sisters attended church together. Mr. Hornbeam joined them. Viola and the major were there, along with his brother, his father, and Mrs. Denby from the poor house, who sat under a plush lap rug in her own wheeled chair, purchased for her by generous Major Hutton.

The family greeted friends and neighbors and answered questions about their new guests. Clearly word had spread about the royal visitors to Sidmouth.

After the service, they returned to Sea View to help Mrs. Besley finish preparing their simple Christmas dinner.

Once she had put away her pelisse, bonnet, and gloves, Sarah went downstairs in her plain long-sleeved day dress. She descended the back stairs, pausing to take her apron from its peg and put it on.

She glanced into the main kitchen and saw Lowen basting two chickens and Mrs. Besley busy at the stove. Sarah turned instead toward the smaller workroom she used as a pastry room and stillroom. Stepping inside, she stopped abruptly, her mouth falling ajar.

Antoine Bernardi stood at the table, working away, as though this were his personal domain.

"What are you doing, Mr. Bernardi?" she asked, her voice sharper than she'd intended.

He spread his hands. "Preparing dishes for the duke's table, as you see."

The pastry chef gestured toward the sugar-paste boughs of holly with bright red berries and the round "kissing balls" coated in green icing and decorated with small marzipan apples and oranges.

"Why here?" she asked. "Why not Woolbrook's kitchen?"

"Too hot and busy in there today. They're roasting every manner of meat for the holiday: turkey, beef, goose—probably a boar's head, for all I know. I needed somewhere quieter and cooler to make these special confections. It is Christmas, after all."

Indeed it was. The reminder stopped Sarah's sour tongue.

He turned to the sideboard, where several large tarts with lattice tops cooled. "I have also baked quince tarts. What is Christmas without something made of quinces? I prepared an extra one for you."

He lifted the tart and held it toward her for inspection. Despite her pique, Sarah could not help bending to sniff. It smelled heavenly—of tangy sweet fruit and warm, buttery pastry.

"Mmm. Th-thank you. Most considerate."

He held her gaze. "Happy Christmas, Miss Summers."

Sarah managed a wan smile in return. "Happy Christmas, Mr. Bernardi."

She decided to leave any further remonstrances about his use of their kitchens until the holiday had passed.

After helping Mrs. Besley for a time, Sarah went upstairs to the dining room. Mr. During came in as she was setting the table.

"Miss Summers, I must go to Woolbrook Cottage to set a festive table for the duke and duchess and their guests." He lifted the handle of the large leather case he'd arrived with, the plate chest and his smaller, personal valise apparently still in his room.

"I have locked my door and have the key." He patted his pocket. "But I don't feel confident leaving the house with any uncertainty about the second key. I don't suppose there is a safe in which you might secure it for my peace of mind?"

Sarah placed the final fork and straightened. "We have a lock box, which we use for payments and petty cash, that sort of thing. Will that suffice?"

"May I see it?"

For some reason, the question made her uneasy. After a moment's hesitation, she led the way to the desk in the library-office, extracted the box from the deep side drawer, and laid it atop the desk for his inspection.

"And who has keys to this box?"

"I do. Although on the rare occasion I leave the house, I leave it with my mother."

"I see."

Sarah placed the extra key in the box and locked it.

"Thank you. That adds a layer of protection, though perhaps not all one might wish." He reluctantly turned to go, and Sarah followed him out into the hall.

"How long will you be gone?"

"Oh, I would estimate two or three hours."

"I am sure we can keep the spare key safe that long."

"Yes, yes. After all, it is not as though many people even know I have the chest here. They would likely assume any valuables would be kept where His Royal Highness is residing. No doubt I worry too much."

He turned back, expression tightening again. "May I ask—

45

are your maids here trustworthy? The chest itself is locked. Even so . . ."

"Yes, Mr. During, I can vouch for everyone's character."

"Good, good. I do hate to ask. But someone in my position cannot be too careful."

Studying his anxious face, Sarah gently asked, "Have you held the office for long?"

He shook his head. "I have served as table-decker for several years, but becoming keeper of the plate is a recently added responsibility, and I am determined to fulfill the charge entrusted to me."

"I understand."

At the tail end of this discussion, Mr. Thomson came down the stairs at a leisurely pace. The two men nodded to one another as Mr. During took his leave.

Mr. Thomson watched him go. "He is a bit . . . earnest, I know. He's been promised a pay rise commensurate with his new responsibility, and as he sends the lion's share of his wages to support his mother and sisters, he could use the added funds. They depend on him for their support."

"I see. That is good of him."

"Yes, I believe he is quite well-intentioned, although his behavior can be rather off-putting at times, I realize."

Sarah nodded, then asked, "Will you join us for Christmas dinner, Mr. Thomson?"

His lips parted in surprise. "Kind of you to offer, but I should not like to intrude on your family celebration."

"You would be very welcome."

He hesitated. "I have been told I might join the upper staff at Fortfield Terrace."

"Ah. In that case, I understand."

He added, "I feel I should attend, although the prospect gives me little joy. I want to stay in General Wetherall's good graces."

46

"And in Captain Conroy's?" she asked.

He winced. "I shall never manage that."

A short while later, the family gathered for Christmas dinner. Simon Hornbeam joined them, as well as his friend Miss Reed from the poor house, who had become far less disagreeable since last summer.

When everyone sat down, Mamma asked Mr. Hornbeam to say a blessing, and he graciously obliged.

They had invited Mr. Gwilt to join them for the meal, but he had politely declined, saying he would eat with Mrs. Besley and Lowen belowstairs, as he usually did since becoming one of their staff.

Sarah wondered how Claire was spending Christmas in Edinburgh. Recalling their great-aunt's strict, stern reputation, Sarah guessed the woman would not countenance a joyful celebration. In all likelihood, Claire would endure a long, somber worship service, plain food, and the avoidance of recreation or entertainment of any kind.

Sarah silently prayed for her older sister as the meal began.

Together they ate slices of savory Christmas pie filled with seasoned pigeon, duck, and forcemeat, and decorated with pastry fruit and leaves. They also had roast chicken and potato pudding, followed by a traditional plum pudding as well as Mr. Bernardi's quince tart. So much for a "simple" dinner.

Mamma lifted another forkful of tart. "Mrs. Besley has outdone herself."

"I agree," Sarah said. "However, Mr. Bernardi made the quince tart—just as Their Royal Highnesses shall be eating today."

"Goodness, we are privileged."

"Indeed. It is delicious," Miss Reed said appreciatively.

Sarah refrained from further comment.

Later, as they were clearing the table, Sarah heard the front door slam. She stepped from the dining room in time to see Mr. During loping up the stairs by twos, case in hand, snow on his hat and shoulders, probably in a hurry to make sure the precious plate chest was still secure.

Recalling what Mr. Thomson had told her about the man's mother and sisters, Sarah's heart softened toward him.

She went belowstairs and filled a plate with food left over from their dinner, in case Mr. During had not been invited to dine with the upper staff as Mr. Thomson had been. She doubted that a table-decker would be considered "upper staff," keeper of the plate or not.

She carried the heaping plate up the back stairs and knocked on the door of the Oak room.

"Yes? Who is it?" came the startled reply.

"It's Miss Summers."

A moment later, the lock clicked and the door inched open. Uncertain blue eyes peered out at her. Apparently assured by her appearance, he opened the door wider.

"Everything all right?" he asked. "The spare key has not gone missing, has it?"

"No, no. Everything is fine. I just wondered if you might be hungry." She lifted the plate in offering.

He glanced at it. "I am hungry, actually. I forgot to eat today in all the excitement."

No wonder the man was so thin.

"Then here you are. Christmas pie, roasted chicken, potatoes, plum pudding, oh, and a small piece of quince tart Mr. Bernardi made. I'm afraid there was not much left. Everyone found it too delicious to resist."

He accepted the plate. "Thank you, Miss Summers. That is very kind."

"I suppose this is different from the Christmas dinners you are accustomed to."

He lifted a slim shoulder. "Not really. I have been in the duke's employ for nearly four years—in Brussels and Germany and London and now here—and holidays are all basically the same. Workdays, sometimes with a glass of cheer in the servants' hall or an extra bob or two on Boxing Day. But before that, yes. Christmases with my mother and sisters were joyous occasions."

"You must miss them."

His eyes took on the look of frosted glass. "I do, yes."

"Well, I hope you enjoy the food. Do let me know if there is anything else you need."

Mr. During nodded, yet his gaze remained distracted, and she knew without asking that he was remembering Christmases far more pleasant than this one.

5

❧

There were ominous signs for the future happiness of this royal family.
—Deirdre Murphy, *The Young Victoria*

Throughout the day, Emily had been keenly aware of her twin's absence. They had never been apart on Christmas before. With her father-in-law and brother-in-law in town for the holidays, Viola had hosted Christmas dinner for them at neighboring Westmount.

But the next day was Boxing Day, and Emily spent part of it with her sister. That afternoon she walked beside Viola as she pushed the wheeled chair along the esplanade, taking Mrs. Denby back to the poor house after she'd eaten luncheon with them.

Thankfully, enough horses, carriages, and foot traffic had passed this way before them that the snow was fairly packed down. Even so, the chair wheels got stuck in a rut. Emily pulled the front handle while Viola pushed from the rear, and soon they were on their way again.

Major Hutton had offered to push the chair for them, but

Emily had insisted she would help Viola. In truth, she had simply wanted to spend time with her twin.

Emily liked Mrs. Denby too, although she was more Viola's friend than hers. Emily did not know the older woman well, not being involved with the poor house as Viola was.

The sunlight faded as they went—the days darkened early now that it was late December. When they reached narrow Silver Street, a cold north wind rushed out at them in an icy blast, snaking under their skirts and threatening to yank the bonnets from their heads.

With a shiver, Emily held on to her bonnet and glanced up the narrow lane.

From its mouth, a dark figure emerged, walking slowly toward them—a woman shrouded in a black hooded cloak, her hands clasped low across her abdomen.

Noticing the oncomer as well, Viola stopped pushing to allow her to pass.

As the woman neared, Emily glimpsed her face. She was an old woman with a hooked nose, her gaze unfocused. She walked by as though she did not see them, as though in a trance.

Emily shivered anew.

When she'd passed by, Emily whispered, "Who was that?"

"I don't know," Viola replied. "Did you recognize her, Mrs. Denby?"

"I did." Mrs. Denby pushed up her spectacles. "That is someone you girls would be wise to avoid."

"Why?"

"I have not seen her in years, but she called herself a fortune-teller back then. I imagine she still does."

"Do you know," Emily began, "I overheard two ladies talking recently. One of them said she hired a fortune-teller to entertain guests at a party. I wonder if that was her."

"Couldn't say." Mrs. Denby shook her head. "Just you stay clear of her. You know the Scriptures warn us to have nothing to do with divination or soothsayers. Promise me you'll remember that."

"We will," they promised in unison, and Emily felt colder than she had only moments before.

———

Because it was Boxing Day, they had given Mrs. Besley, Jessie, Lowen, Mr. Gwilt, and Bibi Cordey—a fisherman's daughter who worked for them a few hours each morning—small gifts as well as the day off. Thankfully, the observance fell on a day they were not obligated to serve dinner to their guests. Even so, Sarah had decided to provide bread, cold meat, cheeses, mince pies, and gingerbread. Emily helped her lay it all out on the sideboard.

That evening, the family gathered in the parlour near the fire, quiet and sleepy after eating their fill of the generous spread, followed by tea and another round of sweets.

Bibi appeared in the doorway, still wearing her cloak. "I've a present for 'ee." Face bright, she thrust forth a strange-looking pie.

The pie contained whole pilchards, with fish heads protruding from the crust as though coming up for air.

Emily regarded it dubiously. "What do you call it?"

"Stargazy pie." Bibi gestured toward the blind fish eyes. "See 'em gazin' up at the stars?"

"Ah. Yes, I do."

"Well, have some." She set it on the sideboard. "Go on. It's my first time making 'em." Bibi's cheeks rounded with a proud, suppressed smile, anticipating their delight.

"Oh. Well, then of course." Sarah retrieved a knife and cut small pieces for everyone.

"Will you have some with us?" she asked.

"No, thank 'ee. Made one more for Pa and my brothers."

They ate tentative bites under Bibi's watchful gaze. Mamma and Emily, Sarah noticed, avoided the pilchards in their portions, tasting the eggy filling instead. Georgie, undeterred, ate a large mouthful of sardine-like fish, leaving only the head and tail on her plate.

Sarah dutifully took a bite and chewed thoughtfully. The fish pie was salty and savory and surprisingly good.

"Mmm . . . Quite tasty," Sarah said. "And the pastry is excellent. Well done, Bibi. Thank you."

The girl beamed. "Glad 'ee like it. Now, I have to get back."

Georgie looked crestfallen. "Aw. Can't you stay awhile?"

"Not today. Made 'em promise to wait fer me before they dig in."

And with that, Bibi wished them a happy Christmastide and hurried out as quickly as she had come.

After they'd set aside their plates once again, Georgiana asked her family to play a game, but no one had the energy or desire.

Georgie's lower lip stuck out in a rare pout. "What a dismal holiday this has been. No music. No dancing. No bobbing for apples or snapdragon. No Viola or Cla . . . other people. I am glad Mr. Hornbeam shared Christmas dinner with us, and Miss Reed. Still, it's not the same as having friends and neighbors in for a party. I had thought at least some of our new guests might join us, but no."

"This is a strange year for us, I agree," Sarah said gently. "Next year will be better, I promise. We shall have a far more festive Christmas then, you'll see."

Georgie pinned her with a look. "I shall hold you to it!"

Later, after Mamma and Sarah had retired for the night, Emily took pity on Georgiana and agreed to play a game of draughts with her. The two sat quietly in the parlour as they studied the board for their next moves.

James Thomson wandered in, book in hand.

Emily glanced up. "Good evening, Mr. Thomson."

He looked at them in surprise. "I did not realize anyone was still in here. I did not mean to intrude."

"Not at all. You are very welcome. There are mince pies and gingerbread there and a pot of tea, although it might have gone cold."

"That's all right." He poured a cup of tea and sat in one of the armchairs with his book.

Emily watched him with interest. "May I ask what you are reading?"

"History."

Georgie sighed. "Here she goes. Don't get Emily started on books, or she'll talk your ear off, I warn you. It's your move, Emily."

Emily halfheartedly shifted her attention back to the game, moving a piece. Seeing Georgiana's devious look of delight, she realized she had made an ill-conceived move.

Emily turned to him once more. "History of what?"

From the title page, he read, "'The General Biographical Dictionary Containing an Historical and Critical Account of the Lives and Writings of the Most Eminent Persons in Every Nation; Particularly the British and Irish; From the Earliest Accounts to the Present Time.'"

"Goodness!" she exclaimed, thinking, *Another long title*.

"It describes notable inhabitants of Bavaria as well. Most interesting."

"You enjoy history, do you?"

"Of course."

"I prefer lighter reading," Emily said. "Travel memoirs, novels, and poetry."

He nodded. "I enjoy those too. As well as current events to aid me in my work. But I am inevitably drawn back to history. There is always more to learn about the past."

Georgiana sighed again, her flash of happy triumph quickly fading as she realized her opponent's attention was no longer on the game.

Emily said, "I agree that learning about the past is valuable, especially if it informs our actions in the present or our decisions for the future. Not merely as an academic exercise."

He quirked one dark brow. "And what does one learn from novels?"

Rising from the table, Emily went and sat on the sofa nearer him. "Novels are stories. And history books, written well, are full of stories, are they not?"

"They are fact."

"Or at least, an author's interpretation of facts. Why, last year I read two accounts of the life of Queen Elizabeth, and I cannot tell you how many disparities I found between them."

"Mistakes?"

"Maybe, or a difference in source or perspective."

Georgiana pushed back her chair with a huff. "If you two are going to be boring, I'm going to bed."

He rose swiftly. "Don't leave on my account. I shall go."

"Stay, Georgiana," Emily urged, realizing she wanted to keep talking to Mr. Thomson but should probably not be alone with him this late in the evening. "Stay, and I promise to talk of pleasanter things."

"Very well." Georgie slouched next to her on the sofa.

Emily turned back to their guest. "You must excuse my sister. She is disappointed that this Christmastide has not lived up to those of the past. I suppose a quiet Christmas in Sidmouth was a letdown for you as well?"

He shrugged broad shoulders. "Much like any other in

recent years. Although last year we were in Amorbach, so the traditions and food were somewhat different."

Georgiana scrunched up her nose. "Amorbach? Where's that?"

"A Bavarian town in Germany, where the duke and duchess resided after their marriage. Otherwise, I have lived wherever Prince Edward was living—in Ealing or London or abroad. I have not been home in years."

"What about when you were younger?" Georgiana asked. "Were you home for Christmas then?"

He nodded. "I was away at school for most of my boyhood, but I went home for the holidays, like other students."

Emily asked, "Where was home?"

"Berkshire. Near Reading."

"Do you have brothers or sisters?" Georgie asked, looking interested again.

"Brothers."

"I have four sisters," Georgie said. "The oldest, Claire, lives in Scotland. But I *wish* I had a brother."

Mr. Thomson's mouth tightened, Emily noticed, and he did not respond.

Oblivious to his change in expression, Georgiana plowed ahead. "Did you have jolly Christmases together? With parties and dancing and music?"

Again his lips thinned. "No. Holidays at home were quiet affairs. My father is not . . . given to frivolity."

"That's a shame. Our father was not given to frivolity either, yet we still had friends over for parties with music and snapdragon and other games." Georgie sighed and looked sincerely forlorn.

"I did not intend to dishearten you further." Mr. Thomson rose, and Emily assumed he meant to bid them good-night. Instead he said, "I don't play snapdragon, but I would play a game of draughts with you, if that might help at all? I know it's a paltry substitute for a party, but . . ."

"Yes, please!" Georgie beamed and hurried back to the table.

Emily sent the man an appreciative smile. For a moment he held her gaze, expression thoughtful. Then he looked away first.

6

The culprit was a local apprentice boy named Hook.
—John Van der Kiste, *Childhood at Court*

The next day, Emily dressed warmly and left the house, book under her arm, intending to walk to Wallis's Marine Library. As she made her way down Sea View's short drive, she saw a woman walking in her direction from farther up Glen Lane. The woman held a bundled child in her arms.

Excitement thrummed through Emily. Might this be the baby princess in the care of her mamma or nurse?

As the woman neared, Emily took in her plain face and simple cape and decided she was likely the nurse. At least, she did not look or dress as Emily would expect a duchess to.

"Good day," Emily greeted her.

The woman returned her smile. "Good day to you. Heavens. Is it always so cold here?"

Emily chuckled. "Hardly ever. At least it has stopped snowing. I live just there." Emily pointed over her shoulder at Sea View and then at Westmount. "And my sister there. Woolbrook is the next closest house, so am I correct in supposing you are staying there?"

The woman nodded. "With the royal party, yes. I am nurse-maid to this wee angel."

Emily leaned closer and asked in hushed tones, "Is this the princess?"

"Yes. Princess Alexandrina Victoria, although we call her Drina."

"How old is she?"

"Seven months and a bit more."

"She's lovely," Emily said, admiring the baby's pale blue eyes, plump cheeks, and rosy little mouth. "I am surprised you two are out in this weather. Does she not mind the cold?"

"It is good for the constitution. Her parents insist upon it."

The baby certainly appeared hale. She was bundled in blankets, so Emily could not see what she wore, but perched on her head was a tartan hat.

"She has pretty eyes," Emily said. "And her hat is adorable."

A man approached from up the lane. A tall, broad man in a long coat and beaver hat. He had ruddy, rather plump cheeks as well, Emily noticed, although his were framed in bushy brown side-whiskers.

"Ah. There is my pocket Hercules," he called.

Emily gulped. Here he was again, the Prince Regent's brother, Prince Edward, the Duke of Kent. Should she quickly retreat? Unsure, she stood there, nerves prickling through her.

As he neared, he asked, "And how is Drina today, Nurse Brock?"

"She is well, Your Royal Highness."

He smiled at the child. "Of course she is. *Vraiment un modèle de force et de beauté.*"

Emily translated the French in her mind: a model of strength and beauty.

Still Emily hesitated, not knowing what to say or do. How was she to behave in the presence of one of King George's sons? Thankfully, the man barely seemed to notice her as he gazed fondly at the babe. Standing closely now, she saw that he had the same clear blue eyes as his daughter.

Nurse Brock said, "Allow me to introduce one of your neighbors. Miss . . . ?"

"Oh, I beg your pardon. Miss Emily Summers." She bobbed a curtsy. "We live in Sea View, just there. We have a few of your staff staying with us."

"Ah yes. A pleasure to meet such a charming neighbor." He bowed his head, then looked from her toward the sea, inhaling a deep breath of icy air. "I like this bracing weather. It's rather . . . Canadian. I was posted there, as you may know." He reached out and stroked his daughter's cheek, and the babe kicked her legs in delight.

"Y-yes. I remember reading that somewhere."

Emily found it difficult to reconcile this doting father with the harsh military leader she had read about.

His attention remained on his daughter, pride evident in his expression. "I am delighted to see my little girl is thriving under the influence of the Devonshire climate."

"Indeed, sir," Nurse Brock said. "Yet I confess I grow cold. We were in the garden for some time before I ventured this way. May I take her inside now?"

"Yes, yes, of course." After a quick kiss to the child's cheek, he waved the woman on her way. "Take good care of her. She may yet be Queen of England."

The nurse walked back up Glen Lane. He, however, remained, turning again toward the sea.

Now what did she do?

Emily wondered how to excuse herself. Did one need to back away from royalty, or only from the monarch?

He relieved her uncertainty by smiling and saying, "If you

will excuse me, Miss Summers, I shall continue my walk. I am told the sea air is excellent for one's health."

She curtsied again, murmuring, "Your Royal Highness," and stepped aside. With another small nod of his head, he strolled away.

Emily watched him go, marveling at the encounter. She had often resented her family's move to Devonshire. Had long wished to return home to May Hill. Yet she was oddly glad to be here now to meet this man and his daughter, one or both of whom might one day sit on England's throne.

After allowing the duke an ample start, Emily walked in the same direction, moving quickly to warm up after standing still too long. She made her way east along the esplanade toward Wallis's to return the volume of poetry and find a new book to read. After her conversation with Mr. Thomson, she was in the mood for something weightier.

She looked through the library's frost-framed window and was pleased to see the proprietor himself bent over some pages at his desk. She wondered what he was working on. Perhaps this would be an opportune time to ask if he might allow her to edit or proofread for him.

When the jingling bell announced her presence, he looked up.

"Ah, Miss Summers." He stood. "Good day."

She blurted, "Guess who I just spoke to."

His face wrinkled in thought. "Um . . . the vicar?"

"No. His Royal Highness!"

His eyes widened. "Did you indeed?"

She nodded and walked closer. "And I met his daughter. Her nurse was out walking with her."

"Ah. Others have mentioned seeing a woman airing a child on the esplanade—and sometimes the duchess herself accompanies them."

"I have not met her yet."

"But you have seen the little princess. What is she like?"

"Lovely. Rosy and sweet with blue eyes."

"Did the duke happen to mention my library? His patronage?"

She gave him an apologetic smile. "I am afraid not."

Mr. Wallis sighed. "I have been appointed bookseller to Their Royal Highnesses, as you know, and yet they have not called in. I am most disappointed, I don't mind telling you."

"I understand. But they have only been here a few days, and you were closed on Christmas, so . . ."

His face clouded. "Oh dear. Do you think that was the problem, that they tried to call and found the library closed?"

"No, no. I don't think so. I did not see them venture out then."

"That's right! Some of his staff are staying with you. You have intimate knowledge of the goings-on in his household."

"Only a little. Though his private secretary is staying with us, and he works quite closely with the duke."

"Well, a subtle reminder to Their Royal Highnesses to act upon their patronage would be most appreciated, Miss Summers, if the opportunity presents itself."

"Oh. I . . . will see what I can do."

She handed over the book of poetry she had been reading.

He accepted it and said, "What will you have next? Perhaps a Gothic romance—*Frankenstein* or *Northanger Abbey*?"

The suggestions were tempting, but Emily shook her head. "Not a novel this time. A history."

A short while later, Emily hurried back to Sea View, a heavy volume of Prussian history in her arms. Entering the house, she set aside the book and looked for her family, eager to share the news of her encounter with the duke.

The first person she found was Sarah, at the desk in the library.

Emily began, "You will never guess who I met today!"

"Prince Edward, the Duke of Kent."

Emily's buoyancy waned. "How did you know?"

"I saw you standing out there a long while. First you spoke with a woman carrying a child. Then a man came and spoke to you both, and even kissed the baby, so I assumed he must be her father. And, after all, we know who is staying just up the lane, so it seemed fairly obvious."

"I suppose so. But I hoped to surprise you."

Sarah grinned. "I *was* surprised to see you talking to him as though he were your long-lost uncle. I considered coming out to rescue you, but I had no idea what to say to a royal duke."

"Nor did I, yet I muddled through."

"Well done, Emily. A little royal favor can only help Sea View's reputation."

Georgiana had grown increasingly restless over the last several days, Emily noticed. Her sister's usually sunny disposition was clouded by the disappointing Christmas season as well as the unusually cold weather. The frigid temperatures curtailed the time she spent out-of-doors, traipsing about the countryside with her friend Hannah or Chips, a local stray, or joining a group of young people on Fort Field for a game of cricket. Most everyone seemed to be remaining indoors presently, except for necessary forays for work or food.

Even so, Emily was somewhat surprised the next afternoon when Georgiana threw down her sampler, stood, and announced, "I'm going out. I cannot sit inside another moment."

"Are you meeting Hannah?" Mamma asked, glancing up from her mending.

"No, she has a cold, which is a pity, especially as it's her birthday."

Mamma said mildly, "Don't venture too far on your own."

"I shan't." Georgiana turned to go.

"And dress warm," Sarah called after her.

Emily set aside her writing slant and rose. "I think I shall go out as well. See how Viola is getting on."

Mamma nodded. "Do be sure and greet her and the Huttons for me."

"And please return in time to help with dinner," Sarah added.

"I shall."

Emily enjoyed a pleasant visit with Viola, Major Hutton, his father, his brother Colin, and his friend Armaan.

She left Westmount for home at around four, but at the sound of a familiar voice, she looked over her shoulder toward Woolbrook Cottage.

Georgiana's voice, sounding stern. "Billy Hook, what are you doing?"

Billy Hook was an apprentice. Emily had seen him once or twice around town, and her sister had mentioned his name.

"Tell me you are not tormenting birds again," Georgie scolded.

"Just sparrows and the like. What's it to you?"

Curious, Emily walked toward Woolbrook, a beautiful white house set in a glen with castle-like battlements and lancet-shaped windows. She followed the voices up a rise and around the side of the residence. Imagining fierce Captain Conroy standing guard at one of the windows, she took care not to get too close.

She wondered what the boy was doing. Throwing rocks

at winter birds perched in trees? Using a sling? She hoped he wouldn't be foolish enough to aim anywhere near the house.

The rear of the property overlooked the western fields. A hedgerow partially enclosed the back garden, lending the place a bit of privacy.

There she saw Georgiana scowling down at a boy a year or two younger than she was, and a few inches shorter—a boy holding a gun.

Emily's heart lurched.

"I don't like seeing creatures harmed," Georgie said, hands propped on hips. Chips sat on his haunches beside her. "It's not as though you intend to eat them. It's wrong to take pleasure in killing. In fact, it's disgusting." At her sharp tone, the terrier's ears went back.

Emily hurried over, hoping to calm the argument before one of the duke's retinue discovered the young people trespassing, especially with Billy armed.

Reaching them, Emily said, "If you must shoot something, pray, not here." She gestured toward the back of the house, visible through a gap in the hedgerow. "You may not have heard an important family is staying here at present, attended by a captain and a general. Not people you wish to cross."

The lad frowned. "But this glen is perfect with a stream and trees and hedgerows. Birds love it."

Georgiana threw her hands in the air. "So do we! At least when you're not shooting up the place."

Perhaps startled by her raised voice and hands, a sparrow flew past and lighted on the hedge beyond. Billy pivoted toward it, arms rising as though of their own accord, gun lifting into position. Georgiana reached out to try to stop him, jostling him as he pulled the trigger.

Crack. The shot rang out.

A second sound followed the first—the sound of shattering glass.

Startled, Chips darted away.

Peering through the gap toward Woolbrook Cottage, Emily saw a spidery hole in an upper-story window.

"Oh no." She pressed a hand to her mouth.

"You shot the house!" Georgie accused. "You may have hit someone."

"It's your fault. You pushed me!"

Pulse pounding, Emily drew a shaky breath. "We had better go and see what the damage is and make sure everyone is all right."

"Not me." Billy turned to beat a hasty retreat, but Georgie grabbed his arm again, this time more forcefully.

"Oh no you don't."

"Georgiana's right," Emily said, stifling her own desire to run. "The worst thing you can do is try to flee."

Georgie added, "If we tell them it was an accident and you're sorry, they'll understand. Probably."

Emily thought again of Captain Conroy's stern looks and the duke's reputation as a harsh military leader. He wouldn't be as harsh with a lad not under his command, would he? And one so young?

"I will go with you," Georgiana said bravely. "It was partly my fault as well."

Emily lifted her chin in resolve. "We shall all go."

Before they had taken two steps toward the house, one of its doors flew open, slamming against the outer wall with a bang. A menacing figure stormed out in their direction—Captain Conroy, posture battle-ready, expression furious. In his hand . . . a gun of his own.

No, no, no. Emily stepped in front of the younger pair.

"Captain Conroy," she said in a rush, lifting beseeching

hands. "A thousand apologies. It was an accident. A foolish mistake. We were just coming to explain."

Mr. Thomson, she noticed, followed the captain outside, his expression serious but less menacing.

"Explain?" The captain jerked an angry hand toward the house. "Explain a shot that broke the nursery window and narrowly missed the infant and her nurse? Glass fell into her cot! The duchess is most exceedingly alarmed. You expect us to believe it was a simple accident? The shot nearly struck the princess. How do we know this was not an assassination attempt?"

"Assass—? 'C-course not, sir," Billy Hook stuttered, his face blanching.

Conroy turned and growled to Mr. Thomson, "Summon the constable or magistrate, or whoever pretends at authority in this rustic place."

Mr. Thomson glanced from one to the other, his gaze lingering on Emily before returning to the man in charge. "Captain, I understand your concern, but no one was harmed. I believe them when they say it was an accident. The lad is young, and the ladies, well, I am acquainted with them, and they are of excellent character."

Conroy glowered at him. "I did not ask for a character reference. I told you to summon a magistrate."

Georgiana spoke up. "Billy was only shooting sparrows, sir. It was partly my fault. I tried to stop him and made his shot go awry."

Billy nodded. "I'm usually a crack shot."

Conroy's black eyebrows drew together. "Crack shot, indeed." He gestured toward the broken pane. "That was not done by simple bird shot. How do you explain the size of that hole? That was caused by a heavier type of shot."

Billy hung his head. "It's all I had at hand. Swan shot."

Georgiana gaped.

"Swan shot!" The captain's face turned the color of beet-root.

Again Mr. Thomson rose to the boy's defense. "An unfortunate choice, I grant you. He probably did not realize the danger. Come. Why do we not all step inside out of the cold and talk this over calmly."

The captain's nostrils flared. Clearly, he was unaccustomed to being contradicted. "Very well. Then you may fetch pen and paper to record the boy's information." He turned and stalked back to the side door, and the others followed more slowly.

As they did, Georgiana again scowled at Billy, whispering, "Swan shot? What on earth were you—"

Emily pressed her arm to silence her. They had more important concerns to address at present.

The two men led them into a small, plain room just off the vestibule that held a desk and a few chairs—a morning room or former steward's office, perhaps.

Inside, the captain gestured toward the desk, and Mr. Thomson reluctantly sat and picked up a quill. Then Conroy whirled on Billy. "Your full name, boy."

The lad swallowed. "William Hook, sir."

"And where do you live?"

"Above Mr. Tucker's workshop. I'm his apprentice. He'll be furious when he hears. Like to tan my hide."

"That is the least of your problems, young man. If I learn there was evil intent or even mischief intended instead of an accident, I will see you punished to the full extent of the law. Do I make myself clear?"

The boy seemed to sway on his feet, and Emily feared he might faint.

"Conroy? What the deuce is going on?"

The stout duke appeared in the doorway wearing a long banyan over shirt and trousers and a matching cap, dark eyebrows drawn low.

Emily's mouth went dry. The duke clearly prized his only daughter, the possible future Queen of England. He would be furious.

She recalled again what she had read. As a military leader, Prince Edward had been vilified as a severe disciplinarian. Ruthless in doling out cruel punishment for the most minor offenses. What would he do to someone who endangered his daughter's life?

Yet in his weary eyes and anxious expression, Emily saw not a tyrant but a mild, middle-aged father. "Nurse Brock says someone fired through a nursery window, narrowly missing the princess in her arms."

Would he exact revenge? Panic tore through Emily's breast. *Please, God, have mercy.*

Georgiana spoke up, her expression humbly contrite. "We are terribly sorry, Your Grace."

"Your Royal Highness," Mr. Thomson quietly corrected.

"Your Royal Highness," she dutifully repeated. "It was an accident. Billy here meant to shoot a sparrow and I tried to stop him, which upset his aim. I beg your pardon and am so glad no one was hurt."

"As am I. Extremely glad." The duke exhaled in obvious relief. He looked from Georgiana to the trembling lad to Emily. He gave her a small nod of recognition, then said, "This seems an unlikely group of assassins, ey, Conroy?"

"Just shooting birds, sir. I swear," Billy said desperately. "Never meant to hit yer house."

"But you did," the captain said between clenched teeth.

"Thank God no real harm was done," the duke said, his

chest puffing out. "My little girl stood fire as befits a soldier's daughter."

"Yes, sir," Conroy said, "but it could have gone very differently."

"True. It is dangerous for inexperienced youngsters to be trusted with guns." The duke took a deep breath and decisively squared his shoulders. "So this is what I want. Write to the local magistrate, George Cornish. Request him to adopt some measures to prevent such an occurrence from happening again. But add that 'Their Royal Highnesses desire most particularly that the boy may not be punished.'"

"Not punished?" Conroy's lip curled. "Are you certain?"

"I am." The duke turned back to the lad. "You won't shoot around here again, I trust?"

"No, sir."

"Good." The big man nodded and retreated into the vestibule.

"Thank you," Emily called after him.

He turned back, and Emily managed a wavering smile and a wobbly curtsy.

The duke nodded at her once more, then disappeared down the corridor.

As soon as he had gone, Emily turned back to the other men. "Now, if you will excuse us." She backed away from the captain, tugging her sister's hand. Georgiana tripped on her hem, but Emily steadied her and all but dragged her out of the house, eager to depart before Captain Conroy could think of some other retribution. Billy followed behind, as eager to leave Woolbrook as she was.

"Thank you, Lord," Emily whispered as they walked away down Glen Lane, relieved they had narrowly missed what might have been a disaster not only for Billy and Georgiana, but also for Sea View's reputation.

While Billy made his way back to the eastern town, Emily and Georgie returned home. There, they summoned Sarah into Mamma's room and explained what had happened.

Sarah's mouth fell ajar. "Good heavens!"

"What if they had blamed Georgie?" Mamma said, expression alarmed. "What if you were both called before the magistrate? Arrested?"

"We were not, Mamma," Emily soothed. "I think the only one of us in serious danger of that was Billy Hook."

"I don't want you to spend any more time with that boy, Georgiana. I don't say that because he is an apprentice, but because he is obviously reckless."

Georgiana pulled a wry face. "I'd like to disagree, but I can't. I do hope Billy won't get into too much trouble with Mr. Tucker. I'd hate for him to lose his apprenticeship."

"Should we do something?" Sarah asked. "Send a note of apology to Their Royal Highnesses? Offer to help with the broken window? Fran Stirling is sure to know 'the very person' to replace the glass."

Emily replied, "I think with the many staff at their disposal, someone has probably already been summoned to repair the window, but I will ask Mr. Thomson if there is anything we can do."

"Good idea." Mamma rose to kiss Georgiana's cheek, then Emily's. "Thank God no one was hurt."

When Mr. Thomson returned to Sea View a short while later, Emily greeted him in the hall.

"Thank you for speaking up on our behalf."

He nodded, lips pressed tight.

She ventured, "Captain Conroy did not appreciate your interference, I noticed."

"No. He has made that perfectly clear. I am not to give my

opinion unless asked, apparently. He gave me a harsh reprimand as soon as we were alone."

"I am sorry."

He shrugged. "Not your fault. He has never approved of me. Most of those who work closely with His Royal Highness—his other secretary, equerry, comptroller, et cetera, are all military men. It makes sense, considering the duke's long military career. I am not one of them."

"You are no doubt very useful to Their Royal Highnesses, despite that."

"I hope so. I have long desired to aid our great country in some manner. And this is the manner currently open to me. Perhaps in time it will lead to a better situation, if I do well in this one."

"Is it unusual for a royal duke to employ multiple secretaries?"

"I don't think so. Prince Edward is an avid correspondent, writing many letters himself and dictating others. As I mentioned, my specific focus is corresponding with the many charities that request his patronage. He cannot sponsor them all, of course, but I help him identify the worthiest. He is surprisingly benevolent."

"I am glad to hear it. Do you know, we have several worthy charities right here in Sidmouth?"

He pursed his lips, clearly impressed. "Is that so? I cannot make any promises, but I would be happy to learn more about them and present them to His Royal Highness."

"Really?" Eagerness sprouted through her. "One charity dear to my sisters is the Poor's Friend Society." She searched her memory and recited, "'Which seeks to relieve the distress of poverty from those who still have a home but are too infirm to work, or those living in the Sidmouth Poor House.'"

He quirked a slender brow at her. "Learnt that by heart, did you? Just waiting for an opportunity?"

Her face heated. "Not exactly."

If there was any censure in his tone, it was alleviated by a glimmer of humor in his dark eyes. Perhaps the first evidence of good humor she'd seen in the man.

Emily said, "I have learned all I can about Sidmouth since we moved here." She had done so in an effort to grow to like the place and overcome her longing for home. "We are personally acquainted with a few people benefited by the charity, and more deserving as well as delightful people I cannot imagine."

A smile touched his lips. "You are uncommonly persuasive."

She returned his smile, admiring the attractive lines of his face, accentuated by the dark stubble already shading his jaw. For a moment, she allowed herself to enjoy the company of a handsome man. Then, recalling her assignment—and her determination to be more guarded—she asked, "Is there anything we can do about what happened today? Help clean up the broken glass? Find someone to repair the broken window?"

He shook his head. "Nothing you need to do. Every particle of glass has been cleared away by diligent housemaids, and Captain Conroy has personally dragged the local glazier from his dinner to see about the window."

"That does not surprise me," Emily said. "Speaking of dinner, I do hope you are hungry. We dine in less than an hour."

He gave another of his tight smiles, almost like a wince. "Actually, I am not very hungry. And I have some correspondence to finish before tomorrow."

"Oh, please do join us," Emily implored. "We are having Mrs. Besley's famous roast beef with Yorkshire puddings. My favorite."

His eyes traced her features, and then he relented. "In that case, I would not miss it."

At dinner that evening, everyone buzzed excitedly about the day's events like bees to bright flowers, asking questions and pressing Emily and Georgiana for details.

"I tried to stop Billy," Georgie said. "I did! Instead I accidentally made his shot go wild."

"It was not your fault," Emily insisted. "He should not have been shooting anywhere near the house, let alone at a bird beneath their window."

Mr. During daintily wiped a table napkin to the corners of his mouth, then said, "I cannot believe a young lad had the hardihood to approach so near the residence of Their Royal Highnesses. I should not have been half so brave at his age."

"Brave, or brazen?" Mr. Bernardi asked. He took an experimental bite of the puffy brown Yorkshire pudding, chewing tentatively. Then setting down his fork, he said, "I'd wager Conroy had fire blazing from his nose and steam from his ears. The man is hot-tempered at the best of times."

Georgie nodded. "He flew out of the house with a gun in his hand!"

"Good heavens," Mamma murmured, pressing a hand to her throat.

"I am surprised he didn't shoot first and ask questions later," Mr. During said.

"I feared the same thing," Emily allowed. "Thankfully, Mr. Thomson was there to help the captain see reason." She sent him a grateful smile, noticing again how handsome he was. Handsome *and* courageous.

Mr. Bernardi looked at him with interest. "How did you manage that?"

James Thomson shrugged. "I did little, truth be told. It was the duke himself who convinced Conroy not to have the boy punished. I think he was so relieved his daughter was unharmed that little else mattered."

"Astounding," Mr. Hornbeam said. "Considering he was known to be merciless in his years as a commander. It is said that wherever the Duke of Kent was in command there were floggings, executions, and desertions. His career ended after an inquiry into his conduct."

Mr. Thomson spoke up. "Though to his credit, he distinguished himself for bravery in the West Indian campaign against the French."

Mr. During added, "And the people of Gibraltar awarded him with a diamond-encrusted garter for his service. It's in the plate chest even now."

Mr. Hornbeam nodded thoughtfully. "Is it not ironic? Some people revere the man, while others abhor him for cruelty. Evidently, he is a man of contrasts. Or perhaps fatherhood has softened him."

Emily said, "He certainly dotes on his daughter."

Mr. Thomson nodded his agreement. "He is devoted to his wife as well. I came to work for him long after his military career had ended. But even in that interval, I have seen a change in him, a softening, as you say. A kindness to others, to animals, and to children."

"And to what do you attribute that change?"

Another shrug. "The love of a good woman, perhaps. And as Mr. Hornbeam said, becoming a father has improved his disposition all the more."

Bernardi lifted his glass. "Whatever the reason, the three of us can be glad he's ceased his merciless treatment of subordinates, ey?"

"Very true," During said, lifting his glass as well, while Mr. Thomson made do with another nod.

Georgiana said, "After today, I count myself in that number."

Emily lifted her water glass to join the mock toast. "Hear, hear."

7

The fine arts are five in number, namely:
painting, sculpture, poetry, music, and architecture,
the principal branch of the latter being pastry.
—Chef Antonin Carême

The next day after luncheon, Sarah went belowstairs. Again, she was unhappily surprised to find *her* room already occupied. Mr. Bernardi stood at the worktable, which was cluttered with mounds of sugar, wooden and glazed-stone molds, and sculpting tools.

"Here again, Mr. Bernardi?"

He looked up with an air of casual ease. "Yes. Busy with sugar work, as you see."

"Is that our sugar? *All* our sugar?"

"Only what was in that box." He gestured toward the storage box with his white-coated sleeve.

"That *was* all our sugar." The wooden box had compartments for a whole sugar loaf as well as for any ground or powdered sugar already made from it.

He splayed both hands toward the sugar-paste structure he was decorating. "A small price for art, yes?"

She shook her head. "Not small. Sugar is terribly expensive."

"Is it? I've not had to worry about that. I suppose that's the comptroller's problem."

"Well, here it is my problem. That sugar was meant for today's tea and for tomorrow's tarts and biscuits."

"What are such trifles to this masterpiece, ey? *C'est magnifique!* You recognize the Brighton Pavilion, yes?"

Frustration mounted. "What is it *for*? Is there to be some grand dinner at Woolbrook I don't know about?"

"Not for some time, which is a pity. Still, one must keep his skills honed."

"It is nearly time for the midday tea tray, Mr. Bernardi. So I suggest you chip off some of those domes for the sugar bowl or fetch sugar from Woolbrook to replace this in the next fifteen minutes."

He pressed a hand to the buttons of his double-breasted coat. "You injure me."

"And you injure me by using up our sugar! I have no budget for more." She planted a hand on her waist. "Nor did you ask permission to avail yourself of this room or our supplies."

"You did not complain the last time I worked here."

"I would have said something, but it was Christmas. Christmas is over."

"Not officially," he grumbled. "Seven of the twelve days of Christmas remain."

She looked at the clock. "You are down to ten minutes."

He pouted, lips downturned. "I can't do it. I won't."

She lifted her chin and held her ground. "Nine minutes."

He huffed. "Oh, very well. But not the domes! Let us begin with the stable block. I shall replace the rest of your sugar later this afternoon."

Sarah retrieved Lowen's sugar-chipping tools—pincher and chisel—and handed them to him.

"You would force me to destroy my own work? Have pity, Miss Summers."

"I could do it for you, *if* you slice cold meat and spread butter on these rolls."

He sighed. "Very well. It will be less painful than destroying my masterpiece."

The chef turned away, unable to watch her chip chunks of sugar from his handiwork, and began slicing the cold beef.

After working silently for a few minutes, she said, "Your name—Bernardi. Italian, is it? Do your people come from that region of the world?"

"I come from London, Miss Summers."

"You know what I mean."

"My father came to England as a steward. But I was born in this country. I am English."

"Yet now and then I hear a faint accent. And you speak French from time to time. Why?"

He nodded as he worked. "Perhaps because my parents did not grow up here. Or because I was educated in France at a renowned cookery school. I studied with the master, Antonin Carême. You have heard of him, yes? Chef to the Prince Regent, Russian tsars, and many others."

"That explains it. Is that your ambition as well? To cook for kings and tsars?"

He lifted one shoulder, not missing a stroke with the knife. "Perhaps. Though I have other ambitions as well."

She tilted her head in question, but he did not explain.

Sarah asked, "How long have you been with Their Royal Highnesses?"

"A few years."

"How did you gain such an appointment in the first place?"

Finished with his rapid-fire slicing, he moved on to the bread and butter. "I was engaged to cook for a gentlemen's club, where I made the acquaintance of many noblemen. Through those connections, I have since been chef de cuisine to several of the nobility. Finally, I was offered this, my first situation in a royal household."

Another long-suffering sigh. "Sadly, so far I am only assistant cook and pastry chef. Mr. Leigleitner is the head cook. Old and set in his ways he may be, but the duke and duchess do not possess refined palates like the Prince Regent's. They are satisfied with simple fare. And the duchess is partial to the food of her homeland. Pork roast and dumplings drowned in thick gravy." He shuddered, then lifted his knife straight up for emphasis. "Thankfully the duke plans to entertain while we are here. And then the dishes will need to be finer, so I must be ready."

Sarah just hoped their kitchen and food stores would survive the ordeal.

Emily looked at the calendar in her miniature almanac. Seeing it was nearly the end of December, a dampening flood of disappointment washed over her. Another year had all but passed, and she had not yet accomplished anything. They had been living in Sidmouth for fourteen months now. She had so hoped her life here, so far from Finderlay, from May Hill, from Charles, would be only temporary. Yet here she was.

Nor had she yet completed a single book. And what she had written still seemed to her a jumble of disjointed scenes. She groaned. Writing a novel was more difficult than she'd ever expected.

Determined to redeem the last days of 1819, Emily sharpened a quill, turned to a fresh page in her notebook, and began to write.

At the end of two hours, she had a sore wrist and a few promising scenes.

Not knowing what should happen next in the novel, she set it aside and instead turned her attention to Mr. Gwilt's parrot adventures, which she had been helping him compose.

She wrote a clean copy of the latest page of his story, correcting spelling and grammatical errors as she went.

At first Parry liked shipboard life, the wind in his feathers, the thrill of flying over the waves. Then he realized he was not the only feathered creature on board. Strange white birds were kept in a large cage on deck. Horror of horrors, day by day, a few more were carried off and into the pot they went.

Parry began to fear he would be next. His life would be over. He would soon disappear, and the world would remember him no more!

The ship's captain, who had captured him, talked to him every day. Parry noticed he did not talk to the other birds. This gave him a small amount of hope for the future. The captain repeated childish words to him over and over, as though he were an imbecile. "Parrot want mango?"

Finally one day, out of sheer frustration, Parry repeated back, "Want mango?" Thinking, Of course I do, you simpleton. Why do you keep asking me?

The man clapped his hands and shouted, "He talks! He talks!" and fed Parry a whole mango. The more words Parry mimicked, the more mango he received. He was soon a very plump parrot.

Parry also learned many other words while aboard that ship of sailors, but most are unfit for young ears and better omitted.

Emily grinned as she reread and revised Mr. Gwilt's humorous yet touching tale. Reaching the end of a page, she began to wonder if Mr. Wallis might be interested in publishing it as a children's book.

Before she dared ask him, she decided she ought to see how the story as written would be received by its intended audience. She had met the master of the local parochial school at church. He would probably allow her to read it to his pupils. A positive report could help to sway Mr. Wallis.

She went looking for Mr. Gwilt and found him polishing silver. She asked, "Would it be all right if I read Parry's story to some school children? I am certain they shall love it as much as I do, and then we can tell Mr. Wallis that when we show him the manuscript."

He looked up, startled. "We? Oh no, not I. I wouldn't know what to say to a man like that."

"Do you have any objection to me showing it to him and asking if he might want to publish it?"

"Publish it . . ." The small man shook his head in wonder, trying and failing to restrain a grin. "Thought makes me a bet giddy, I own. Go on, then, if you really think he might like our wee tale."

"I do."

The next day, with the schoolmaster's blessing, Emily read the story to the students at the Sidmouth School and their enthusiastic response emboldened her. So on the last day of the year, she carried Mr. Gwilt's manuscript to the Marine Library and waited in nervous silence while Mr. Wallis read. As he turned the pages, she gauged his progress, mentally summarizing the story in her mind. She knew when he'd reached the part about Parry living with the ship's captain in a rented room after he retired from sea. She knew when he read about the captain dying and Parry finding himself in a curiosity shop, poorly fed and tormented by mean-spirited youths. And then the tentative joy of being rescued by a small, quiet man. The man was not named in the story, but of course Emily knew the character was based on Mr. Gwilt himself.

The story went on to recount their early days together. Parry did not talk to the man or repeat his greetings at first. He was tired and sickly after months in the shop and disillusioned with humans. Instead, he watched and waited to see what sort of human had brought him home.

This man was kind to Parry and fed him delicious treats, yet grief hung heavy over the man—grief caused by the woman in her bed, still and silent, although alive. This, Emily knew, described Mr. Gwilt's wife.

The man dutifully cared for the woman, although she spoke not a word to him and barely seemed to know who he was.

Parry, who had long feared being forgotten, felt the deep sadness of this and longed to cheer the man. Hearkening back to a phrase he had not repeated in a long, long time, Parry praised him with a "Good boy."

This earned Parry a smile from the sad man—a treat far sweeter than mango.

Every night before the man went to bed, he would say to Parry, "Good night. Sleep well. I love you."

And Parry would repeat, "G'night."

The other words were unknown to him, but he concentrated and kept listening.

Then one day, Parry heard the man weeping over the

woman in bed. And soon after, people came and carried her away.

After that, the poor man sat beside Parry's cage for hours as the rooms darkened, not bothering to light a lamp. Yet he never forgot to feed Parry.

Eventually, the shroud of grief lifted and the man began to talk to him once more. He told Parry he was good company. A godsend, whatever that was.

All Parry knew was that he looked forward to spending time with the man and liked his soothing voice. Is that what "love" was?

A peaceful time passed. A few months, perhaps more. Then Parry began to lose his appetite. To sleep more and to talk less. Even his favorite treat of mango lost its appeal, although he pecked at it to please the dear man, who watched him with mounting concern.

One day the man lifted Parry's weak body from the cage and held him gently on his lap, stroking his feathers.

"Oh, Parry. Will I lose you too?"

Parry saw tears in the man's eyes and his little heart swelled. Parry no longer cared if the world remembered him after he was gone. As long as this kind man, his true friend, never forgot him, he would be content.

"G'night," Parry said. "Love you."

And those were the last words he ever spoke.

Mr. Wallis pulled a handkerchief from his pocket and swiped at his nose. Then he removed his spectacles and dabbed his eyes.

Emily wondered if he found the story moving, or if he was thinking of his own dearly departed wife.

After a moment, she ventured softly, "Affecting, is it not?"

With a final sniff, he stowed his handkerchief and straightened. "Depressing, I'd say. Surely not a children's book."

She huffed and countered, "*Robinson Crusoe* was not initially considered a children's book, and it has become a treasured tale for adults and children alike."

"This is no *Robinson Crusoe*."

Emily felt her defenses rise and her mouth fall open in dismay.

He raised a consolatory palm. "Admittedly, I may not be the best judge. I do not publish children's books as a rule."

"But you publish games for children. And just last year you published *Sketches of Juvenile Character*, which included stories like 'The Curious Girl, Cured,' and 'The Life of an Angry Boy.'"

He winced. "That was primarily my brother's doing. Moralistic twaddle, I thought."

"Those are far more depressing than this story."

"Perhaps, but parents buy the books, and they want cautionary tales to scare the naughtiness out of their children."

Emily had thought some of the tales horrid yet refrained from saying so. It would better serve her—and Mr. Gwilt—to remain in the publisher's good graces.

Instead she said, "There are lessons to be learned in Mr. Gwilt's tale too. Lessons of kindness and loyalty and friendship. I read it to the children at the Sidmouth School, and they seemed to truly enjoy it."

He straightened the pages and pushed them back across the desk to her. "I am afraid I cannot help you. This is not something I am interested in publishing. It is nothing personal, you understand."

He twisted his mouth to one side, then added, "While we are on the subject, your sister mentioned that you are writing a novel. . . ."

Heat rushed to Emily's face. She was not prepared to tell anyone about that, and certainly not this esteemed professional. It was not ready. *She* was not ready.

"Which sister?" she blurted. Had it been Viola, her biggest supporter? Or it might have been Georgiana, who could not keep a secret for love or money.

He studied her face, fair eyebrows rising. "Is it such a secret? I have no wish to cause a quarrel." He went on before she could reply. "A Gothic novel, is it? A romance? Never mind. At all events, I thought it prudent to mention that I am not looking to publish novels for young ladies at this time." He gestured toward the shelves. "You know my publications better than I do: games, prints, maps, scenic guides, and the occasional sermon."

Glancing in the direction he pointed, Emily saw Mr. Wallis's clerk emerge from the back room and begin dusting those shelves.

Mr. Wallis cleared his throat. "Well. I decided I should tell you now to avoid misunderstandings or injured feelings later. I value our literary conversations and of course your patronage, but if you are hoping to curry favor—publishing favor, that is—I thought it kindest to disabuse you of that notion without delay."

The clerk sent her a sympathetic look. Having an audience to her humiliation only made the situation worse.

Embarrassment seared through Emily. She wanted to shout at Mr. Wallis that she'd never had any idea of asking him to publish her novel, that he was the last man on earth she would think of asking! She longed to turn and flounce from the establishment, slamming the library door in her wake. Instead, she bit the inside of her cheek to keep from crying.

Again he studied her countenance. "Oh dear. I am afraid I have offended you."

Emily clasped her hands together until the fingernails cut into her palms, and schooled her features.

"Not at all, Mr. Wallis. I thank you for making your position plain."

In a haze of mortification, Emily walked blindly along the promenade, past Hodge's Medical Baths and the York Hotel.

She glanced up and found herself standing outside Marsh's Library and Public Rooms.

This competing library had been in operation for some time, yet Emily had never ventured inside. Not only was the Marine Library closer to Sea View, but she liked Mr. Wallis and enjoyed their discussions about books and authors. She'd been too loyal to him to patronize his competitor—impressive building notwithstanding.

Now she felt a crack spreading through that solid wall of loyalty until the invisible barrier crumbled and seemed to fall away.

With a deep breath, she pushed open the door and crossed the threshold.

The interior was well-appointed with reading chairs and inviting displays. The large windows offered a lovely view of the beach and sea.

She looked around and quickly cataloged an extensive range of reading materials as well as shelves filled with beautiful seashells and ornamental Devonshire marble.

"May I help you, Miss Summers?"

With a start, Emily turned. She had not noticed anyone nearby.

Here he was, the same man she had encountered twice on the esplanade, and now for the first time in his private domain.

He was again dressed in gentlemen's attire, yet his coat of red-and-black plaid contrasted vividly with his striped waistcoat and gold cravat. Most gentlemen wore coats in solid colors over simple waistcoats and plain white cravats. He was definitely a showy dresser. Or perhaps color blind.

His dark wavy hair flopped over his brow in unruly abandon, and she was not sure if he looked more like a rogue or
a little boy in need of a haircut.

Emily still wondered how he knew her name when they had
not been introduced. She said, "Pardon me, but have we met?"

"No, and I am the poorer for it, I assure you."

"Then how do you know my name?"

"My dear lady, what man with eyes and taste does not know
the name of Miss Emily Summers? You and your sisters have
lived here for over a year now, and your reputation as a local
beauty has spread."

She hesitated, both flattered and discomfited by his words.

"Pray forgive the presumption and allow me to introduce
myself." He bowed smartly. "John Marsh, at your service."

She gave a shallow curtsy, unsure if she should. To her memory, she had never curtsied to Mr. Wallis.

"This is your first visit to my establishment, I believe."

"Yes."

"Such a pity. I have felt your absence most keenly." His mouth
quirked, and this hint of humor eased the awkwardness of the
words.

Emily said, "I have always frequented Wallis's. It was nothing personal," she hurried to add. "It is simply nearer our
home. I have a subscription there, and I . . ."

"And you what?" he prodded, a teasing gleam in his bright,
gemlike eyes. "Worship the man?"

"Of course not!"

"Why? Everyone else does."

"Not I. Although I do enjoy discussing books with him,
and his upcoming publishing projects, that sort of thing."

He glanced at the manuscript pages in her hands, interest
kindling in his expression. "And what upcoming publications
might those be?"

"I . . . could not say."

"Ah. So she is discreet and clever as well as beautiful."

There was something in his tone she did not like. She lifted her chin. "Yes, she is. Now, if you will excuse me, I shall not trespass any longer." She turned toward the door.

"Not at all, Miss Summers. You are very welcome." He hurried over to forestall her. "Please, forgive me. I meant no disrespect to you or to Mr. Wallis. Why would anyone not respect the man? After all he has accomplished? I certainly look up to him, although from afar. In fact, I consider him something of a mentor. An example to emulate. As you are probably aware, many credit him with pioneering, or at least popularizing, the inclusion of illustrations within books."

She took this in, feeling somewhat mollified. "Do they? I did not realize."

"Yes. And now he has the royal seal of approval. Something I can only aspire to."

"He has been fortunate, yes."

Nodding slowly, Mr. Marsh added, "He has been most fortunate indeed to gain your friendship and good opinion."

Puzzled, she regarded him through narrowed eyes.

He explained, "I have noticed you leaving his . . . fine library, book in hand, on more than one occasion. You must browse my collection before you leave. Surely there must be something you are longing for, something Mr. Wallis cannot supply?"

With effort she pulled her focus from his magnetic gaze and shook her head. "Another time, perhaps."

He seemed about to object, but at that moment the door opened, and two other ladies walked in. He turned to greet them with his charming smile, and Emily took the opportunity to slip away.

When she returned to Sea View a short while later, she

found Mr. Gwilt helping give the house a thorough cleaning—the only New Year's tradition they were observing that year. While Mrs. Besley and Lowen went through the larder, throwing away any food going off, Mr. Gwilt helped Jessie remove ashes from the fireplaces to start the year fresh.

"Ah, Miss Emily." Kneeling before the hearth, he lifted grimy hands. "Please excuse the state of me."

"Not at all." She bit her lip, hating to disappoint him. "I am sorry to tell you that Mr. Wallis is not interested in Parry's story. He said it's nothing personal. He's simply not publishing children's books at this time."

Robert Gwilt rose with a pop of his knee and turned to face her, revealing a sooty streak on his cheek. "That's all right, Miss Emily. Don't you fret. Never really thought he'd be interested in a silly story about my wee *dutty*."

"I did. And it's not silly."

"Don't give it another thought, my dear. I only hope you don't regret the time you spent on it."

"Not for a moment. And I have not given up yet."

8

Saturdays and Tuesdays are the chief market days.
Poultry and eggs are brought by the country-people . . .
and the supply is commonly equal to the demand.
—*The Beauties of Sidmouth Displayed*

Sarah knocked at the door of Broadbridge's Boarding House, intending to pay a friendly call on Fran Stirling, as she liked to do whenever she found herself nearby and with time to spare—which was not often enough.

Fran smiled upon seeing her on her doorstep.

"Miss Sarah, what a pleasant surprise. Do come in."

Behind Fran stood Mr. Farrant, local carpenter and all-around handyman. It was not the first time Sarah had encountered him at Broadbridge's. Sarah glanced from him to Fran, brows raised in question. "If you are busy, I can come back another time."

"Not at all. Mr. Farrant was just leaving." Fran sent him a significant look.

"Oh. Right." He glanced around the room. "Just came to, uh, take a look at that crack in the plaster there. I'll bring lime and horsehair when next I call." He caught Fran's eye. "Soon."

The broad-shouldered man of perhaps forty sauntered from

the room. Sarah looked back at Fran and saw her friend tracking the man's exit with an appreciative gaze. Leslie Farrant was ruggedly masculine with his muscled forearms, merry eyes, and thatch of dark hair. Sarah could understand the appeal.

After he'd gone, Fran returned her attention to Sarah. "I am so glad you've come. Will you stay for tea?"

Sarah held up the parcel of biscuits she had brought. "I was hoping you'd ask."

Over tea and the biscuits, the two women commiserated about the challenges of hosting strangers, and shared memories of the old days at Finderlay, when Miss Stirling had been Mamma's lady's maid. It struck Sarah that what had been the "good old days" for the rest of them might not have been the best for Fran.

She asked abruptly, "Was it awful, being in service? I never asked."

"No, my dear. Not with your family. I could tell you horrid tales about my previous situation, but I shan't. Your mother was always kind and gracious to me, and you girls were as well. I am grateful to have a place of my own now, of course, although at times I wish the work—and the people—were half as pleasant."

The two shared a long smile.

Sarah sipped, then tentatively began, "You seem to find Mr. Farrant most . . . pleasant."

Fran blushed. "He has been very helpful to me since I moved here. I have come to rely on him."

"And he clearly admires you."

Fran looked down and then up again, a troubled look crossing her pretty face. "He does. In fact, he . . ."

"He what?"

"Oh, Sarah. He asked me to marry him."

Sarah drew in a sharp breath. "Has he indeed? And have you given him an answer?"

Fran shook her head, nibbling her lip with uncertainty. "I am tempted, I own. I like him a great deal."

"But you don't . . . love him?"

"I don't know. I could do, I think. I am less enamored with the prospect of the name *Fran Farrant*. Although I suppose I could grow accustomed even to that."

"Then what is it? Would you not want him here with you, in the boarding house?"

"That's just it! He has his own house. A fine house and workshop, by all accounts, on the outskirts of town."

"So you would have to give up this place?"

"He has not said as much, but really, it would not be practical to keep two houses. I could not do justice as landlady nor as wife if I tried to do both."

"And he would not give up his home to live here?"

"He built that house with his own hands with help from his dear papa, God rest him. I could not ask it of him, but nor am I ready to give up my livelihood. I have become accustomed to being an independent woman."

"I understand. So will you refuse him?"

"I don't know. I told him I needed to think about it."

Sarah squeezed her hand. "Of course you do. Take your time. There is no rush."

Leaving Broadbridge's a short while later, Sarah glanced over at the marketplace, topped by its ball and weathercock.

The market's brick walls protected shoppers and sellers alike, and in two corners stood metal barrels containing warming fires to ward off the worst of winter's chill. There were not as many stalls as in spring and summer, when area farmers brought in fruits and vegetables, but the local greengrocer and fruiterer were there, with modest displays of hothouse-grown offerings and imported produce. Several bakers offered bread and cakes for sale. Meat, poultry, and eggs could be bought at the market, or people could arrange to have them delivered right to their door.

Seeing the poulterer reminded Sarah of something. Mrs. Besley had told her they'd not received their usual delivery of eggs that morning. Assuming it was an oversight, Sarah approached the poultryman to mention it and to buy a few dozen now.

"Good day, Mr. Bidgood."

"Miss."

She gently mentioned the missed delivery, keeping any criticism from her tone.

"Sorry, miss. We'd no eggs to deliver. And none to sell 'ee now, sad to say."

"Why? I do hope your hens are in good health?"

"Oh aye. Though them lay fewer eggs when it's cold."

"I don't recall a shortage of eggs last winter."

"No, miss. But there were no royal party at Woolbrook last winter. Them want a great many eggs. A great many. Not that I've seen a farthing for a one of 'em yet."

"Oh dear. How unfortunate."

"Aye. But I'll do me best to deliver some to 'ee in a day or two."

"Thank you, Mr. Bidgood."

She turned away, wondering how long they would get by with the few eggs they had on hand, and what they might serve for breakfast instead of eggs, which were a staple.

The cake she had thought of making would have to wait.

She noticed Mr. Bernardi then, a straw market basket over one arm, talking or perhaps bargaining at one of the stalls.

He waved to her. "Miss Summers! Do come and lend your advice."

That the confident chef would ask advice about anything surprised her, but she drew her mantle more securely around herself and walked over to join him.

"What do you think of this veal?" he asked, pointing. "It is not so large as what I found in London markets, but nor, by excessive bleedings, rendered so white. The butcher assures me it is very sweet."

"We don't often serve veal, but I trust Mr. Drewe."

"In that case, I shall take it." He turned to the butcher. "Please send it to Woolbrook Cottage."

The man nodded and waved to his boy to wrap up the meat.

Mr. Bernardi gestured for her to proceed him, and the two walked on together, stopping briefly at the next stall. "Look at these iced buns." He gave a tsk of disapproval. "So puny. You could no doubt do better."

"Thank you. I think."

He lifted his basket and explained, "Besides our regular fare, I am beginning to search out ingredients for the duke's party next week."

"I see. I am sure you are looking forward to the challenge."

"True." He glanced around the market. "Fruits and vegetables are not as plentiful as I should wish, but at least the meat is in good supply. Beef, mutton, pork. All seems adequate."

"Speaking of adequate, there are not enough eggs to go around with such a large party at Woolbrook. I don't suppose you have any extra to spare? We are nearly out and there are none for sale."

"For you, Miss Summers, certainly. I shall bring some to you from our stores. A dozen, perhaps? Two?"

"Two dozen, if you can spare them. Thank you."

He nodded and turned his attention to the next stall. His gaze landed on something, and his bushy brows rose.

"Ah, here is a find indeed. Radicchio. First cultivated in northern Italy."

Sarah studied the round maroon heads. "What do you do with it?"

"Eat it, of course."

"Ha ha. I meant how do you prepare it?"

"It can be bitter, so I soak it in cold water first. Then I grill it until crisp and brown, which brings out a sweet, nutty flavor. I will make some for you."

He added a bunch to the basket.

"If you'd like."

She walked beside him as he strolled past more stalls, now and again stopping to sniff an imported orange, a wedge of cheese, a link of sausage, or a handful of shrimp, adding some items to his basket and directing others to be delivered to Woolbrook and billed to the Duke of Kent's comptroller.

Then he lifted a bunch of dried garlic and inhaled deeply through his rather prominent nose. He extended it to her. "Smell this."

Sarah tentatively complied.

"I adore garlic," he said, "especially sautéed in butter or with bacon. Sadly, I've learned many English people prefer their food bland."

"Don't forget, you told me you are English too."

He ducked his head, looking mildly abashed. "True. Yet my mamma does not cook like an Englishwoman, and of course there were my years spent in France to educate my palate. From Mamma, I learned the importance of quality ingredients."

"And from France?" she asked.

"Ah." He raised a finger. "In France I learned that butter makes everything better."

As they left the marketplace, Sarah pointed out Broadbridge's Boarding House, explaining it was owned and managed by their friend Miss Stirling.

At least for now, she added to herself.

He nodded and his expression turned wistful. "Sometimes I think of that, of having an establishment of my own. An eatery, or a small hotel where I might cook for my guests."

Sarah looked at him in surprise. "You astonish me. I would

not have thought a humble hostelry could compete with cooking for a royal household."

Perhaps she ought to have introduced Mr. Bernardi to Miss Stirling. Then, remembering the look on her friend's face when she gazed after Mr. Farrant, it seemed too late to do so now.

He lifted one shoulder. "Serving royalty is not as pleasant as one might think. Consider, when the duke went to Germany, I went to Germany—far from my family, and living in a place where I did not speak the language. Thankfully my French is passable after training in Paris. The duchess speaks German and French, but little English. Understanding one's orders is not always easy in such an environment.

"Then we moved to Kensington Palace, where I was assigned the most menial tasks, assisting the senior kitchen staff like a lowly minion. I began to think I would lose my place until the duke decided to move to the West Country for the winter. Yet even here I am under Leigleitner."

"So it's not all sugar work and accolades?" she asked.

"Sadly, no." He sighed. "In my younger days, I longed for recognition. To prepare delicacies for the most noble palates and make my mark among the great chefs. Yet now, when I think of my parents living happily above their own shop, which they manage as they see fit . . ." He looked thoughtfully toward the boarding house once more.

Sarah said, "I imagine owning a business severely limits one's free time. Shop hours would keep one tethered in place."

He nodded. "That was true, in the early days. But they have reached a modest level of success and have been able to engage a shop clerk, so they can enjoy a bit of leisure from time to time."

"I am glad for them."

His face took on a distant look. "Nothing smells as good as my family's home. Basil and fennel and marjoram . . ."

"Don't forget garlic," she teased.

"I don't forget! In fact, allow me to prepare for you one of Mamma's favorite dishes, hm?"

She grinned. "Garlic stew?"

His eyes glimmered with challenge. "You shall have to wait and see."

When Sarah returned from town, she sewed with Mamma and a reluctant Georgiana for a time while Emily wrote at the table nearby. Since it was the first of the year, the duke had given most of his staff the day off, so the men joined them in the parlour, looking rather bored.

Sarah served tea, then suggested they might walk to the billiard room or join the card games at the assembly rooms. With discouraged glances at the sleet-speckled windows, the three decided to remain indoors.

Mr. Bernardi sat down with a cookery book, Mr. During borrowed writing supplies and began a letter to his mother, and Mr. Thomson retreated to his room.

He returned a few minutes later with the long, narrow case he'd carried when he first arrived, and opened it on the parlour table. Inside the velvet-lined interior were two swords and two foils with blunt practice tips.

Intrigued, Georgie crowded close.

Mr. Thomson looked at Selwyn During, who sat sipping his tea as primly as a dowager. "Do you fence, During?"

"No. Never." He sipped again, little finger raised. "Ask Bernardi."

"I have. Many times. The answer is always the same."

Mr. Bernardi raised a hand without lifting his gaze from the recipe he was perusing. "The only weapons I wield are kitchen knives and my favorite pestle."

Thomson turned back to Mr. During. "Might come in handy to know how to defend yourself, if you are to protect the plate chest."

During winced. "I don't know. Violence is not really my way. I think they merely expect me to watch over it, and to keep things polished and in good repair should we suddenly face some state occasion. Unlikely here in remote Devonshire! Besides, with both General Wetherall and Captain Conroy in our number, who would dare try to rob the duke?"

"Then do it to humor me. I need the exercise," Mr. Thomson urged. "I don't like sitting idle for hours on end."

Mr. During set down his cup and pushed himself to his feet. "If you insist. But I'm afraid you will soon discover I am not very athletic."

Mamma spoke up. "Not in here, gentlemen, if you please."

"Where would you suggest?"

Mamma considered. "I don't know . . ."

"The hall?" Mr. Thomson asked.

"That is rather in the middle of everything."

Georgie said, "The attic has plenty of room. There's the old servants' sitting room, or the nursery is even bigger."

"But, Georgie, that's near your room," Mamma said.

Mr. Thomson hesitated. "We might make a fair bit of noise, tromping around up there."

"I don't mind," Georgie replied. "Especially if I can watch you fence."

He turned back to their mother. "Is that all right with you, Mrs. Summers?"

"I suppose so. Although if plaster begins raining down on our heads, you shall have to find another place."

"Of course."

"I'll show you where it is," Georgie said, leading the men upstairs.

Emily laid aside her quill and notebook. "I think I shall watch as well."

Sarah and Mamma continued with their sewing. Half an hour or so later, Emily returned.

"How is it going up there?" Sarah asked, looking up from her needlework.

"Mr. Thomson is all patience, but Mr. During's technique leaves much to be desired. I shall demonstrate." Taking up her quill again, Emily brandished it as though a small sword, striking out with timid, mincing jabs while her feet shuffled in a lumbering gallop.

"Oh dear." Mamma pressed a hand to her mouth to stifle a laugh.

Sarah bit back a grin. "We should not make fun of our guests."

Emily ceased her pantomime, amusement shining in her eyes. "Then let us just say, Selwyn During is an honest man and sadly correct about his athletic ability."

That night, Emily dreamed she was dancing with Charles Parker. He held her close as they whirled to the music. Heavenly.

Mr. Thomson appeared and tapped her shoulder. When she turned, he handed her a fencing foil.

"Time to rise."

Rise?

The music faded.

"Emily?" Sarah's voice. "Wake up. It is time to get ready for church."

"Ugh." Emily pulled the counterpane over her face.

Sarah said strategically, "I wonder if Mr. Thomson shall attend this morning."

Down went the counterpane, just as her sister had known it would.

"How long do I have to dress?"

Sarah consulted her watch pin. "Thirty minutes."

"What!" Emily threw back the bedclothes and launched from the mattress. "You should have woken me earlier."

"I did try. More than once."

Emily hurried to the basin and began to wash. "May I borrow your Oldenburg bonnet? I think it becomes me rather well."

"You may. It's on the dressing chest."

Mamma had mentioned the service time to their guests the night before. Mr. Bernardi had declined, but Mr. Thomson and Mr. During had expressed interest. Emily dressed quickly.

After helping Emily fasten the laces of her stays and frock, Sarah said, "I am going to make the rounds and see if all is in order. Don't be long." She left the bedchamber, closing the door behind her.

Emily tied up her stockings and slipped into shoes. Then she set to work on her hair.

She wished she were more skilled in arranging it. Carefully brushing it upward, she gathered the brunette length into a thick rope and coiled it at the back of her head, holding it in place with one hand. She grabbed a pin from the dressing table and stuck it in, then ran her fingers over the tabletop searching for another but found none.

She looked around for more pins, opened a drawer with her free hand and shuffled through the contents. Where had Sarah put all the hairpins? She did not have time to let her hair fall and start the process all over again.

With a frustrated huff, she rose and pushed open the door. As she stepped into the passage, the coil shifted and she raised her other hand as well, holding her hair in place as though a priceless crown.

Hearing something, she looked diagonally across the stairwell toward the water closet. Over the balustrade she saw the open door and heard rustling from within. Perhaps her sister tidying up?

Tentatively, she called, "Sarah?"

More rustling.

"Sarah," she called again. "I can't find the hairpins."

A moment later a figure emerged, but it was not her sister.

Mr. Thomson stood there in trousers, waistcoat, and shirt-sleeves, a towel around his neck and a razor in hand.

"Sorry. It is only me."

Emily felt foolish to be caught in the passage like that, both arms over her head. At least she was mostly dressed.

His warm gaze traveled over her, up her arms to the top of her head. How self-conscious she felt standing there with bare arms and lifted bosom. She wished she had put on a fichu before starting on her hair.

"Is something wrong?" he asked.

"I . . . just need hairpins."

"None of those, I'm afraid." His lips quirked softly.

"Of course not."

For a moment, they both stood where they were, looking at each other across the distance. Emily felt oddly breathless. Perhaps her stays were too tight.

At that moment, Sarah came up the stairs. "Emily, are you almost ready?"

She looked from Emily then through the balusters to Mr. Thomson. "Is . . . everything all right?"

Emily said, "I can't find the hairpins. I was coming to ask you."

"I put them in the lacquered box on the dressing chest, remember? I was tired of finding them spread all over the place."

That's right. Emily had forgotten.

Sarah turned and nodded to their guest. "Excuse us, Mr. Thomson."

Emily quickly retreated into their bedchamber, face burning.

A short while later, Emily and the others set out for St. Giles and St. Nicholas together. Mamma, whose health had improved, had begun attending divine services with them, to the delight of her daughters.

The church was about a ten-minute walk away, in the eastern town. Due to the cold weather, Major Hutton sent his carriage for the ladies, while the men planned to go on foot. Georgie, however, insisted Mr. Hornbeam take her place in the carriage while she walked with their guests. She had never minded the cold, so Mamma agreed to the suggestion.

When Emily, Sarah, Mamma, and Mr. Hornbeam arrived at church, they waited inside the entry porch for Georgiana and the two guests to join them, as well as the Huttons and Mrs. Denby.

By the time they had all assembled, the service was about to start. Emily decided introductions would have to wait. They processed through the nave together in silence.

Emily noticed Mr. Thomson drop a few coins into the alms box as he passed. Ahead of her, Mamma linked arms with Sarah but seemed less and less to need the support.

Mamma and Sarah sat first, followed by Georgiana. Mr. Thomson gestured for Emily to precede him into the pew, and she did so, sliding over as far as she could next to her sisters. Mr. Thomson sat beside her, several inches of space between them. Then Selwyn During squeezed in on his other side, jostling Mr. Thomson nearer, until his coat sleeve pressed against her shoulder and his thigh in snug pantaloons brushed her skirts.

Together they filled the family's usual pew as well as the one behind. Major Hutton, wearing a black silk band over his damaged ear, positioned Mrs. Denby's wheeled chair against the end of the pew. Viola sat beside her, followed by the major, his father and brother, Mr. Hornbeam, and Miss Reed. Their servants sat nearer the rear, and Mr. Gwilt chose to sit with them.

As the service began, Emily found herself all too aware of the man beside her.

She dutifully gave the responses and repeated the prayers, but all the while she remained attuned to him, listening to his low, earnest voice. When the organist began to play, Emily looked for another hymnal, but Sarah and Mamma were already sharing one, while Georgiana held the other. Georgie shifted hers closer to Emily, but it remained out of view of the men.

She was about to extract it from her sister's hands when she realized Mr. Thomson was singing the hymn from memory, his baritone rich and true.

"'O God, our help in ages past, our hope for years to come, our shelter from the stormy blast, and our eternal home . . .'"

She liked his voice very much indeed.

After the service, Mr. During quickly exited the pew. Mr. Thomson, however, lingered.

Emily turned to introduce him to Viola and the major. She wondered how he would react to meeting the couple. Like Viola, the major also bore scars. His were more extensive, as he'd been injured in an explosion while serving in India.

"Allow me to introduce one of our guests," Emily began. "Mr. Thomson is private secretary to His Royal Highness, the Duke of Kent. And this is my sister, Mrs. Hutton, and her husband, Major Hutton."

James Thomson bowed. "A sincere pleasure to meet you. Miss Emily speaks of you both often and highly."

Emily watched as he looked from Viola with her unusual lip to the major with his burn scars and covered ear. She saw no signs of revulsion, nor did he seem in any hurry to turn away.

Viola glanced toward Mrs. Denby, likely planning to introduce her, but the elderly woman was surrounded by old friends, smiling and chatting. How much Mrs. Denby's life had changed since the charity had asked Viola to read to a poor-house resident with no family of her own. How much both of their lives had changed.

With this in mind, Emily added, "Mr. Thomson has oversight of the duke's charitable interests, and is willing to learn more about the Poor's Friend Society, if you'd like to arrange a meeting."

Viola beamed. "Indeed I would. Would tomorrow evening at Sea View suit?"

"Perfectly."

"And may I invite two committee members to join us?"

Mr. Thomson glanced at Emily. "If that is all right with my hosts."

Emily nodded. "It is."

The major leaned toward his wife. "Sorry to interrupt, but if we don't return home soon, Chown will burn the roast mutton again."

"Good point. Pray excuse us."

Mr. Thomson bowed. "Of course. Until tomorrow, then."

The couple took their leave, pushing Mrs. Denby's wheeled chair ahead of them.

Mr. Thomson returned his gaze to Emily. "And Chown is . . . ?"

"A former soldier learning to cook as he goes. Our Mrs. Besley has helped him a great deal. Speaking of which, I am starved. I did not have a bite of breakfast."

He grinned. "Too busy searching for hairpins?"

Her cheeks heated at the memory, and his smile widened. "Exactly."

9

WARM SEA BATHS established by Mr. Hodge. Having been exclusively used by their Royal Highnesses the Duke and Duchess of Kent, are best known as *the Royal Baths*.
—*The Beauties of Sidmouth Displayed*

On Monday, Viola and Emily accompanied Mamma to the warm brine baths, traveling there in the Huttons' carriage to avoid the frigid weather. Emily had no plans to repeat her one disastrous experience bathing in the open sea, but she enjoyed the heated indoor baths on occasion. And on such a cold day, a long soak sounded heavenly.

The carriage descended Glen Lane, then turned left, traveling east past Fort Field and the Marine Library to Mr. Hodges's Medical Baths, located near the middle of the beach.

A single carriage stood outside the premises, a bundled-up coachman and shivering groom waiting to carry home the bathers there before them. The place was certainly less busy than it usually was, with nary a sedan chair in sight.

They entered, paid their fees, and followed an attendant into the ladies' dressing room. There, they changed into the provided brown linen petticoats and jackets with tie waists.

When they were ready, they stepped out and descended the stairs into the large sunken bath. The warm water enveloped Emily's body like a welcome embrace.

On the other side of the bath, two women sat with water up to their necks. The younger one wore a stylish hat sporting an ostrich feather, while the older woman was bareheaded, as they were.

They looked up as the Summers ladies joined them, nodding across the water in acknowledgment. Then the women returned to their own conversation, in another language. German, Emily guessed.

Viola leaned near and whispered, "That is the duchess with, I believe, her lady-in-waiting."

Emily looked again with more interest.

The pretty woman was in her early thirties, with dark hair, large eyes, and an aquiline nose over thin lips.

"How do you know?" Mamma whispered back.

"The major and I met them when she and her husband walked past Westmount with their daughter."

Emily regarded the woman in admiration. "I should have known. Only a duchess could look so elegant in these drab costumes."

An hour or so later, the Huttons' carriage dropped them back at Sea View. After bidding Viola farewell, Emily retreated into the library to write, while Mamma went to her room to rest.

When Mr. Thomson returned from work that day, Emily greeted him. "Good afternoon, Mr. Thomson. How are things at Woolbrook?"

"About the same. The duchess is busy with her English lessons and taking sea-water baths."

"Yes, we saw her there today," Emily interjected.

He lifted his chin in acknowledgment. "And the duke remains busy with correspondence. He is making plans to return to Bavaria soon."

"And you would go with him?"

He glanced up quickly, as if surprised by the question. "Yes, of course. Why?"

"Oh, I . . . just curious. Silly question, I suppose." She quickly changed the subject. "Thank you again for agreeing to meet with the ladies from the Poor's Friend Society this evening."

"My pleasure. Will you join us for the meeting?"

"Oh. I am not sure if my presence would be helpful. Viola will be here, but I certainly could attend as well, if you'd like."

He held her gaze. "I would."

Her pulse skittered and her stomach felt oddly tingly. "Very well, then."

After dinner, Viola arrived early from Westmount for the planned meeting and joined Emily and Mr. Thomson in the drawing room to await the others' arrival.

He bowed. "A pleasure to see you again, Mrs. Hutton."

Viola curtsied. "And you, Mr. Thomson."

They chatted for several minutes until their visitors arrived.

When they had all gathered, Emily began, "Mrs. Fulford, Mrs. Robins, allow me to introduce Mr. James Thomson, private secretary to the Duke of Kent, with oversight of charities."

He bowed to the ladies.

A squeal escaped from timid Mrs. Robins, and she quickly pressed a handkerchief to her lips to suppress another.

Mrs. Fulford, tall and elegant, and the obvious leader of the pair, showed no such sign of being intimidated. Rather, her countenance shone with eager speculation.

"Delighted to meet you, Mr. Thomson. We appreciate this opportunity to acquaint you with a charitable organization dear to us all."

Once the ladies were all seated, Mr. Thomson sat as well. Emily served tea and a plate of pastries prepared by Mr. Bernardi. She took a bite, and the crumbly pastry melted in her mouth. *Goodness* . . . She privately vowed not to tell Sarah that his pastries were even better than hers.

Mrs. Fulford sipped her tea, then set the cup and saucer on the side table. She faced Mr. Thomson squarely and began, "The Poor's Friend Society endeavors to check neglect and disorder of the poor here in Sidmouth, whether living in our local poor house or elsewhere. We also solicit donations of cast-off clothes, so we are able provide those in need with decent apparel. Since the formation of the society, relief has been afforded to sixty-four families and individuals, and not less than two hundred and sixty distinct visits have been made by committee members or volunteers. In fact, Mrs. Hutton here is one of our most active volunteers."

He nodded. "Most impressive. May I ask how the charity is sustained and governed?"

"Of course. Our work is made possible by the generosity of subscribers. We carry out our mission under the superintendence of local magistrates and other leading gentlemen of Sidmouth. Here is a list of our governors." She handed it over.

"And how might His Royal Highness be of most assistance at this time?"

Again Mrs. Robins stifled a giddy squeal behind her lace handkerchief. With her free hand, she clutched her pearls.

Ignoring her, Mrs. Fulford smiled and calmly replied, "How kind of you to ask. If His Royal Highness would perhaps consent to become our royal patron?"

Clearly astonished by the bold request, Mrs. Robins's eyes widened. Sharing the woman's tense anticipation, Emily held her breath.

"I would be happy to present the good work of your society

to him," Mr. Thomson said. "Although naturally I cannot make any promises."

"Of course, of course." Mrs. Fulford handed over a page of ornamental script on fine stationery. "Here is a list of our current subscribers, any of whom would be willing to provide a positive report on our work."

"Excellent. Thank you."

A short while later, Mrs. Fulford and Mrs. Robins departed.

Viola lingered. "That went well," she said. "At least from my point of view."

"I agree," Emily said. "But Mr. Thomson must be the judge." They both turned to him.

He nodded. "I was impressed by the little they shared."

Viola tilted her head as she regarded him. "What might truly sway you is to see some of the good works for yourself. Perhaps you might visit the Sidmouth Poor House?"

"I shall indeed. At my first opportunity."

Taking Viola's admonition to heart, Mr. Thomson asked Emily to direct him to the poor house the very next day.

She readily acquiesced. She had already seen Viola pass by in the carriage, on her way to read to the residents as she often did on Tuesdays and Thursdays. Being more familiar with the place, her sister would be better qualified to give him a tour. If Emily and Mr. Thomson left soon, they could walk to the poor house and meet Viola there.

Together they set off for the eastern town. Thankfully the day was milder, with barely a hint of wind and plenty of sunshine to warm them.

As they walked from Fore Street onto Mill Lane, they passed the Sidmouth School, its yard enclosed within a brick wall.

Through its gate, they saw a group of boys kicking a ball over patchy grass worn to dirt in places by many feet. Only a hint of snow remained around the perimeter. The boys were supervised by the schoolmaster, Mr. Ward, who had graciously allowed her to read Mr. Gwilt's tale to his pupils and had even asked for his own copy.

She waved to the man now. "Good day, Mr. Ward."

He returned the wave and gestured for them to come closer. As they did, he opened the gate, and Emily and Mr. Thomson walked into the yard.

"I wanted to thank you for that story. The children asked to hear it again and seemed to enjoy it as much the second time."

Emily smiled. "I am glad. I shall pass along their praise to the author."

His eyes glinted with interest. "Not you, then?"

"No indeed. Mr. Gwilt, our bookkeeper at Sea View. He will be delighted to know the children are still enjoying it."

She turned to her companion. "Allow me to introduce Mr. Thomson. Mr. Thomson, this is Mr. Ward, the schoolmaster."

"A pleasure, sir."

"Mr. Thomson, is it? Not the Duke of Kent's private secretary?"

"The same, sir."

"Ah. Mrs. Fulford was here a short while ago. She mentioned meeting you and presenting her society for His Royal Highness's consideration. Most charitable woman. Am I correct in guessing you are on your way to view the poor house?"

"We are, yes," Emily replied.

"Before you go, I would be remiss not to mention our school here." He turned and swept an arm toward the simple whitewashed, two-story building. It possessed two front doors, one bearing a stone plaque marked *Girls*, the other *Boys*.

"The school was established for the education of the infant

110

poor," Mr. Ward explained, "according to Dr. Bell's plan, and is supported by voluntary subscriptions. More than fifty children are now being educated here."

"Goodness," Emily breathed. "I had not realized there were so many."

Mr. Thomson observed, "Impressive."

For a moment longer they watched the game, and then Mr. Ward said, "I don't suppose you could watch over this lot for a few minutes so I can nip home for a lesson book I left there? I live just next door."

"With pleasure, sir." Mr. Thomson glanced at Emily. "That is . . . if it's all right with you?"

Emily glanced at her watch pin. Viola was likely to be at the poor house for another half an hour, so they had about twenty minutes to spare. "Certainly. Take your time."

Mr. Ward called to the boys. "Mr. Thomson and Miss Summers will oversee the play yard for a few minutes. Be on your best behavior!" And with that admonition, he hurried away.

The children paused in their game. A few grinned shyly at Emily, but they eyed their male visitor warily.

Emily offered a general nod, while Mr. Thomson addressed the boy holding the ball. "May I see that?"

The lad hesitated, then reluctantly complied, tossing the ball to the stranger.

Mr. Thomson eyed the rough ball, then dropped it. For one second, Emily feared he'd found it too dirty or in too poor a condition. Instead, he kicked it into the fray. Then he ran to join the others, whacking the ball into the makeshift goal to the cheers of his new teammates.

Then he began playing defense, attempting to block the older boys' drives with skill but without aggression, and at the last moment, allowing a smaller boy to hit it through the goal.

The informal game continued for a quarter of an hour or

so. Mr. Thomson encouraged and good-naturedly teased the youngsters as he blocked and kicked and feinted a miss to a chorus of groans and cheers.

Watching his antics, Emily could not help smiling.

"Join us?" he called to her.

"No thank you. I have never played this game."

He expertly kicked the ball toward her, and the children turned to watch.

"Come on!" one shouted encouragement.

Halfheartedly, Emily attempted to kick it back. It rolled only a few yards.

"Try again," Mr. Thomson urged.

She reeled back her half boot and kicked it again as hard as she could, sending the ball a little farther, before an impatient lad came and retrieved it.

"Told you!" Emily called back to him. His warm smile in reply melted away any embarrassment she might have felt.

When Mr. Ward returned, Thomson handed the ball back to the lad who'd originally given it to him. "That's all for today, I'm afraid. Miss Summers and I must be on our way."

This announcement was met with more good-natured groans.

"Already?"

"Will you come back and play with us again?"

He glanced at Emily, then placed a hand on the smallest lad's head and ruffled his hair. "If at all possible."

The two continued to the poor house. Once inside the neat brick building, Emily went and found Viola, who was just leaving one of the residents' rooms. "Oh good. You are still here. Mr. Thomson took your advice. Do you have time to show him around?"

"Yes, of course." She smiled at Emily's companion. "A pleasure to see you here, Mr. Thomson."

He bowed. "Thank you for encouraging me to come."

For a moment, Viola's eyes glimmered with interest as she looked from one to the other, and then she gestured down the main corridor. "Shall we?"

She led them around, pointing out the residents' rooms, a small kitchen, and the communal dining room overlooking the River Sid. Viola described the simple rooms and meals, and the society's efforts to improve the lives of the residents.

The door marked *1* opened, and Miss Reed stepped out dressed in an old-fashioned gown that had once been fine. Her face still bore the faded pockmarks of smallpox. When she saw them, she smiled, and the expression smoothed her skin. "Mrs. Hutton, it is good to see you, as always. And Miss Emily! This is a pleasant surprise."

Emily felt self-conscious and a little embarrassed for Mr. Thomson to hear that she was not a regular visitor to the poor house, not as active in good works as her sister.

Even so, she politely returned the woman's greeting. "Miss Reed. How are you?"

"Better than I ever expected to be again."

Studying the older woman's cheerful countenance, Emily wondered if the improvement in her spirits was due to the amount of time she'd spent in Simon Hornbeam's company in recent months.

After introducing Mr. Thomson, the three moved on, greeting another resident, Mr. Banks, on their way to Mrs. Denby's room.

Mrs. Denby was Viola's favorite, Emily knew. The older woman's sight was dim after years of lace making, but her outlook and smiles were always bright.

Viola knocked, and hearing a muffled "Come in," opened the door. Viola gestured her sister and guest into the humble room.

Frail Mrs. Denby beamed up at them from her chair.

"Ah! You're back, Viola. And with Miss Emily too. Let me put on my spectacles so I can see you properly. And who, pray, is this handsome young man?"

Emily spoke up. "This is Mr. Thomson. He is staying with us at Sea View. He oversees the Duke of Kent's charitable interests and is here to learn more about this place."

"I see—well, a little," the woman joked. "Welcome, welcome! Yes, Mrs. Fulford and her committee have been very generous. But it's Viola here who has stolen my heart and changed my life. If the duke wants to help old folks like me, he'd find a way to make many more dear souls like her! And Miss Sarah has been generous too, with all the baked goods she sends over. And Miss Emily and Miss Georgiana are kind as well. They sometimes deliver gifts on their sister's behalf."

Again, Emily felt sheepish at this comparison to her sisters. At least Mrs. Denby made her sound as charitable as Georgie.

Mr. Thomson asked, "And how long have you lived here, Mrs. Denby? If that is not an impertinent question?"

"Not at all, young man. Though I'm afraid it's many years now. After Mr. Denby died, I shared a pair of rooms with my sister. Sadly, she reached her eternal reward not long after my husband did. My eyesight had grown worse by then, so I was no longer able to take in sewing to pay the rent. I thank God a room here was offered to me, for I had nowhere else to go."

"What about your spiritual needs? Or medical care?"

"Spiritual needs? If that's a fancy term for praying for us, then yes, the vicar comes by now and again, although it's Mr. Butcher, a dissenting minister, who visits most often. And when one of us falls ill, the local apothecary comes when he can."

"And how is the food?"

"Good. Wholesome."

"Who prepares it?"

"Mrs. Novak cooks for us. She is older than any of us here, if you can believe it! But spry as well as kind."

Mrs. Denby leaned closer and said in conspiratorial tones, "The treats Miss Sarah sends over taste better, but you did not hear it from me!"

She giggled like a girl, and Mr. Thomson smiled at her. "Your secret is safe with me."

Emily felt the warmth of that smile in her own heart. *Careful, Emily*, she admonished herself. *Don't let your head be turned simply because he is kind to children and old people. Charles would be kind as well. Any gentleman would be.*

After visiting with Mrs. Denby a few minutes longer, they thanked her for her time and bid her farewell. As they walked out together, he said, "I look forward to telling His Royal Highness about the society and its good work. And to recommending his support."

"Thank you," Viola replied.

"Yes, thank you," Emily echoed. And again she was aware of her twin's speculative gaze studying the two of them.

10

[The Duke of] Kent encountered a fortune teller
in Sidmouth, who told him, "This year two
members of the Royal Family will die."
—A. N. Wilson, *Victoria*

Later that day, after Mr. Thomson went to Woolbrook, Emily walked to Marsh's Library and Public Rooms with a copy of Parry's story. She had not confided her plan to Mr. Gwilt, for she did not want to raise his hopes should they be dashed once more.

"Miss Summers." The owner rose and bowed when she entered. "A pleasure to see you again, and here in my humble establishment."

"Mr. Marsh." Emily held Mr. Gwilt's manuscript tightly to her chest, not certain why this man disconcerted her so.

Perhaps noticing her discomfort, he did not approach but remained where he was.

His gaze, however, lowered to the pages in her arms.

"And what have you there? Another book Wallis plans to publish?"

"No. This is a manuscript. A story. I wondered if . . ."

"Ah! Something by your own hand. You are a writer."

Her sister again, Emily supposed, irritation flaring. "Who told you that?"

"No one told me. It was only a guess. After all, you are carrying a manuscript as though a beloved child. Also, you are clearly an avid reader. Which, in my experience, is the best training for a writer."

Emily agreed with his assertion wholeheartedly. But before she could compose a reply, he went on.

"In fact, I'd wager you have read everything published about Sidmouth, its history and environs, and know Mr. Butcher's guide cover to cover."

"Perhaps. However—"

"I knew it!"

"While I admit I am an aspiring author, this manuscript was written by a friend of our family. I have helped him revise and edit this copy, but the tale, the emotions, the imagination are all his."

His mouth quirked. "One of your many admirers, I assume?"

"Not at all. He is at least fifty. I look on him as more of an . . . uncle." An odd, eccentric uncle, but she did not mention that.

Mr. Marsh raised his chin in understanding, then expelled a fatalistic sigh. "You want me to read it."

"I do, yes. I believe this has merit and want to see it published." She tentatively laid it on his desk.

He wrinkled his nose as though smelling something foul. "I would be more interested if you had written it."

"Why?"

He held her gaze, eyes alight with . . . something . . . she could not fathom. Not attraction, which she was familiar with. This was something more . . . speculative.

"Because you interest me." He sat back down and inhaled

slowly, fingers tapping on his desk. "I'd like to see a sample of your work."

"My work?" For a second she thought he'd meant a sample of the most common type of women's *work*—needlework, a skill she sorely lacked. Then she realized what he must mean. "A sample of my editing abilities? Pages I have corrected?"

He shook his head. "A sample of your writing."

"Of my . . . handwriting?"

"Come now, feigning ignorance does you no credit. I want to gauge your writing skill—your way with words, your ability to communicate, to describe, to inform, to entertain, to impress."

Goodness. He expected her writing to do all that? Her palms began to perspire.

She could show him a few pages of her novel, she supposed. Viola had read the opening chapters and given her suggestions for improving them. Emily had already made the changes and had polished the first chapter too many times to count. Even so, the thought of showing it to this man filled her with abject fear.

Reluctantly, she admitted, "I have written several chapters of a novel, but it is not yet finished."

"A tantalizing Gothic romance destined to be all the crack and make us both rich?"

"I . . . would not describe it like that, no."

Another sigh. "Even so, I should like to see it. Bring me something tomorrow."

"To what end? I highly doubt you would be interested in a"—she recalled Mr. Wallis's description—"novel for young ladies."

"I shall be the judge of that. In the meantime, I have a different project in mind for you. Before I explain particulars, I need to determine if your skills are sufficient to the task."

She bristled, pride and insecurity wrestling within her. "I did not come here seeking employment for myself."

"I know. But if you do as I ask, I will consider this uncle's manuscript." He tapped the pages on his desk before sliding them back to her.

"You haven't even read it yet."

"I shall, in due course. First, bring me something of yours. I know I shan't be disappointed."

"Your confidence in me is unmerited."

Again his blue-green eyes glinted. "On the contrary, I think I see in you something very valuable indeed."

A few moments later, Emily left Marsh's Library and started for home, walking west along the esplanade.

Behind her, slow and steady footsteps crunched the snow. Emily looked over her shoulder and saw a woman in a hooded cloak, head bowed against the cold. Was she following her? Or simply walking in the same direction?

Emily picked up her pace, ears attuned to the trailing footsteps. The woman quickened her pace as well.

Emily was relieved to reach the old fort and turn up Glen Lane. There were only a few houses on this narrow track. Surely the woman would continue along Peak Hill Road or turn back after reaching the end of the esplanade.

Ahead of her on Glen Lane, Emily spied the duke in a heavy coat and hat, again out taking the air.

Noticing her, he raised a hand in acknowledgment, and Emily returned the gesture, glad to no longer be alone.

He smiled as he drew nearer. "Miss Summers, we meet again. What brings you out today? Taking the sea air, as am I?"

"I went to the library, Your Royal Highness."

"Ah, yes, I met the man. Wallis, was it? He gave us a long print of Sidmouth."

Guilt rose at his assumption that she'd been to Wallis's library. Remembering Mr. Wallis's plea that she remind the duke of his patronage, Emily felt another stab of disloyalty for having visited his competitor's establishment. She decided not to correct the duke.

Instead she said, "Mr. Wallis told me how pleased he was to meet you. And to be appointed bookseller to Your Royal Highnesses. He was exceedingly honored."

"That's right." The duke nodded. "I shall have to visit his library one of these days." He looked at the slim stack of pages in her hands.

"That doesn't look like a book. Did you find nothing interesting to read there?"

"Oh. I . . . Not today. But I have borrowed many wonderful books from Mr. Wallis in the past."

"Good, good."

He looked over her head and his eyes narrowed. "I say, who is that?"

Emily turned and her nerves jangled. The woman who'd been following her had turned up Glen Lane as well.

As she walked closer, Emily recognized her with a jolt. The fortune-teller.

Where was she going? Surely no one at Westmount or Woolbrook had invited her to come and tell their fortunes.

In the brighter light of day, Emily better saw the old woman's face. Her eyes, once again in a vague, trancelike stare, were heavily lined with kohl.

Emily hoped the woman would continue past them without a word, as she had the time she, Viola, and Mrs. Denby had encountered her.

Instead, the woman stopped dead when she reached the duke, and turned her strange eyes on him with no change in expression. Did she even know who he was?

Before Emily could think how to prevent her from speaking to Prince Edward, the woman cracked open her wrinkled lips and said, "This year two members of the royal family will die."

Apparently she did know who he was.

Emily's stomach twisted. She wanted to apologize to him, to do *something*, but then the woman turned her eerie stare to Emily and said, "And you, my pretty, shall break your heart. Lose it . . . utterly."

For a moment Emily stared in dismay and shivered, much as she had upon first encountering the woman. Then anger flared at her presumption and disrespect. Emily opened her mouth to tell the woman to go on her way, but the fortune-teller turned of her own accord and slowly retreated the way she had come.

How very odd, Emily thought, watching her go.

Once the woman had walked away, the duke exclaimed, "*Quelle horreur!* Who was that?"

"I don't know her name. She is rumored to be a fortune-teller."

"Horrors," he repeated. "Perhaps it is a good thing my family came to this healthful place, then." He glanced at Emily, then hesitated. "Is she . . . often correct?"

"I don't know that either," Emily replied. "I have only been warned to stay away from her."

He drew a long breath. "Well, I would not give her predictions much credence. After all, my father the king has long been ill, so predicting his death does not require supernatural powers. And as far as a second death?" He shrugged. "The royal family is a large one. And none of my older brothers enjoy good health. The Prince Regent is grossly overweight, and the Dukes of York and Clarence are heavy drinkers. Thankfully, my wife has recovered well from childbirth, and our daughter and I are both perfectly hale." He pulled a handkerchief from his pocket and wiped his nose. "Apart from a trifling cold."

He pocketed the handkerchief and looked again at Emily.

"And as for what she said about you, it does not take a great deal of imagination to predict a young lady might have her heart broken, now does it?"

"No, I . . . suppose not." She shivered again, and this time he noticed.

"You are cold. Forgive me. I shan't keep you standing out here much longer. But allow me to say one more thing."

She nodded, and he continued.

"Many young women break their hearts over unworthy men, but you will discover that you shall have more than one chance at love in this life. At least I have. Despite the mistakes of my past, this old soldier now has a much-beloved wife and daughter, and I am grateful."

Again Emily nodded. What to say . . . *I am happy for you?* Why should he care what she thought? She settled on "You are blessed indeed."

"I am. And I hope you will be similarly blessed one day as well."

She managed a small smile as he went on his way.

Emily had planned to go straight home, but after the strange encounter, she longed to talk to Viola. So she walked farther up Glen Lane and turned at Westmount's wooded drive, her mind reeling from the duke's platitudes to the strange woman's prediction.

Had she lost Charles for good? Is that what the woman's words meant? Was Emily soon to learn of his upcoming marriage to someone else? That would certainly break her heart. Was she destined to be unhappy always? A spinster? Or might they have a second chance, as His Royal Highness had said?

Reminding herself of Mrs. Denby's admonition to have nothing to do with fortune-tellers, Emily tried to banish the image of the woman's eerie lined eyes, their inner corners yellow and veined.

Silently she prayed, *Forgive me, Lord, for entertaining her words for even an instant.*

Reaching Westmount, Emily pushed through the wrought iron gate and stepped under the porte cochère.

Major Hutton's friend, Armaan Sagar, opened the door before she'd even knocked. "Good day, Miss Summers. I saw you on the drive. Come in out of the cold."

"Thank you." She stepped inside and then noticed how he was dressed. "Going riding?"

"With the major, yes, although I do not know where he is at present." He glanced over his shoulder. "Perhaps he forgets or is busy."

"Is my sister at home?"

He nodded. "In the sitting room, last I saw her." He took Emily's mantle and gestured down the passage. "Shall we go and see?"

"Yes, please. I am eager to speak to her."

Together they walked to the sitting room, and he pushed open the door. There was Viola . . . locked in the major's embrace, kissing quite passionately.

Emily let out a squeak of surprise.

Armaan sent her a wry look, slowly shaking his head. "New-wed people."

Noticing them, Viola immediately attempted to pull away, but the major only slowly, begrudgingly released her. He scowled at his friend and seemed about to curse, but seeing her, he refrained.

"Good day, Emily."

"Jack. Sorry to . . . intrude."

"Ah well. Is that not what pesky little sisters do?" He winked at Emily, his sister by marriage.

She knew he expected her to tease back, but Emily barely managed a grin.

Viola gave her husband a playful push. "Now, go on your ride. Shoo."

"If I must."

When the men left, Emily looked back at her twin and found Viola studying her in concern.

"What's wrong? Are you upset about something?"

"I am. Though I hope you will tell me I am being silly."

"Let's sit by the fire."

Viola closed the door. They sat in armchairs near the fireplace, but Emily felt chilled despite the flames.

"What's happened?" her sister asked.

"I met Prince Edward in the lane just now. As we were talking, that frightening old woman approached us."

"What woman?"

"The fortune-teller. Remember we saw her once before?"

Viola nodded. "Mrs. Denby warned us to stay away from her."

"I know. And I certainly did not seek her out. She came up the lane as though specifically to speak to His Royal Highness. After she had said her piece to him, then to me, she turned and left."

"What did she say?" Viola asked, eyes wide.

"I hate to think of it, let alone repeat it. She said, 'This year two members of the royal family will die.'"

"Oh no! How awful. What a terrible thing to say."

"I agree. Thankfully, he seemed to brush it off as claptrap. For the most part."

"And what did she say to you?"

Emily swallowed. "She said that I would utterly break my heart."

"Oh, Em!" Viola reached over and took her hand. "I am

sorry. But remember, she knows nothing. She is a stranger to you. And we don't go in for that sort of thing. Mrs. Denby was right. We ought to have nothing to do with her."

"I agree. Even so, it gave me gooseflesh." Emily shuddered, then added, "Of course I thought immediately of Charles— that she was telling me I had lost him for good."

"You still hold out hope for a reconciliation?"

"You know I do. You would tell me, would you not, if you'd had news from home—learned he was engaged to someone else?" She heard the plaintive note in her voice but made no effort to conceal her fear. Not with this sister.

"I would. And I have not heard any such news. But, Em, after all this time . . . you must prepare yourself for that possibility."

"I know," Emily said bravely, and then realized she was shaking her head. She stopped and added, "In the meantime, I will probably have nightmares about that woman."

Viola squeezed her fingers. "I shall pray that you don't."

Her sister insisted she stay until the shock had passed and Emily was warmed through. She asked Chown to bring them tea for the purpose.

As they sat near the fire, sipping their hot drinks, Emily considered telling her about Mr. Marsh's request to see a sample of her writing.

In the end, she decided against it, in case it all came to nothing. And after the day's unhappy predictions for the future, Emily feared that was exactly what would happen.

11

I have been learning to fence. It is quite the proper thing
nowadays for women to learn how to handle the foils.
—Nellie Bly, *The New York World*

Early the next morning, the duke sent a footman to tell
Mr. Thomson not to bother coming over that day as he
wouldn't be dealing with any official correspondence
nor need him to take dictation. Instead he planned to rest
his sore throat. The prospect of a day of leisure did not seem
to cheer the private secretary, who clearly chafed under the
confinement.

After breakfast, Emily sat with her writing slant in the parlour, rewriting a clean copy of the first few chapters of her
novel for Mr. Marsh, wondering all the while if she would
actually find the courage to allow the man to read them.

Nearby, Mr. During sat with an issue of *Ackermann's Re-
pository*, apparently content to sit still for hours. He was not
needed at Woolbrook either.

James Thomson entered the parlour in fencing attire and
asked During to fence with him.

The table-decker groaned. "No, no. Please don't insist.

Once was enough punishment for us both, I should have thought."

Mr. Thomson sighed.

Georgiana spoke up. "I'd like to learn," she said. "Would you teach me?"

He hesitated, then said, "I have never had a female opponent before."

Noting his reluctance, Emily assured him, "Georgiana is a natural-born athlete and excels at most sports."

"I have no problem believing it," he said, turning back to Georgie. "Very well. I can show you a few basics, although I am no teacher."

"Wonderful!" her sister enthused. "What shall I wear?"

"Something comfortable that gives you freedom of movement. And sturdy shoes."

"Very well." Georgie's blue eyes shone. "Give me just a few moments." She hurried away.

Mr. Thomson looked at Emily, expression intent. "Will you join us?"

She set aside the slant and stood. "I think I will."

It wouldn't be proper for her sister to spend time in the secluded attic alone with a man. Or so Emily justified in her mind as an excuse to accompany them.

She added, "It is not that I don't trust you, of course. I do."

He smiled softly. "I am glad to hear it."

"That I trust you, or that I will join you?"

"Both."

Emily walked with him up to the attic, to a large room that had once served as nursery and perhaps schoolroom. There, he surveyed the child-sized table and chairs, and a few small desks pushed to the perimeter of the room.

"Reminds me of my old schoolroom."

"Mine too."

He returned his gaze to her. "Were you educated at home?"

"Yes, by a series of governesses, poor things. You as well?"

"Briefly, until my father sent me away to school at the age of eight."

She gasped in sympathy. "So young!"

"I certainly thought so. And later I of course attended university."

"Cambridge?"

"Oxford."

Charles Parker had also attended Oxford. The men were of similar age. She wondered if their paths might have crossed. Yet for some reason she did not want to mention Charles to this man. Besides, with so many different colleges at Oxford, the chances of the two being acquainted were slim.

Mr. Thomson asked, "And how old is Georgiana?"

"Barely sixteen."

He nodded. "Don't worry. I shall go easy on her."

Emily laughed. "At your own peril! You had better be on your guard with Georgie, and I mean that literally!"

When her youngest sister entered, all eagerness, Mr. Thomson began the lesson, while Emily sat on one of the small chairs to watch.

He began by showing her the practice foil with its blunt tip, explaining how it was different from a sword used in actual fighting.

"Always keep the broad side up and strike your opponent with this point."

Then he began showing her the various positions, demonstrating, for example, how to assume first position by facing her, heels together. Georgie followed suit.

Looks simple enough, Emily thought. *Even I could do that. Maybe even Mr. During . . .*

As the lesson continued, Emily found her attention straying

to novels she had read that included sword fighting. *Waverly, Rob Roy, The Heart of Mid-Lothian.* She also thought of Robinson Crusoe trying to survive on his desert island. He had salvaged broadswords from the wrecked ship and used one as a sickle to harvest his corn crop. Imagining polished James Thomson doing the same, she chuckled.

He glanced over. "Are we amusing you, Miss Emily?"

She looked up guiltily. "Not at all. I was thinking of something else."

Suddenly she remembered that later in the book *Robinson Crusoe*, swords had been used to kill people, which was not at all amusing. Her mirth quickly faded.

Mr. Thomson said, "Thankfully your sister has excellent focus. Concentration is key in fencing."

"Thank you." Georgiana beamed.

"Well, you can't blame me," Emily teased. "All that advancing and retreating—forward and back, forward and back—is rather hypnotic. At least I was only daydreaming when I might have fallen asleep!"

Returning the foils to the case, he shook his head, expression tolerant. "Next time we shall have a real bout and endeavor to keep your attention."

"I shall look forward to it."

Georgiana clapped. "And so shall I!"

Later that day, Emily did some advancing and retreating herself, pacing the floor of Marsh's Library and Public Rooms, heart pounding in her ears, as its proprietor sat reading her opening chapters.

Without looking up he said, "Do stop pacing like a caged animal. You are distracting me."

"Sorry."

Clasping her hands tightly, she went to stand at the window, blind to the passersby and view of the sea beyond. How uncomfortable this was. How her nerves writhed!

She longed to snatch back her pages and hide them from his scrutiny. Instead she forced herself to endure the excruciating wait, feeling every moment like a butterfly pinned to a board for close inspection . . . and imminent death. At least, death of her ambitions.

Reminding herself yet again that she was doing this for Mr. Gwilt as well, Emily remained where she was, anxiety heating every pore. She pulled a handkerchief from her reticule and dabbed at the perspiration beading along her hairline. Then she leaned nearer the chilled glass, feeling a refreshing draught of cold outside air.

Behind her, she finally heard pages being tapped against the desktop to straighten the thin stack.

She turned, forcing her gaze to his face, afraid to see what expression he wore. Disappointment? Reluctance to give her bad news, just like Mr. Wallis?

He rose and carried one of the armchairs from the reading area closer to his desk. "Please sit down."

When she had done so, he interlaced his fingers and rested his elbows on the desk. "You have talent, Miss Summers. That is obvious. I cannot speak to the plot and characters after so brief a sample, but your writing is vivid and compelling."

"Th-thank you," she murmured halfheartedly, waiting for the *but*.

"So here's what I propose. As you are probably aware, it is common practice for publishers like Wallis and me to hire others to write for them. The Reverend Edmund Butcher wrote *The Beauties of Sidmouth Displayed*, yet whose name is on the title page? *Printed for John Wallis, at The Marine Library*."

"I noticed that."

"We know it sells well, as they are printing a new edition. So I would like you to write a guidebook to be printed for me and my establishment." He raised an eloquent hand as if writing the words in the air. "*The New Sidmouth Guide, with an accurate description of the situation, scenery, and climature of that much-admired watering place. Printed for John Marsh at his library and public rooms.*"

Emily stared at him, stomach churning. *She* was to write a book to compete with the popular guide written by an esteemed clergyman, a man who had written and published other books besides?

"I am not qualified."

He wagged a finger. "I believe you are uniquely qualified. You admitted you have already read everything there is about Sidmouth. Books like Mr. Butcher's and anything else you could find about your new home?"

"Well, yes, but I—"

"And are you not acquainted with many people of the town—nobility, gentry, and tradespeople alike? Have you not hosted visitors in your own home, and learned what local information they most need and value?"

"I suppose that's true."

"You would not receive the credit. It would be work for hire, as many writers before you have started out. And I could not pay you much. But if you complete the project in a timely manner and I am satisfied with it, then I will read your friend's manuscript and consider yours besides. And *that* you could publish under your own name—unless you prefer to shield your identity under a pen name, as many women do."

Emily's pulse quickened and she began to perspire once more. "How soon would you need it?"

He screwed up his mouth, then said, "A few weeks? A month?

It need not be very long. Seventy or eighty pages and many of those filled with lists of tradespeople, available services, and coach times. Rather like Butcher's slim volume."

"A month?" she asked incredulously.

"Or sooner, if you can manage it."

Again she was on her feet, pacing once more. "Goodness. I could not work here round the clock. I have responsibilities at Sea View: advertising, corresponding with guests, helping in the office. . . ."

He rose as well, then came around the desk and leaned against its edge. "You may work on it at home, as best suits your schedule. I have no need to supervise your progress day-to-day."

He handed her an embossed leather portfolio containing an outline for the envisaged guidebook along with the scrawled notes he had made so far.

She paused to glance over it, but her thoughts were of Sea View. Being able to work on this at home would make things easier. She often fit in some writing during her shifts in the office or when her other tasks were finished.

He extended a hand as though to lay it on her shoulder, then crossed his arms over his chest instead. "Work hard and demonstrate your talent. Help me succeed, and I will do the same for you."

When she still hesitated, he leaned nearer, eyes intense.

"Come, Miss Summers. This is a rare opportunity. What are you waiting for? What have you got to lose?"

"I don't know. The prospect frightens me."

"My dear young lady, do you not think I face down fear every time I sink money into a new building or publishing venture? All men of business . . ." He corrected himself. "All *people* of business take risks every day. No risk, no reward."

Emily studied the man's animated expression. He was undeniably persuasive, with passion sparking in his eyes. Yet beyond her own doubts about her abilities, Emily was still plagued by a sense of loyalty to Mr. Wallis, who had been so kind to her over the last year.

Then again, he had not been willing to consider Mr. Gwilt's manuscript, nor hers. And her name would not appear in this guidebook, so perhaps Mr. Wallis need never know.

She took a deep breath and exhaled. "Very well, I shall do it."

He beamed and extended his hand to her. She had rarely shaken a man's hand before, and certainly not to seal a business arrangement.

But she reminded herself that Mr. Marsh was neither stranger nor suitor. He was a colleague. And with that thought, she shook his hand.

That afternoon when Sarah stepped into the dining room to spread a fresh cloth for dinner, she drew up short, taken aback to find Mr. During inching open one of the drawers in the sideboard, peering in at the family silver.

Noticing her, he snapped upright like a soldier, heels together, arms at his sides. "Selwyn During, table-decker to the Duke of Kent, entrusted with the royal plate."

Sarah blinked. "Yes, Mr. During, I remember. Might I help you with something in here?"

"I . . ." He glanced longingly at the china atop the sideboard. "I only wondered . . . Might I set the table for tonight? It's what I do, you know. But with the Royal Highnesses entertaining so little, the old fingers start to itch from inactivity. I notice you have some lovely china and silver. Nothing as fine as the Portuguese silver, nor of course the Grand Service, which is made of gold."

Sarah looked at the patterned plates and soup bowls. "These

are my mother's. We brought them with us from Gloucester-shire, along with the table linens." Father's heir had not been pleased to learn the household linen, plate, many books, and this china, along with the family's handsome pianoforte, were not included in the entail, as they had been gifts from Mamma's own family.

"Lovely pattern. Simple. Elegant." He dragged his gaze from the plates to her. "So . . . may I?"

Sarah laughed, amused and ill at ease at once. "If you truly want to set our table, be my guest. Literally."

Clearly missing her joke, he rubbed his long thin hands together in eager anticipation. "Thank you."

The man's entire form was long and thin, his shoulders narrow. He must be stronger than he looked to be entrusted to protect the valuable items of silver and gold owned by the royal pair.

He donned white gloves and spread the table cover, attempting to smooth out the wrinkles. Then he extracted a ruler from one pocket and a polishing cloth from the other and went to work, positioning the plates the exact same distance from the edge of the table.

With a bemused shake of her head, Sarah stepped from the room.

In the passage, she encountered Mr. Bernardi, just returned from Woolbrook after a morning spent in their kitchen. "Ah. Good afternoon, Mr. Bernardi. All done for the day?"

He nodded. "An early day for me. Leigleitner has already prepared one of the duchess's favorites for dinner. *Schweinsbraten* and sauerkraut." He shuddered. "There was little for me to do."

He glanced behind her at the man busily employed in the dining room and rolled his eyes. "A piece of work, that one. I gather he asked to do that?"

"Yes. He seems to miss his role in royal entertaining as much as you miss yours."

Bernardi made a face. "Do not liken us, I beg of you."

She followed his gaze to where Mr. During was holding up each fork, knife, and spoon for inspection, pausing to polish away any smudges before laying them, just so, on the cloth.

"I suppose it makes sense for the person in charge of the plate to perform the role of table-decker as well."

"Actually he was only the table-decker until we returned to Kensington Palace. The previous plate keeper was from Coburg and did not want to uproot himself to move to England. Had a sweetheart there and no command of the language here. Conroy tried to assure him the duke would be returning to Germany after the child was born on English soil, but . . . not all of the duke's promises are kept."

She nodded her understanding. "So they added his duties to Mr. During's to avoid having to hire someone?"

"Yes. And in any case, overseeing the plate chest is not overly taxing. At least not for the Duke of Kent, who hasn't amassed the valuables his older brothers have. Selwyn agreed to take on the responsibility while we're here for a slight rise in pay. Not that he's likely to see a farthing for some time with the royal finances as they are."

Sarah's stomach pinched with disquiet. The Duke of Kent's servants had not been paid? Would they in turn depart Sea View without paying for their stay?

Mr. During appeared in the doorway. "Miss Summers. As flowers are out of season, might I have permission to find an ornament or two from other rooms to adorn the table? I promise to return everything to its proper place."

"Oh, um. Of course. Make yourself at home."

In sardonic tones, Mr. Bernardi said, "Shall I create a pastry replica of Sea View for the table? An arrangement of sugar flowers? A tower of fruit?"

Again missing the irony, Mr. During gave a little gasp, eyes rounding in delight. "What a wonderful idea! Very generous, Antoine. I am most appreciative."

The pastry chef sent Sarah a telling look. He opened his mouth, but Sarah cut him off before he could rescind the offer and steal the man's pleasure.

"Let us leave Mr. During to his work, shall we?"

Bernardi frowned but followed her down the passage without another word. Near the back stairs, he paused and huffed a long-suffering sigh. "Dash the man. Now I shall have to create a dessert befitting the table." And with that he disappeared belowstairs, apparently on a mission to do so.

Yet Sarah did not think he genuinely minded the task.

Aware of the trouble Mr. During was going to, Sarah quietly spread word to the others, suggesting they dress with extra care for dinner. She attended to some tasks for a few hours but left time to follow her own advice. Going up to her room, she donned a more formal than usual evening gown and added earrings, which she rarely troubled to wear.

Emily came in and looked at her in surprise. "You look lovely."

"Thank you."

"What shall I wear?"

"Anything you like. What about the pale pink? You have not worn that in ages."

"Hmm . . . Maybe."

Sarah didn't wait to see what Emily chose. Her sister would look pretty in whatever she wore. She always did.

When Sarah entered the dining room to see if all was in readiness, she stopped and stared.

The room had never looked more beautiful.

Their best linen had been ironed to shiny smoothness and re-laid. Candelabra gleamed along the table's length, filled with long straight tapers. Mr. During must have gathered extra from different rooms of the house. The base of each candelabrum wore a wreath of flowers. Had the man walked to a shop in town for hothouse blooms?

On closer inspection she realized the flowers were fashioned of silk, satin, and the like. A strip of embroidered fabric he'd studded with polished seashells ran down the table's length. And at the center stood the promised tower of fruit. Its shape conical, like a pine tree, the centerpiece consisted of bright oranges and lemons adorned with artfully placed leaves, and had been placed on a porcelain cake stand for added height.

Mr. During came in, now dressed in evening attire.

"My goodness. You are an artist, Mr. During."

He beamed. "My pleasure, Miss Sarah. And I would be remiss to not mention Mr. Bernardi provided the fruit."

Behind him, Mr. Bernardi entered, similarly dressed. Gone were the white coat and apron he wore in the kitchen. Both men looked unusually handsome.

Bernardi shrugged. "Why not? There were lemons and Seville oranges languishing in the Woolbrook larder. But Selwyn is the one who created the tower with them."

Sarah supposed she should protest the use of Woolbrook stores but was relieved not to have to bear the expense of imported fruit. "Well, it all looks splendid."

Emily and Mamma entered next, both elegantly dressed, and both exclaiming over the grand appearance of the dining room.

Sarah pulled back the chair at the head of the table. "I think you should sit here tonight, Mr. During, as you are the one responsible for all this beauty."

"Truly?" He touched his heart. "I would be most honored. That is extremely kind."

Georgiana walked in looking older and quite feminine in a

pretty blue gown. She'd joined arms with Simon Hornbeam. "Oh! Mr. Hornbeam, I wish you could see it! The table is beautiful. Flowers, and candelabra, and a tower of oranges and lemons."

"The fruit, I can smell. And I feel the warmth of many candles."

The ladies sat first, and the men followed.

"I assume we have you to thank for this display?" Mr. Thomson asked the table-decker as he came in and seated himself.

"Indeed," Sarah answered in the man's stead.

Together, they were a party of eight, everyone in their best frocks or frock coats. Sarah noticed Mr. Thomson's appreciative gaze linger on pretty Emily, and her sister's eyes shine as she smiled back at him. Sarah could not deny the tall secretary was striking in formal attire, and she wondered if this man might succeed in driving thoughts of Charles Parker from Emily's mind and heart at last.

Joining in the spirit of the evening, Mr. Gwilt laid a white cloth over his arm and offered the guests small glasses of champagne.

During the main course, Mr. During looked around the table, shaking his head with both wonder and satisfaction. Then he turned to Sarah. "I am obliged to you, Miss Summers. You don't know what this means to me. For all the hundreds of tables I have set over my career, this is the first I have been able to sit down to and personally enjoy. I admit, when I first learned I would be assigned to secondary lodgings as nonessential staff, I felt discouraged. But now I am grateful, for otherwise I should never have had this unforgettable experience."

"You are very welcome, Mr. During. We are all enjoying the fruits of your labors." She shifted her gaze to the pastry chef. "And yours, Mr. Bernardi."

"My contribution was minor compared to Selwyn's. But indeed it is my pleasure to add to the night's festivities."

Mr. Bernardi lifted his glass. "A toast. To Selwyn During, table-decker and plate keeper to Their Royal Highnesses, the Duke and Duchess of Kent."

Everyone around the table lifted their glasses. "To Selwyn During."

Mr. During's dimples blazed in an effort to suppress a giddy grin. "Thank you all." He lifted his own glass. "And to Antoine Bernardi, pastry chef extraordinaire."

"Hear, hear."

"Speaking of which . . ." Mr. Bernardi rose. "I have a little something more." He slipped from the room.

While they waited, they exchanged looks of questioning anticipation. A few moments later, he returned. In his hands he held another porcelain stand, this one bearing a large iced cake decorated with a colored sugar crown and *pastillage* swans.

Georgie gasped in delight and leaned close to explain the new arrival to Mr. Hornbeam. Around the table, people began to clap.

"Well done, Mr. Bernardi."

He gave a modest shrug. "It is Twelfth Night, after all."

Was it? Sarah stared in surprise. She had forgotten. Next year, she reminded herself, they would celebrate the holiday season properly.

12

There is a certain romantic appeal in fencing.
—Kay Geyer, *The Sportswoman*

The next day, Sarah gave Emily and Georgiana each a list of chores to accomplish. With only one housemaid and a few hours' help from Bibi, they all had to lend a hand with the cleaning. Emily resisted complaining, for she knew Sarah's list would be far longer than either of theirs.

An hour later, she and her younger sister worked in the library together, Georgie on the ladder dusting shelves and Emily polishing the windowpanes. Sarah had rightly assumed that if she'd asked Emily to dust the shelves she would be distracted by the books and not get any work done. Georgie was clearly distracted, but not by the books. She glanced often at the clock as she worked.

Finally, she said, "I had better go up and change for my fencing lesson."

Emily sent her a knowing smirk. "Since when does it take you more than five minutes to dress?"

A rattling sound drew Emily's attention outside, to a small cart coming up the drive. Georgie hurried down the ladder and joined her at the window. "It's Hannah!"

She jogged from the library to open the front door, and Emily followed, curious. Georgie's friend Hannah usually came on foot.

Mr. Gwilt was there before them, hastily donning a coat as he strode to the cart. He helped the girl down and held the horse.

"I'll be just a moment," she called to him over her shoulder.

Hannah came to the door, smiling eagerly at Georgiana. "Mother wants to take us to the York Hotel for tea and cake. A belated birthday celebration, now that my cold is better."

"When?"

"Now. I know it's last minute, but please say you'll come. Mother let me have the pony cart to come and fetch you. She will meet us there."

"I would like to go. Let me ask Mamma."

Georgie ran across the hall to Mamma's room and returned in less than a minute. She looked at Emily imploringly, eyebrows high. "She says I may go if you will clean the bath and gather the towels for me. The dusting can wait, but that cannot." She clasped her hands in supplication. "Please!"

Emily sighed. "Very well."

"Huzzah!" Georgiana retrieved her cloak from the closet, then paused, eyes wide. "Oh! I forgot. My fencing lesson . . ."

"I am sure Mr. Thomson will understand."

"You will explain?"

"I shall. Now go and enjoy yourself."

A short while later, at the time appointed for Georgiana's fencing lesson, Emily removed her apron and went up to the attic alone. Mr. Thomson was already there, stretching his long limbs.

A Winter by the Sea

Emily averted her gaze and cleared her throat. "My . . . Um, my sister asked me to tell you she will not be able to fence with you today. Her friend came and invited her to take tea at the York Hotel. It was all rather last minute, and Georgie could not refuse."

"I don't blame her. Though unfortunate for me. I was looking forward to the exercise. I don't suppose you would take her place?"

Emily hesitated. "I . . . am not as athletic as Georgiana, as you surely know from my poor attempts at kicking that ball. And the only experience I have with fencing comes from the books I've read. You would have to start from the beginning."

"You watched us. Well, that is, until you almost nodded off."

She chuckled. "True. And I admit to attempting to advance in the parlour while wielding a quill, but that is the extent of my practice."

"Come. Have pity on me. I could use a diversion."

"Very well. Though I hope you won't regret asking me."

"Never. Now, what is this?" He held up the blunt-tipped practice sword.

"A foil."

"See, you know something already. Please remember to strike your adversary—that's me—with only the blunt tip."

"I shall try."

"To start, we salute. Hold the foil before your face, like this." She did so.

"Now stand in first position." He faced her, heels together. She mirrored his stance.

"Hold the foil in your right hand, slide your left partway along the foil, then raise it with both hands above your head."

He made the move look easy, but Emily found it hard to emulate.

142

"When you hear 'On guard,' or '*En garde*,' point the foil at your opponent with your right hand while stepping forward with the right foot. On guard!"

Again Emily tried to follow his instructions, but she felt awkward and clumsy as she attempted it.

"Bend at the knees. Breathe!" he encouraged. "This is only an exercise. There will be no examination, I promise you."

"That's a relief." She tried again, this time more fluidly. Then she lost her grip on the foil.

He set his aside and walked toward her. "Keep your hand firmly clasped around the hilt, or your opponent could disarm you." He took her hand in his and positioned it correctly. "Like this. The back of your hand down, the nails up."

She liked the warmth of his hand on hers. The gentle patience of his voice. *Careful, Emily*, she reminded herself.

"Now, the next move is to strike out. Hold your arm straight, point the foil at my chest, and as you do, straighten your left arm. Ready? On guard; strike out!"

Emily did so and almost lost her balance. She steadied herself and tried again.

"Balance, balance . . . good."

Inwardly, Emily groaned, knowing she cut a poor figure as a fencer. She wished he could see her dancing a quadrille instead.

"Next, step out with the right foot, and strike me with the tip of your foil. Ready? On guard; strike out; attack."

At her weak noodle-armed attempt, his serious expression crumpled and his shoulders shook with laughter. "No, no. You would never best an opponent if you struck him like that."

They returned to their former positions and practiced the movements for some time until they gradually became easier for Emily. By then she was breathing heavily.

Next they worked on advancing. "I retreat while you advance.

Bring the right foot forward and then the left, keeping them in the same position."

Again he retreated and Emily advanced.

"Very good," he encouraged. "Very graceful."

"It is rather like a dance," she observed.

His mouth quirked. "If you are accustomed to dancing with a weapon, I suppose."

"Do we always take turns advancing?"

"Only in practice. In a bout, I would try to force you to keep retreating off the mark." He demonstrated, advancing and advancing again until she was forced to retreat all the way to the end of the room, her back coming into surprising contact with the wall. For a moment he pinned her there with a practice tip and a pair of intense brown eyes.

Holding his gaze, Emily felt more breathless than before.

She licked lips that were suddenly dry as her heart beat hard. Voice not quite steady, she said softly, "N-now what?"

For a moment longer he held her gaze, and then his focus dipped lower, to her mouth.

Was he going to kiss her? Did she want him to? But what about Charles?

Instead, he inhaled deeply and stepped back.

After they both caught their breath, he continued the lesson.

Again they advanced and retreated, their foils clanging together. Emily was grateful for the blunt button-shaped tips.

"Fencing becomes you," he said. "Your color is high, your eyes bright from the exercise, and your posture elegant."

Finally, she bent over in surrender, hands resting on her knees, panting. "Sorry. I am done in. So much for my elegant posture."

He chuckled.

"Fencing is more taxing than I would have guessed."

He nodded. "No better exercise. It employs every muscle and instinct and trains the mind to think quickly."

She straightened with a final long breath followed by a whooshing exhale. "I think I've had enough for one day."

"Good session." He held out his hand to her.

After a moment's hesitation, she put her hand in his. "Opponents shake hands, do they?"

"In friendly matches, yes. Thank you, Miss Emily, for obliging me. I have sincerely enjoyed your company."

"And I yours." She added tartly, "Though if I cannot walk tomorrow, I shall know whom to blame."

Later, after wiping down the tub and tidying the bathroom, Emily gathered a load of towels for the laundry, every muscle sore from fencing. She carried the pile toward the water closet to see if there were any damp towels in there. Turning the corner, she heard the door knocker echo from the hall below. She paused at the banister and peered down.

The housemaid, Jessie, hurried to the main entrance and opened the door.

A masculine voice asked, "Is this the Summers residence? Have I the right place?"

"Yes, sir. Who may I say is calling?"

"Charles Parker."

Emily's heart lurched. Charles! At last!

She started toward the stairs.

Suddenly realizing her arms were full of dirty laundry, she looked wildly one way, then the other, and tossed the towels through the open door of her bedroom.

She yanked off her apron and pressed a hand to her chest. Had he come to see her? To renew his addresses?

Below, Jessie took his hat and glanced around the empty hall. "I don't know where everyone is at the moment. Please wait here while I look." She laid his hat on the side table and headed toward the parlour.

Emily walked to the top of the stairs and gripped the newel post tightly. With her free hand, she smoothed the front of her bodice, wishing she were wearing something more becoming than an old day dress.

Perhaps hearing her footsteps, he glanced over his shoulder and turned toward the staircase.

At this first full look at his face—his devastatingly handsome face—Emily's breath hitched. Despite his cold-chapped cheeks, Charles Parker was as attractive as ever with thick, dark blond hair and darker eyebrows, well-shaped nose, and full lower lip. *Oh, those lips . . .*

As his gaze alighted on her, a rapid series of emotions flickered over his features. His eyes brightened, and a slow smile replaced his serious expression. He took an eager step forward only to stop before he'd reached the bottom of the stairs. Was he unsure of his welcome?

As well he should be.

Emily descended slowly, hand trembling on the rail.

He followed her descent, eyes tracing over her hair, her face, her form. Once again she wished she were better dressed, better prepared physically and emotionally to meet Charles Parker after more than a year apart.

When she reached the hall landing, he bowed. "Miss Emily."

She dipped a shallow curtsy in reply. As she did, she noticed the potted hyacinths in his hand.

He followed her gaze to the flowers and said, "For your mother. I did not presume . . ."

"Of course. I am sure she will enjoy them."

An awkward silence passed. She wondered why Jessie had not taken his coat. Did he not intend to stay long?

Clearing her throat, Emily opened her mouth to say something more but every line she thought of seemed leading. *What are you doing here? What brings you to Sidmouth?*

She made do with "I am surprised to see you."

"Are you? I did write to . . . Well, never mind. My sister has had a baby and is unable to travel, so—"

"Already?" Emily blurted before she could stop herself. Amanda Parker married shortly after the Summerses left May Hill. Emily once thought Amanda would ask her to be her bridesmaid, but no. Now she'd had a child and Emily had not even known she was expecting.

"Yes. So we went to her home for the holidays. Amanda and her husband live in Wells, not sixty miles from here."

"I see. And you are traveling with . . . your parents?" *Please, not another woman.*

He nodded. "Since we had already gone that far, we decided to continue to the south coast, hoping for milder weather. No luck."

With effort, she kept her tone casual and hopefully her expression as well. "Sadly, it has been unusually cold here lately."

He glanced around the hall, looked at her, then away again. "I . . . understand many people overwinter here."

She nodded. "And some even sea-bathe year-round."

Pulse pounding, Emily was barely aware of what she said. She couldn't believe they were standing there talking about such trivial things.

But at least they were talking.

She wanted to ask him why they had chosen to come to Sidmouth. If they wanted the south coast, Weymouth would have been somewhat closer. Was it his parents' choice, or his? Had she figured into the decision at all?

As if guessing her unspoken question, he said, "Mamma thought it would be pleasant to see your mother while we are here."

This surprised Emily. She had assumed his family would want nothing to do with them after they'd come down in the world—both from Claire's disgrace and the change in their financial circumstances.

He added, "And I thought I would call on you . . . and your sisters."

Emily swallowed hard. "And where are your parents now?"

"Settling in at the York Hotel. I decided I had better call first instead of all of us descending upon you at once."

Emily glanced again at the flowers. Purple hyacinths, she knew, symbolized deep regret.

He followed her gaze, then looked back at her. "You know what they mean?"

"Yes," she murmured.

Stepping closer, he locked eyes with her, expression earnest. "And I do so regret—"

The door flew open with a blast of cold air. Georgiana hurried inside, returning from the outing with her friend. Seeing them, she stopped abruptly, her mouth falling ajar. "Charles!"

She seemed about to throw her arms around their old neighbor, but at the last moment he thrust out a hand. Georgie grasped it in both of hers. "How wonderful to see you!"

Her youngest sister had always idolized Charles, some ten years her senior. To his credit, he had never ignored the youngest Summers but had instead treated her with kindness.

"And you, Georgiana. You've grown."

"So the dressmaker tells me." She laughed. "I knew you'd come to visit us! You are the first from home to do so."

He smiled—a bit sheepishly, Emily thought.

Looking around the hall, Georgie unclasped her cloak, then asked Emily, "Where are the others? Everyone will be so happy to see him." She turned back to Charles. "I shall have to tell Viola. She married last summer and lives next door with her husband. And you do know Claire moved to Scotland? She is staying with our great-aunt there."

Nerves thrumming, Emily held her breath, awaiting his reply.

"Ah yes." He glanced from one to the other, then down to his hands. "I remember . . . hearing something about that."

"Oh! And did you hear the Duke of Kent is staying up the lane, in the house next to Viola's? We have some of his staff here with us. It's terribly exciting!"

"No, I did not know. Quite impressive."

"We rent out rooms now, like a guest house. But if you want to stay, you would be more than welcome. We would not charge an old friend."

Emily felt her face heat. "Georgie. The Parkers are staying at the York Hotel."

"Oh. That's nice too. I just took tea there. The cakes are remarkably good. . . ."

Georgiana chatted away and Emily stood there, hands clasped, torn between disappointment at the untimely interruption and a flare of hope. This was not how she'd imagined a reunion with the man she had loved all her life. But he *was* here, and that was a start.

———

Sarah was sitting in Mamma's room, talking over menus, when the sound of voices from the hall drew her attention—Emily's, uncharacteristically subdued, a man's low tones, followed by exclamations from Georgiana.

Sarah rose. "I shall see who it is. As far as I know, we are not expecting anyone today."

She poked her head out the door, looked into the hall, and jerked back in astonishment.

"Who is it?" Mamma asked.

Sarah quietly shut the door and lowered her voice. "Charles Parker."

Her mother's eyes widened. "Is it? I did not think he would come. For Emily's sake, do you think?"

"I don't know. I had only a brief glance, but it did not look like an entirely happy reunion. Georgie was the only one smiling."

"He's given Emily plenty of reason not to smile," Mamma said dourly.

She glanced around the sunny room and at the neatly made French sofa bed. "Ask him to come in for a private word, please. Wait—do I look all right?" She stepped to the mirror and smoothed back her hair. "I don't want him to tell Louise I have let myself go."

"Not at all, Mamma. You look lovely. But here . . ." Sarah handed over the rouge pot. "Just a touch on your lips, I think."

Mamma accepted it. She glanced at Sarah and said, "Take off that apron before you go out there."

Sarah did so, then took a deep breath and walked into the hall to greet their guest.

"Charles. This is a surprise." She glanced at Emily, but her expression was difficult to read. "What brings you to Sidmouth?"

Charles returned her greeting, then explained, "My parents and I visited Amanda over Christmas and thought we would come here for a short holiday before returning home. We are staying at the York Hotel."

"Ah." Sarah managed a smile. "Our mother would like a word, if you don't mind." She gestured down the passage.

"Of course not. With pleasure." He nodded to Emily and Georgiana and then followed Sarah to Mamma's room.

Mamma had positioned herself in one of the room's armchairs but rose when he entered. "Charles. A pleasure to see you again."

"Mrs. Summers." He bowed, then handed her some hyacinths. "These are for you."

Mamma looked from the purple blooms to Charles and back again. Sarah wondered if he knew what they symbolized.

"Thank you." She set the flowerpot on the nearby table.

"You are looking well," he said to Mamma. "You are in good health, I trust?"

"Daily improving, thanks be to God and sea-bathing."

"Charles is here in Sidmouth on a short holiday with his parents," Sarah explained.

"I see."

Not sure what her mother intended or if she wished to speak to the young man privately, Sarah asked, "Shall I leave you two to talk?"

"Please stay," her mother replied. "But do close the door."

Feeling uneasy, Sarah complied. She glanced at their guest and wondered which of the three felt more nervous.

Her mother sat and gestured to the chair near her. Charles sat as bidden.

"I received your letter," Mamma began.

Surprise flashed through Sarah. Mamma had said nothing about a letter.

"I did not mention it to the girls because . . . well, I did not wish to raise hopes, should your visit not come to pass."

He nodded. "I understand."

Mamma drew a deep inhale, then said, "You are aware that my eldest daughter is living in Scotland, are you not?"

"I knew she had gone."

"And you also know why?"

His Adam's apple bobbed above his cravat. He looked away as he replied, as though addressing the doily on the table. "My . . . former . . . friend did tell me what happened, but—"

"His version of what happened," Mamma snapped back.

Charles flinched. "Yes. But he did not divulge particulars."

Mamma gripped the chair arms. "Sarah and I are aware of what transpired. We had hoped the situation would not become known outside of our family. I suppose that was too much to hope."

"If it helps," he said, "I told no one. Not even my parents."

"Really? I am relieved to hear it." Mamma exhaled, some of the tension leaving her.

"Emily and Viola have pieced it together somehow"—here she shot Sarah a look—"but Georgiana knows next to nothing. So please be discreet in her company. Perhaps not telling her is a mistake, but she was quite young at the time. She, therefore, talks more freely about her eldest sister than the rest of us do. We rarely speak of her."

"She mentioned your eldest went to Scotland to stay with a relative, apparently."

"Apparently. She lives there as companion to my husband's aunt. That woman and I have never been close. Nor do we correspond with . . . either of them. It was my husband's decision, and I have chosen to honor his request, even though it is difficult for us all."

He solemnly nodded. "I understand." He added softly, "And I am sorry."

"Are you?"

He nodded and looked down at the floor like a chastised boy. "I cannot help but feel I might have prevented it somehow."

Sarah's heart twisted. *She* might have prevented it.

Mamma sighed, and when she spoke again her tone had gentled. "You are not alone in having regrets. There, I have said my piece. Now. How is your mother?"

"She is well."

"Do greet her for me."

"Actually, she would like to call on you while we are here, if you are willing to receive her?"

Mamma hesitated, lips parted.

Sarah guessed Mamma was not eager for a friend from May Hill to see her in their new circumstances, forced to rent out rooms to make ends meet. Sarah was about to suggest she might meet Louise at the York Hotel when Mr. Parker spoke up.

"If you would rather not, I am sure Mother will understand."

Eugenia Summers lifted her chin. "Louise is welcome to call, of course."

"Excellent. I shall let her know."

Mamma rose, signaling the end of the interview. Sarah and Mr. Parker followed her example.

"Thank you for calling, Charles, and for the flowers. I hope you enjoy your stay in Sidmouth. And do take care where Emily is concerned. I don't wish to see her hurt again."

"Nor do I." He bowed and left the room.

When he had gone, Sarah looked at her mother with interest. "What did he say in his letter? Only that he might call on us?"

Mamma shook her head. "He expressed belated sympathies for your father's death and regret for not being of more help to us during his illness and our time of grief. He did mention he hoped to call on us in future, but no specific date."

"Nothing about Emily? Or . . . Scotland?"

Another shake of her head. "I suppose it was rude of me not to reply. I did not feel it my place to extend forgiveness on our family's behalf. For I am not the one he most injured."

Emily told herself not to wait in the hall for Charles. Not to appear so eager, so desperate. She forced herself to go into the library-office instead, even as her ears remained alert for sounds of him exiting Mamma's room. She guessed what they were talking about and groaned. Why did it have to happen? If it had not, she might be engaged to Charles even now.

Perhaps already married! Emily wished yet again that Lord Bertram had never come to May Hill. Never set eyes on her sister Claire.

She heard footsteps on the hall's marble floor, and her pulse jumped. She hurried to the door, then slowed, trying to look casual.

But it was not Charles in the hall. It was James Thomson, freshly dressed in frock coat, waistcoat, and trousers.

He smiled softly when he saw her. "We meet again."

"Mr. Thomson, are you . . . going out?" Emily was torn between politeness and wanting to hurry him away so she might speak to Charles alone.

He walked closer, his smile fading into concern. "Are you all right? You look upset."

"Do I? That is not the look I was hoping for."

"Has something happened?"

"It's . . . well . . . I have just had a surprise, that's all. An unexpected visitor from home—our former home."

His eyes narrowed as he studied her face. "A welcome visitor?"

Her reply came out in a breathy whisper. "I hope so."

A door opened and another set of male footsteps sounded.

They turned in unison and watched Charles cross the hall. If anything, Mr. Thomson looked more surprised to see him than Emily had been.

"Parker," he muttered.

Charles's eyes widened. "Thomson. What the devil are you doing here?"

"I live here."

"Live here? You must be joking." Charles glanced at her, then at Thomson standing close to her, and his brow furrowed.

"Temporarily at any rate," Mr. Thomson amended. "I am a guest, along with a few other members of the Duke of Kent's staff."

"Ah. Miss Georgiana said some of his staff were lodging here. And what is your position with him?"

"Private secretary with oversight of charities."

"Secretary, hm? Thought you intended to take up the law."

Emily stood there, witnessing this unexpected reunion with astonishment. The men's stiff postures, measuring looks, and stilted tones told Emily theirs had not been a particularly warm friendship.

"And you, Parker. What is your profession? A man of leisure, I expect, as eldest son?"

"Not at all. I have been busy learning all I can about estate matters and endeavoring to improve our properties and farm methods. My father's health is not all it once was, so I have already taken over much of the day-to-day management."

"Yet here you are."

"We spent Christmas with my sister, then came to the coast hoping for a reprieve from winter. My father's physician thought the sea air might do him good."

"I hope it does. Have you taken rooms here at Sea View?"

"No. We are at one of the hotels. But we are old friends of the Summerses, so I called to pay my respects."

"That is quite a coincidence."

"Yes." Again Charles glanced at Emily before turning back to Mr. Thomson. "Still fencing?"

"Occasionally. I have little time to practice these days. And few worthy opponents."

"Have foils with you?"

"I have."

Charles held his gaze. "Then I may take you on while I'm here."

After a few more moments of tense conversation, Charles left, and Emily asked, "How do you two know each other?"

"We were at university together," Mr. Thomson replied. "And you? An acquaintance from home, you said?"

"Yes, we grew up near one another. Neighbors. Family friends."

Mr. Thomson looked away and his eyes seemed to harden. "The young lady from home . . ."

"Excuse me?"

He made no reply, simply staring into the distance.

"And you were at Oxford together?" she asked.

"Balliol College, yes."

"Were you . . . friends?"

His eyes narrowed. "Not exactly."

"Enemies?"

He shook his head. "Rivals."

"In fencing?"

He hesitated, then gave a terse nod.

"And which of you was the better swordsman?"

"Parker was always the victor. On the fencing strip and off."

His stern expression and clipped voice spurred her to ask, "Was he not well-liked? I always imagined he was."

"Forgive me. I did not intend to suggest otherwise. He was well-liked. Respected. Admired."

"But not by you?"

"I did admire him, until . . ."

"Until he began to best you in fencing?" she teased.

He remained serious. "No, Miss Summers. And I did not begrudge his triumphs . . . in most things."

She stared at him. "Whatever do you mean?"

Again he remained quiet.

"Come, Mr. Thomson, you are being rather mysterious."

He said nothing more for a moment, then diverted the topic. "I met his parents on more than one occasion. They seemed like excellent people."

"I always thought so. Although I imagine my mother is not keen on them calling here and discovering we are now humble boarding-house keepers."

He looked at her in surprise, dark brows rising. "Miss Summers, you and your family have no reason to be ashamed. You have a beautiful home in a fashionable seaside resort." He added with a wink, "And you were selected to host several *important* members of the Duke of Kent's household."

Emily smiled at him. "You are very kind to say so. Thank you."

At dinner that evening, Mamma was quiet. Apparently her talk with Charles that day had worn her out. In her stead, Emily kept the conversation going by talking about the weather and the latest news. Then she began asking their guests about their backgrounds and families.

"Where are you from, Mr. During?"

"London, born and bred."

"I believe you mentioned having a mother and sisters?"

He looked up with wide, almost fearful eyes. "Why would you mention them?"

Startled, Emily faltered, "Oh, I . . . no reason. Only making conversation."

His face flushed. "Of course. Sorry. Yes, I have two younger sisters, and the kindest of mothers."

"Is your father . . . gone?"

"Hm? Oh no. He is there as well. At least, usually. We are not close. I did not mean to imply that he . . . It is just that I am much closer to my mother and sisters and miss them a great deal."

Mamma spoke up. "Very natural. Your feelings do you credit."

"And was your father in royal service before you?" Mr.

Hornbeam asked, likely thinking of his own son, who'd disappointed him by not following him into government service.

"My father? Heavens, no. He's a former wine merchant who drank his own inventory." Mr. During gave a bark of laughter, but it was an awkward sound. He gazed down at his glass, running a distracted finger over the rim.

No doubt noticing his colleague's discomfort, Mr. Bernardi spoke up to fill the gap. "My father was a steward—not in a royal household, but in a noble one. He saved his wages to buy a small business, a grocery focusing on delicacies imported from the continent, primarily Italy and France. He and my mother were successful enough to send me to the Parisian College of Cooking."

Mr. Hornbeam nodded his approval. "You were fortunate indeed."

"I was."

Sarah added, "And we have been fortunate to sample some of your culinary creations."

"My pleasure." The chef looked at his neighbor. "Your turn, Thomson."

Mr. Thomson set down his fork and began, "There is not much to tell. I am a younger son. I read law at university in hopes of an eventual career as a civil or Crown servant. This position with the Duke of Kent was the first opportunity that presented itself. I was glad for a chance to do meaningful work, and to see something of the world."

"Probably thought you'd spend your days meeting heads of state, negotiating treaties, and changing the world," Mr. Bernardi teased.

Mr. Thomson modestly ducked his head. "I admit this position is not all I imagined, but it is a privilege to serve one of His Majesty's sons."

Emily asked, "You mentioned being a younger son. How many brothers do you have?"

"Two. We should have been the perfect trio: an heir, a second son for the military, and a third for the church. Is that not what tradition decrees?"

"There are many exceptions," Mr. Hornbeam said mildly.

"My eldest brother is heir, of course."

"Learning to manage the estate one day?" Mr. Hornbeam asked.

"Not really. To his credit, he might take a more active part if allowed. But our father likes things to be done as he has always done them."

"And your other brother?" Emily asked.

"My next older brother showed aptitude in both strategy and fighting and planned to join the army, to my father's delight. Unfortunately, he was badly injured and is now an invalid."

"Oh no," Emily breathed.

"Injured in battle?" Georgiana asked.

"No." Mr. Thomson grimaced. "He never made it into the army. He was injured in a shooting accident before he left home. He was only seventeen."

"How dreadful. I am sorry."

Mr. Thomson nodded his agreement, expression pained.

After a respectful moment of silence had passed, Emily asked, "Did your father want you to go into the church?"

"Hardly. He esteems clerics even less than men of law. He wanted me to go into the army after Arthur was injured, as a replacement, I suppose."

"You did not want that?"

"No. Father was not pleased."

"Did *you* want to go into the church?"

Thomson shrugged. "I did not sense a vocation for the

church, beyond being a dedicated parishioner. But I do wish to do good. That the duke has given me oversight of charities suits me well. I hope it is not vain to say I have long been interested in charitable organizations. And in this profession, I also employ the attention to detail and rhetoric I learned at university."

Mr. Hornbeam lifted his chin. "Sounds not dissimilar to my duties as clerk assistant of the House of Commons. Until, that is, the loss of my sight put an end to that career."

Mr. Thomson looked at the man, eyes alight with admiration. "Impressive indeed, sir."

"Although the career you chose was not his preference," Mr. Hornbeam said, "your father must be proud of you now."

James Thomson chuckled, more sardonic than amused. "Not in the least."

Mr. Hornbeam slowly shook his head. "Then he must be more blind than I am."

13

The Duke had caught a cold, but insisted on going out
and walked some distance with Captain Conroy, looking
after the horses. He came back chilled through.
—Cecil Woodham-Smith, *Queen Victoria*

The next morning, Emily bundled up and walked to
the parish church, notebook and a graphite pencil in
hand. According to Mr. Marsh's outline, she needed
to describe the church for the new guidebook. Although she
had been there dozens of times, she had never really studied
it with a writer's eye. Now she walked slowly around the
exterior, composing in her mind:

The church is a handsome stone structure built in a
tasteful style, having been repaired and beautified at
various times over the years. The tower has an air of
grandeur and is of considerable height. It bears a fine
clock face, which has lately been put up for the conve-
nience of residents and visitors alike.

Then she went inside, thankful to get out of the cold wind.
She sat in a pew for several minutes making notes.

*The church's interior is neat and pleasant, contain-
ing seats for a numerous congregation. The church
possesses a small organ, lately erected by subscription.
Solemn memorials of the dead adorn the walls, many
of whom came to Sidmouth as a last hope for the re-
storative power of its mild air.*

It seemed to Emily that most of the memorials were for young
people, however she doubted she should mention such a thing
in a guidebook for visitors. She would probably revise it later.

On her way back, Emily stopped first at the post office to
pick up the mail. There she encountered Miss Charlotte Cornish, daughter of the magistrate, George Cornish. Charlotte
was a few years younger than Emily. The two had met at church
and at a few social events, yet they remained polite acquaintances rather than friends.

"Miss Summers," Charlotte began, her expression lighting
up upon seeing her. "I heard there was a shocking incident
near your house recently. A dangerous shooting at a very important residence."

Because of her father's position, Charlotte often learned
of things before others did.

Emily nodded. "Yes, it was an unfortunate accident."

"So His Royal Highness maintained in the letter he sent,
asking for leniency. But the culprit was one of those parish
apprentices, so one wonders what truly happened."

"I don't wonder," Emily bluntly replied. "It was an accident. I was there."

"Were you indeed?" Charlotte seemed to shrink before her
eyes, having lost her cherished role as revealer of secrets.

A moment later she brightened again and stepped conspira-
torially close. "What can you tell me about it? Who else was
there? How did His Royal Highness react?"

162

Emily smiled at the girl's enthusiasm. "Perhaps another time," she appeased. "Now I really must go. Pray excuse me."

Emily left the post office and hurried to Westmount, eager to tell Viola about Charles Parker's unexpected visit the day before.

She found her talented sister in the drawing room, where she was playing the pianoforte, as she often did. Emily sat nearby and listened until she finished the piece. When Viola turned her full attention to her, Emily told her the news.

Viola's eyes grew large as she listened. "And how did you feel, seeing him after all this time?"

"I felt . . . I don't know . . . so many emotions! For so long now I have hoped to see him again, but truth be told, it was somewhat awkward. We were alone only briefly and mostly made small talk. We even spoke of the weather!"

"Maybe he was nervous."

"I certainly was."

"Do you think he came to apologize, or at least explain?"

"I think so. He brought purple hyacinths for Mamma and seemed about to apologize to me, but Georgiana came in and took over the conversation. He was polite and kind to her, of course."

"He always was."

Emily nodded. "Then Mamma asked to speak to him in her room."

"About what?"

"Claire, I imagine. Or perhaps to warn him to say nothing to Georgiana. I don't know. And when he came out again, Mr. Thomson was there. It turns out they were at Oxford together. Rivals."

"Rivals? In what way?"

"In fencing, among other things."

"What other things?"

163

"I don't know. That's what Mr. Thomson said. When I pressed him, he changed the subject."

"Hmm. That's interesting."

"Or troubling."

"Will Charles come back again, do you think?"

Emily shrugged. "His mother plans to call, so it is possible Charles and his father may accompany her."

"Do you want to see Charles again?"

"Naturally I do. What a question!"

Viola tilted her head to one side. "It's only that I . . . thought I noticed signs of partiality toward Mr. Thomson."

"I can't deny I like and admire Mr. Thomson—what little I know of him. But you know I have loved Charles for years."

"Still? Despite everything?"

"Yes! And I don't know all the particulars, do I? Perhaps he has long regretted cutting ties with us. Perhaps he had a good reason."

"And if that reason has not changed?"

Emily looked at Viola, then away again, uncomfortable under her sister's scrutiny.

"We shall have to wait and see. If he returns, I shall at least hear him out."

"Of course." Viola pressed her hand and gave her a small smile. "I just don't want to see you disappointed again."

"Me either." Emily rose and gathered her mitts and notebook. "Are you coming to Sea View this afternoon? I believe Miss Stirling plans to join us."

"I shall be there—even though it will mean seeing *you* twice in one day." Viola gave her a playful nudge, and Emily embraced her before taking her leave.

On the short walk home from Westmount, Emily saw two men coming up the lane.

As they drew closer, she recognized them as the Duke of

Kent and Captain Conroy. She stiffened at the sight of Conroy, even as her heart warmed to see Prince Edward again.

Conroy seemed about to pass by with the barest of nods, but the duke smiled and paused. "Ah, Miss Summers. A pleasure to see you again."

"And you, Your Royal Highness. You have picked another cold day for a walk."

"I know. Conroy and I went out to see about the horses, and he insisted we walk a bit farther. The sea air is supposed to be good for the health, remember?"

A chill wind snaked up the lane, and he shivered. "Though at the moment, I question that wisdom." He turned his head and coughed.

Emily bit her lip. "That does not sound good."

He waved a dismissive gloved hand. "A trifling cold. Don't mind me. I have always been as strong as an ox. Stronger than any of my brothers."

"I am glad to hear it. And your wife and daughter? Are they in good health?"

"My dear wife is depressed. She worries our beloved *Vickelchen* has a sore throat. When she opens her little mouth to cry, one gets a good view. Perhaps it is a little red." He shrugged. "I am not the best judge." Again he turned away to cough, then asked, "Have you seen her lately? My wee princess?"

"Not in a few days. But when I did, she seemed quite hale. Pretty too."

He beamed. "Ah. Your words gratify me. Yes, she is lovely as well as strong. Cut her first teeth without the slightest inconvenience. She is now between seven and eight months old yet looks like a child of a year!"

Emily smiled at this display of paternal pride despite the man's red nose and obvious discomfort.

Captain Conroy glanced significantly up the lane toward Woolbrook and cleared his throat.

"Well, I shan't keep you," Emily said, taking the hint. "I am sure you want to go indoors and get warm and dry."

"True, true."

"You don't want to catch your death," Emily added, then wished the words back as soon as she'd said them.

"Heavens, no," he replied. "That would not do. Good day, Miss Summers. I bid you *adieu*."

Sarah looked out her small bedroom window to gauge the weather. Grey storm clouds gathered in the east. Movement caught her eye from below, and she glanced down. Another storm seemed to be brewing right there on the grounds.

Selwyn During paced in agitated strides across the side yard, one way, then back again. He lifted something to his face—a letter by all appearances—before crumpling it in one hand and running his other through his hair. His hat, she saw, had either fallen or been tossed aside where it lay topsy-turvy on a frosty garden bench nearby. The man was usually fastidious in the care of his attire.

What sort of news had the letter contained to so upset him? He was clearly overwrought with strong emotion—anger or something akin to it.

Should she go down to see if he wished to talk? Offer help or at least a listening ear? Then again, he might not want anyone to see him in his current state.

Sarah went downstairs, going first to the office to see if Emily knew anything about the letter.

When she entered, Emily quickly slid one piece of paper under another before lifting her face with a guilty look. Was she carrying on a secret correspondence with Claire? Sarah didn't think Emily would hide that from her, but perhaps she'd feared it had been their mother approaching. Mamma would definitely not approve.

Sarah decided not to pry. Instead she said, "I saw Mr. During just now. He received a letter, apparently?"

"Yes. I gave it to him a short while ago. He seemed pleased about it."

"Did he happen to say who it was from?"

Emily considered. "Not exactly. Something about 'News from home. Good news, I hope.'"

Having witnessed Mr. During's reaction, Sarah doubted it.

Sarah thanked her sister, retrieved her mantle, and went to find the man, nervous to intrude but compelled to offer comfort if she could.

He was still outside, now sitting on the garden bench, head in his hands.

Hearing her footsteps on the gravel path, he glanced up and straightened. His face looked sickly white, his eyes large and almost glazed. He blinked and gathered himself with visible effort.

He started to rise until Sarah said gently, "Please, stay as you are. May I join you a moment?"

He said nothing but moved his hat to make room for her.

"Mr. During, are you all right? I don't mean to intrude, but I noticed you from the window, and you are obviously upset."

"I . . ." He hesitated, staring off into the distance, then he frowned and said, "I don't know what you mean."

"Really? Well, then, forgive me. I saw you pacing. I thought perhaps something in that letter upset you. Emily mentioned a letter from home."

He glanced down at the crumpled paper poking out from his fist.

"Oh, that. Well. Not the best news, no. But nothing you need be concerned about."

Sarah studied his countenance. He was clearly reluctant to confide in her.

She asked gently, "May I help in some way?"

"Ha." The chortle was a bleak one. "Help is an expensive commodity. And one few of us can afford. No, nothing you can do, Miss Summers. I will manage things." He glanced up, and perhaps seeing her dubious expression, added, "Even so, thank you for asking. Very kind of you to concern yourself with the private affairs of your guests."

Message received. It was none of her business.

Sarah rose. "Very well. If you change your mind, please do let me know."

That afternoon, Sarah joined her family in the parlour. Viola and Fran Stirling came over as well. As usual, they were all eager to catch up on the latest news in town and in each other's lives.

After enjoying tea, small cakes, and general conversation for a time, Fran set down her teacup and announced, "I have news, ladies. I am engaged to be married. You are looking at the future Mrs. Farrant."

They all congratulated her and asked questions about her upcoming nuptials and plans to sell Broadbridge's.

But privately, Sarah was surprised. When she had last spoken to Miss Stirling, she had seemed reluctant. What had changed?

As if reading her thoughts, Fran turned to her and said, "I am not getting any younger. And Mr. Farrant is a kind, hardworking man."

Viola nodded encouragingly. "Not to mention skilled, respected, and if I may be so bold, rather handsome."

Fran blushed, eyes shining. "I quite agree."

"We ought to do something to celebrate," Mamma began. "Let me think on it. . . ."

Mr. Gwilt knocked softly on the doorframe. "I beg yer pardon, ladies, but there is a Mrs. Parker and a Mr. Parker come to call."

"Oh!" Mamma started, and she and the girls looked at one another with varying expressions of unease. Emily pressed a hand to her chest, clearly nervous.

Only Georgie seemed purely delighted. "Excellent! They are friends from home. Our former neighbors."

Mamma recovered her composure. "Thank you, Mr. Gwilt. Do take their coats and show them in."

"Righty-o, madam."

Sarah glanced at the teapot and still-full plate of queen cakes and added, "And after, please ask Jessie to heat more water."

"Will do. I'll bring it up in a jiffy." He bowed and swept from the room as regally as a trained butler.

Fran whispered anxiously, "Shall I go?"

"Heavens no," Viola answered with tart precision.

Mamma looked less certain.

Georgie hopped up to carry a chair from the perimeter of the room and add it to their circle. Emily joined her, carrying a second.

A moment later, Mr. Gwilt showed in their newly arrived guests, and everyone rose to greet Mrs. Parker and her son.

"Welcome, Louise. Charles. Please, be seated." Mamma gestured to the two additional chairs.

Mr. Gwilt again backed from the room, pulling the doors closed as he did so.

Louise Parker glanced in his direction. "You have a butler here. I did not think . . . That is, he seems quite efficient."

Sarah decided not to correct her misapprehension, saying only, "He has been a godsend in many ways."

Mamma asked, "Is your husband not with you?"

"We left him at the hotel," Mrs. Parker replied. "He tried the medical baths earlier, and it drained his strength. His health is not all we would wish it to be."

"I am sorry to hear it."

Louise Parker's gaze swept over her old friend. "You look well, I must say, Eugenia. Better than you have in years."

"Thank you. Yes, the combination of sea air, sea-bathing, and long walks has done wonders for me."

Louise nodded. "Then let us hope Mr. Parker shall likewise benefit from his time here." She added, "It is also good to see you out of your widow's weeds. And you too, Sarah."

Sarah had worn mourning gowns for a long time after the death of her betrothed. She was surprised to realize she had not thought of Peter in some time.

Next Mrs. Parker's gaze shifted to the new bride. "I understand congratulations are in order. Is that right?"

Viola smiled. "Yes, I suppose so."

"You married a major, Charles tells me. Astounding."

Emily bristled on her twin's behalf. "Is it so astounding?"

The older woman looked at Emily and placated, "I did not mean to imply anything untoward. Viola, you are looking very well and very happy."

"I am happy, thank you."

"Good."

Mamma said, "And I hear you are to be congratulated as well, Louise, on your first grandchild."

"Yes! Amanda presented her husband with a son, and a

mere twelvemonth after their wedding. Oh, and before I forget, she sends her regards to you all."

Sarah had not known Charles's sister well, as she was several years younger, nearer in age to the twins. Amanda and Emily had been close as girls, but less so as they grew up.

Mrs. Parker continued, "And what about you, Emily? Is there romance in the offing for you as well?"

Emily's cheeks pinkened and she studiously avoided looking at Charles. She sipped her tea, then murmured, "Not at present."

Georgie grinned and added, "Although she always has plenty of admirers."

At that Charles raised an eyebrow at Emily, who looked down as though fascinated with the dregs in her cup.

Mrs. Parker did not ask Georgie about suitors, due to her youth. Nor did she ask Sarah, probably assuming she was resigned to spinsterhood.

Mrs. Parker's gaze landed next on Fran Stirling. Frown lines appeared as she narrowed her eyes in concentration. "Forgive me. You look familiar, but I can't quite place you."

Sarah said, "This is our friend Miss Stirling."

"Stirling . . ." She turned to Mamma. "Did you not have a lady's maid called Stirling?"

"I did."

"That's me," Fran said with a humble smile. "One and the same."

Mrs. Parker did not return the smile. "This is most irregular. And I thought you left service some time ago."

"I did."

Viola explained, "Miss Stirling owns her own home here in Sidmouth. A charming boarding house much in demand. She is remarkably successful."

The woman's lip curled. "A boarding house, but surely . . ."

Then, glancing around the tight-knit circle once more, she did not complete the sentence.

Charles, Sarah noticed, shifted uncomfortably in his chair. Had he not told his parents about their own new venture?

He began, "Mamma, I meant to tell you. The Summerses are—"

Georgie blurted, "We keep a kind of boarding house here too, although Mamma prefers to call it a guest house. More genteel, do you not think? We've had some interesting guests, I can tell you. It's been rather diverting, although a fair bit of work, I don't deny."

Mrs. Parker blinked. "You . . . take in . . . lodgers? Strangers?"

Mamma lifted her chin. "Yes, we do, Louise. Many in Sidmouth do."

"But surely it's beneath . . ."

Charles interjected, "In fact they have some impressive guests staying here at present. Officials from the Duke of Kent's own staff."

"Really?"

Charles's words pleased Sarah, and she noticed Emily send him a grateful smile. *Officials* was a bit of an exaggeration, but no one corrected him.

His mother said pensively, "Someone in the hotel mentioned the Duke of Kent was residing in Sidmouth."

"Yes. He is our neighbor," Emily said. "And surprisingly friendly."

Mrs. Parker's eyes widened. "You have met him?"

"Oh yes. He passes our house on his walks and always seems happy to stop and chat. We've seen his daughter too. She's adorable."

"Goodness."

An awkward silence passed. Sarah was relieved when Mr. Gwilt quietly came in with a fresh pot of tea.

Mamma poured for their guests, and Sarah passed them the plate of small currant-dotted cakes.

"Sarah makes those herself," Georgie offered.

She was trying to be helpful, but Sarah doubted a woman like Louise Parker would be impressed to learn a gently bred lady performed kitchen tasks.

Charles took a bite and said politely, "Delicious."

"Yes," his mother agreed, although her smile seemed tight.

"It's nothing," Sarah said, feeling self-conscious.

Another pause, filled by the tinkling of china cups on saucers.

Mrs. Parker set down her barely touched cake. "And what of Claire? Is she still in Scotland with a relative? Your husband's aunt, I believe you said."

Charles, she noticed, frowned at the question.

Mamma's own smile tightened. "Yes, still in Scotland."

"Seems a pity. Such a lovely girl. Sad that she should waste her bloom as a companion to an old woman. And one you never liked, as I recall."

"Yes. A pity."

"I think it was very kind of Claire to go," Georgie said. "Though I miss her terribly. We all do."

Again the family members glanced awkwardly at one another. Mrs. Parker observed them with interest.

Charles cleared his throat. "Well, Mamma, perhaps it is time we take our leave. See how Papa is getting on after the baths."

"You are right. We should not leave him on his own too long."

She rose, and the other ladies did as well, followed by Charles. Together they walked into the hall.

They gathered near the door, exchanging polite thank-yous for the call and hospitality while they waited for Mr. Gwilt to retrieve their coats and hats.

As Emily stood there with the others, James Thomson came down the stairs.

Mrs. Parker looked up and paused, recognition widening her eyes. "Mr. Thomson?"

"Ah. Mrs. Parker. I am happy to see you again."

"And I you. Don't tell me you are one of the Duke of Kent's officials?"

With a quick glance at Emily, he replied, "I . . . yes, I am."

"Well done. Charles does not often see his schoolfellows. What a lovely surprise. You two will have to catch up while we're here. Talk of old times." She turned to the others and explained, "These two were at university together."

Turning back to Mr. Thomson, she asked, "And how are your parents? In good health, I trust?"

"I believe so. I saw my mother a few months ago. She came to Town to visit me while their Royal Highnesses resided at Kensington Palace. We had dinner at her hotel and a good long talk. She seemed quite well."

"Excellent. And your father?"

His smile fell. "Estate affairs kept him at home, as often happens."

"Yes, yes, I sympathize. Were my husband not determined to improve his health, I doubt we could have convinced him to come away for a holiday."

Concern softened his features. "I am sorry indeed to hear it. He was always kind to me when he visited the college. I shall pray for his recovery."

"Thank you."

The two continued to speak for a few more minutes, the rest of them standing awkwardly as silent observers.

Emily found herself waiting beside Charles, somewhat removed from the others.

She glanced at him and said quietly, "Mr. Thomson mentioned you were rivals at Oxford."

"Did he? And he still resents me, I suppose?"

"He did not speak a word against you. In fact, he said you were well-liked and respected. Although I don't think he liked it that you always won."

"Not always."

She studied his somber profile. "I don't remember you mentioning this rivalry during school holidays."

He grimaced. "It is not something I would confide to a young lady. Especially you."

"Why ever n—?" She broke off and looked at him sharply, realization dawning. "We are not talking about fencing, are we."

"Fencing? Of . . . course we are."

Yet Emily noticed a flush creep above his cravat.

"Look, this was all a long time ago," he said, voice low. "Clearly this so-called rivalry meant far more to him than to me."

Emily continued to study him. Was Charles prevaricating? Once, she had known him so well. But that was a long time ago too.

Charles turned toward his mother and spoke more loudly. "Well, Mamma. Shall we go, or keep everyone standing here all day?"

"Oh yes, yes. Forgive me. A pleasure to see you, Mr. Thomson. And thank you all again."

Together they ushered the Parkers out the door with a collective sigh of relief.

14

A friend loveth at all times, and a
brother is born for adversity.
—King Solomon, Proverbs

Now that she'd gleaned there was a female involved, Emily regretted teasing Mr. Thomson about his rivalry with Charles, and hesitated to mention it again. Had both men courted the same woman? Had Charles pursued someone else while at Oxford, then come home at holidays and spent time with her, building her hopes, leaving her none the wiser? Charles was an exceedingly handsome man. She should not be surprised if other women had sought his attention. But that he had, perhaps, reciprocated? It was foolish to be jealous—but she was.

That evening, when Emily came downstairs dressed for dinner, Mr. Thomson was there before her, waiting in the drawing room for the others to gather.

She began, "Mrs. Parker was clearly pleased to see you again. Apparently you were acquainted with Mr. Parker senior as well?"

"Somewhat. He visited Charles several times at Balliol. More than was customary. Mr. Parker clearly doted on him—

brought him gifts from home. Treated him to fine dinners. And he often invited a few other students as well. He never failed to greet me by name and ask how my studies were going. That sort of thing. It may not sound like much, but it meant a great deal to me."

Emily studied his profile. Remembering what he'd said about his father not being proud of him, she asked softly, "Your father was not . . . like that?"

He shook his head. "Mr. Parker showed more interest in my studies and well-being than my own father ever did. At least once I'd refused his offer to buy me a commission."

"So is your eldest brother the golden boy of your family?"

He grimaced. "The truth is, none of us have lived up to Father's expectations. All of us have disappointed him in one way or another. Arthur was his favorite, until he was injured."

"Your father is disappointed in him because of that? When it was not his fault? Surely he does not blame Arthur!"

"No." A muscle in his jaw pulsed. "He blames me."

Emily gaped. "Oh no. What happened?"

"The three of us went hunting in the wood behind our house. Edward said we had Father's permission, but he lied." Another grimace. "I honestly don't know how it happened. I took a few shots at birds high in the treetops, but that was all. Then suddenly, Arthur was on the ground and there was blood everywhere. It was the worst moment of my life. How I thanked God when the surgeon announced he would survive, even though Father's military aspirations for him would not. Of course Father was furious and took Edward to task for it."

James Thomson shook his head. "But nothing is ever Edward's fault. He has always blamed others for his sins. Sent down from Oxford? That was a schoolfellow's fault. Overspending? Dishonest tradesmen taking advantage. And when this happened, he insisted I was to blame. Said it must have been me as I was the least experienced with a gun and had been shooting wild. I tried to protest, but Father did not believe me."

Realization trickled over her. "Is that why you came to that boy's defense when he shot the Woolbrook window?"

"It certainly brought all the memories rushing back. But I believed the lad—and you and Georgiana—when you said it was an accident, that no harm had been intended, and thank God, no harm had been done."

Emily's heart squeezed. She longed to take Mr. Thomson's hand in hers, but she resisted.

"How old were you when that happened?"

"Fifteen. After that, Father washed his hands of me."

"I am sorry, James." Emily realized she had called him by his Christian name. He shot her a curious look, clearly noticing as well. But she did not mention it and neither did he.

When they sat down to dinner that evening, Mr. During was absent. Sarah wondered if he might be standing guard in his room again.

She asked conversationally, "Does anyone know where Mr. During is?"

The others shook their heads.

Mr. Gwilt spoke up as he laid a platter of poached cod on the table.

"Off to the Old Ship Inn, I'd wager, I would. Asked me where a man might have a pint and meet the locals."

"Really? How unexpected. Thank you, Mr. Gwilt." Sarah had not thought Selwyn During a tippler, nor sociable, nor interested in local customs or people. She had clearly been wrong.

Mr. Bernardi viewed the plain pale fish with keen disappointment. He looked up and said, "That's odd. He always refuses when I ask him to go out for a pint. Says he must save every farthing for his family."

"Seems he made an exception," Mr. Thomson said equitably.

They began to eat.

A few bites later, Sarah heard the front door open. Soon, Selwyn During entered the dining room, unwinding his long, crudely knitted muffler as he came.

"A thousand apologies for my tardiness," he said. He brought with him the smells of ale, pipe smoke, and fried fish, but his eyes were clear. He sat down with the squeal and thump of chair legs, still wearing his coat.

Bernardi asked, "Did you actually go to a public house alone when you always refuse to go with me?"

During's eyes widened. "How did you know?"

He glanced warily at Mr. Gwilt, but Bernardi answered, "It's obvious from the smell on your clothes."

Selwyn lifted a sleeve and took an experimental sniff. "Oh dear. I shall have to remedy that posthaste. And I only had the one. To be friendly. You know I am very careful with my limited funds."

"If you say so."

"I do. You know I don't drink as a rule." He rose with another squeal of wood. "I came straight in because I was late, but I shall take my things up to my room."

"No need, sir. Allow me." Mr. Gwilt divested the man of his outer coat, hat, and muffler and carried them away, much of the unpleasant scent leaving with them.

"Well," Sarah said as Selwyn During sat back down. "Let us not continue to question Mr. During as though he were on trial. Allow him to eat in peace."

The conversation moved on with Mr. Hornbeam changing

the subject, to Sarah's relief and most likely Mr. During's as well.

He said, "I understand Their Royal Highnesses are hosting an evening party in two days' time. You three must be busy getting ready for that."

Mr. Bernardi brightened. "Definitely! At long last, we are able to entertain again."

Selwyn During nodded. "Hear, hear."

Over the previous week, word had begun to spread throughout Sidmouth that the duke had asked people in for an evening party. Everyone wondered who would be privileged to attend. Rumor had it he had invited several members of the local gentry, who no doubt looked forward to this rare opportunity to speak with members of the royal family.

The Summerses had not been in that number.

Emily said, a note of hurt in her voice, "I am sure those invited are all eagerness to attend."

An awkward silence passed.

Mr. Hornbeam cleared his throat and turned the topic to other news. "I read in the newspaper today—that is, Miss Georgiana read it for me—that the duke's creditors are still causing problems in London, despite his removal to the West Country."

Around a bite of fish, Mr. During grumbled, "Blasted unfair, if you ask me. He gets in debt, he goes to the seaside, while common folks are sent to the Marshalsea."

Mr. Hornbeam looked up, face stilling at the man's tone. "Vile place, I understand."

Mr. During stared across the table. "Is it?"

"From what I have read. I have not been there myself."

"Nor I, of course. Nor I."

That night, Emily sat up late reading in the parlour. The fire in the hearth burned low, but she had a blanket around herself for warmth, and a candle lamp for light, so she remained where she was long after Mamma, Georgiana, and even Sarah had gone to bed.

The house was quiet, save the occasional hiss and crackle of the fire.

Her eyes grew sleepy, but she soldiered on and turned the page.

She heard footsteps approach and glanced up, mildly startled.

Mr. Thomson entered the room, book in hand. He wore a waistcoat over a shirt and dark trousers, but no frock coat. His white collar rose above a jawline shadowed with late-evening whiskers.

Seeing her on the sofa, he stopped midstride. "Sorry. I thought everyone had gone to bed. I saw the light in here, but if you prefer to read in peace, I . . ."

"Not at all, Mr. Thomson. I am capable of reading through thunderstorms and even Georgie's chatting. The company of a fellow reader shall not disturb me in the least."

This was perhaps not absolutely true, for even were he silent as a mouse, she would still be aware of—and *slightly* distracted by—his presence.

"Very well."

He moved to sit in an armchair some distance away, but Emily said, "You may as well sit here and share the light. It's difficult enough to read with only one branch of candles and a dying fire. Yet I am so deliciously cocooned that I have not been able to rouse myself from this spot."

"I shall stoke it for you. For us."

"Thank you."

He poked the fire and added a log before sitting on the opposite end of the sofa.

She nodded toward the arm. "There is another blanket there, if you are cold."

"Good idea." He laid it over his lap, then looked at her. "You do indeed look quite snug."

She noticed his gaze drift downward and a smile touch his lips. She followed his gaze and saw her stockinged toes propped on a footstool, peeping out from the blanket. She self-consciously drew them back under, her cheeks warming. She told herself not to be silly. If he could sit there in his shirtsleeves, then she could sit there without shoes.

"Another novel?" he asked with a nod toward the thick volume in her hands.

"No, actually. I hope you are duly impressed that I am reading a history book I selected from the circulating library. It's about the reign of Frederic William II, King of Prussia."

His dark brows rose. "Prussia? I *am* impressed."

"Good. However, I've had it for nearly a fortnight and confess it is slow going. I have promised myself I can pick up a novel again after I finish one more chapter."

"Like a spoonful of sugar after foul-tasting medicine?" he asked. "You don't have to read it, you know."

"I challenged myself to do so, so I shall."

"What if I tell you that I am already deeply impressed with you, history or no?"

Despite her resolve, her heart fluttered. He was likely only teasing her, she decided, and she matched his light tone. "And now you shall have all the more reason."

Emily glanced at the book in his hand. "And you? Another dry, dense history, I imagine? It is not half as thick as mine."

"Will you think less of me if I tell you I am reading a novel?"

She chuckled. "On the contrary, you shall only rise in my estimation!"

"Then I am definitely reading a novel."

"Which one?" she asked, all enthusiasm.

"It's called *Persuasion*. Have you heard of it?"

"Heard of it? I adored it." She leaned closer. "How far along are you?"

"Nearing the end. I am enjoying it overall, although I admit that some parts are as slow going for me as your history is for you. Lots of description and introspection."

"If you find that one cumbersome, then I would not recommend *Sense and Sensibility*. I love it, of course, but even *I* find some sections difficult."

"Duly noted," he said. Then he went on, "I must say, I was rather confused by Captain Wentworth for a time. Him flirting with the young Miss Musgroves and blustering that he'd marry any woman who praised the navy. And meanwhile poor Anne had to suffer through it in silence. He certainly was not very gallant toward her at first."

Emily considered. "I think he was still wary because of her rejection of him years before. Probably feared Lady Russell would once again persuade Anne that he was not good enough for her. And perhaps he was bitter initially, yet he makes it all up to her with that letter!"

Emily quoted, "'I have loved none but you. Unjust I may have been, weak and resentful I have been, but never inconstant. . . .'"

His eyes, warm and glimmering, rested on her face.

She said, "I hope I have not given away anything."

"I had just come to that part. Quite moving. Also quite intimidating for an ordinary mortal. I don't know that I could ever write something so affecting."

"You should not have to, not if you were honest about your feelings all along and expressed them to the woman you admired."

His gaze still lingering on her face, he said softly, "I shall remember that."

With effort, Emily pulled her gaze from his and went on, "Wentworth's mistake was in underestimating her constancy and his own worthiness."

"That is little wonder." A corner of his mouth tipped up. "After all, he was a younger son as well."

She chuckled at his joke, but he soon sobered.

"I suppose you adore this novel because it is about lovers who were unjustly separated, and then later, have a second chance at romance, and finally achieve their long-awaited happy ending."

She narrowed her eyes. "I thought you still had one chapter left?"

"It is a foregone conclusion. After all, the final chapter begins, 'Who can be in doubt of what followed?'"

"I loved *Persuasion* on its own merits," she insisted.

"I am glad to hear that."

Secretly, Emily wondered if her fondness for that novel *was* related to her disappointment over Charles. Possibly. She pushed the thought aside and said with resolve, "Now, I am going to finish this chapter if it kills me . . . or puts me to sleep. And you finish yours."

"Very well."

Emily, cold and uncomfortable, awoke while it was still dark, her neck aching. The bedroom fire had gone out, and she must have slept in an awkward position. She gathered her blankets around herself and shifted, trying to find a comfortable place on her pillow—a pillow that seemed surprisingly hard as she drifted off once more.

She awoke again as faint dawn light began seeping into the room. At least she was warmer and far more comfortable than she had been earlier. She cracked open her eyes and stilled.

She was not in her bed. She was still on the parlour sofa, her head resting on Mr. Thomson's shoulder. She must have slid closer to him while she slept. He sat low on the sofa, his head resting on the back, eyes closed, breathing deeply. She, meanwhile, half reclined on the cushions, using the man as her pillow.

Oh dear.

Emily straightened gingerly, hoping not to wake him.

Getting quietly to her feet, she gazed down at him, looking relaxed in slumber. Younger. She spread her blanket over him and tiptoed from the parlour.

Going upstairs, she slipped into the room she shared with Sarah, hoping not to wake her either.

But her sister, who regularly rose early, was sitting up on the edge of her bed. "Oh! There you are, Emily. I was worried to wake and find your bed not slept in."

"Sorry. I fell asleep reading downstairs."

"Did you? That must have been cold and uncomfortable."

"Um, a little, yes. Would you mind terribly if I slept for a bit longer? I am still tired."

"And no wonder! Very well, but don't sleep too late. I shall need your help clearing up after breakfast."

"Thank you, Sarah."

"Never mind. Now, get some sleep."

Emily yawned and climbed into her own bed.

After she had washed and dressed for the day, Sarah went downstairs. On her way to the breakfast room, she glanced into the parlour to see if Emily had left any used teacups or blankets to tidy.

She was surprised to see Mr. Thomson standing in the

room, folding a knitted blanket and returning it to the arm of the sofa.

For a moment she stared at him, her thoughts whirling. Nothing untoward had transpired between him and Emily last night, had it? No. Surely not.

Not wishing to embarrass him, she turned and walked quickly and quietly away.

Was she right to worry, or had Claire's fall from grace made her overly sensitive?

Either way, she decided to caution Emily the next time she saw her.

15

Despite the very cold weather, the duchess, her
daughter and nurse were seen on the Esplanade.

—Nigel Hyman,
Sidmouth's Royal Connections

Emily slept for another hour or so. Then she washed and
dressed for the day and went downstairs.

She had just donned her cloak when she saw Mr. Thomson leaving the house, greatcoat collar turned up against the wind. Pulling on her gloves, she picked up Viola's work bag and hurried outside to catch up with him.

"Mr. Thomson!" she called.

He turned, and seeing her, he walked back, meeting her halfway. "Good morning. How did you sleep?"

She felt herself flush. "Remarkably well, considering. You?"

"For some reason," he replied archly, "I awoke with a crick in my neck."

"I can't imagine why. But perhaps the less said about that, the better. Going to Woolbrook?"

"Yes. To see if His Royal Highness wishes to dictate any letters or has made a decision about becoming a patron of the Poor's Friend Society."

"How do you view our chances?"

"Above average. Despite his debts and unenviable reputation, he is quite charitable."

"Glad to hear it. I am on my way to Westmount. Do you mind if I walk with you?"

He shook his head. "How could I mind that? I always enjoy your company. Awake or not."

She chuckled and they walked on.

He said, "Pardon my impertinence, but did you not just see Mrs. Hutton yesterday?"

"I did. I am returning her work bag. She left it in the parlour when we were surprised by the Parkers' call."

"And it could not wait?"

"I don't mind. I am always happy for an excuse to see her."

He said, "I admire your closeness with your sisters, especially Mrs. Hutton. I suppose it is because you are twins?"

"Perhaps, though we have not always been close. There used to be more discord between us than anything else. Thankfully, that rift has been repaired."

He looked at her, dark eyes alight. "How did you bridge the gap?"

Emily shrugged, thinking back. "Apologies. Talking. Time. Oh, and she nearly drowned last summer, which scared the life out of me and made me realize how much I love her."

"Well, I don't wish my brothers to nearly drown, but I do wish we were closer."

"Do you and your brothers not often talk?"

"Barely at all in the last few years."

"You *have* been away a great deal."

"True. Though we rarely talked even before I moved away."

"Perhaps you might try writing a letter?" She ventured a small grin. "I understand you are quite skilled at correspondence."

He returned her grin, but it did not reach his eyes.

Nurse Brock came down the lane from the direction of Woolbrook Cottage, wearing bonnet and cape, the small child again wrapped in many blankets in her arms.

As they neared, Mr. Thomson greeted her. "Good day, Mrs. Brock. How is the princess today?"

"She is much better, thankfully."

Emily smiled at the woman. "A pleasure to see you again. And your little charge."

The woman tried to smile in return, but her teeth were chattering. "His Royal Highness insists upon these daily airings. And I agree they do her good. Me, however . . . Oh, the wind does pierce this old cape—and the bones beneath it."

Mr. Thomson offered, "Shall I fetch you another cloak? Or your shawl, perhaps?"

"You'd never find it. And it's too soon to take this wee one back inside. Here." She stepped closer and shifted the bundled child to Mr. Thomson. "Hold her for me for a few minutes, will you? I shall dash into the house for my shawl and return directly."

"Of course." He wrapped his arms around the babe and settled her against his chest.

The nurse hurried away. Emily watched her go, but Mr. Thomson's focus remained on his precious burden.

"Mrs. Brock must trust you a great deal."

"I suppose she does."

The sweet child looked up intently at the man holding her. Wisps of pale golden hair showed from beneath a knitted cap. Delicate eyebrows, just visible, framed blue eyes that revealed no alarm, only mild interest.

"She trusts you as well."

"It is not the first time I've held her." He gently swayed from side to side.

"You seem to know what you are doing."

He shrugged. "I've learned a few things. You must have experience with babies, having a younger sister."

Emily considered. "Georgiana is nearly six years younger than I am, but I don't recall being entrusted with her care." Perhaps Emily had been too immature or too wrapped up in her own pursuits to offer to help. Mamma had employed a nurse and also shared in the care of her baby. Sarah had been eager to help as well. But Sarah had been born responsible.

James glanced up from the child's face to hers. "Do you not like children?"

"Oh, I do. I simply have not been around babies much in years."

His gaze returned to the little princess. Emily took in the picture they made, the tall man holding the child with competent ease and infinite care. Her heart softened and seemed to stretch, to reach toward him.

At that moment Chips bounded up the lane toward them. A squirrel scurried across his path and the dog began to bark, chasing the flash of red tail into a nearby field.

At the sharp sound of barking, the child's face wrinkled, and she began to wriggle in agitation.

Mr. Thomson spoke to her in soothing tones and gently rocked her in his arms. "Shh. There, now. You are all right, Your Highness. Just a silly dog and now he's gone. There, there. You're all right. . . ."

Emily's heart turned to warm toffee.

In her mind, a scene appeared as if drawn by a painter at high speed. James holding another baby in his arms. Their baby. Glancing from his beloved child to Emily, love and adoration in his dark gaze. Her chest tightened. She had never imagined another man as father of her children. Only Charles. Charles, who had come to see them. Charles, who had wanted to apologize. Charles, whom she had long loved. What was wrong with her?

She blinked away the surprising, tantalizing image and found
James looking at her in mild concern.

"Sorry," she blurted. "Did you say something?"

"I asked if you felt all right. An odd look came over you."

"Oh. I . . ." *Don't be a fool*, she inwardly scolded. *Don't
fall for a man you barely know when Charles has just arrived.
This man will be gone as soon as the royal party leaves. Gone
to far-off Germany, most likely. And you will still be here.*

"I am well. Just . . . thinking."

Later that day, Emily wrote a clean copy of the newest section of the guidebook and added it to the first batch of pages.

Then she put on her mantle and gloves and set off for
Marsh's Library and Public Rooms, the man's leather portfolio in her arms. She wanted to show him a draft of the pages
describing the town and church, not wanting to progress too
far until she knew she was on the right track.

Emily walked briskly along the esplanade, past Fort Field,
a cold breeze tugging at her hood. She regretted not wearing
an extra flannel petticoat under her dress. Glancing ahead,
she noticed one of Mr. Wallis's sons on the library veranda,
sweeping off the snow. Mr. Wallis himself stepped out and
gestured to the stair he'd missed.

Seeing him, nerves jolted Emily and she faltered, her steps
slowing almost to a halt. She suddenly wished she'd taken the
longer way through town.

Tightening her grip on the portfolio, she ducked her head
and walked on, hoping he would not notice her.

"Miss Summers?"

She looked up guiltily. "Oh, good day, Mr. Wallis. Lost in
thought."

"I just received the newest *Waverly* novel and thought of you at once."

"H-how kind. Perhaps another time? I am just . . . out on an errand."

He glanced at the portfolio she clutched to her chest like a muff . . . or a shield.

"Of course." His eyes narrowed behind foggy spectacles, and his small mouth cinched tight. Curious, or suspicious?

Emily forced a smile. "Well. Good day."

She walked away, pressing her eyes tight against another wave of guilt.

I am doing nothing wrong, she reminded herself. Yet she didn't wholly believe it.

Emily felt, or at least imagined, Mr. Wallis's gaze following her. Would he watch her walk all the way to her destination? She was tempted to turn up Fore Street so he wouldn't see which door she entered. Instead, as she neared the York Hotel, she risked a glance back and saw with relief that the veranda was now empty. Perhaps the cold had overridden his curiosity.

A few minutes later, Emily sat in nervous silence before John Marsh's desk. She clenched gloved hands together in her lap while he read the pages, often dipping his quill to scrawl a note or addition in the margins. She began to think he hated it. He probably did. He was most likely sorry he'd ever asked her.

He looked up. "Excellent. Good start. Keep going." He stowed his pen and handed the portfolio back to her.

Relief.

They spoke for a few minutes longer, then Emily stepped outside in a daze of satisfaction, so much so that she did not pay attention to where she was walking. Sidestepping to avoid a delivery boy, she landed on a patch of ice. She slid, free hand flailing, then her feet flew out from under her. She tried to stop her fall with the same hand, the other clutching tenaciously to the portfolio.

Crunch. She landed hard on the walkway and pain shot up her arm.

The door behind her opened and rapid footfalls approached.

"Miss Summers!" Mr. Marsh squatted beside her. "I saw you from the window. Are you injured?"

"I don't think so. Only my dignity." She tried to push herself up and cringed. "Oh no. I've hurt my hand."

Taking her other arm, he gingerly helped her to her feet. "Let's get you to Dr. Clarke."

"I am sure I don't need a doctor."

"A surgeon, then."

"Emily? Are you all right?"

She looked up. Charles Parker stood there, just outside the York Hotel. She imagined she looked a fright, with her hat askew and a long hank of hair hanging down, having come loose in the fall.

"I just slipped on the ice."

Charles looked pointedly at the man still holding her arm.

Mr. Marsh released her, explaining, "She has injured her hand. I was trying to persuade her to see someone about it."

Again Emily began to protest, "I don't think that is—"

"I agree." Charles spoke over her demur. "Mr. . . . ?"

"John Marsh, at your service." He bowed and gestured toward the library windows, with their displays of books, prints, and gifts. "This is my establishment." He turned back to Charles and ran a speculative gaze over his fine attire and aristocratic mien. "And you are . . . ?"

"Oh." Emily spoke up. "This is Mr. Parker. A family friend. He and his parents are here visiting."

"Ah."

"Thank you for coming to Miss Summers's aid," Charles

said politely. "I would be happy to escort her wherever she needs to go."

Mr. Marsh touched a hand to his chest. "That would be most appreciated. And as you are old friends, I have no qualms about leaving Miss Summers in your care. In fact, you are a godsend, sir. As I really should not leave my library unattended, and it is my clerk's half day."

Charles nodded and offered Emily his elbow. She tucked the portfolio under her arm and placed her good hand on his sleeve. As they walked away, Charles asked, "Does your hand hurt? Tell me honestly."

She sighed. "Yes. And my wrist is throbbing."

"Then come," he said warmly. "Let's get you taken care of."

An hour later they returned to Sea View, Emily's hand and wrist wrapped tight. Charles insisted on seeing her safely home.

As they approached the door, he said, "By the way, I know it is not my place, but do you not worry about strangers staying here? After all, you are ladies without a man's protection."

"Not at all. We have Lowen and Mr. Gwilt."

As if on cue, Mr. Gwilt opened the door to them, took their coats, and fussed over her injury. He led the way into the parlour, where her mother sat sewing in her usual chair.

Mamma glanced up and her eyes widened in alarm. "Emily, oh no! What happened?"

"I fell on the ice. Don't worry, it isn't broken, only sprained. We stopped at Dr. Clarke's office to be sure. He said I should keep it wrapped for a few days, however."

"That is a relief."

"Yes," Emily agreed, though inwardly, she lamented the accident. How was she to write with her hand like this? And if she could not write, how would she meet Mr. Marsh's deadline?

Mamma looked up at Charles. "Thank you so much for bringing her home."

He dipped his head. "My pleasure. I am glad I came upon her when I did."

"Why do you not join us for dinner?" Mamma said. "It is the least we can do."

"I would enjoy nothing more, but I'm afraid my parents are expecting me."

"Send them a note. I am sure Mr. Gwilt would deliver it to their hotel."

Robert Gwilt nodded eagerly. "That I would, madame. Happy to do it."

Charles hesitated. "Are you certain it would not be too much trouble to add to your number at such short notice?"

"Not at all. In fact, Mr. Thomson was asked to dine at Fortfield Terrace tonight, so he shan't be joining us. We won't even have to set an extra place."

"In that case, I gratefully accept. It will be like old times."

"Excellent. We dine at six."

He glanced at his watch. "Normally I would dress for dinner, but . . ."

Mamma's gaze swept over his dark, immaculate attire. "No need. You are perfect as you are. Now, if you will excuse me, I shall just let Sarah and Mrs. Besley know."

When she had gone, Emily stood there, unsure what to do. Then she said, "We have a little time. Would you like to see more of the house? I think you saw only the parlour when last you were here."

He looked at her earnestly. "I would very much like to see where you spend your time nowadays. I can tell you May Hill has not been the same since you left."

At his words, Emily's heart leapt.

She led him through the more formal drawing room into

the dining room. There, his gaze was drawn to the patterned china already set on the table. Sarah's work, no doubt.

He mused, "Ah, the many meals I have eaten from these."

Emily felt a rush of pleasure that he should remember them.

"Your parents kindly invited me to join you for many dinners at Finderlay, you may recall. Birthdays, holidays, or simply when I happened to be there and put off taking my leave until the dinner hour. Your family meals were more enjoyable than ours, filled with pleasant talk and friendly teasing. Far more so than at our house, where every meal was like a lesson in table manners and decorum."

Yes, his mother had always been a stickler for proper behavior, a trait she had passed on to Charles and his sister.

Emily said, "I think Papa liked having another male around the place."

"Yes. 'Reinforcements,' he'd call me."

They walked on, through the breakfast room and back to the parlour. Emily added, "I think he saw you as something of the son he never had."

Charles nodded. "He even took me shooting a few times. Fishing too. Those were good times for me."

Emily's eyes heated at this fond memory of her father. She'd too often allowed the difficult months after his apoplexy to blot out the happier years before it. He had been so angry after Claire's departure, although at the time Emily had not known about the failed elopement and attempt to retrieve her, nor understood his bitterness.

Charles said, "I am sorry I was not there to support you when he had his attack."

"Perhaps you should be glad not to have witnessed the change in him."

Charles shook his head. "I am not glad. It was wrong of me to leave you all the way I did."

196

Emily wanted to ask him why he had. But courage failed her.

Georgiana and Sarah joined them in the parlour, and Emily relayed the story of her fall to explain her bandaged hand. Mr. Gwilt returned from the hotel and told Charles his message had been delivered and Mr. and Mrs. Parker wished them all a pleasant evening.

Just before six, they made their way into the dining room together. Mamma was already there, lighting the candles, and Jessie and Mr. Gwilt stood ready to wait at table. After a moment's qualm, Emily directed Charles to sit in James's usual place, and introduced him to their other guests.

Despite her initial reservations, it was a delight to have Charles at their table once again. He was charming throughout, teasing Georgiana, recounting good memories of Papa as well as anecdotes from their shared childhoods. Emily enjoyed watching the faces of her mother and sisters, awash in nostalgic glow, as they listened and laughed and offered memories of their own.

Mr. Hornbeam asked a few insightful questions, while Mr. Bernardi and Mr. During seemed content to remain quiet, allowing the ladies to converse unimpeded with an old friend from home.

Emily wondered if the mood would have been more constrained had Mr. Thomson joined them. Perhaps she should be relieved he had not.

Later that night, after Charles had left, Emily retreated into the office and sat down to see if she could write. Thankfully, Sarah had already lit the library lamp.

First, she tried holding the pen in her wrapped right hand. The tight, bulky bandages made it almost impossible to grip the thin quill, and the first word she attempted was illegible.

Then she tried dipping the quill and writing with her left hand. The result? Even worse.

Emily clumsily set down the quill, held her head in her good hand, and groaned aloud.

She could ask someone in her family to help her, yet she hesitated to do so. Sarah was always busy. Viola was newly married and active in charitable works. Mamma needed her rest now that she was helping more around the house. And Georgiana . . . well, her scrawl was atrocious.

Plus, asking for help would mean confiding what she was doing.

Emily was not completely certain why she had not told her family she'd agreed to write a new guidebook for Mr. Marsh. She supposed she was afraid they might not approve, either of the work itself or due to loyalty to Mr. Wallis. Or perhaps because Emily reasoned that the fewer people who knew, the less likely it was to get back to Mr. Wallis that she had been the one to write the book, which would compete directly with his. Or perhaps because she feared she would fail. That the guidebook would be criticized as far inferior to the work of Wallis and Butcher, and she would not want her name to be associated with it. With a veil of anonymity, she could fail in her first publishing endeavor and still show her face around town.

A veil of anonymity . . . The phrase brought to mind Viola, who used to wear a physical veil whenever she went out in public. Emily felt belated compassion for her twin, although their reasons for wanting to shield themselves were far different. Thankfully, Viola no longer felt the need to hide her scar. Love and marriage had given her new confidence.

Emily had never, ever dreamed she would be jealous of her sister, scarred and reclusive as she had been for most of their lives, but now she almost was. Emily too longed for love.

She thought of Charles gallantly assisting her after the fall. Escorting her to the physician's office and then home, taking care not to let her slip once more. Charles calling her "Emily" in his surprise at coming upon her on the walkway, when he had been calling her a formal *Miss* before. And then there was his charming presence at dinner. . . .

She became aware of another person's presence and glanced up, half expecting to see the man of her thoughts appear before her.

Instead Mr. Thomson stood at the desk, staring down at her hand, his handsome face lined with worry.

"What's happened?"

"Oh, I fell on the ice. It's only sprained, thankfully."

"Does it hurt? I heard you groan from the next room."

"It throbs a bit, but that's not why I was groaning. I can't write with my hand like this."

He stepped closer. "I could write for you. It's something I am good at, after all."

"Really? No. I could not ask it of you."

"Why not? I dislike being idle, and I would like to be of help to you. It will be far more pleasant to listen to your voice than His Royal Highness's. Especially when he has a cold." He grinned, adding, "Although I did enjoy hearing him agree to become patron of the Poor's Friend Society today."

"Did he? Wonderful! The ladies will be so pleased. And how was dinner at Fortfield Terrace?"

"Pleasant enough. I have eaten my fill and have plenty of energy for dictation."

Even so, Emily hesitated. "It is kind of you to offer. But I would be far too self-conscious. Besides, most of the time, I don't know what I want to say until I have a quill in my hand."

"We could at least try." He tilted his head to the side. "What is it you want to write? Correspondence? Nothing too personal, I trust. And please tell me it's not a love letter."

She laughed. "No, it's not. It's something of a . . . private project. May I trust you to keep it between us?"

His eyes glimmered. "Need you ask? I am entrusted with government secrets, after all."

"In that case, I am writing a new guidebook for a local publisher and bookseller."

"And why is that a secret?"

"My name won't be on it."

"He is paying you, I hope."

"Yes. Well, a little. Regardless, I would like to do a good job."

"Of course." He brought a second chair close and took from her the quill and paper. "Shall we begin?"

"Now?"

"Why not?"

"Again, I have never tried dictating to someone else. I shall likely hum and haw."

"You shan't be the first. Remember, we can always revise it later."

"True. In that case, let's give it a go." She consulted her notes and began.

"Over the last twenty years, Sidmouth has rapidly advanced from an obscure fishing town, containing a few—" She broke off. "No. Composed of? Comprising? Sorry. . . . Consisting of a few handsome, I mean, homely cottages . . ."

Face heating, she glanced over and found him writing away, unperturbed, pausing to dip the quill every five or six words.

He appeared completely at ease, and she wished she felt half as comfortable. Along with being nervous, she was distracted by his attractive profile and the warm, masculine scent of his shaving soap.

She pressed her lips together, then went on. "To an attractive
. . . Scratch that. To a populous and well-built watering place,
possessing every convenience desirable to those who wish to
enjoy sea-bathing, healthful exercise, cheerful society, or elegant
amusement."

Again she glanced over. "Do I need to repeat any of that?"

"I think I have it. Just one minute more . . ."

The man must have an incredible memory.

When he stopped writing, he looked up at her expectantly.

For a moment she sank into his dark eyes, her concentration
crumbling once again. She told herself such feelings were only
natural, not disloyal. She would be distracted by any attractive gentleman sitting this close to her. Charles most of all.

He gently prompted, "Whenever you are ready."

She inhaled deeply and continued, "Besides sea-bathing,
the town also offers two libraries furnishing opportunities of
general information and social converse. As well as a public
walk, and ball and assembly rooms, beaming with the smiles
of youth and beauty."

She looked at him with a wince of embarrassment. "Over-
done?"

"Not at all. Very vivid. You express yourself well."

"You are kind to say so."

He said, "These ball and assembly rooms you mentioned.
Do you attend balls there?" He looked down as if self-conscious
at the question.

"On occasion."

He opened his mouth to say more. Glanced at her, then
away again.

Seeing his hesitation, she asked, "Do you like to dance,
Mr. Thomson?"

"I do, yes. Although I admit I am somewhat out of practice."
He swallowed, then added, "Perhaps we might . . . attend . . .

together? Once your hand is better? In the spirit of writing an accurate description, of course."

"Of course," she echoed, then stilled. Had she just agreed to more than the need for an accurate description? Had she agreed to go with him? She pushed her uncertainties aside and focused again on her notes.

They continued for another half an hour, until Emily realized it was growing late.

"Enough for tonight, I think. A good start. And I certainly accomplished far more than I thought I would, thanks to you."

"My pleasure. Let me know when I might help again."

"Thank you. That would be most appreciated."

16

On Sunday his cold was still worse, but he had asked
people in for the evening and would not cancel the party.
—Cecil Woodham-Smith, *Queen Victoria*

I n church that Sunday, Emily made a point not to sit next to
Mr. Thomson, attempting to put some distance between
them, physically and otherwise. Instead she wedged herself
between Sarah and Georgiana. If he noticed, he made no sign.
He opened his prayer book and held it between himself and
Selwyn During, silently offering to share. Mr. During angled
himself for a better view.

Emily recited the responses and prayers and tried to concentrate on the service. Despite her efforts, her ears singled out
his voice among the others, especially when the congregation
sang a hymn.

She glanced across the nave, and her heart gave a guilty
start when she saw the Parker family: Charles's perfect profile in fashionable morning dress, his proud mamma beside
him in all her finery, and distinguished Mr. Parker, shoulders
slightly stooped, on her other side. Charles stared straight
ahead, seemingly not struggling to remain focused on the

service as she was. She noticed, however, that he did not sing a single word.

After the divine service concluded, everyone rose and began to file from their pews. Viola touched Emily's arm to forestall her, clearly eager to chat. Emily stopped, happy to oblige her. Viola asked about her wrapped hand, the bandage visible above her short glove. Emily told her what happened and insisted she was all right.

All the while they talked, Emily watched Mr. Thomson from the corner of her eye—thanking the vicar as he passed down the aisle, bending low to greet Mrs. Denby, and then shaking hands with Mr. Parker senior, who beamed at him and clapped him on the shoulder.

The Parker family approached them next, offering polite greetings to Mamma and the girls. Viola spoke up, pleased to introduce her husband to them. Emily was proud of Vi for speaking so confidently, so unlike the wallflower she had once been.

Mr. Parker nodded and murmured the appropriate responses while his wife blinked rapidly and quickly turned away from the major, either repulsed by his scars or trying not to stare.

Charles reacted more warmly, shaking the major's hand. "A pleasure indeed to meet Viola's husband."

If Major Hutton was surprised or offended at Charles's use of Viola's given name, he did not show it. "My wife has spoken of you as a neighbor and family friend. It is . . . good to put a face to the name."

He did not, however, say that meeting Charles was a pleasure. Viola had probably told him that this former neighbor had disappointed her sister. Did that account for his cool, if civil, greeting?

Once the Parkers had moved on, Emily became aware of the low hum of conversation around her and overheard more than one person talking about the party to be held at Woolbrook Cottage that very night.

Charlotte Cornish stood nearby with two younger girls. She was fashionably dressed as usual, and she glowed under her audience's rapt attention. Charlotte was telling them that her family had been invited to the party. Her tone conveyed mild indignation. Apparently attending a social event on the Sabbath bordered on the scandalous.

"It is the first time in my life that I will pay such a visit on a Sunday, and I hope it will be long before I do so again. Yet we cannot disappoint Their Royal Highnesses, now, can we? Especially when the duke wrote such a *gracious* letter to Papa over the matter of the Hook boy. I am sure he looks forward to furthering his acquaintance with our entire family."

Noticing Emily watching them, Charlotte raised a hand and called, "Good morning, Miss Summers." Emily returned her greeting but did not step closer to talk.

Emily knew the duke had not written that *gracious* letter himself, but bit back the words. Saying them would be petty and smack of sour grapes. She told herself she had no right to be bitter. It was not Charlotte's fault the Summerses had not been invited.

Of her family, only Viola would attend. As a former officer and next-door neighbor to Their Royal Highnesses, Major Hutton and his wife had received a coveted invitation.

Emily turned her attention back to her sister and managed a smile. "And what shall you wear to the party tonight?"

"My green silk, I thought." Viola's mouth turned down in sympathy. "I am sorry you cannot join us."

"That's all right." Emily felt another rare flash of envy. She had now envied her twin sister twice. When she had married the man she loved, and now.

"I promise to tell you everything, in great detail." Viola

watched Emily's face, concern coloring her features. "Or if you mind us attending, I could decline. You know the major is not keen on social events. At the merest hint that I don't want to go, he would pen our regrets himself."

"No, no. Don't decline on my account. I am simply feeling sorry for myself. Do please take note of every detail. Who is there and what they wear. Oh! And especially what the duchess wears! Also, what each room looks like, and the food they serve. Although I suppose I can extract that information from Mr. Bernardi."

Viola asked wryly, "Shall I conceal a small notebook in my reticule?"

"Good idea."

Viola rolled her eyes. "I was being sarcastic."

"*I* was in earnest!"

Viola squeezed her hand. "Oh, very well. Anything to chase that sad look from your face."

After church, Mr. Thomson went to Woolbrook to see if he was needed. Emily and the others, meanwhile, returned to Sea View.

After they took tea and a light meal to warm themselves, Georgie requested and received permission to go and visit Bibi Cordey. Mamma and Mr. Hornbeam went to their own rooms for Sunday afternoon naps, and Sarah retreated into the office. Meanwhile Emily, Mr. Bernardi, and Mr. During gathered around the fire in the parlour. The two men had only an hour or so to relax before they were due at Woolbrook to complete their preparations for the party.

Mr. Thomson returned a short while later and reported that the duke's cold had worsened. The duchess blamed a long walk with Conroy, saying her husband had returned chilled through and with wet feet.

Mr. Bernardi threw up his hands. "There goes the reception we have been working toward."

"Oh no." During groaned.

Emily nodded thoughtfully. "He looked rather unwell when I last saw him and had a bad cough. I would not blame him if he did cancel." She sent the two men an apologetic smile. "Sorry."

"Actually," Mr. Thomson said, "the duke has no intention of canceling the party. He insists on going ahead with it."

The chef raised a triumphant fist. "Huzzah!"

During rose. "Well then, it's almost time we went over."

He and Bernardi left the parlour together to change.

Mr. Thomson looked at Emily, some suppressed emotion flickering over his lean, handsome face. "Why do you not look similarly pleased?"

Emily shrugged. "It makes little difference to me, although I know many people would have been disappointed."

"But not you?"

"I am not invited. None of us here are."

"Are you quite certain?" He pulled something from his pocket. "Then I wonder what this is?" He unfolded it. "It looks very like an invitation to me. And see—your names are written just there. *Mrs. Summers and the Miss Summerses.*

She took it from him, studied it, then looked up into his face. "This is your handwriting. You did this."

"I did. With the duke's consent."

"If he does not really want us there, then . . ."

"An oversight, I assure you. When I reminded him who you were and described your family, he was most agreeable. He remembers meeting you on his walks and said of you, 'Ah yes, a charming young lady.'"

For a moment vanity wrestled with longing. Should she decline for pride's sake?

The twinkle in his eyes began to fade. "You don't wish to go?"

She bit back a grin and replied, "Well . . . I *would* like to see more of Woolbrook Cottage. I got no further than the morning room on the day of the shooting."

The light returned to his eyes, and the grin she was trying to suppress won out.

"Then I shall take great pleasure in giving you a tour."

Emily quickly found Sarah and showed her the invitation. They let Mamma nap for a time and then went into her room to share the news with her as well. Mamma decided that it was enough for Sarah and Emily to go and represent their family. She and Georgie would stay home.

Emily could not resist putting on her cloak and dashing over to Westmount to tell Viola the good news. When he heard two of his sisters-in-law would be attending, the major insisted on sending his carriage for them, even though it would take longer to ready the horses than to make the walk of about a hundred yards.

That night, Emily took pleasure in donning an evening gown in a vibrant color the magazines called *celestial blue*. The dress was several years old, but Emily still liked it. The blue satin slip had a pleated bodice and short sleeves. With it she wore a long sleeveless robe of white crepe trimmed in lace.

Sarah helped with her hair and fastenings, as Emily's injured hand was too clumsy to manage alone. Sarah also helped her wrestle on white kid gloves, even over the bound hand. Her fingers were stuffed tight as sausages, but at least the long glove disguised the ugly bandage. Sarah, meanwhile, wore an elegant high-necked gown in a dull shade of lavender-grey. Emily thought the style a bit matronly but made no comment.

When the Huttons' carriage arrived for them, Emily and Sarah climbed inside, and the vehicle bore them down their

sloped drive and then up Glen Lane. Though bitterly cold, at
least it was not snowing, and the lingering snow on the lane
had been packed down by a procession of tradesmen making deliveries and other guests arriving before them in chairs
and chaises.

Passing Westmount, they soon reached Woolbrook Cottage, its short drive lit by torches. In their glow, combined
with moonlight, the house shone creamy white. Snug in its
snow-covered glen, it looked like a small fairyland castle.

When they alighted, the door was opened by a footman,
and the sisters stepped into the modest entry hall, where a
servant took their cloaks. With a few whispers to Sarah, Emily
pointed out the morning room, where they had been ques-
tioned after the gunshot. Emily thanked God yet again for
the merciful outcome.

From there, they followed the sound of voices past a stairway into a larger reception room with tall windows and pa-
pered walls, where guests stood mingling and waiters served
drinks from a cloth-covered cart.

The room was not large, and guests flowed from it through
an open archway into the adjoining room. Even with fires
lit and the growing crowd, the house was still barely warm
enough to forgo one's cloak. Emily wished she had thought
to bring her long silk scarf.

At one end of the room stood the duke and duchess, greeting guests as they filed past singly or as couples or families,
the guests offering bows and curtsies to thank their hosts for
inviting them.

The duke wore a red coat with gold braid and epaulets
over light pantaloons, a blue sash across his chest. Without
a hat, his bald pate gleamed by candlelight, or perhaps with
perspiration.

The duchess wore an evening dress with a flounced neckline

and puffed oversleeves over sheer full-length sleeves. Dangling earrings caught the candlelight and swung as she nodded to those she met. A small plumed hat sat atop her head, and dark hair curled on both sides of her face. She looked lovely, yet her demeanor was reserved, and Emily noticed her glance at her husband more than once in measuring concern.

She and Sarah joined the queue, looking around in curiosity and occasionally exchanging greetings with people they knew, Mrs. Fulford among them.

Charlotte Cornish noticed Emily and stopped to speak to her in the receiving line. "Miss Summers. I did not expect to see you here."

"Did you not?"

"Well, no. Your family is not . . . That is, you did not mention you were coming when I saw you at church."

"That is true."

"I suppose you were invited on account of your sister's husband?"

"Not at all. I wonder you should think so."

Their turn came, and from the corner of her eye, Emily saw that Miss Cornish lingered, perhaps curious to witness the Duke of Kent's reception of two boarding-house keepers.

"Ah, Miss Summers!" he boomed, a smile brightening his plump, sweaty face. "How good of you to come."

A wave of pleasure swept through Emily at this mark of kind remembrance. She was glad Charlotte was near enough to hear Prince Edward use her name.

He turned to his wife. "My dear, this is one of our near neighbors. I believe I mentioned her. Mr. Thomson is staying with them, as are a few others." He added something in German and the duchess nodded and smiled at her.

Emily turned to include Sarah. "Please allow me to introduce my sister, Miss Sarah Summers."

Sarah curtsied.

Emily added, "And you probably met another of our sisters earlier—Mrs. Hutton?"

"Ah, the major's wife, yes. You are all very welcome. Do help yourself to refreshments in the next room."

He turned to hide a cough. "It seems I could use a cup of tea myself. Pray, excuse me. Throat is a bit dry."

But Emily knew more than a dry throat was ailing him.

They thanked the royal pair and moved on.

Emily glimpsed Mr. Lousada and nodded to Sir John and Lady Kennaway. Lady Kennaway paused to greet them, asking after their mother's health.

As they stood chatting, Emily saw James Thomson, striking in full evening attire, talking with an equally well-dressed gentleman perhaps ten years his senior.

"Who is that?" Emily wondered aloud.

Lady Kennaway looked over. "I don't know the younger man, but the other is Sir Thomas Acland, baronet and former member of Parliament."

Emily wondered what the two men were talking about so earnestly.

A short while later, Lady Kennaway's attention was claimed by someone else in the crowd.

Mr. Thomson nodded farewell to the baronet and stepped over to greet Emily and Sarah.

"I am glad to see you here." He bowed. "You both look lovely."

"Thank you for inviting us."

"You are a guest of Their Royal Highnesses. I am but a hired pen." He sent her a sly wink. At his veiled reference to her secret occupation as writer for hire, Emily bit back a grin.

The three spoke for a few moments longer, then Sarah turned to greet the vicar. Suddenly, James took Emily's hand

and pulled her through a curtained door she had not even realized was there. Together they climbed a curved, sconce-lit stairway.

"Where are we going?" Her question came out as a laughing whisper.

"You said you wanted a tour."

True, though she had not thought he'd really meant it.

Reaching the first floor above, he led her through double doors into a large room with many tall, narrow windows topped with velvety swags and tied-back curtains. Moonlight spilled in through them onto the patterned carpet. French doors led to a terrace, their many panes of glass allowing in yet more moonbeams. Large mirrors in gilt frames also reflected the light so the room seemed illuminated even though no candles were lit and the fire in the hearth had burned to embers. Matching chaise longues faced the fire. A tall upright cabinet piano stood at one wall, and an elegant writing desk on the other. On it sat a birdcage, swathed in white cloth as its feathered occupants slept.

Looking around, Emily quietly observed, "This is a lovely room."

"I agree. The duchess favors it."

"I can see why." Emily would love to curl up on one of the chaise longues with a cup of tea and a thick book.

He led her next to a room with simple furnishings and a larger desk. "The duke uses this as his study. I spend a lot of time here."

"It's freezing."

James nodded. "His bedchamber is even colder."

Emily stood at the window. "Look." She pointed. "You can see our house from here."

He came to stand next to her, shoulder to shoulder. "Yes. I glance over often while at work and think of you there."

She turned to him in surprise.

He gazed down at her. Moonlight painted his features in muted light and shadow. She leaned closer, eyes locked on his.

A squat mantel clock tick, tick, ticked as they stood there, mere inches apart. Then he took her hand. "There's more."

He led her up a narrower set of stairs leading to the higher floor. "The nursery is up here. And several of the servants sleep here as well."

"Then let's be quiet," she whispered. "I'd hate to wake the princess."

He pointed out the room in question, and they tiptoed past. It was quite dark—despite faint light from the landing lamp and a small window at the far end of the corridor. Perhaps they ought to have brought a candle.

Ahead, a golden glow showed from beneath one of the doors.

"Ah. Herr Eckardt is working," James said and softly knocked.

A man in his late thirties opened the door. "Ah, Herr Thomson!" He said something more in another language—German, she assumed.

James replied in the same tongue and then turned to make the introductions. She heard her own name in an incomprehensible string of words. Then James said to her, "Sebastian Eckardt came from Bavaria with Their Royal Highnesses to paint and sketch. He understands a little English but speaks almost none."

Emily dipped a curtsy to the man. He opened the door wider, and they both stepped into the room. Inside, an easel stood near the window, with many candle lamps arranged nearby.

Mr. Thomson asked him something in German, and the older man shook his head, gesturing to the easel.

"What is he saying?" Emily whispered.

"He says large parties do not interest him. No one sits still and there is no focal point."

Seeing the twinkle in the man's eyes, Emily chuckled.

"May I?" She gestured to a few pieces on a narrow side table, propped up against the wall.

The artist nodded.

She walked over and saw a chalk drawing of the duchess, and another of her infant daughter. There was also a detailed watercolor of the duchess's salon.

She pointed to it. "This is excellent! We were just in there and it's a perfect likeness."

Clearly understanding the gist of her praise, Mr. Eckardt smiled and gestured to a chair, indicating for her to be seated. Knowing he could not politely return to his stool until she sat, Emily complied.

He sat and continued sketching as he and Mr. Thomson spoke in German for several minutes longer.

Emily began to wonder if they would be missed downstairs. She didn't want Sarah to worry, nor tongues to wag.

She tentatively rose. "It was a pleasure to meet you, Herr Eckardt. Now I had better return to the party."

"Yes, of course," Mr. Thomson agreed. He said something to the artist, who held up an index finger, asking for a moment. He added a few lines to his sketch and then stood, handing James a small rectangle of paper.

He glanced at it, and if the candlelight didn't lie, his face reddened.

"What is it?" Emily asked, curiosity piqued.

After a moment's hesitation, he showed her.

It was a sketch of Emily herself. Head and shoulders. Quickly done but definitely her, and rather flattering.

"Goodness. That was fast." She looked from it to the artist. "Is it for me?"

Apparently understanding her question, he shook his head and pointed to James. In heavily accented English, he said, "Fur him."

She glanced at James's embarrassed expression, and her own face heated at the implication.

⌒⌒⌒

Sarah had somehow managed to lose track of Emily in the crowd. Hoping to find her, she made her way slowly toward the adjoining room, nodding to a few other acquaintances as she went.

In the dining room, she saw a banquet laid out beautifully on a long table lit by four tall silver candlesticks and decorated with hothouse flowers and towers of fruit—Mr. During's work, she supposed.

Sarah thought she might sample a few dishes and try to guess which Mr. Bernardi had prepared so she could compliment him later. At the moment, however, there was a line to reach the food, so she decided to wait. She felt mildly self-conscious standing there alone. A waiter offered her tea or sherry, and she accepted a cup of tea, glad for something to busy herself with while she waited.

She glimpsed Mr. Bernardi in the background, slipping in through a door to surreptitiously survey the trays of food and then slipping out again, probably into the larder or pantry. He was dressed not in kitchen whites but in butler black to allow him to serve at the event.

He returned a few minutes later, holding a silver tray mounded with something. He nodded to one of the waiters, indicating he should remove a nearly empty tray to make room for the full one.

Sarah made her way over to him as he settled the heaping platter in its place.

Sidling close she whispered, "How is it going?"

He whipped his dark head toward her in surprise. "Ah, Miss Sarah. All is going well and quickly. West Country people eat a great deal, it seems. Although they don't seem to be fond of *les cuisses de grenouilles* or *les oursins*. Perhaps they don't know what they are." He gestured toward two of the dishes.

She cast a dubious glance at the first. Whatever it was looked like long, skinny . . . legs? The second dish contained spiky half circles with orangey innards like preserved peaches. "What are they?" she asked.

"Frog legs and sea urchins."

"You must be joking."

"No. Why?"

Sarah blinked. "Never mind. I am sure everything is delicious. It all looks wonderful."

"Thank you, though I cannot take the credit. We all did our part. Oh! You must try these while you are here." For a moment she feared he would expect her to try a frog leg and was relieved when he indicated the platter of puff pastry cases, their hollow centers filled with something that looked like a thick stew.

Taking up a small plate and serving fork, he scooped one onto it and handed it to her, announcing, "*Vol-au-vent.*"

She took a tentative bite. The flaky pastry shattered into crumbs and melted in her mouth. The savory filling was deliciously flavorful.

"What is the filling?" she asked.

"Chicken and mushrooms in a *velouté* sauce."

"This is excellent. I like it very much."

His face lit with satisfaction.

"You have talent, Mr. Bernardi," she said. "I hope your employers appreciate it."

"Thank you. I hope so too."

At that, Mr. Bernardi recommenced his duties and Sarah turned. She glimpsed Emily hurrying into the dining room, looking flushed and winded. Mr. Thomson entered a few steps behind her, his neck also red above his cravat.

Concern flared through her. Emily could be naive and easily have her head turned by a handsome man, and after what had happened to Claire, Sarah felt wary at seeing the two reappear together. As the older sister, she ought to have been more on her guard—made more of an effort to protect Emily when she had failed before. She did not distrust Mr. Thomson specifically, but an unmarried woman could not be too careful.

Emily pressed through the crowd to join her.

"There you are!" Sarah exclaimed. "I was beginning to worry. Are you all right?"

"Yes. Sorry. Mr. Thomson showed me more of the house."

"Alone?"

Emily dipped her head, blush intensifying. "I did not stop to think how it might look. Nothing happened, I promise. He was a perfect gentleman. He even introduced me to a painter the duchess employs who is staying here as well."

Sarah studied her face. Emily certainly seemed in earnest.

"Are you sure everything is all right?"

"Perfectly. Just sorry to worry you."

Sarah sighed. "Let's hope others did not notice you leave with him."

Mr. Thomson joined them, his expression somber. "I apologize, Miss Sarah. I should not have shown your sister around without asking you to accompany us. That was badly done. Please forgive me."

Emily sent Sarah an imploring look.

Sarah said, "You are forgiven, Mr. Thomson. But do take care in future. A young woman's reputation is a fragile thing."

He nodded. "I understand."

"Now, come!" Emily insisted. "This is supposed to be a party. So far it is not a very jolly affair, what with the duke clearly miserable and his wife worried and unable to talk with most of the guests. We must do our part. Let's eat some of that divine-looking food and be merry!"

Emily's enthusiasm was contagious, and Sarah found herself grinning.

Mr. Thomson looked from one to the other with evident relief, glad to have the mood lightened. "I quite agree."

With a rare streak of mischief, Sarah gestured to the silver trays. "In that case, may I suggest you start with the frog legs or sea urchin?"

17

[The duke] became so feverish that the duchess called in his physician, who was much concerned by his case.

—Christopher Hibbert,
Queen Victoria: A Personal History

Early the next day, Sarah hurried around the breakfast room, making sure all was in readiness for the morning meal. Hearing voices outside, she stepped to the window and looked out. Tall, lanky Mr. During was speaking to an older, stocky man in coarse clothing, a donkey-drawn wagon loaded with split logs and stacks of turf behind them. She recognized the man as Mr. Mutter, who delivered wood and turf to most of the big houses in the area. He was no doubt very busy at this time of year. With the recent cold spell, fuel for fireplaces would be in high demand.

She wondered what Mr. During wanted with the man. Mr. Bernardi, she might understand. He could be inquiring about fuel for the ovens. But the table-decker?

The older man removed his flat cap, scratched his mop of steely-grey hair, and shrugged before replacing the cap.

Mr. During said something more adamantly—though what,

Sarah couldn't make out. Finally the other man nodded, then climbed back into the wagon.

Bibi Cordey, who helped them make beds and tidy guest rooms, walked past with a housemaid's box in hand.

"Bibi, are you acquainted with that man?"

The girl joined her at the window and squinted out as the older man gathered the reins and started off. "Aye, miss. That's Abraham Mutter, what delivers wood and such."

Sarah nodded. "Yes, but what else do you know about him?"

"Not much," Bibi replied. "Lives between here and Otterton, somewhere over Peak Hill."

Together they watched as the wagon disappeared up Glen Lane, then Bibi looked back at Sarah. "I could ask Pa. He knows most everything 'bout folks round here."

"Yes, please do."

Mr. During disappeared down the outside steps leading to the kitchen entrance—traditionally the servants' entrance. Usually, Mr. During and Mr. Thomson used the front door, and only Mr. Bernardi—accustomed as he was to spending much of his time belowstairs—seemed to prefer the back.

Something had clearly unsettled Mr. During's customary habits and demeanor. Sarah wondered again what that might be.

After breakfast, their three guests went to work at Woolbrook Cottage as usual. Mr. Thomson, however, returned half an hour later, expression somber.

"What is it?" Emily asked.

"The duke's cold has taken a violent turn. He is sick in bed with orders from his personal physician to stay there."

"Oh no. I am sorry to hear it."

James nodded. "I offered to take dictation from his bedside, but Dr. Wilson sent me away, insisting the duke rest undisturbed."

"Probably wise. I would not worry. He will recover soon. He told me himself that he is strong—stronger than all his brothers. And it's only a cold, after all."

"I am sure you are right. At all events, as I find myself with free time, and you with only one good hand, why do I not help with your secret project?"

Gratitude swept through her. "Yes, please!"

The two sat down in the office and returned to work on the guidebook. Emily consulted Mr. Marsh's outline to see what came next, reviewed her notes on the geography and history of Sidmouth, and began to dictate.

When she got ahead of him, she stopped speaking for a time and waited for him to catch up. She should have been consulting her notes to rehearse the following paragraph but instead found herself inspecting his profile: his head bent to the task, a dark fall of hair over his brow. The slightly upturned tip of his thin nose. The well-sculpted side-whiskers. The shadow of stubble darkening his cheeks, which looked pleasingly masculine.

He glanced up and caught her staring.

"Ready when you are," he said, meeting her gaze with his deep brown eyes.

Ready for what? she thought, then swallowed hard. *Ready for more words, of course. Don't be such an idiot.* Face warm, she looked down at her notes and cleared her throat to begin anew.

She heard the front door knocker sound and Jessie calling that she would answer it. Taking a moment to gather her thoughts, she went on, "Sidmouth is situated at the extremity of the valley of the River Sid and . . ."

Jessie brought a caller to the office door, announcing, "Mr. Parker, miss."

Emily looked up in surprise. "Charles!"

Beside her, James stiffened.

Charles too seemed to still at the sight of his old school-fellow seated so close to her. His focus shifted from one to the other.

"Thomson, we meet again."

"I am a guest here, after all."

"Right." Charles turned back to Emily. "I came to see how you were getting on since your fall."

"I am doing well. My hand barely hurts any longer. I should be able to remove the wrapping in a few more days."

"Excellent. In time for this week's ball, then?"

"I . . ." She glanced awkwardly at James and back again.

Mr. Thomson rose. "Excuse me. I will leave you to your caller."

"Actually," Emily blurted, "Mr. Thomson and I were discussing Sidmouth's ball and assembly rooms just the other day. He is interested in attending as well."

James faltered. "I don't . . . that is . . . I have no wish to intrude."

"Not at all, Mr. Thomson," Emily insisted. "We are all friends here, are we not? You two are old friends, and Mr. Parker and I are old friends. It only makes sense that we go together. Is that not right, Charles?"

Words he had once spoken whispered through her mind. *"We are friends—that is all."* She pushed the memory aside and added, "Perhaps Sarah might join us as well. I will ask her."

Charles hesitated, fleeting irritation in his expression. Then he said evenly, "As you wish."

He turned back to Thomson. "You mentioned fencing when last we met."

"Actually, you raised the subject," James corrected.

Charles held his gaze. "Then I challenge you to a bout, at your convenience."

"Now would suit me."

"I am not dressed for it," Charles said. "Tomorrow?"

"I shall look forward to it."

But pleasure was not what she saw on either man's face.

After that, Mr. Thomson did excuse himself, while Charles remained.

Emily rose, wondering what to say. She began, "Mr. Thomson was not needed at Woolbrook today, so he was helping me."

"Helping you how?"

"Helping me write a few . . . lines. He is a secretary, after all, and I am responsible for our correspondence and advertisements and things."

"Do you mind?"

Unsure of his meaning, Emily licked dry lips. "Do I mind what?"

"Having to rent out rooms, having to advertise, having to dine with strangers?"

"Oh, that. I certainly minded at first. I did not want to give up my room, or clean, or play hostess. In fact, I argued against the idea, although not as vehemently as Viola did. She detested the thought of having strangers here. You know what a recluse she used to be."

"I do."

"But Sarah insisted we all had to either assist with the guests or earn income some other way. With a little . . . prompting, Vi began reading to invalids, and that's how she met her husband. It has been so good to see her emerge from her shell and truly live."

Emily stretched out her hands. "So while I would not have chosen any of this . . . nor would I go back and change it, not considering the outcome for Viola."

"And for you?"

She looked up and held his gaze, trying to decipher what she saw there. She was tempted to say, *"That is up to you."* But she did not.

Instead she said, "Well. Shall we go and find Mamma and Georgiana? They will want to see you."

"Very well."

When they stepped into the entry hall, Charles's attention was caught by the large landscape on the wall. He walked toward it. "Finderlay. Can't believe I did not notice it when last I was here."

Emily followed him, and the two stood beneath the gilt frame, gazing up at the painting of the Summerses' former home—a fine house set among lime trees, well-tended gardens, and sprawling parkland.

He added, "It was like a second home to me."

"Do you never go there now?" she asked. Since her father's death, their Gloucestershire estate, entailed through the male line, had gone to a relative they barely knew.

"No. I paid one call to your father's heir to welcome him to the neighborhood, and to see what kind of man he was. I confess I found him rather cold and unwelcoming."

That had been Emily's impression as well, the few times she had met him after Papa's death.

For several minutes, Charles and Emily stood there, talking about their former neighbors and other people they knew, village life and fêtes, their adolescent treks up May Hill, and a few childhood escapades they had *not* shared with Mamma. And the longer they talked, the more the formality and awkwardness between them faded. Emily began to wish she had not suggested seeking out Mamma and Georgie.

"Do you know," Emily confessed, "there was a time I thought you liked one of my older sisters."

"Really?" He chuckled and shook his head. "I admit I thought Claire pretty—all the lads did—but she was older and seemed far above me. And I've always liked Sarah though not romantically. No, there was only one Miss Summers I was ever interested in."

Emily's throat tightened. "Was there?"

He nodded. "Although not at first. At first she was just a pesky neighbor girl. Following me about. Asking endless questions. Begging me to read to her when her sisters refused." A fond smile teased his lips.

"I remember."

"But as she grew into adulthood, she grew in beauty and self-assurance. As I spent more time with her, my regard for her grew as well."

Pulse racing, Emily whispered, "I remember that too."

Their gazes caught and held. Emily felt herself sway toward him, very like that final night of the house party when she had been so sure he'd been about to kiss her, and to ask for her hand.

Georgiana came skipping into the hall. "Charles! I thought I heard your voice!"

Emily jerked back.

"Georgiana," he said. "How are you?" If he was annoyed at the interruption, he hid it well.

"Excellent, thank you. Though I wish the weather would warm. I have not been able to play cricket in ages. You were the one who taught me, remember? It seems like forever ago, does it not? I play with some of the local lads when I can. Do you still play?"

Charles listened to the younger girl prattle on and answered her questions patiently, now and again glancing at Emily, a hint of longing in his eyes. Longing laced with remorse? Promise? Whatever it was set her heart to racing.

Soon Mamma joined them as well, ending any hope of more private moments between them.

Before he left, they finalized plans for the ball on Wednesday evening. He offered to come in his family's chaise to collect her . . . and whomever else she chose to bring along.

Later that day, Mr. Thomson once again appeared in the office doorway, a leather ball in hand. He tossed it in the air and caught it with a boyish grin. All traces of his earlier pique had disappeared.

"What do you have there?" Emily asked.

"A new ball for the school."

"Where did you get it?"

"One of the shops."

"That was very kind of you."

He shrugged. "I was hoping you might go with me to deliver it. We could visit the poor house again while we're at it."

A week had passed since Mr. Thomson's first visit to the school and poor house. Perhaps now that the Duke of Kent had agreed to act as patron for the Poor's Friend Society, he was eager to become more involved.

Emily hesitated before answering. She probably shouldn't go with him. But she did want to take another look at the two main hotels in town, which were on the way to the school.

She asked, "Would you mind if we made two brief stops on the way? To help with the guidebook?" She had been to the London Inn more often because that was where the balls were held. She was less familiar with the York Hotel, although she had been inside a few times.

"I don't mind—as long as we reach the school in time for outdoor recess."

They put on their warm outer things and, after Emily told Mamma where she was going, the two left Sea View.

As they walked, she pointed out the fort—dismantled after the Battle of Waterloo—residences of note, the medical baths, bathing machines, and other businesses. She gave him details about the owners, the ages of various buildings, and the services each one provided.

"You know," he said, "you are a living, breathing guide. Who needs a book?"

"Mr. Marsh does. And hopefully many other people."

She did not take him into the Marine Library, because she could already describe it in great detail with her eyes closed. Besides that, she was not keen to face Mr. Wallis, especially during her current mission.

Emily explained, "The London Inn is situated in the most crowded part of town, with no view to speak of. The York Hotel, however, was built facing the beach. It's newer and has excellent views."

"Careful," he teased. "Or you shall have me wishing I had stayed there instead."

When they reached the York Hotel, she said, "I just want to ask about the number of bedrooms and public rooms, meals served, that sort of thing."

"Are you also hoping to see the Parkers while you're here?"

"No."

He appeared skeptical but held the door for her. Once inside, Emily approached the reception desk and spoke to a young man stationed there.

Without stating her ultimate purpose, she asked her questions, which he politely answered. She wrote a few things in her notebook and thanked him, and they left a few minutes later. Emily did glance around the vestibule but saw no sign of Charles or his parents.

After a brief stop at the London Inn to ask similar questions, they continued to the school.

When they arrived, Mr. Ward again invited them into the yard. With his permission, Mr. Thomson presented the lads with the new ball, and after they'd cheered, they all began to play with it. The schoolmaster stood beside Emily, and they watched the game.

"Where are the girls?" Emily asked him.

"Most are inside. They prefer to play spillikins indoors when it's cold."

"Most?" Emily echoed. She looked again at the group playing ball and only then noticed a muddy skirt hem peeking out from under a long coat, and black stockings, which Emily had mistaken for trousers. A knitted cap hid the girl's hair as she ran and kicked with the rest of the children.

Emily nodded in her direction. "What's her name?"

"That's Cora."

"Does she often play with the boys?"

He nodded. "Not fond of sitting still, that one."

"I see. Reminds me of my younger sister."

Above the heads of the children, James caught her eye and called, "Play with us!"

Emily hesitated.

"Come on!" he urged.

Beside her, Mr. Ward encouraged, "You'll get frightfully cold standing here watching—as I know from daily experience."

"Oh, very well, then. Will you hold my things?"

"Happily."

She handed over her notebook and reticule and joined the fray.

Emily had little idea what she was doing, so she attempted to imitate Cora's movements, running back and forth after the ball. The girl managed to kick it from time to time, while Emily never got close enough.

As the schoolmaster had implied, however, she quickly grew warm.

After a few more minutes, she again joined Mr. Ward on the edge of the schoolyard, huffing and puffing.

"Clearly I am not the sportswoman Cora is."

"You were willing to play with them, Miss Summers. That is what counts."

Emily considered that as she caught her breath.

Perhaps she should ask Georgiana to come and play with the children now and again. She could teach them all a thing or two—herself included.

After half an hour at the school, they continued next door to the poor house. When they reached the entrance, they met Viola about to go in as well. She smiled. "Good day, you two. This is a pleasant surprise. What brings you back here?"

"I wanted to see Mrs. Denby again," Mr. Thomson replied. "She has stolen my heart."

Viola's smile widened. "She seems to have that effect on people."

Unintentionally, they walked in during the residents' mealtime.

On the communal dining table lay a hunk of bread tinged with mold, a few pieces of bruised fruit, and one smoked sausage, which Miss Reed cut into equal segments for all.

Mrs. Denby looked up when they entered. "Viola! Miss

Emily!" she called. "And Mr. Thomson, if my old memory serves. What a pleasure to see you all again."

She turned to the gathered residents and introduced a few Emily had not met before.

"We would ask you to join us, but I'm afraid this is all there is today."

Mr. Thomson frowned. "Mrs. Denby, I don't understand. You told me the food here was good, wholesome, and plentiful."

"And it was! Until a few days ago. I told you about kind Mrs. Novak, who cooks for us. She fell, poor dear, and injured her ankle. Do pray for her, if you would."

"I will, of course. But who is cooking in her stead?"

"We make do. The baker sent his lad over with last week's bread, and there's a bit of smoked sausage from the butcher, and just yesterday, Mr. Cordey brought us a few of his famous smoked herrings. Oh, and the greengrocer often gives us bruised fruit and other produce going off. With a knife to cut off the bad spots, we can cobble together quite a feast. Sometimes poor eyesight is a blessing!"

She laughed, but Mr. Thomson managed only a small smile in return.

"I am sorry to hear it." He shared a look with Emily.

Viola spoke up. "You ought to have told me straightaway. I am sure Sarah would send more food than usual. The major and I will as well. And how is Mrs. Novak getting on? Perhaps we might take a basket to her to aid in her recovery."

"How generous."

Emily felt a twinge of contrition. That thought had not even crossed her mind. "Yes, an excellent idea," Emily said, admiring her sister's charitable spirit. How her twin had grown and changed in recent months!

"Do you know where she lives?" Viola asked.

"With her daughter and son-in-law," Mrs. Denby replied. "Above the print shop, I believe."

"Very well. We shall do what we can."

From the window, Sarah saw Emily, Viola, and Mr. Thomson alight from the Huttons' carriage. The three hurried to the door, no doubt eager to escape the cold.

Sarah crossed the hall to open it for them.

"Come in. Come in," she greeted them. "You must be freezing."

"Less than we would have been," Emily said, "thanks to Viola offering us a ride back."

Mr. Thomson added, "We are obliged to you, Mrs. Hutton."

Sarah looked again at the waiting carriage, its driver ensconced in a caped coat and blankets, his hat pulled low. "Is that Taggart?" she asked, squinting to identify the major's footman and sometimes coachman beneath the many layers.

Viola glanced over her shoulder. "Yes. Don't worry. I shan't leave him sitting there for long."

Once Sarah had shut the door behind them, Viola said, "At least he went to the trouble of bundling up and harnessing the horses for more than one errand. Before taking me to the poor house, he dropped the major at the billiard room. He was invited to play with General Wetherall and Captain Conroy—and he actually agreed, if you can believe it."

"Goodness. Are there to be no hermits left at Sea View or Westmount?"

"Thankfully not." Viola grinned, then it faded. "But I am afraid I stopped in with less pleasant news."

"Oh?"

With a glance at Emily and Mr. Thomson, she explained,

"We have just learned that Mrs. Denby and the others are making do with stale bread, spoilt fruit, and a few scraps of meat or cheese."

"What?" Sarah's mouth parted in dismay.

"Their cook fell and injured her ankle and is supposed to stay off it for a while. So she can't come to the poor house."

"Oh no. First Emily fell, now Mrs. Novak! How long until she can cook for them again?"

"I don't know. We just found out. I shall have to pay a call on her and ask."

"Shall I prepare some food?" Sarah asked. "Mrs. Besley is busy, but I will help as much as I can."

"I was hoping you would say that. I am going to ask Chown to help as well. His skills have improved, thanks to Mrs. Besley. He still has a long way to go, but he could certainly do better than stale bread and cheese."

Sarah nodded. "Perhaps we might come up with a schedule. Rotate the responsibility between a few of us until Mrs. Novak is back on her feet."

"Good idea. Who else should we ask? Mrs. Fulford?"

"Yes, and perhaps Mrs. Butcher and the vicar's wife?"

"Good plan. But are you sure you can fit this in with your other responsibilities here?"

Sarah tilted her head, an idea striking her. "I shall find a way."

While they readied for bed that evening, Emily asked Sarah, "Will you go to this week's ball with me, Charles, and Mr. Thomson? I will feel awkward attending on my own."

Sarah's eyebrows rose. "You are going with the both of them?"

"It could not be helped! Mr. Thomson asked if I ever attended balls at the assembly rooms and suggested we might go together sometime. We made no specific plans, but then Charles came over and asked if my hand would be recovered enough that I could attend this week's ball. He asked right in front of Mr. Thomson. I could not ignore him, not when he had suggested attending as well."

Sarah groaned and shook her head. "Oh, Emily. The trouble you get yourself into!"

"I did not intend to. I don't think either man is pleased with the arrangement, but both have agreed to it."

"So . . . what? You plan to go to the assembly rooms together, just the three of you?"

"I would ask Viola, but neither she nor the major would be eager to attend a public ball. And you know Vi would not dance if she did. She always refused to join us for lessons with the dancing master."

"I remember."

"If it helps sway you, Charles will collect us in his carriage."

"Kind of him. Will he deliver you home again afterward?"

"I don't know. I did not think to ask."

Sarah settled into bed. "In all honesty, I have little desire to go, but nor do I think going out at night without a female chaperone would be wise."

"So will you go with me?"

Sarah sighed. "Let me think about it."

"Very well." Emily climbed into bed and blew out the candle, heart heavy with doubts.

She thought back to last summer, when a former guest, Mr. Stanley, had walked her home from a ball alone. That moonlit stroll *had* been a little uncomfortable. And later, Viola had seen him kissing another woman. Emily still cringed at the memory. Yes, she certainly did land herself in awkward situations.

18

Fencing brings to mind thoughts of tragic duels at dawn.
—Kay Geyer, *The Sportswoman*

The next morning, Sarah approached Antoine Bernardi in the breakfast room, where he lingered over coffee and a cookery book. She noticed a small plate of bonbons nearby. He must have made them himself.

"Mr. Bernardi, I wonder if you might help me with something?"

He looked up with interest. "With your mortar-and-pestle technique? I was hoping you'd ask." His hazel eyes glinted with humor.

"No. I am hoping you will help prepare a few meals for our local poor house. The woman who does so is recovering from a fall, and the elderly dears are getting by on fruit, a bit of meat, and stale bread."

He scrunched up his face in displeasure.

Before he could refuse, she went on, "You said you were bored! And that you had extra time on your hands now that the duke is eating only invalid food and the duchess has lost her appetite."

He turned a page in his book. "There is plenty to do in roasting joints and boiling potatoes and making plain custards for people who would not know *grande cuisine* if it kissed their lips. But sadly, little call for fine pastries or my other works of art."

The man certainly had a high opinion of his abilities, Sarah thought acidly. Then again, having seen and tasted some of his creations, she really could not blame him.

Even so, she would not give up so easily. She paraphrased a Proverb, "Whoever is generous to the poor lends to the Lord, and He will reward him for his deeds."

He looked up at her, expression flattening. "That is low. I did not suspect you of being a manipulative woman, Miss Summers."

Irritation rose. "Then forget I asked. Heaven forbid you should lay aside your bonbons and receipt books to help someone in need. I shall keep that privilege for myself. After all, 'it is more blessed to give than to receive.'"

She turned in a huff and quit the room, even as her face flamed and remorse singed like melted tallow, burning her heart. What a hypocrite she was! He was right. Using Scripture to persuade him had been manipulative. She was ashamed of herself for doing so. Especially when she considered how she had neglected Scripture reading and prayers of late, busy as she was with the guest house. She had no right to hurl verses at him like weapons. *Forgive me, Lord.*

With a heavy sigh, she retreated into the office. She hesitated to ask Mrs. Besley to do more when cooking for their guests clearly sapped her strength and her aging bones were not fond of the cold weather. Not to mention Lowen was often laid low with his rheumatism. Mr. Gwilt was always eager to help and filled in where he could but had little experience in the kitchen. No, she would find a way to do it herself.

In the end, Sarah put together a simple meal for the poor house on her own: cold meat, cheese, fresh rolls and muffins, good butter, and bottled fruit. The meal would win no awards, but it would be nutritious and filling. Georgie helped her carry it over to the poor house and serve it to the residents, who were all graciousness and gratitude. All for this, her simple fare. Mr. Bernardi did not know the blessing he was missing.

Late that afternoon, Emily, Georgiana, and James Thomson gathered in the hall, awaiting Charles Parker's arrival for the promised fencing bout.

He arrived promptly and greeted James with an arched brow and a smirk. "Ready to lose?"

Mr. Thomson's thin nostrils flared. "Are you?"

"Boys, boys, boys," Emily admonished. "No need to posture like bulls in a ring."

Charles gave her a more genuine grin. "Only teasing him. I may have once been champion, but that was years ago. These days, I fence only twice a week with a local master."

James shook his head. "Of course you do."

"And you, Thomson?"

"As I said before, I've had little time to practice lately, and few worthy opponents."

"Hey!" Georgiana interjected. "Don't forget about me."

Charles looked from Georgie to James Thomson in question.

Emily explained, "Mr. Thomson has kindly been teaching Georgiana to fence." She hesitated. "And I have had one lesson as well."

"Have you indeed?" Charles's brows lowered. "Then perhaps you would like to witness our bout."

Both men looked at her, expressions sober and expectant.

Hoping to lighten the competitive atmosphere, Emily was about to decline. Before she could, Georgiana enthusiastically answered for them both. "To be sure she would, and so would I!"

The men marched up the stairs to the former nursery in the attic. Georgiana followed eagerly—Emily less so.

"My apologies, ladies. . . ." Charles removed his coat. Beneath it he wore pantaloons and a loose white shirt. "I am afraid I did not bring my fencing kit with me."

"That's all right," Georgiana assured him.

Mr. Thomson wore buff knee britches and a white fencing coat buttoned down one side. He opened his case, and each man chose a foil.

The bout began.

Emily sat in one of the small chairs pushed to the side of the room, and her sister sat beside her. As they watched, Georgiana quietly commented on the moves she recognized.

"Advance, lunge, retreat. Strike-parry-riposte. Feint-parry-riposte."

On and on, the pattern continued, until Charles jumped forward in a maneuver Emily had not seen before.

"Oh! I think that was a balestra," Georgie observed. "I'm not certain."

Charles seemed more graceful and his form finer. James, however, was also skillful, as well as quick and determined.

In short order, however, Mr. Thomson was breathing hard, while Charles seemed at ease. James's recent lack of practice clearly hindered him compared to Charles's conditioned endurance.

As Mr. Thomson tired, his guard slipped, and he gave his opponent an opening to land a strike.

"Charles scored!" Georgiana whispered excitedly.

The bout continued. Charles struck hard again, and this time James parried. James lunged and Charles attempted to counter, but James scored a hit.

"Bravo," Georgiana cheered.

"Well done," Charles acknowledged. "You are better than I recall."

Mr. Thomson leaned over, panting to catch his breath. Charles, meanwhile, wiped his forehead with a handkerchief.

It reminded Emily of the monogrammed handkerchief of his she had kept all these years, pressed flat in a girlhood diary.

After a brief respite, the men faced off again, advancing and retreating across the sun-striped floor, attacking on the inside, then outside of their foils, up, down, above, and under.

Emily was very glad they were using foils with blunt, protective tips instead of sharp swords. She did not like the fierce gleam in each competitor's eye. Even so, she could not help but admire Mr. Thomson's broad shoulders, speed, and agility. Nor could she fail to notice the outline of Charles's chest and arms through his thin, damp shirt.

She was grateful neither man could read her thoughts at that moment.

With a look of determination, Charles advanced and advanced again, until Mr. Thomson was forced to retreat all the way to the wall. Finding his opening, Charles struck James in the chest with the tip of the foil and a fierce shout.

"Hit acknowledged," James conceded between heavy breaths. "You defeat me yet again, as you always did."

"It was a near thing," Charles graciously allowed. "My regular bouts with a fencing master gave me an advantage."

James nodded but said nothing more.

Charles looked to their audience and added, "Fencing with novices cannot compare. Pray do not be offended, Georgiana."

Georgie lifted her chin. "I shall try not to, Charles. But give me a year with your fencing master, and I would best you both."

Charles met her gaze. "I do not doubt it for a moment."

Mr. Thomson excused himself to wash and change. Georgiana remained in the attic, going to her room for something.

Emily walked downstairs with Charles alone, stopping at the linen cupboard to retrieve a towel for him to mop his face and neck. Then they continued to the ground floor and into the quiet hall.

"This rivalry of yours," she began. "It was clearly about more than fencing."

He hesitated, then said, "Yes."

"Tell me."

He grimaced. "There was a young lady he admired in Oxford. Daughter of a local solicitor, who had answered some questions of law for him during his studies. Apparently, Thomson began to call on this young lady, but she did not return his esteem. Thomson blamed me."

"Why? Were you acquainted with her too?"

"I was. We danced together a few times. And she flirted with me, I don't deny."

"And you flirted back?"

"I may have done, though not intentionally. This was several years ago, remember. Before you and I . . . Before I . . ."

"Before you what?"

"Began seeing you as a woman, instead of one of the little neighbor girls."

"Little!" Emily sputtered.

"You are four years younger than I, after all, which seemed a large divide . . . then. But that gap dwindled to insignificance when you were nineteen and I three-and-twenty."

Emily wondered at that, then tilted her head to study his expression. "Were you interested in this Oxford girl?"

"For a time, maybe. It was never anything serious. At least on my part."

"But if you knew your friend liked her . . . ?"

"Thomson and I were not close. And I did not intentionally encourage her. She was a pretty girl, and I can't pretend I did not enjoy the attention. But if memory serves, she flirted with several fellows."

"Hmm," Emily murmured, not sure what to think. Her sisters had often accused her of flirting indiscriminately, sometimes unknowingly. She should not jump to conclusions about this girl. Charles may have misjudged her intentions.

"Any other questions?" he asked, the light of challenge again in his eyes.

She regarded him somberly. "I have many questions. Probably few you'd like to answer."

His brow furrowed, and he took a step nearer, his expression softening. "Emily, I realize I disappointed you in the past, but I hope you know you can still trust me."

Could she? She slowly nodded.

He glanced at the mantel clock. "Well, I had better return to the hotel. I should not miss dinner with my parents again. The ball is tomorrow, so I will see you then, yes?"

Again she nodded. He reached out and pressed her hand. "I am looking forward to it."

For most of her life, Emily had trusted Charles implicitly. Did she still? A conversation she'd had with Mr. Thomson came to mind, about history being "fact," and her rebuttal that histories were an author's interpretation of facts. Sometimes there were glaring discrepancies when two people experienced and later described the same events, whether by mistake or a difference in perspective.

Emily decided she believed Charles was telling her the truth. At least, his version of it.

After Charles left, Georgie came back downstairs, eager to talk over the fencing match.

A short while later, Mr. Thomson came down as well, washed and dressed in his usual gentlemen's attire, and joined them in the parlour.

He said to Georgie, "I hope seeing your supposed teacher lose today did not disappoint you overmuch."

"Not at all," Georgie replied. "I thought you were both magnificent. In fact, I am more determined than ever to learn all I can."

"I am glad to hear it."

"Perhaps tomorrow?" Georgie suggested.

Thomson grinned. "I admire your spirit."

"Now, if you will excuse me, I am going to tell Mamma all about it." Georgiana hurried from the room.

When the two were alone, Emily said, "I asked Mr. Parker about the rivalry between you. Over a lady, it seems, as much as fencing?"

"I am surprised he told you."

She summarized what Charles had told her about the young woman.

His eyes widened even as his dark eyebrows drew low. "He said that?"

"Yes. Why?"

James shook his head. "Miss Moulton did not flirt with 'several fellows.' She was a sweet, genteel young lady. I received her father's permission to call on her and even to write to her. And despite what Parker told you, she *did* return my regard, at least initially. But once he began to show her attention . . ." Again he shook his head, expression rueful. "And why would she not be smitten? Eldest son and heir. Good-looking. Confident. After meeting him, she quickly changed toward me. Became distant."

Emily knew how that felt. "Did you love her?"

James considered the question. "I cannot honestly say I loved her, as our acquaintance was not of long duration. Yet I thought . . . and believed . . . we would fall in love—in time. But it was not to be. Parker began courting her, and my hopes for the future were dashed. He even introduced her to his parents."

Did he? A painful lump lodged in Emily's throat. Charles had not mentioned it.

"But his attentions toward Miss Moulton did not last long."

"Why not?"

James shrugged. "I gathered his mother did not approve. Beyond that, I don't know the particulars. I do know he cut Miss Moulton's acquaintance and she broke her heart over it. You may not believe me, but I felt no satisfaction—I did not like seeing her hurt."

"Did you . . . renew your addresses to her?"

"No. I did not come begging like a loyal dog, hoping for a pat. I was polite and, I hope, kind when our paths crossed, but I did not attempt to rekindle a romance."

"Do you ever regret not doing so?"

He looked at her steadily. "I once had second thoughts, but no longer. Now I am glad to be free."

She met his gaze. Was he saying what she thought he might be? For a moment longer she held his gaze, then looked down. Was she free? Unattached? Or did Charles Parker still own her heart?

As her silence lengthened, he cleared his throat. "Of course, living with and serving His Royal Highness as I do, going where he goes, I am not really free at all, am I? I could not offer . . . anyone . . . a future."

His words provoked a surge of sorrow, followed by confusion. Why was she sad? She had always known he would be leaving. He'd never misled her.

Once again, she resolved to cease thinking of James Thomson in any romantic sense, reminding herself sternly not to become attached. She might be attracted to the man, but there was no future in it. And if she was not careful, she could ruin her chance at happiness with Charles over a foolish, futile attraction.

19

The assembly and card rooms are at the London Inn.
Balls are frequent and the floor has an excellent spring.
—*The Beauties of Sidmouth Displayed*

As they dressed for dinner that evening, Emily glanced at Sarah and asked, "Have you decided about the ball?"

Sarah hesitated. "I have thought about it, and I agree the situation is awkward. And I would like you to be able to enjoy yourself."

"So?" Emily prompted, anxiously awaiting her answer.

When Sarah said nothing further, Emily rushed on, "Perhaps we might invite Mr. Bernardi too? Maybe even Mr. During, to be polite. It would be good to offer our guests some entertainment while they are with us, would it not?"

Sarah frowned. "I would not want to ask either man individually, as that might be misconstrued. And I should warn you, Mr. Bernardi is unlikely to accept any invitation from me, as he and I quarreled this morning."

"About what?"

"Oh, I asked him to help me with something and I handled

it poorly. But perhaps you might issue a general invitation at dinner."

"Really? Does that mean you will go with us?" Emily asked in surprise. Sarah had not once attended a local ball.

"I am not saying I shall dance—I doubt I remember how— but perhaps I would enjoy an evening out as well."

Emily's heart lifted. "Oh, thank you, Sarah! That makes me very happy!"

Once they were all seated in the dining room and the meal began, Sarah sent Emily a significant look.

Emily nodded and announced, "We were thinking some of you might like to attend a ball with us at the local assembly rooms? Tomorrow night. There will be music, dancing, and refreshments."

Sarah added, "Mr. Thomson is planning to attend, I believe. As are Emily and I."

At this, Emily glanced across the table at Mr. Thomson for confirmation, and found him regarding her with a furrowed brow. He said nothing.

Mr. During sent her an apologetic wince. "Kind of you to offer, but I shall have to decline."

Emily turned toward the pastry chef. "Mr. Bernardi?"

With a pointed glance at Sarah, he replied, "You would not want me there. I never learned to dance. They didn't exactly teach that at cookery school."

Emily said, "Our local dancing master and his wife call out the patterns for the newer country dances. It makes things much easier, since people come from all over and are not always familiar with the same dances. You might find it is not as difficult as you think."

Sarah added, "If you can follow a recipe, then I imagine you could follow dance instructions as well."

"Just that easy, ey? What—no proverbs to sway me?" He shook his head. "I am not keen to dance."

A tense moment followed while the others exchanged uncertain glances.

Then Bernardi spoke again. "However, I would not mind seeing what passes for refreshments at a seaside assembly."

"Then you will go?"

He shrugged. "I shall."

Emily sent Sarah a satisfied look. "Excellent."

After the meal, as they left the dining room, Mr. Thomson stepped near Emily and said in a low voice, "If you did not wish to attend with me, you might simply have said so. No need to invite the whole house to avoid spending time with me."

"Not at all. I am glad you are going. But Mr. Parker will be there as well, and a trio could be awkward. This way no one shall feel like a gooseberry."

His mouth pinched. "We shall see about that."

The next morning, the laundress's lad delivered a load of clean towels and sheets. Sarah paid the boy, then carried them upstairs and stowed them in the linen cupboard. Glancing down the passage, she noticed Mr. During's door stood slightly ajar, a crack of sunlight spilling through it into the dim corridor.

Curious, she walked toward his room.

"Mr. During?" She tapped on the open door with her knuckles.

No reply.

Footsteps marched behind her and she turned. Here came Mr. During now.

"Miss Summers, what is it?"

"Oh, there you are. I was surprised to see your door open and wanted to make sure everything was all right."

He frowned. "My door . . . open? How did that happen? Did you unlock it with your own key?"

"No. It was open when I came upstairs."

"Nonsense. I would never leave the door unsecured. Must be a fault of the lock." He jiggled the latch.

"The lock is fairly new, but we could have Mr. Farrant out to confirm it is sound, if you are worried about it."

"Oh." He looked upward, as if struck by a thought. "I suppose I may have . . . Well, I only stepped out for a moment to, um, use the water closet. That must explain it. I would never otherwise leave my door unlocked." He went inside and looked around the room, then bent to study the plate chest.

"Don't worry, Mr. During. I shan't report you to Captain Conroy." She said it as a lighthearted jest, but he looked up in alarm.

"Good heavens. I should hope not!"

"I was only teasing." Sarah glanced over his hunched form and observed, "Thankfully there is a lock on the chest as well for added security."

"True, though I open it from time to time to polish the pieces and keep them in readiness, should another occasion arise to use them."

He rose to his feet with a sigh of relief. "No harm done."

She regarded him with compassion. "I gather you miss setting out all the royal finery?"

He nodded. "Yes, although this is only the small plate chest. It holds little tableware beyond four magnificent silver candlesticks."

Sarah nodded. "I believe I saw those at the party Sunday evening."

"You may have, yes. The chest also contains items of a more ceremonial nature. The Duke of Kent has received several awards, like the Freedom of the City—as did his brother, the Duke of Sussex."

"What is the Freedom of the City?"

"A mark of gratitude from the city of London. The certificate was presented in a gold box of exquisite workmanship."

"Goodness," Sarah breathed. "His Royal Highness must indeed trust you."

His head jerked up at that, his gaze almost wary. "I suppose so. Although I don't think he values those awards as he ought. I am sure he would prefer their value in legal tender. He could never sell them, of course, as they are inscribed to him and are too well-known. Although with his financial situation as it is, he would no doubt otherwise be tempted."

Sarah tucked her chin, taken aback by his words. "I hope that is not true." She studied Mr. During and added tentatively, "He might be tempted, but I trust he would resist. That his better nature would win out in the end."

Despite the cold and the prospect of a ball that night, they still needed to bring in provisions to feed their guests. So Sarah and Georgie bundled up and walked over the esplanade and past Heffer's Row to visit their favorite family of fishermen. Chips ran alongside.

Mr. Cordey sat cleaning fish near his humble cottage. Sarah saw his sons, Punch and Tom, down the beach, dragging one of their boats to shore.

"Good day. How was the fishing this morning?" she asked.

"Slow. Caught some herrings and a few cod. Not large, mind, but still good eatin'."

"I am sure they will be." Sarah selected enough fish for dinner, and Mr. Cordey placed them in her basket.

Mr. Cordey opened his mouth to speak, then with a glance at Georgiana, shut it again. He looked toward the cottage's small window, where Bibi stood bent over the stove. "Why not go in and see how 'er crab soup's comin' along?"

Georgie followed his gaze and returned Bibi's wave. "Happily. I'll lend her a hand."

When Georgie had loped away, Chips wandered off as well.

The older man returned his gaze to Sarah. "Bibi said 'ee was askin' 'bout Abraham Mutter. That right?"

Sarah nodded. Keeping her tone casual, she said, "I saw one of our guests deep in conversation with the man, which made me curious. I wondered what the two could have to talk about."

Mr. Cordey frowned, which deepened the sunbaked lines around his eyes and mouth. "Fellow called During?"

Sarah looked at him in surprise. "I suppose Bibi mentioned his name?"

He shook his head. "Heard an incomer been loiterin' in the Old Ship Inn, chatting with the salts who frequent the place, and askin' questions."

Mr. During had returned to Sea View smelling of fried fish and ale more than once, although never visibly intoxicated.

"What sort of questions?"

"Don't like castin' suspicion on a fellow I never met, but as he's stayin' with 'ee, I think I better do." He worked his jaw a moment, then said, "He asked how a fellow might go 'bout selling somethin', quiet-like."

"Selling what?"

"Don't know. Don't wanna know."

What did Mr. During want to sell? Sarah wondered. Surely not something from the plate chest—at least she prayed not. If he were trying to sell something valuable, a few old fishermen would be unlikely buyers.

She said, "I don't understand."

Mr. Cordey looked behind himself, then lowered his voice. "The Old Ship is a favorite haunt of free traders."

Sarah frowned in confusion. "Free traders?"

"Smugglers."

Her mouth fell ajar. "Oh."

"A mate o' mine were there and told him, 'Mutter is yer man. But don't tell 'im I sent 'ee.'"

"The same Mr. Mutter who delivers fuel for our fires?" Sarah asked, confusion again muddling her thoughts.

"Aye."

Sarah said, "He sells wood and turf, delivers it in his cart. There's nothing wrong with that."

"Wood and turf ain't all he delivers. Contraband too. Seems the biggest houses buy a great deal of fuel *and* brandy. So regular visits by Mutter's carts rouse no suspicion."

"Smuggled brandy? He cannot have the time to sail to France in between all his wood chopping and deliveries. Especially not in winter."

"No, miss. There's others do that. They land cargo in small boats and stow it in sea caves west o' here. After dark, they haul it up the cliffs to avoid excise men. Tricky business, mind, with tides risin' regular-like and fillin' the caves. Takes a fellow with skill to time it right."

Sarah raised one eyebrow. "You, Mr. Cordey?"

"In younger days, aye, I shan't deny it." He scrubbed a hand over his bristly face. "But the missus begged me to stop, fearin' our lads would follow me into the trade. Ain't worth the risk, she said. And when her died, I stopped in her memory. Better late than never."

"Is Mr. Mutter dangerous?"

"Naw. Not unless you threaten his livelihood. But the man he works fer? I'd not cross him fer an ocean o' Frenchie brandy."

"Who does Mr. Mutter work for?"

"That I shan't tell 'ee, maid'n. Fer yer own good."

"But you know who he is?"

"Know his reputation, and that's enough. He's been caught many a time and always gets away. Soldiers cornered him in a public house on this very coast, and he fought 'em all off with only a knife. Best hope yer Mr. During steers clear of that fellow."

"Yes," Sarah whispered, and a shiver crept up her neck that had little to do with the cold. She prayed there was some other explanation for Mr. During's odd behavior.

That night after dinner, Emily and Sarah changed into the best of their old ball gowns and helped each other with their hair. Emily's hand felt much better, but Sarah convinced her to wear a thin bandage for support under her long gloves, just in case.

"I hope it is not obvious how out of fashion our gowns are," Emily murmured, trying in vain to smooth down a wrinkled length of ribbon trim.

"My dear, you are so pretty, no one shall notice the dress, except how well you look in it."

"Thank you." Emily regarded her sister, who wore a gown of white-and-blue-striped gauze with a modest yet flattering V-shaped neckline.

"You are the one who looks pretty tonight, Sarah. I have not seen you wear that dress in . . . heavens, I can't recall."

"I have not worn it since Peter left. I fear it's too young for me now. Do I look like mutton dressed as lamb?"

"Not at all. You look lovely. Truly. And I shan't be the only one to notice."

"Oh dear. I am not sure I want that. Though I was curious to try this on again. Honestly, I am surprised it still fits me after all the pastries I've been baking—and sampling."

A short while later, they donned their mantles and joined the men in the hall to await the Parkers' carriage. It arrived as promised, a coachman in a many-caped coat at the reins.

Charles stepped out and helped the ladies inside. "Good evening, Miss Emily. Miss Sarah." He nodded to the other men, then entered after the sisters.

Seeing how crowded the interior was, Mr. Thomson hesitated. "Perhaps I should sit on the bench with the coachman," he offered.

Mr. Bernardi looked at him, then through the window to Emily. "No, I should be the one to do so." He climbed up before anyone could argue, and soon the coach was carrying them along the esplanade.

As they went, Emily found herself tongue-tied in the presence of both men. Thankfully Sarah took over the conversation, asking Charles about his sister, the new baby, and mutual friends from home.

Soon, they turned up Fore Street and came to a halt near the London Inn entrance. Mr. Thomson alighted quickly and assisted first Sarah down and then Emily, taking care not to press her hand too hard. "Does it still pain you?"

"Hardly at all, thank you."

Mr. Bernardi climbed down from the bench more gingerly, hugging himself against the cold.

Arriving at the assembly rooms, they paid their fees, removed hats and cloaks, and then left their outer garments with an attendant. Mr. Bernardi blew into his cupped hands to warm them.

Charles was formally dressed in knee breeches, an expertly tied cravat, and a dark, well-tailored coat. With shoulders straight and head held high, he looked extremely confident and handsome.

In turn, his gaze swept from Emily's curled hair to her ball gown. She hoped he did not notice it was a dress she'd worn a few years before.

He said only, "How beautiful you look," and offered her his arm.

Together, they entered the spacious rooms lit by candelabra and heated by a roaring fire at one end, as well as by the warmth of energetic dancing. The gathering was not the crush it had been in the summer, but it was still large enough, and the music lively enough, to fill the room.

Charles touched Emily's hand and leaned close to say, "Pray excuse me a moment. Mamma decided to come, and I promised to find her as soon as I could."

"Oh, of course," Emily murmured in surprise. She had not expected Mrs. Parker to attend.

Charles walked away, quickly disappearing into the crowd.

While she waited, Emily surveyed the room. In a nearby alcove, the promised refreshments were arrayed, available for an additional few shillings for those who wished to partake. The table within held a punch bowl and cups, accompanied by a meager arrangement of food: thin slices of buttered bread and lump-like ratafia cakes.

Mr. Bernardi did not look impressed. Perhaps more dishes would be brought out later.

Emily turned her attention to the assembled company, searching for anyone she might know. She noticed people congregating in separate groups. There, the well-dressed aristocrats. And there, country squires and their daughters, who ogled dragoons in close-fitting jackets. And finally, a huddle of tradesmen and their wives.

She saw Mrs. Parker's feathered headdress before she saw

the rest of her. There she was, wearing a dark evening gown and a turban toque adorned with white ostrich feathers. Charles stood beside her. The two were surrounded by several young ladies and their mammas.

Someone greeted Sarah and asked to meet her companions, but Emily walked on alone, barely hearing, all her focus on the clutch of people ahead.

She drew near enough to the fawning women to overhear their conversation.

"Mr. Parker, what a pleasure to see you again. I believe the last time we met was at Almack's last season."

"Was it? Ah yes."

A second woman said, "I did not know you planned to over-winter here. You did not mention it."

"We planned the trip since last we spoke—and will probably stay only a fortnight."

"Pity. You will be in Town for this year's season, I trust?"

Charles looked over and caught Emily watching him. "I have yet to decide."

"Oh, you must!"

The women, dressed in the height of fashion, went on to cajole him and flirt with him. Emily felt too intimidated to join them, so instead she walked past them to greet Colin Hutton, the major's younger brother and Viola's brother-in-law.

"I did not know you were coming," she said. "You should have told us. We would have given you a ride—tried to squeeze you in, at any rate. Did you walk?"

"Yes. But better me than you in those drafty dresses and thin slippers you ladies wear."

"I suppose that is true. And how was Christmas at West-mount?"

"Far more cheerful than it would have been, thanks to your

sister. Left to his own devices, I doubt Jack would have bothered with greenery or gifts or any other festivities."

"Well, hopefully next year, we can all be together for a proper Christmas."

"Yes, I understand Sea View was besieged by royalty this year."

"Not quite 'besieged,' and our guests are not royal, but yes, certainly not a usual Christmas for us. Now, do you know plenty of people here? If not, I'd be happy to introduce you to some pretty young ladies." She looked around the room to spy out acquaintances.

He grinned. "Knew I liked you, Miss Emily. Send *all* the pretty ladies my way."

Mr. Thomson appeared at her side and asked if he could bring her a glass of punch. Emily introduced them. "Mr. Thomson, please meet Colin Hutton. Viola is married to his brother, Major Hutton. And Mr. Thomson is our guest and one of the Duke of Kent's private secretaries."

"Ah." Colin nodded. "You must be one of those bookish fellows. Knows how to spell and where to dot the *i*'s and cross the *t*'s and all that. I was never a good student, I'm afraid. But I doff my hat to you, sir."

Mr. Thomson shrugged and said easily, "There are other, more important abilities."

"Thank heavens. And mine are dressing well and flirting. Now if you will excuse me, I see a lovely young miss in need of a dance partner."

He winked, bowed, and turned away. Emily and Mr. Thomson watched him cross the room, bent on his mission.

"Pleasant young man," Mr. Thomson observed.

"I have always thought so."

He turned back to her. "And are you also a lovely young miss in need of a partner?"

Emily hesitated. She did not want to disappoint James, but she'd assumed Charles planned to dance with her. After all, he had made such a point of asking her to come and had even collected her in his carriage. It would be ungrateful to not dance with him first.

She opened her mouth to decline as she glanced toward him, several feet away. Charles looked at her and stepped in her direction, but his mother caught his elbow.

"Charles, you simply must dance with Miss Ferris. Her mother and I were at school together."

Suppressing a sigh, Emily looked back at Mr. Thomson. "Apparently I am."

He had not missed her hesitation, nor the looks exchanged with Charles, but instead of appearing resentful, his expression was decidedly sympathetic. He offered her his hand, palm up. How could such a small gesture speak so? With a grateful glance, she placed her gloved fingers in his.

He led her onto the floor, where couples were lining up, men and women facing one another. Charles and his partner joined them.

The violinist played the introduction, the music plaintively sweet, and the stately dance began with a bow and curtsy. Then they joined hands, moving toward one another, and away. Each gentleman turned his partner under his arm to change places. Then again, back to their original positions. Each woman turned toward the next gentleman, joined hands with him, and together turned in a slow circle before returning to her partner.

Etiquette directed each dancer to look into the face of his or her partner in friendly acknowledgment. Holding Mr. Thomson's gaze felt intimate and strangely thrilling.

Even as she held Mr. Thomson's hand, she was aware of Charles nearby, his eyes often upon her.

The couples formed a star, joining hands to turn.

Soon each dancer again faced his own partner. The pattern brought them side by side, hands clasped at each other's backs. Joined that way, they craned their necks to look into each other's eyes as they turned.

When it was time to release hands, Mr. Thomson's lingered at her waist before moving away.

The pattern continued.

His expression remained serious throughout, studying her. She stared into his eyes, so dark and filled with intensity.

As she sank deep into those eyes, the music faded. Again they stepped forward, hands between them, and she forgot to step back. Forgot to breathe. He stilled as well. For a moment, they stood there, nearly chest to chest, lost in each other's gazes.

The next pattern brought the neighboring couple toward them, and at the last moment, they parted to let them pass.

Inwardly, she cried, *Emily, what are you doing?*

She braved a glance at Charles and saw him look from her to Thomson and back again. He did not look pleased at all.

After the first set concluded, Charles approached her. "Sorry about that. I had hoped to dance with you straightaway, but Mamma had other ideas."

"So I saw. I hope she did not have to walk here, while we rode in your carriage?"

"No. I had our coachman drop her here first." He gestured toward the gathering couples. "May I have the pleasure of the next dance?"

She was tempted to refuse, torn between feeling cross with Charles and guilty about her reaction to James, a man with no future to offer. Remembering James's sympathetic response, she decided to offer the same.

257

Gently, she said, "I would be happy to dance with you, Charles. But please don't feel obligated. You are obviously acquainted with several other ladies here, all no doubt wishing for partners."

He held her gaze. Leaned closer. "I did not come all this way to dance with them."

His eyes searched her face, and Emily's heart thumped. How she had longed for Charles to look at her like this. Was this one of her romantic daydreams, or was it really happening? When she became aware of Mrs. Parker watching them, reality won out and felt more unnerving than thrilling.

Together they danced the figures of a quadrille. Four couples gathered in square formation, with each couple facing another across from them, and two others on the sides. Gentlemen bowed to their corners and then to their partners, and the dance began.

Determined not to embarrass Charles or herself, Emily struggled to concentrate on the entwining figures: meeting the opposite man in the middle of the square and performing small kicking movements, then one-hand turns, and two-hand turns.

The ladies formed a star and skipped in a circle one way, then the other. Then the gentlemen joined them. It was an energetic dance with opportunities to flirt and show off one's footwork.

"You always were an excellent dancer," Charles said when the dance brought them close.

"Thank you."

Charles too was a skilled dancer—his posture erect, his every step correct. Did he enjoy dancing as much as she did? It was difficult to tell.

While Emily danced with Charles, Mr. Thomson danced with Sarah. It was good to see her dutiful, practical sister dancing and laughing and, for once, not working. Emily began to think she and Sarah would both enjoy the ball.

But as soon as the set ended, Mrs. Parker came over and introduced her son to yet another young lady he "simply must" dance with, and with a regretful bow, Charles left her side.

Once word circulated that Mr. Thomson was from the duke's retinue, he too became an in-demand dance partner, leaving Emily standing alone more often than she liked. Sarah, meanwhile, was talking with some of the musicians' wives, who had no dance partners either.

Emily looked hopefully toward Mr. Bernardi, but he had struck up a conversation with the landlord of the London Inn, who'd come to see how the ball progressed. The two began talking about favorite dishes to serve at parties, the trials of finding quality ingredients at good prices, and so on.

Emily was glad not to be included in that conversation.

As she stood near the wall, sipping punch, she noticed someone carrying the strong scent of sandalwood at her elbow.

"Should you not be home writing?"

She looked up, startled.

Mr. Marsh stood there, smirking down at her.

"This is research," she defended.

"Right."

Emily was pleased to see him and relieved to have someone to talk to. She glanced at him and teased, "Are you here to persuade all the well-to-do book lovers to visit your library?"

"No. Though a laudable idea."

"Then should you not be at your desk, poring over your next great publication?"

"You are still writing it."

"Shh!"

She saw Sarah look over at her curiously.

Emily lowered her voice. "I have not told my family I am writing for you, so please don't say anything when I introduce you."

Sarah bid farewell to the musicians' wives and walked toward her. Mr. Bernardi strolled in their direction, looking bored. When Sarah joined them, Emily introduced the man simply as Mr. Marsh, whom she had met a few times at his library and public rooms. Sarah in turn introduced Mr. Bernardi, and when the chef learned the man was a publisher, the two began talking about the possibility and profitability of publishing a cookbook together.

Emily sighed, and she and Sarah exchanged wry looks. Now they had lost two more potential dance partners.

Meanwhile, Charles danced with one pretty partner after another, his mother looking on with pleasure and approval. Always polite, Charles did ask Sarah to dance once, his eyes promising Emily that she would be next.

Mrs. Parker came and stood beside Emily, her gaze remaining on the dancers. "It is always so pleasant to see young people enjoying themselves. I did not realize we would meet so many acquaintances here. Charles, as you have probably noticed, is highly sought-after. He will soon make an excellent match, I do not doubt."

Emily managed a tight smile, her stomach sinking.

"And now I think I shall retire. My work here is done." She looked over at Emily, expression softening. "Please don't misunderstand. I have always liked you, Emily, but Charles must think of his responsibilities. Our daughter married a man of impeccable character and family. I trust Charles will do the same." The older woman patted her arm. "Good night."

As she stood awkwardly alone once again, memories of another uncomfortable experience in these very rooms returned to nettle her. Emily had attended a ball here last summer and had been surprised to see a few acquaintances of Charles Parker's in attendance, Lord Bertram along with Mr. Craven and his sisters. Mr. Craven had danced with her first, hands lingering overlong, his every look cloying. At one point he'd whispered in her ear, "I have heard of the beauty of the Summers sisters, and you exceed my imaginings."

At the time, Emily had been discomfited to learn that she and her sisters had a reputation among strangers, though she did not understand why. She had even agreed to dance the next with Lord Bertram, who was, at least, polite. Polite or not, she would never have agreed to dance with him had she known then what he had done to Claire.

Now Emily pressed her lips together to hide their tremble and gave herself a mental shake, trying to dislodge the memory.

Thankfully, Colin came to her rescue, partnering her for two energetic reels. He compensated for his unfamiliarity with the steps with boyish grins and jigging enthusiasm.

Finally, the last dance was called. By then Emily had given up hope of dancing with Charles again and wanted nothing more than to go home and drown her sorrows in cake. From the look of Sarah's drooping shoulders and eyelids, she was ready to go home too.

Charles appeared before her then, a genuine smile on his handsome face.

"Now that my mother has retired, I may dance with whomever I like. And I would very much like to dance with you." He held out his hand, and Emily was powerless to resist.

She was vaguely aware of Mr. Thomson's face, set in resolute lines. After she reminded herself again that he would be leaving, the secretary faded from view.

A moment later, she was in Charles Parker's arms. Dancing with the man she had long loved. And he was smiling into her

261

eyes and holding her close, his hands warm and sure as they held hers and led her confidently through the steps.

It brought back memories of the last time they had danced together, at the Parkers' house party, when she had been so certain he loved her.

Seeing the light of admiration in his eyes now, she thought perhaps he still did.

This was real, she told herself. Possible. A future with James Thomson was not.

When that final dance ended, Charles helped the ladies don their cloaks and ushered them from the assembly rooms to his waiting carriage, having instructed the driver to return for them after delivering his mother to the York Hotel.

"I won't accompany you this time," he said. "That way, there shall be ample room for everyone."

Before anyone might protest, Mr. Bernardi clambered in. James entered next, to avoid having to step over the ladies, then Charles handed Sarah inside.

Emily was the last to enter. She stood facing Charles on Fore Street, only vaguely aware of the crowds of people milling around them, calling for a chair or their gig to be brought round.

Charles took her hand and for a moment simply stood there holding it, gazing down into her face. Then he said, "It was a pleasure to spend time with you. To dance with you again. It certainly brought back memories of happy times."

"Yes," she agreed in a small whisper.

He said, "We are visiting a friend of Father's tomorrow, near Exeter. But may I call on you on Friday?"

Aware of the others beyond the thin carriage window, Emily made do with a nod.

Charles smiled and helped her into the carriage, his hand holding tightly to hers before pulling away.

When he closed the door behind her, Emily braved a glance at her companions. Sarah glanced from her to Mr. Thomson and back again, looking concerned, while Mr. Thomson stared straight ahead, wearing a blank expression.

It was a cold and silent drive home.

20

Mutter's Moor, on the fringes of Sidmouth,
takes its name from Abraham Mutter, one
of Jack Rattenbury's accomplices.
—Richard Platt, *Smugglers' Britain*

T he next morning, Emily almost skipped breakfast,
not sure she was prepared to see Mr. Thomson, nor
that he would wish to see her.

Then again, she longed for a cup of tea. And pastries.

Perhaps she could slip in and out again before anyone else
came down to eat. She hesitated outside the breakfast room
door and heard the low rumble of male voices within. So
much for that plan.

She took a deep breath and entered.

Mr. Bernardi looked up. Mr. During, however, continued
to stare at his toast and jam as though they were of great
scientific interest.

She steeled herself and said, "Good morning, gentlemen."

Mr. Thomson lifted his chin as though it weighed a full
stone. "Miss Summers," he said, his demeanor cool, although
perfectly polite.

Mr. Bernardi asked, "And how is the belle of the ball this morning? You survived the dance mania? Or are your feet begging for mercy?"

She managed a weak grin. "I am well, thank you. My feet survived and the rest of me also." *For the most part*, she added to herself, aware of an ache in her chest at Mr. Thomson's detached expression.

He folded his table napkin, set it aside, and rose. "If you will excuse me, I would like to get to Woolbrook early this morning and see how the duke fares."

Mr. Bernardi said over the rim of his cup, "I shall follow shortly."

James turned to the table-decker, who continued to stare at his plate, his thoughts clearly elsewhere. "During?"

"Hm? Oh yes. Excellent tea."

The other two men exchanged a look, and Mr. Thomson departed alone.

Emily drank her tea and nibbled a pastry. Then, after helping Jessie clean away the breakfast things, she went into the library to work on the guidebook, not expecting to see Mr. Thomson again until almost dinnertime.

Yet an hour later, he returned.

Seeing him approach Sea View through the window, Emily went into the hall to meet him. "Is the duke's cold not any better?"

"I am afraid not. Worse, by all accounts."

"I am sorry. Can we do anything? Mrs. Besley makes an excellent chicken soup that has seen me through many a cold."

"Unfortunately his condition has progressed beyond soup. Dr. Wilson proposed leeches."

"Oh no. Poor man."

He nodded. "The duchess asked us all to help move the

duke's bed into another room—one that is slightly warmer. The house is frightfully cold. Hopefully the move will help."

"I hope so too."

"In the meantime, I have no work to do and am again at your disposal. Might I be of some assistance with your project, or have you moved on without me?"

Emily blinked, surprised he should offer after last night's ball. She knew she should politely decline. Her hand was better. She did not need him any longer. What she needed was to keep her distance. But the words would not come.

Instead she said, "I have been able to write and have nearly finished the Sidmouth sections. However, I still need to write about the surrounding villages, like Mr. Butcher did in his guide. I have not yet visited them all. Mr. Marsh said I should simply use other published guides as my source, but I would like to see at least some of them for myself."

"Understandably. When will you go?"

"I don't know. I have not yet figured out how to manage it. We have no carriage, and even if we did, I could not go out of town on my own."

"I could accompany you, if that would be helpful." He hesitated, then added, "Perhaps with one of your sisters as . . . companion."

He'd meant *chaperone*, she knew. Was he trying to keep a distance between them, as she was, or simply concerned for her reputation?

Emily said, "Georgiana would be pleased for an outing, I'm sure. She is always chafing at being confined to the house."

"I sympathize, and I would enjoy seeing more of the area myself. Where would we go first?"

We. What a weighty word. Again she told herself, *Say no. No thank you. Ask Charles to accompany you instead.*

266

Although that would mean telling him she was working as a jobbing writer. Besides, Charles had gone to Exeter with his father.

"I was thinking of Otterton to start."

He asked, "How far is that?"

"About three miles. Too far to walk in winter. Not to mention with steep Peak Hill between here and there." Emily tapped her chin as she considered. "I could ask to borrow Major Hutton's carriage. He has been exceedingly generous in lending it."

"I have an idea," James interjected. "Let me ask our head groom first. He was complaining just now about the duke's horses needing exercise."

"Really? Do you think he would allow it?"

He shrugged. "Won't hurt to ask."

Half an hour later, Mr. Thomson returned from Woolbrook and joined her in the library.

"Good news?" Emily asked.

He nodded. "The groom is happy to have an excuse to take out the horses, with the caveat that he will drive them himself, and he even requested that we take a different team the next time. That is, if there is a next time."

"And a carriage?"

He nodded. "I doubted Captain Conroy would grant permission, so I asked General Wetherall. Going around Conroy will earn me another dose of the man's vitriol, but it will be worth it, if it helps you."

She smiled at him. "You are very kind."

For a moment he simply looked at her, his gaze tracing her mouth, her cheeks, her eyes. Then he seemed to recall himself to the present. "What time shall we plan to depart?"

"As soon as possible."

Emily told Georgiana that Mr. Thomson wished to see more of the surrounding area and asked her to go along. As expected, her adventurous sister eagerly agreed and went to change into warmer clothes.

Emily returned to the library to think about what to say to Mamma and Sarah. She considered telling them the same story, but in the end, her conscience would not allow the deception.

She found Sarah in Mamma's room, the two going through some invoices and bills. Emily shut the door, took a deep breath, and broached the subject.

"I have asked Georgiana to accompany Mr. Thomson and me to Otterton and some other villages."

"Yes, she was just in here, bubbling over with excitement at the thought of getting out of the house. Apparently Mr. Thomson is keen to see more of the area?"

Emily winced apologetically. "That is what I told her. She is a dear, but you know she can't keep secrets."

Mamma frowned. "Secrets? What sort of secrets? Tell me you and Mr. Thomson are not plotting something that will further break my heart."

"No, Mamma! Of course not. Nothing like that. It's just . . . I think it's best if we keep it quiet."

"Keep what quiet?" Sarah asked, clearly wary.

Emily released a long sigh, relieved to be unburdening herself, while at the same time anxious about their reactions and the possibility that neither would approve.

"The truth is, I am writing a new Sidmouth guidebook for Mr. Marsh."

Mamma screwed up her face. "Mr. Marsh?"

Their mother, who had been an invalid and primarily housebound until late last summer, was not as familiar with the local businesses as her daughters were.

"Of Marsh's Library and Public Rooms," Emily supplied.

"Ah. You have spoken of Wallis's library almost daily since we moved here, but I don't recall you mentioning this Mr. Marsh before."

"His establishment is at the far end of the esplanade, beyond the York Hotel," Sarah explained. "I met him last night at the ball. He is a competitor to Mr. Wallis."

"Competitor, yes. That's just it," Emily said. "I feel a bit guilty for agreeing to do this for Mr. Marsh when Mr. Wallis has always been so kind to us. My name will not appear in the publication, so I hope Mr. Wallis might not discover my involvement."

"Few things remain secret in a small town," Sarah said.

"Is he paying you to do this?" Mamma asked.

"A little. But he has also agreed to consider Mr. Gwilt's story as well as my novel someday, should I write the guide for him. Mr. Wallis, however, made it clear he is not interested in either."

Emily looked down at her clasped, ink-stained hands. "Was I wrong to agree?"

"I do wish you would have told us straightaway," Mamma replied. "But I am glad you have told us now. This family has suffered enough secrets, I think. Will this project injure Mr. Wallis? Professionally, I mean?"

"I can't imagine it having much impact. A few people might buy Mr. Marsh's guide instead of his, but he is better established and has many publishing interests beyond the one guide. Beyond even his library."

"Then why do you feel guilty?"

"Because I have always felt loyal to Mr. Wallis, and this seems like a betrayal."

"Then perhaps you ought to tell him now, before the guide is published," Sarah said. "Explain you did it to aid Mr. Marsh and further your own writing career, but you mean him no ill will."

"What if the guide is a miserable failure? Do any of us really want my name associated with it if it is?"

"My dear." Mamma tucked her chin. "We all know you are talented. Why on earth should it be a failure?"

"I don't know. I just feel ill at the thought of people reading and criticizing words I wrote—even if they only describe the age of the church, the commodious attributes of each hotel, or the local purveyors of Bath chairs."

Another frown from Mamma. "What has all this to do with Mr. Thomson?"

"He knows about the guidebook—he wrote for me while my hand was bound. And he has offered to accompany us. Even secured the use of one of the royal carriages for the purpose. Mr. Butcher's guide describes the surrounding villages and churches, for those who wish to take day trips, I suppose. Mr. Marsh has asked me to do the same."

"Well, as long as your sister goes with you, I don't see any harm." Mamma looked to Sarah. "Do you?"

"There is nothing wrong with it, or at least nothing immoral about writing a competing guidebook. As far as your loyalty to Mr. Wallis and the guilt you feel . . . that is between you and your conscience. Did you pray about this before agreeing?"

Emily hung her head. "No, I simply plunged in, as usual." She sighed. "I hope I won't live to regret it."

Early that afternoon, an enclosed carriage rattled up Sea View's drive. On its box sat a young groom bundled up in greatcoat and muffler, a fur wrap covering his legs.

Emily, Georgiana, and Mr. Thomson climbed inside. Once they were settled, Mr. Thomson rapped on the front window and the carriage started off.

At the bottom of Glen Lane, they turned west up Peak Hill Road. The horses hauled the carriage up the steep incline far more quickly than they could have managed by donkey or by foot, the animals' steaming breaths the only evidence of their exertion.

Soon they reached the summit, and Emily glimpsed the English Channel in the distance to the south. Inland, to the north, stretched a patchwork quilt of frosty fields and stands of silvery trees in winter's slumber. Georgiana remained glued to the window in fascination while Emily found herself glancing at Mr. Thomson's profile now and again, wondering what he was thinking.

After descending the western side of Peak Hill, they soon reached Otterton, one long street of ancient cottages, neatly thatched and whitewashed. A brook ran along the length of the street, and this, along with a stand of fir trees at the center of the village, gave the place a rustic air.

They alighted and looked around for a time. With the shelter from hills on the east and west, the temperature in the Otter Valley was remarkably mild, and the surrounding hills and fields were pleasant to look upon, even in winter.

They walked up a steep lane to St. Michael's. The church was built on a rise and possessed a tall bell tower. The ragged building appeared to have been partly pulled down, suggesting it had fallen into a sad state of neglect but had recently undergone repairs. Now it seemed to be patched together in irregular style.

The interior was more pleasing, with many Gothic arches, stone pillars, and a wide central aisle leading to a fine altar.

Emily paused to write descriptions in her notebook.

Georgie asked, "What are you writing? Your novel?"

Emily hesitated, then shook her head. "Notes for a . . . future book."

They returned to the carriage and continued on, crossing a scenic stone bridge over the River Otter.

Not far outside of Otterton, they came to a small sign marked *Budleigh*.

"Are we not going there?" Mr. Thomson asked.

"I had not planned to, but we certainly can, if you like. Do you know of it?"

"I read that Sir Walter Raleigh was born in a farmhouse near here."

"Really? You are a fount of knowledge."

He shrugged. "I read a lot of history."

Surprised and impressed, Emily made another entry in her notebook. "And I, for one, am benefiting from it."

After again knocking to draw the groom's attention, they made a detour to see the house near East Budleigh, which had long since changed hands with another farm family. Then they stopped at the All Saints churchyard, where Sir Walter Raleigh's parents were buried. Together they explored the fourteenth-century church until they found the Raleigh coat of arms on one of the pew ends.

Georgiana, meanwhile, was more interested in befriending a village cat that had followed them into the churchyard.

A short while later, they climbed back into the carriage and moved on. They traveled north along a narrow lane bordered by stone walls and bristling hedgerows.

"Now where?" he asked.

"Bicton. There's a church there I want to see."

They approached St. Mary's, a modest cruciform church surrounded by great groups of tall, mature trees. The stone tower and walls were grey with age but still in good repair. There was something reverent and pleasing about the church, standing by itself in that lonely place, rising majestically from the surrounding trees and winter gloom.

For a short time, they walked around the quiet, shadow-laden churchyard filled with ancient headstones, Celtic crosses, and other monuments.

Thomas Gray's famous lines began whispering through Emily's mind, and she recited a few aloud.

"Lo, how the sacred calm that breathes around,
Bids every fierce tumultuous passion cease;
In still small accents, whispering from the ground,
A grateful earnest of eternal peace."

James nodded with approval and identified the poem. "'An Elegy Written in a Country Churchyard.' Quite apropos."

She looked at him in astonishment, pleasure warming her. "You, Mr. Thomson, are a wonder."

Emily was thoroughly enjoying herself and could have continued for hours. Georgiana, however, had clearly grown bored. Cold grey churches were not her idea of an adventure. It was time to head back.

"May I ride on the box?" Georgie asked plaintively. "Perhaps try my hand at taking the ribbons?"

The groom looked to James. James glanced at Georgiana and then back to the young man.

"Would you mind, Ralph?"

"Not at all, sir."

Next, James turned to Emily. "Are you all right with this? Ralph is careful and trustworthy, I assure you."

"Very well. It will make Georgiana's year, I know, so why not. Though I warn you, Ralph, be on your guard and ready to reclaim the reins. My sister is not the least timid and may take it into her head to break some speed record."

Georgie pulled a face. "Not on my first try."

Mr. Thomson helped Georgiana up onto the box, then

offered Emily a hand into the carriage. A moment later he closed the door on just the two of them.

Emily immediately felt conscious of the change. The unspoken possibilities of being alone with him. She gripped her hands in her lap and tried to appear unconcerned.

She knew it was Georgie at the reins as soon as the carriage lurched into motion and the velvet curtains, swinging wildly with each movement, slid nearly closed. Emily pretended not to notice.

She stole a glance at Mr. Thomson, saw his prominent Adam's apple rise and fall.

He began, "If you are not comfortable . . ."

"I am perfectly comfortable," she quickly insisted, although it was not perfectly true.

They rode on in heavy silence, the tension between them palpable. Did he feel pressured to somehow take advantage of this rare private moment? To say something? To . . . do something?

As Georgie turned the horses back onto Peak Hill Road, the vehicle careened sharply to the side, throwing Mr. Thomson against the wall of the carriage and Emily toward its window, her bonnet flying off.

His arms flew out, capturing her against himself to stop her fall, her head coming to rest against his chest.

The breath left her. "Ohh!"

She blinked up at him, startled to find herself reclining against him, her head mere inches from the windowpane. Angling her head, she looked from the glass back to his face.

Words came to mind. Empty words like *"That was close"* or *"Thank you for catching me."* She did not utter them—wasn't sure she could form them if she tried. It seemed a waste of speech. A waste of this moment.

She should sit up. Move away. Apologize for crashing into him.

Instead she looked solemnly into his face as he gazed down at her. His dark eyes shone. Sparking with . . . what?

His arms were around her. One arm beneath her, the other over her midriff.

He pressed his own lips together, and his focus lowered to her mouth, then away again.

He was the first to speak and said, somewhat shakily, "Are you . . . all right?"

She ran a nervous tongue over her lips. "I . . . think so."

The arm that lay over her shifted, and she instantly missed its warm weight. He lifted it slightly, his hand rising toward her face, brushing back a strand of hair that had fallen across her brow.

"Are you hurt?" He ran his fingers experimentally over her temple, then brought his hand forward again, framing the side of her face. His thumb stroked her cheek.

"I . . . don't think so." She almost wished she were, so his fingers would have a reason to linger.

Again his gaze dropped to her mouth.

If he leaned down a few inches, he could kiss her.

Did she want him to?

Yes, she found that she did.

He slowly lowered his head, looking into her eyes to gauge her reaction, her willingness.

What about Charles? Unbidden, Charles's face appeared in her mind's eye. His eyes fixed on hers, his head slowly dipping toward her . . . that near kiss on the veranda during the ill-fated house party. She tried to blink away the untimely image.

Perhaps he noticed her look of unease, because Mr. Thomson's expression changed, and he pulled back.

At that moment, the carriage staggered to a halt, and angry voices arose from outside.

Suddenly on full alert, James used the arm beneath her to easily lift her back up.

Emily straightened on the seat, looking out the window in concern. "What is it? Why have we stopped?"

"I don't know." He pushed aside the curtain and from his taller vantage peered out the front window, past Georgiana's back as the groom descended the box.

"What's happening?" Emily asked.

"Ralph jumped down. Probably to set chocks behind the wheels so we don't roll back. There's someone on the road."

Emily pressed her face close to the window to look out and recognized one of the men. "That's Mr. Mutter, who delivers our firewood and such."

"And the other man?"

"I don't know."

The second was a burly, broad-shouldered man in his forties with an impressive head of hair and a deep frown line above his prominent nose.

"I don't like the look of him," Mr. Thomson murmured.

"Nor I. I wish Georgie were inside with us. Are they blocking the road?"

James's jaw clenched. "Appears that way. I shall go out and see."

Glad he did not try to forbid her, Emily followed, descending the carriage after him. In the distance stretched Mutter's Moor, a scrubby heathland broken by crooked paths and windswept trees.

The unfamiliar man scowled at them as they emerged. "Who are 'ee and what do 'ee want?"

"We are heading back to Sidmouth," the groom said.

"For what purpose?"

"We live there," Mr. Thomson explained.

"You a preventive man?"

Mr. Thomson frowned. "Do I look like one?"

"Mayhap."

Emily pushed aside her fear. "We live at Sea View," she said. "Mr. Mutter there delivers our firewood."

The burly man turned to his companion. "You recognize 'em, Abe?"

"The maid'n, aye."

The big man considered. "Very well. On yer way. We was just havin' a little meeting. A private meeting."

Mr. Thomson quickly helped Georgiana down from the box and ushered her inside the carriage. Emily felt the men's eyes searing her back all the while. After Georgie was inside, Mr. Thomson offered a hand to help Emily in as well.

Their gazes met and held, concern and regret passing between them.

When they reached Sea View, Mr. Thomson helped the ladies down, then climbed back in, saying he would go on to Woolbrook to learn if there had been any change in the duke's condition.

Sarah met the returning sisters in the hall and asked how the outing had gone. Georgie told in excited tones about her turn at the reins, saying the groom had called her an "excellent whip." She then hurried to Mamma's room to relay her adventure. Emily lingered.

Sarah studied her face in concern. "You do not look as pleased."

"It started out well. Mr. Thomson was a helpful and insightful companion. Then on the way back, we encountered two men on the road. They seemed almost threatening and all but accused Mr. Thomson of being a preventive officer."

"Who were they? Did you recognize them?"

"One of them was Mr. Mutter, who delivers our fuel. I did

not recognize the other man. Big and angry. I did not like the look of him."

Sarah slowly shook her head, worry evident in the down-turned corners of her mouth. "This is the second time I have heard Mr. Mutter spoken of with misgivings about the company he keeps. If his companion was the man Mr. Cordey warned me about, let us hope we have seen the last of him."

"Good heavens!"

"Yes." Sarah drew herself up. "In any case, I am glad you made it back safely. Now, I had better see how dinner is progressing. Oh! I almost forgot. Charles called while you were out."

Emily bit her lip. "Did he? Did he say what he wanted?"

Sarah dipped her head and looked at Emily through her lashes. "Need you ask?"

"Yes, I do! Especially as he told me he would be visiting a friend of his father's today, and that he would not call until Friday."

"Apparently their plans changed."

Emily swallowed. "Did you tell him where I'd gone?"

"I told him you went to visit a neighboring village. He asked if you went alone. I assured him Georgiana went along, and he said, 'And Mr. Thomson, I assume?'"

Emily groaned.

"I don't like to lie, so I said, 'Why, yes. He wished to see more of the surrounding area.' To which Charles rather dryly replied, 'Of course he did.'"

Emily's stomach dropped. "Oh dear."

"If he was displeased, do you blame him? He came here to apologize and be reconciled with us—especially with you. And yet you are spending a great deal of time with another man."

"Charles has nothing to fear there. Mr. Thomson has made

it clear he is not in a position to marry. He will leave when the royal party leaves. Probably back to Germany."

"Then perhaps you ought to tell Charles that to put his mind at ease. Assure him Mr. Thomson has no designs on you, and that you and he are just friends." Sarah tilted her head to study Emily's face. "You are just friends, are you not?"

Emily sighed. "I don't know, Sarah. We are hopeless—that's what we are."

"Well. Hopeless or not, you had better hurry and change for dinner. It will be ready soon, whether you are or not."

Sarah walked away, concern for her sister churning inside her. Must relationships between men and women always be so difficult? She started toward the kitchen. As she descended the stairs, she thought of Mr. Bernardi. In the days since his refusal to help prepare a meal for the poor house—and her angry reaction—there had lingered an awkward unease between them. They had passed each other with polite nods, shared meals civilly, and attended the same ball, yet their former camaraderie had crumbled.

Entering the kitchen, she was relieved to find Jessie busy grinding the after-dinner coffee and Mrs. Besley stirring a pot of soup on the stove.

"How is dinner coming along?" she asked.

"Not bad. The soup will soon be ready, and Jessie is preparing the coffee before she takes the aspic out of the mold."

"Anything I can do?"

"Would you mind fetching cream from the larder? I need to add a pint in a few minutes, just before I send it up."

"I don't mind at all."

Chown, the cook from Westmount, hurried in, out of breath. "Might I borrow some butter, Mrs. B.? Oh, sorry, miss."

"That's all right," Sarah reassured him. "I was just on my way to the larder." To Mrs. Besley, she added, "I shall bring butter as well."

Sarah walked into the workroom she and Mr. Bernardi had often shared, struck anew with regret, and by some unusual aroma.

She walked into the cool larder for the cream and butter. On a larder shelf, she saw a covered plate and a small card beside it marked *Miss Sarah*. Mr. Bernardi's doing, she guessed. Curious, she walked over and removed the cover. On the plate was a salad made of the radicchio he had promised to prepare for her when they had strolled through the market together. The small purple heads had been sliced and grilled, then sprinkled with white cheese and tossed with some sort of dressing.

After delivering the cream and butter, Sarah returned to the larder and carried the plate to the workroom table. Bending low to inhale the tantalizing aroma, Sarah set down her burden and picked up a fork.

She took an experimental bite. *Mmm*. As Mr. Bernardi had said, grilling the vegetable had given it a slightly sweet and smoky taste that paired well with the tangy cheese and savory dressing. The bitterness had gone.

The chef came in and, seeing her, paused just over the threshold, uncertainty etched on his brow.

She smiled at him. "You were right. This is delicious. Although I imagine it's a dish not everyone enjoys."

He slowly nodded. "It's something of an acquired taste." He dipped his head in a self-effacing manner. "Like me."

"Thank you for making this for me."

"I am glad you enjoyed it." He looked at her from beneath his dark lashes. "Truce?"

"Truce."

From the adjoining kitchen, Mrs. Besley called, "Soup is ready, Miss Sarah!"

Sarah rose and moved to retrieve the heavy ironstone tureen with its lid and platter, but Mr. Bernardi intercepted her. "Please. Allow me to carry it for you."

21

Away with your fictions of flimsy romance;
Those tissues of falsehood which folly has wove!
Give me the mild beam of the soul-breathing glance,
Or the rapture which dwells on the first kiss of love.
—Lord Byron, "The First Kiss of Love"

After completing her chores around the house the next morning, Emily returned to her bedroom to write alone, glad her hand cooperated. She had enjoyed Mr. Thomson's assistance and his company during yesterday's research trip, but after their ill-advised tête-à-tête in the carriage, she decided she would be less distracted and more productive working someplace she would not hear his voice and be tempted to seek him out.

From her notes, she added to the section headed *Environs of Sidmouth*, writing descriptions of Otterton and the other villages and the churches they had viewed.

Despite the quiet room and her efforts to concentrate, she found her thoughts returning to the previous day. Had James Thomson wanted to kiss her in the carriage? She had thought so at the time. But she had been wrong before.

She had once thought Charles Parker intended to kiss her, but that was more than a year and a half ago and he had not done so.

What would it have been like? Uncertain? Awkward? She certainly had little idea what to do. Or would it have been perfect—the stuff of every novel and every romantic poem she'd ever read?

In her current mood, Emily was tempted to be cynical about the power of a kiss. Could pressing two mouths together really be that wonderful? Maybe. After all, mouths smiled and sipped warm chocolate. Then again, those same mouths ate onions and drooled.

Would she ever know?

With a sigh, she reached into the drawer of her side table and once again pulled out the notebook she kept for inspiration, the one filled with excerpts of literary kisses she had read about in books. She flipped through the pages, stopping at some Byron excerpts.

Did Byron have the right of it? She skimmed through the lines she had copied down.

> *When heart, and soul, and sense, in concert move,*
> *And the blood's lava, and the pulse a blaze,*
> *Each kiss a heart-quake . . .*
>
> *As if their souls and lips each other beckoned,*
> *Which, being joined, like swarming bees they*
>   *clung . . .*

"Goodness," Emily breathed aloud, both intrigued and ill at ease at the thought.

Yet Byron should know what he was talking about. He was reckoned one of greatest Romantic poets in English literature. Then again, he'd had many notorious affairs that had shocked society.

She turned next to a few lines by the Scottish poet Robert Burns. Perhaps he had the right of it when he wrote in dreamy fashion:

> *Honeyed seal of soft affections,*
> *Tenderest pledge of future bliss*
> *Dearest tie of young connections.*
> *Love's first snowdrop, virgin bliss.*

That sounded sweeter. Purer.

Such extremes.

Emily moaned in exasperation. Perhaps she ought to ask Viola, her one and only married sister, what kissing was really like.

<hr>

"Lips joined *like swarming bees*?" Viola's eyebrows rose. "That sounds painful and potentially dangerous."

Emily's twin sister regarded her from an armchair near the crackling fire in Westmount's sitting room, her mouth quirked and eyes glimmering with mirth. "I think someone has been reading too much Byron again."

"Don't tease me. I want to know."

Viola set down her teacup. "He is right about one thing—it is beyond the physical. The heart, and soul, and senses are all involved when you kiss the man you love. Although I have nothing to compare it to, as the only man I've kissed is my husband, which is perhaps as it should be."

Emily sighed. "Then chances are I shall never know what it's like!"

"Oh, Em. Don't say that. You will marry one day. I am sure of it."

"That makes one of us. And in the meantime, how am

I supposed to write a novel that convincingly portrays two people falling in love and kissing if I've never experienced it myself?"

"You have a good imagination."

"At least tell me which poet was correct. Is kissing more 'tender pledge' or blazing 'heart-quake'?"

"Both, at different times. Sometimes it's a tender expression of affection, of our pledge to love and honor each other. And other times there is blazing passion and beating hearts. But please don't ask me for details or I shall die of embarrassment!"

"We can't have that," Emily wryly replied. "I would miss you too much, and the major might miss you just a little as well."

Her sister chuckled, then said, "I admit that we did not wait to kiss until we married. We kissed once or twice before he proposed, and *several* times after." Viola attempted unsuccessfully to restrain a girlish grin. "But he is the only man I have ever loved or wished to kiss."

"I am so happy for you, Vi."

Viola slowly nodded, countenance awash with joy. "Me too."

Seeing her twin's wistful, doe-eyed expression, Emily felt a stab of longing. She hoped she too would one day love a man who loved her back.

When Emily returned to Sea View, she asked Sarah a similar question.

"May I ask . . . have you ever been kissed? I mean, you were once engaged."

Sarah looked down, and Emily instantly regretted asking. Had she done more than embarrass her sister, perhaps saddened her as well?

She quickly added, "I am sorry. If it's a painful subject, you need not answer."

Sarah looked up, her cheeks pink and bemusement tilting her lips. "What's brought this on?" Her expression turned wary. "Although after your outing yesterday, I am not sure I want to know."

"I simply want to know if the poets and novelists are right— that's all. If it is a thunderous, transporting experience. Or if it has all been exaggerated and I've been longing for something that does not exist."

"You have never . . . ?"

Emily shook her head, her face heating.

Sarah paused, then began tentatively, "After Peter asked me to marry him, we did seal our agreement with a kiss. A chaste, awkward kiss, truth be told. We were both nervous."

"Was that the only time?"

"Goodness! You ask a lot of questions! No, he kissed me a second time, just before his ship sailed."

"And?"

"And let's just say, that kiss was longer and more . . . impassioned." Sarah's blush deepened.

"Do you regret kissing him? When things turned out as they did and you did not get to marry him after all?"

"I don't regret it. Not for an instant."

"I am glad. And Mr. Henshall? Did he . . . ?"

"He most certainly did not!" Sarah's eyes flashed but her tone quickly softened. "Well, to be honest, that is not precisely true. He did kiss my hand before he left. And I learned that a kiss to one's hand can be far more affecting than I'd ever imagined."

That afternoon, Emily dressed in her thickest pelisse, woolen stockings, boots, and a knitted cap, which were warm although not at all fashionable. She retrieved one of the blankets from the parlour sofa and carried it out with her onto the deserted veranda. She brushed lingering snow from one of the chairs and sat down, cocooning herself in the blanket. She wanted to be alone. To be quiet. To look at the water and think.

In the distance, the winter sea churned frothy grey, the swells formidable. She hoped no one would be foolish enough to go sea-bathing on such a day. She thought again of the time she and Viola had attempted it last summer. The sea had been choppy that day too, although nothing to this. A rogue wave had knocked over the bathing machine—knocked the two of them over as well. Emily had surfaced first. And for those few seconds when she could not see her twin and feared the worst, she had prayed like never before.

Emily wondered about that—how prayer worked. Why some prayers were answered and some were not. She had prayed for Papa to recover, for Claire to return to them, for Mamma to regain her strength, and for Charles to renew his affections. Some of these requests had been answered with a resounding no. Thankfully Mamma seemed much stronger than she had even last year. And Charles *had* come to Sidmouth. Had called on them, apologized, and even danced with her. Might it all lead to something more? Might her prayers about him be answered at last?

Did she want those prayers to be answered?

Emily blew out a long exhale, a white stream in the cold air, and let her thoughts wander. Her rebellious memory returned to the final night of the house party the Parkers had hosted in honor of Charles's visiting friend, Lord Bertram.

Charles and Emily had danced together several times that night. He'd held her close during the waltz, smiling warmly into her eyes, and she had truly believed he loved her.

The room had grown too warm and suddenly seemed far too crowded.

They stepped out onto a veranda much like this one to cool down and catch their breath. A foreign silence hung between them—a new tension like a reverberating harp string. Emily was often prone to chatter on when nervous, but she found herself uncharacteristically silent, her throat tight, her heart beating hard.

Was he about to propose? She remembered her mother's hints and hopes for the two of them, as well as her own.

Together they stood at the veranda railing, gazing out over the garden. Emily gripped the railing tight, seeing little, her every sense centered on the man beside her.

He turned toward her, and she slowly turned to face him, looking up into his glimmering golden-brown eyes.

"Emily. I . . ."

"Yes, Charles?"

After a glance at the French doors, which cast light on them from within, he gestured toward a bench to one side. "You must be tired from dancing. Please, sit down."

"I . . . yes. Thank you."

She did so, and after a moment's hesitation, he sat beside her.

"I suppose we should not tarry out here alone," he began. "But I wanted to . . ." He paused and angled toward her on the bench, his knee brushing hers, and his face very near.

She knew he was conscious of propriety, but Emily did not worry. The Parkers were old friends. Her parents trusted Charles. His family and friends were right inside, along with her sister Claire.

His gaze lowered to her mouth. Was he about to kiss her? She certainly wanted him to. Is that what *he* wanted? For a gentleman like Charles, would a kiss not be tantamount to an offer of marriage?

She leaned slightly closer, hoping to encourage him without being too forward.

He leaned in as well, focused on her mouth. Her eyes fluttered closed in anticipation.

The French doors abruptly opened, and Charles pulled way, leaping to his feet.

Disappointment stung. Emily glanced over to see who had interrupted them, already resenting the perpetrator in her heart.

Lord Bertram.

"Ah. Here you are, Charles. We think alike, I see. Miss Summers and I wondered what became of you and her sister."

He turned to someone behind him, revealing Claire. "Here they are, safe and sound."

Claire and Emily had been the only two Summerses in attendance that night. Viola, as usual, had refused to attend, and Sarah was still in mourning for her betrothed, even though he had been dead for more than a year.

Bertram grinned at Claire. "Perhaps we had better chaperone the pair? They looked rather cozy just now."

Charles clenched his jaw, and Emily felt her neck heat at the man's implication. Nothing had happened!

She expected a gentle reprimand from Claire, but Claire only smiled vaguely in Emily's direction before her dreamy gaze returned to the man beside her, her hand tucked into the crook of his arm.

Emily had been so wrapped up in her own romantic longings that she had not paid much attention, had not taken note of her sister's uncharacteristic behavior with a man she had known for less than a fortnight.

How different that scene now appeared in her mind with the benefit of hindsight.

There on Sea View's veranda, Emily closed her eyes and tried to return to the more pleasant portion of that memory. Of Charles looking at her with admiration and perhaps desire. His face, his lips nearing hers . . .

Elbows on the chair arms, hands tented fingertip to fingertip, Emily pressed her fingers to her mouth, imagining the pressure of his lips on hers.

The door from the drawing room opened and Emily jerked upright, startled and embarrassed to be caught kissing her own hands. She hoped it was not obvious and was thankful her thoughts were not visible.

Charles Parker stood there, hesitating in the doorway.

"Am I intruding?" he asked. "I have been sitting with Georgiana for a quarter of an hour, hoping you would join us. She told me you had come out here, although one wonders why. It is awfully cold."

"I was only thinking. I like to sit out here and look at the sea."

"May I join you?"

"If you'd like." She gestured toward the nearby chair.

He hesitated again, then shut the door behind himself and sat down, turning up his coat collar against the chill.

"You'll freeze. Here." Impulsively, she spread half of the large blanket over him.

Only after she had done so, and noticed his stiff posture, did she realize that such an act was probably not appropriate.

He began, "I am not sure we should—"

Illogically irritated, she turned her face away. "Throw it off if you want, but don't blame me if you get frostbite."

From the corner of her eye, she saw him glance at her in surprise, then look toward the sea as if to discover what she found so fascinating. He did not, however, remove the blanket.

After a few moments, Emily stole another peek at him. Might

he be thinking of the last time they tarried on a veranda together, sitting side by side much as they were now? She wondered if he even remembered.

She said, "I suppose you don't recall the last time you and I sat on a veranda together."

He sent her a sharp glance. "I do, actually. Are you a mind reader? I was just thinking of that. I must say, the weather was much finer then."

"True. And we were interrupted by Lord Bertram. If only I'd known then what I know now, I might have helped Claire. Warned her."

"Yes," he murmured. "My thoughts exactly." A grimace creased his handsome features.

She went on, "I have often thought of that house party. The pleasure and hope I felt during those days, before the bitter regret to follow."

He nodded. "I as well. I went into that last evening with such anticipation. Looking forward to seeing you. Dancing with you. You may recall that I danced with you several times, even though I knew doing so would signal my attachment. I did not care."

Emily nodded. "I remember."

Perhaps it was brazen, but after more than a year of wondering, she very much wanted to know. "I thought you were going to kiss me that night."

He flashed another glance in her direction. "I thought so as well. I was certainly tempted." He sighed and rubbed a hand over his face. "You don't know how I have tortured myself. Wondering how differently things might have turned out if I had foreseen what Bertram intended and somehow prevented it. I did not tell my parents what happened. They had their suspicions, but I covered it over as best I could. You know how exacting they can be."

"How exacting you can be."

"I can't deny it. Thankfully their suspicions waned during the intervening months when no word of your sister's disgrace was bandied about and Lord Bertram continued on his unencumbered way. They asked once why I did not invite him back. I considered doing so, merely to allay any lingering suspicions they might harbor about him and Claire. But in the end, I could not stomach the thought of that man in our house again."

He turned to her, sought her hand beneath the blanket and grasped it. "Emily, I want you to know how sorry I am. I realize I am partly to blame. I never guessed he would do such a thing. Never imagined what inviting him to our house would lead to."

Emily swallowed a painful lump. "You cut ties with all of us. For something I had no part in. Something entirely beyond my control."

He hung his head. "I know. It was wrong but please don't think the worst of me. I had my own sister to think of. A duty to protect her future."

"And now? Why did you come here? To alleviate your guilt?"

"In part. I came to apologize, yes. You don't know how I have regretted my inaction. Letting you go like that. Would that I could go back and make different decisions. I have missed you so much." His hand beneath the blanket drew her closer. "And I still wish . . ."

His head dipped toward hers.

Again the drawing room door opened. Charles reluctantly pulled back. Emily glanced over and saw James Thomson standing there, mouth slack, staring in dismay. Her own heart plummeted. What must he think of her?

"Mr. Thomson." She forced a lightness to her tone she did not feel. "We were just . . . discussing old times. You may join us, if you like."

James looked from her to Charles, eyes flattening, mouth tight. "I think not."

"Mr. Thomson, we were not—"

But he retreated without a word, closing the door behind him, and for some reason tears heated Emily's eyes.

"Let him go," Charles urged. "I am trying to tell you how sorry I am for distancing myself from you and your family. Especially with your poor heartbroken father suffering as he did." Charles shook his head and Emily saw a sheen of tears in his eyes as well.

She looked away, staring off into her memories. "I remember him being more angry than heartbroken."

"Can you blame him? When he discovered what Claire and Bertram had done?"

She said, "What Bertram did."

"Claire was a willing party," he gently reminded her. "You cannot paint her as innocent victim in what happened."

"How would I know?" Emily asked. "I have never been allowed to ask her. To hear her side. I have written to her but received only a brief, stilted reply. You know how I looked up to her. Loved her. To come home after spending time away to discover Claire gone? And no chance to say good-bye?"

"I am sorry for that too. Yet maybe that was for the best. Perhaps the separation kept rumors from overshadowing you and your other sisters. That was a mercy, was it not?"

Emily considered and grudgingly nodded. "I suppose so." But losing Claire did not feel like a mercy.

"Come." Charles stood and offered her his hand. "Let us go inside before one of us takes a chill."

Emily put her hand in his and allowed him to help her to her feet. For a moment they stood like that, hand in hand, face-to-face. Then Charles opened the door and ushered her inside.

Charles joined them for dinner again that evening. James Thomson did not.

After Charles left Sea View, Emily went in search of Mr. Thomson. She did not find him in any of the public rooms. And when she knocked on his bedchamber door, there was no answer. Georgiana came down the passage, and Emily asked if she had seen him.

Georgie nodded. "He went out."

"To Woolbrook?"

"I don't know."

An hour later he returned, wiping his shoes and taking off his outer things.

Emily waited near the stairs, hands clasped. "Good evening, Mr. Thomson."

"Miss Summers," he said, tone civil if curt.

"Where have you been?" she asked. "If that is not too prying a question."

"I went to Fortfield Terrace to talk to the captain. See if there might be a room for me there."

Remorse jabbed her stomach. She pressed her hands to the spot and asked softly, "Has your stay here been so unbearable?"

"Only in one respect."

She looked at him, waiting for him to expand on his reply.

He huffed a sigh. "Please understand. I have no interest in trying to come between you and Charles Parker. Ill-fated rival is a role I have played before and am not keen to repeat. You and he clearly have a long history, a bond, that I cannot compete with. I fooled myself for a time, but it is clear you still have feelings for him."

"I . . . well, yes. I cannot deny we have a history. But that does not mean you and I cannot be . . ."

"Cannot be what?"

"Friends?"

"I have enough friends, thank you," he retorted. Then he sighed again and ran a hand through his hair. "Look. I don't mean to be churlish or petty. Just tell me. Are you and he going to . . . Have you reached an understanding?"

"No."

"Do you want to?"

"I once wanted nothing more. Now I . . . well . . ." Her sentence hung there, unfinished.

"If you decide to marry him, that is your choice," he said, dark eyes glittering. "With my life as it is, there is nothing I can say or do to stop you, but I don't want to be here to see it."

"Are you leaving?" Emily's voice hitched.

His mouth tightened. "I cannot, as it happens. There is one spare room there but not for long. They've sent a messenger to London asking for an experienced royal physician to come immediately. The duchess hopes Sir David Dundas will arrive by Monday. So for the present, you are stuck with me."

She exhaled in relief. "And I am very glad to hear it."

22

TAKE two chickens and dress them very neatly.
—Mrs. Glasse,
The Art of Cookery Made Plain and Easy

When her turn came to provide another meal for the poor house, Sarah decided she could do a little better than cold meat this time, with or without Mr. Bernardi's help.

She resolved to try a warm entree but something simple like chicken and rice. When she'd flipped through a cookery book the day before, she had also considered a recipe called Scotch chickens, in no small part because the final line read, *The Scotch gentlemen are very fond of it.* Then she had reminded herself that she'd already had her chance with a handsome Scottish gentleman and had not taken it.

She pushed that thought aside and regarded the two chickens lying dead on the worktable. She had purchased them at the market early that morning for a good price. Perhaps she should have paid a few extra pence to have them plucked and cleaned. She had thought Lowen might do that for her, or Jessie, but Lowen was in bed with his rheumatism again, and Jessie was run off her feet helping Mrs. Besley as well as cleaning the house.

Sarah picked up a knife and studied the chickens, wondering where to start. She became aware of someone watching her and looked up. Mr. Bernardi stood in the doorway, leaning against the frame. She had not asked for his help again but was not terribly surprised to see him, since he often took the liberty of using their kitchen or this workroom.

Mr. Bernardi stared at the fowl, brows high. "Do they not come plucked and drawn?"

"These were less expensive," she said. "Lowen usually cleans them, but he is feeling poorly today."

"Let me guess. You have never cleaned a fowl yourself?"

She shook her head. "I don't imagine you are required to do so either."

"Not now. But as a lad, oh, how many I cleaned for Mamma." He straightened and stepped inside. "Come. I shall have pity on you."

He held out his hand and she passed him the knife.

Sarah said, "I thought you were not interested in helping prepare food for the poor house."

He lifted one shoulder. "I have changed my mind. Besides, the duke is still unwell, and the duchess will not leave his bedside. I must cook for someone."

In sure, rapid motions, he sliced an incision, drew out the entrails, and cut off the head. He plucked the feathers, singed the pin feathers over the fire, trimmed the feet and wings, rinsed the inner cavity, and dried the whole.

"Now, are we trussing these for boiling, or roasting them on a spit?"

Sarah hesitated. "What would you suggest?"

"Do these people have teeth?"

297

"What a question! Yes . . . I think so. At least I have not noticed the lack."

"How were you planning to prepare these?"

"I thought a simple dish of chicken and rice. With vegetables and bread rolls?" She looked at him warily, anticipating a scoff.

Instead he nodded. "Good idea. Simple but quite flavorful, if done well. I presume you have rice?"

She went to fetch some. They worked side by side, him directing, her assisting and gathering ingredients. They boiled rice in white broth, which he had prepared previously and kept on hand. He poured a few cups of the broth into a saucepan, added a scraped carrot, onion, cloves, mace, a bay leaf, and a bouquet of parsley, green onions, and thyme, tied together neatly.

"Now we set it to boil. We must pay strict attention to prevent scorching." He handed her a long-handled, perforated copper skimmer, which he called a scummer. "Then skim well, and simmer gently at the side of the stove."

She attended to the sauce while he trussed the birds with string and placed them in an oval stew pan along with an onion stuck with cloves. He poured in more of the reserved broth to cover the breast of the fowl and placed the lid on the pan.

"That will want about an hour over a slow fire."

"What shall we do in the meantime?"

He raised his hands. "The rest!"

The chef put Sarah to work cleaning and cutting the vegetables, while he prepared a second sauce for them. Then he asked, "And for dessert?"

"I had thought of a custard, but . . ."

His face fell.

"But that was when I thought I would be cooking it all

myself. Attempting to, at any rate. You may make whatever you like."

He brightened and set to work.

Soon he was blanching almonds and crushing them with his prized mortar and pestle. He mixed these with sugar ground fine, amaretti biscuits crushed, egg yolks, butter, and salt. Then he whipped cream with a whisking motion so fast the implement appeared a mere blur.

He added the cream to the other ingredients. Then he prepared puff pastry, rolling it into a nearly perfect circle. Then he rolled out a second, slightly smaller one. He laid the smaller circle on a baking tray and mounded the almond and cream filling in the middle. He laid the larger circle over the first, pressing down the edges. After brushing an egg glaze over it, he took a sharp knife and cut an intricate pattern into the top—a star with curved rays.

"Take care not to cut all the way through the pastry," he said as he notched around the edge and made horizontal slashes in the pastry.

"What does that do?"

"Helps it rise at the edges."

She regarded the dessert, which looked like something between a pie and a cake. "What is it called?"

"*Gâteau Pithiviers.*"

He slid it into the oven. "This will want half an hour. Perhaps a bit more."

While they waited, he roasted mocha coffee beans over the fire, stirring the berries with a wooden spoon until they were light brown. Then he blew away the burnt particles before grinding the beans in his personal coffee mill. To the grounds, he added boiling water and let it brew near the fire before clarifying it with isinglass.

As he worked, he said, "This reminds me of my parents.

They frequently cook together, Papa often stealing a taste"—he grinned—"or a kiss."

Sarah could not imagine her parents doing so, neither cooking together nor playfully stealing kisses. "You are blessed to have parents who so clearly love each other."

He poured strained coffee and a dollop of cream into two cups. "I agree. It was love at first sight for them both. Whereas my first love is pastry. And yours?"

She hesitated, then said softly, "His name was Peter. We were to be married. Sadly, he died before we could."

His expression sobered. "I am sorry to hear that."

"Thank you. It was a few years ago now, but he will always be my first love." Sarah thought fleetingly of what she used to say, that she'd had one great love in her life and did not expect to have another. She had not said those words since last summer.

"I understand," Mr. Bernardi replied. "Although . . . may I tempt you to discover a new love?"

She gaped up at him in alarm, until he handed her a cup of coffee with another cheeky grin.

Sarah raised the cup to her lips and sipped, closing her eyes to savor the strong, rich drink. This was not Mrs. Besley's coffee.

"Delicious," she pronounced.

When the cake was golden brown, he sifted finely granulated sugar on top, and returned it to the oven for five more minutes.

Sarah inhaled deeply. "Mmm. Smells heavenly."

"That, my dear mademoiselle, is the smell of a French patisserie—Carême's patisserie."

When the chicken was done, he drained the fowls, removed the trussing strings, and placed the birds on a serving dish. To the boiled rice, he added white sauce, egg yolks, pepper, grated nutmeg, and a pat of butter. He formed the mixture into egg shapes and arranged them around the chickens.

"We will serve this with a creamy béchamel sauce."

Sarah shook her head, both impressed and amused. "Not exactly the simple dish of chicken and rice I had in mind."

"You are not pleased?"

She held up her hand. "Do not mistake me. I am more than pleased."

Then Sarah added, "Although I do feel bad for Mrs. Novak. She shall have her work cut out for her to match this when she returns."

Word of the forthcoming meal spread around the house and Mr. Thomson was quick to offer his help. He hurried over to Woolbrook to borrow a carriage and horses to transport the covered dishes and those serving the food.

Knowing Mr. Hornbeam often visited his friend Miss Reed at the poor house, Sarah invited him to join them for the meal, and he cheerfully agreed.

Then Sarah went to Mr. During's room to ask if he might like to set the table for them. His door was open, and she found him sitting at the small table within, a letter spread before him, his head in his hands. When she knocked on the doorframe, his head shot up and he quickly refolded the letter.

"Yes? What is it?"

She explained the reason for her visit. For a moment, his fair eyes lit, then he looked down at the table. "I am afraid I shall have to decline that pleasure, but thank you for asking."

She followed the direction of his gaze. "You received another letter?"

He winced. "Yes." But he did not expand on his reply.

His reaction and his refusal surprised Sarah, since the man

clearly delighted in any opportunity to display his skills. She decided not to press him.

Soon the carriage from Woolbrook arrived. Mr. Thomson and Mr. Gwilt carried up the side dishes and sauce boats from belowstairs, while Mr. Bernardi admonished them to be careful and not to spill. The men delivered their burdens to the waiting carriage and returned for another load. Mr. Gwilt took up the tea-making supplies, and Mr. Bernardi carried the heavy serving dish of chicken and rice. He entrusted Sarah with the prized *gâteau*.

Holding it carefully, Sarah surveyed the workroom and spied one last remaining item. "Mr. Thomson, if you might carry that basket of utensils?"

"Of course."

Once he'd lifted it, Sarah looked around to see if they had forgotten anything and only then noticed Emily left standing by the door, empty-handed.

"Oh. I did not realize you wanted to help." Her gaze skimmed the now empty work surface.

"Perhaps you might . . . set the table when we get there."

With no change in expression, Mr. Thomson silently pulled a serving spoon from the basket and handed it to her.

She wanly accepted it, her customary sparkle absent. Sarah wondered if the two had quarreled.

When they reached the poor house, Emily began laying the table. They had brought linens from Sea View but had decided to use the poor house's modest tableware. Emily was no Mr. During, but she did the best she could, smoothing the cloth over the rough, nicked table, setting the plates, forks, knives, and spoons in place, and folding the serviettes into simple rectangles.

The poor house did not have a fully equipped kitchen, only a simple room with a pump and sink, cabinets that held a few essential utensils, and a small stove for heating water or pots of soup.

Sarah assisted Mr. Bernardi in the small workroom as he grumbled about the insufficient space, insufficient stove, and insufficient utensils.

"That is why we brought what we needed from Sea View. Stop complaining. The residents might hear you, and this is supposed to be a pleasant occasion."

He grumbled something more that she did not understand. Something rude in French or Italian, perhaps.

As the scheduled mealtime approached, the residents emerged tentatively from their rooms, eyes wide and uncertain.

"Come, everyone. Be seated," Sarah said with a friendly smile. "We are nearly ready."

Miss Reed, Mrs. Denby, Mr. Banks, and two other elderly men she had not yet met sat down. Mrs. Denby introduced them as Mr. Satterly and Mr. Pring, retired fishermen. The latter grinned, and Sarah saw that he was indeed missing several teeth. She hoped the chicken would be tender enough.

Discovering Mr. Hornbeam had joined them, Miss Reed made no effort to conceal her pleasure.

Mrs. Denby said, "Whatever that is smells delicious."

Mr. Bernardi brought out the large serving dish of chicken with rice "eggs." He set it on the table to a chorus of delighted ohhs and ahhs. Sarah followed with two bowls of vegetables, while Mr. Thomson carried out the rolls, and Emily, the butter.

"Goodness," Mrs. Denby said. "We ought to give thanks for such a feast. Mr. Pring, perhaps you would oblige us?"

"Oh, aye." Mr. Pring bowed his head and the others followed suit. "Thank 'ee, Lord, fer this foine catch and them what cooked it. We'm grateful."

"Hear, hear," Mr. Hornbeam said.

Mrs. Denby nodded. "Amen."

The meal began.

Mr. Banks, sitting in the middle, dished out portions of chicken and rice while others passed the vegetables and rolls.

Mr. Pring bypassed his fork and scooped a heap of sauce-covered rice with his spoon and regarded it curiously. "What's this, then?"

"Have you never eaten rice, Mr. Pring?" Miss Reed asked.

"Only in rice pudding!" He laughed and ate a bite, smacked his lips, and proclaimed, "Whatever it be, it tastes like more!" And he quickly scooped a second bite.

The others chuckled.

Miss Reed chewed more delicately, then said, "This chicken is incredibly tender and flavorful." She looked at the hovering helpers and insisted, "Come. You must try some of this too. Bring in extra plates. There is more than enough for everyone."

The helpers were quick to agree—it really did smell delicious—and soon Mr. Thomson, Mr. Bernardi, Emily, and Sarah each held plates of food, the ladies sitting on spare chairs, while the men stood, leaning against the sideboard.

"Not bad, if I say it myself," Mr. Bernardi allowed.

"Talented *and* modest?" Sarah teased.

After a time, Mr. Bernardi bent his head to Sarah's and whispered for her to stay where she was and enjoy herself. He and Thomson would see to the tea and dessert. The two men excused themselves.

From down the passage came the sound of the outer door opening. A moment later, a middle-aged couple entered the communal dining room. Mr. and Mrs. Robins. Mr. Robins was the treasurer of the Poor's Friend Society, as his wife was forever reminding people. What were they doing there?

The laughter around the table died and smiles faded. Even Mr. Hornbeam seemed aware of the sudden change in the room's atmosphere and put down his fork, the bite uneaten.

Mrs. Robins, holding a quartern loaf of bread and wedge of cheese, looked with wide eyes from the serving platters to the plates mounded with food, her mouth stretched in dismay. "What in heaven's name is going on here?"

"In heaven's name . . . How accurate!" Mrs. Denby exclaimed. "Is it not grand? I do hope you have come to join us."

"Not at all. We heard Mrs. Novak was unable to perform her duties, but I never expected this. Such excess. Such . . . extravagance."

Her husband nodded his agreement. "They seem to eat better than we do."

The small woman lifted her chin. "We regularly describe the poverty and mean state of the residents . . ."

Sarah noticed Emily frown and open her mouth to retort, so she quickly laid a staying hand on hers.

". . . to encourage donations from potential donors. And this . . ." Mrs. Robins gestured toward the table. "This makes liars of us all. Thank goodness we have not brought a potential donor with us today. They would be shocked indeed, as we are!"

Sarah took a calming breath and said, "Now, now, Mrs. Robins. This dinner has not been funded by the society but by my family and the generosity of Mr. Bernardi, pastry chef to the Duke of Kent."

Perhaps hearing his name, Mr. Bernardi emerged from the kitchen, wiping his hands on a towel. Mr. Thomson followed, carrying a teapot.

The woman's eyes widened. "Mr. Thomson! Is this your doing?"

He shook his head. "I am just here to help, ma'am. And happily so."

The birdlike woman sniffed in offense and turned with her bread and cheese. "Come, Mr. Robins. Our offering is not needed or wanted."

"Nonsense," Mrs. Denby called. "We will happily eat it tomorrow."

But the couple stalked out, their exit punctuated by a slamming door.

After a beat of silence, Miss Reed looked to the others. "Now, where were we?" she said, her good humor undiminished. "Ah yes, enjoying a delicious meal."

When everyone had finished eating, Mr. Thomson began pouring tea while Emily and Sarah cleared the empty plates.

Mr. Bernardi brought out the prettily decorated *gâteau* and displayed it to more exclamations of delight. Then he carried it to the sideboard to cut into pieces.

When everyone had been served, Mr. Hornbeam took a bite and looked up in astonishment. In his younger days the educated, successful man had traveled widely and probably eaten many fine meals. "This is incredible!" he enthused. "This must be Carême's famous *gâteau Pithiviers!*"

His neighbor, Mr. Pring, looked at him with a bland expression, clearly unimpressed. "Aye, certainly. What else would it be?"

Sarah restrained a chuckle, then took a bite, closing her eyes to relish the marriage of luscious flavors. When she opened them again, she found Antoine Bernardi watching her with interest.

"Oh my . . ." she breathed.

"You like?"

"Very much."

Minutes later, someone else barged in—this visitor more unexpected than the last.

Captain Conroy.

Sarah gulped. *Good heavens.*

He surveyed the room, demanding, "Is During here?"

"No, sir," Sarah replied.

"I went to Sea View and your mother told me all of your guests had gone out."

Sarah felt her brow furrow. "Mr. During was there an hour or so ago. He must have left on some errand after we departed."

The man's ever-stern expression darkened further. Then he looked from the table to Bernardi and Thomson.

"Was this meal paid for with the duke's funds?"

"The duke's?" Mr. Thomson's eyes bulged, and an incredulous laugh escaped. "Uh . . . no. He has lent his name and patronage to the charity, but this meal was provided by our generous hosts at Sea View."

"You and Bernardi are complicit in this?"

"Complicit?" Mr. Thomson echoed on another laugh. "In providing a meal? Why yes. Guilty as charged."

Conroy shifted his angry gaze to Bernardi. "We are not paying you to cook for other people."

"Actually no one has paid me in some time," the chef replied, "but let us not split hairs. I had time on my hands."

Emily spoke up. "And what better use of his time than helping others, than serving the community that has received all of you so warmly?"

The captain turned to her, eyes glinting. "Ah. Miss Summers, defending stray lads again, I see."

Emily lifted her chin. "Yes, I suppose I am."

"Hmm . . ." He frowned at her before turning back to his subordinates. "If you see During, tell him to report to General Wetherall without delay. Understood? As comptroller, the general wants to inventory the plate chest to verify all items are accurate in Prince Edward's will."

Emily drew in a sharp breath. "Why? Surely it has not come to that. His Royal Highness only has a cold."

Conroy opened his mouth, seemed to think better of whatever

he'd been about to say, and muttered, "Just in case." Then the captain pivoted on his bootheel and stalked out.

After a moment of silence, Sarah said tentatively, "On that note, perhaps we had better pack our things and head back."

Effusive thank-yous were given, and everyone helped tidy the kitchen, while Mr. Hornbeam picked up a towel and dried plates.

Amid the bustle, Sarah saw Mr. Thomson approach Emily, his manner serious rather than flirtatious. He said, "That was brave of you, standing up to Conroy like that."

Emily replied with a quote from a favorite novel, "'My courage always rises at every attempt to intimidate me.'"

He raised his chin in recognition. "*Pride and Prejudice?*"

She looked at him, clearly astonished. "You, James Thomson, are the most well-read man I know."

After Sarah returned to Sea View, she helped put away the serving dishes and then tackled a few chores.

She was sweeping dust and cobwebs from the upstairs passage when Selwyn During trudged up the back stairs.

"Mr. During, there you are. I trust you received Captain Conroy's message?"

He looked up in confusion. "What message?"

"He was looking for you an hour or two ago. General Wetherall wants to inventory the plate chest."

The man's eyes widened. "Does he? Why? Has he some reason to think all is not as it should be?"

"No, nothing like that. Apparently, he wants to ensure everything is correct in the duke's will."

"Why should they care about a few medals and things?"

"Surely that is not so strange. You mentioned some of the

items are quite valuable, like the silver candlesticks and gold Freedom of the City box."

"I said that, did I?"

Sarah nodded, studying his pale face in concern. "Is there . . . a problem?"

He swallowed. "No, no, of course not. I am only surprised. And the timing could not be better, actually. I shall see to it directly."

"Good," Sarah replied.

He continued to his room, and Sarah returned to her task. Yet a sense of disquiet remained, like a cobweb out of reach.

Emily returned to Sea View feeling both gratified and a little low. She had found it pleasant and satisfying to help at the poor house, to share good food and conversation with people whose lot in life could be difficult and lonely.

She had feared Mr. Thomson might be cold to her after last night's scene on the veranda followed by his efforts to leave Sea View. Instead, he had been polite but kept his distance, focusing on the tasks at hand and talking primarily with Mr. Bernardi and the residents, which, she told herself, was exactly as it should be. Even so, the change in their relationship would take some getting used to.

That evening, Emily sat writing by candlelight in the office when Sarah showed Charles Parker inside, saying, "Here she is."

Emily looked up, startled. She had been concentrating so intently she'd not even heard the door. "Good evening, Charles."

"Emily. I came by earlier, but your mother told me you were helping with a meal at the poor house?"

"That's right. It was mostly Sarah's doing, although I enjoyed lending a hand."

"And Mr. Thomson was there as well."

"Yes. The duke has recently become the patron, so Mr. Thomson is understandably interested, as well as quite charitable himself."

"Admirable."

Recalling Sarah's advice to put Charles's mind at ease, Emily added, "You do realize Mr. Thomson will leave here when the royal party does? They had planned to stay the winter, but with the duke's poor health, who knows if they will stay even that long. I think Mr. Thomson wants to help all he can during the brief time he's here."

For a long moment Charles held her gaze, and a look of understanding passed between them.

Then he glanced down at the desk. "And what are you busy with?"

Emily hesitated, unsure whether to tell him. Then she steeled herself and said, "I am writing."

"Letters?"

"A book, actually." Only a slim guide, perhaps, but a book even so.

He nodded. "That's right. You've always fancied yourself a writer."

She lifted her chin. "I *am* a writer."

"I did not intend to imply otherwise." He gestured to a nearby chair. "May I?"

"Of course."

Charles sat in one of the chairs by the fire. She rose from the desk and joined him there.

She took a steadying breath and said, "In fact, I am writing it for a publisher in town."

"Really? What sort of book is it to be?"

Was that disapproval in his voice, or was she assuming the worst? "A guidebook. He hopes to publish it as soon as may be."

"And will your name appear on this work?"

She wanted to say, *"Yes, in big bold type."* Instead she told the truth. "No."

"Probably wise."

"Why?" She had her own reasons for wishing to remain anonymous but wanted to hear his.

He considered, then said with gentle diplomacy, "Not everyone believes ladies should write books."

"And you, Charles? What do you believe?"

"I admire you as you are. Becoming published would not change that. I also believe a woman must tread carefully. Guard her reputation."

"Yes, you have made that abundantly clear. I have been thinking about what you said, how our separation from Claire was a mercy."

"Only in that it spared you and your sisters from being tainted by association."

"You seem awfully ready to blame Claire. Have you talked to her in all this time? Heard her side of the story?"

"No. But I spoke to Bertram shortly afterward."

She looked at him in surprise. "He returned to May Park?"

"Only to gather the rest of his belongings and his footman."

Emily leaned closer. "Tell me everything, from the start."

Charles sighed. "I can never think of it without regret. I saw Bertram flirting with Claire during the party. Dancing with her too often and holding her too close. I should have said something, but at the time my thoughts were of you. Of us. Even so, I never thought he would do anything so dishonorable.

"The morning after the party, I learned Bertram had left in the night, took his traveling chaise and a valise but left his trunk and footman. I remembered he had asked me about Claire's dowry and was instantly alarmed.

"Your father came to May Park soon after, clearly anxious.

He told me Claire was gone and demanded to know Lord Bertram's whereabouts. I spoke to him privately—told him what I knew or guessed. Furious, your father stalked out to go after them, to try to catch them on the road and make certain they wed. I offered to go along, but he said it would cause less talk if I stayed home and pretended nothing was amiss. Knowing Bertram had been there at my invitation left me sick with remorse. Yet I thought he would at least marry her, and the manner of their wedding might be covered up somehow.

"When Bertram returned to May Park alone, I learned the situation was even worse than I'd feared. He had not married Claire. Instead he'd abandoned her at an inn along the road to Scotland. I was livid, insisted his duty was to marry her, to repair her reputation, and to spare her family deep disgrace. He merely scoffed."

"Did he never intend to marry her?"

"He said he meant to but changed his mind." Charles winced. "In fact, he blamed me. Said I had led him to believe Claire's dowry was larger than it was. Bertram has gaming debts and needs to marry an heiress. He thought she had fifteen thousand pounds."

"Fifteen! That's the amount settled on all five of us together."

"I know. He misunderstood, or I failed to clarify—I don't know. Perhaps I was guilty of letting him believe you all had greater dowries so he would approve of my interest in you. *If* I exaggerated, it was you I had in mind, not Claire. I had no thought of promoting his interest in any of your sisters. My thoughts were only of you."

It should have been a lovely thing to hear, but Emily was too indignant to enjoy it.

"And for that he abandoned her? After ruining her reputation? You know Claire would never have agreed to run away with him except with marriage in mind."

Charles nodded. "True. Although she should not have done so under any circumstances."

Again lifting her chin, Emily said, "We all make mistakes."

"Not of that magnitude." He looked at her sadly, imploringly. "Like it or not, your sister's behavior reflects poorly on your entire family. You may judge me harshly, but if you think I am the only gentleman who would abhor such scandal, then you would be mistaken and do me an injustice. Many gentlemen would not even consider connecting themselves with a family who had been thus disgraced. Or would be, should it become generally known."

It was just as Sarah had said last summer, Emily realized, when she had pressed her for the truth. *"I love her,"* Sarah had said. *"Yet I cannot deny how materially the credit of the rest of us must be hurt by her false step."*

At the time, Emily had groaned at the news. Now she felt defensive on Claire's behalf. On her entire family's behalf. It all seemed so unfair.

"I saw him, you know," Emily said. "Last summer. Lord Bertram came to Sidmouth with friends. Mr. Craven and his sisters?"

Charles's expression hardened.

Emily went on, "Mr. Craven flirted with me shamelessly. His hands lingered and his words dripped with innuendo. I could not account for his behavior. He made me quite uneasy."

"I can account for it. The man's a vile libertine." Charles shook his head in disgust.

"Lord Bertram was more polite," Emily continued. "He asked if my sisters were all in good health. His stilted questions and veiled looks surprised me. I remembered he had been attentive to Claire during the house party, and she had obviously been smitten with him. But nothing ever came of it, as far as I knew. Of course, at the time, I did not know the whole. You probably don't remember, but immediately after your house party, I left with Miss Smith, who had invited me to spend a fortnight with her in Cheltenham."

"I do remember. I was sorry to see you go."

Emily absorbed that small consolation. "By the time I returned to Finderlay, Claire was gone. I was told she'd moved to Scotland to serve as companion to Papa's ailing aunt. I was stunned. And that was not the only unhappy change awaiting me." She looked him full in the face. "You showed me such marked attention at the party. Your kind words, our many dances. I foolishly thought you were about to propose." She chuckled bleakly. "There, I've said it. Mortifying, I know, but it is what I thought. And I was not alone in thinking it. Your behavior led my entire family to think so. To expect . . ."

"I intended to propose when you returned."

Emily's breath caught. "Did you?" A lump of hope and regret rose in her throat, a tasty morsel shot through with gristle.

She swallowed hard and pressed on. "Instead you became a distant stranger, one who would barely meet my eye. Do you remember what you said to me before we left May Hill? 'If I have led you to believe my intentions were more than they are, I apologize. We are friends—that is all.'"

He stared at the floor. "I know."

She spoke with effort, her throat tight. "When you began treating us with cold formality, I was left to cast about for answers. I am ashamed to say I thought you broke things off because of Viola. That it had been one thing to befriend us, but you had decided you didn't want to marry someone whose twin had been born with a defect."

He looked up, clearly stunned. "No."

"It was either that, or our reduced circumstances. What else was I to think?"

He said, "I could not explain, not without telling you about

Bertram and Claire, which I knew your parents wished to keep secret."

Charles inhaled deeply, then said, "When I realized there was nothing I could do—that the damage had been done—I told Bertram the least he could do was to not speak of what had happened, and to order his servants to remain silent as well. Bertram agreed, although I hoped more than believed him sincere. After all, he had already proven himself to be a man without honor."

Remembering his friend's innuendo, Emily said, "He was not as discreet as you have been. He must have at least told Craven."

"Evidently." Charles grimaced. "I never breathed a word to anyone, but after Bertram's abrupt departure, followed by news of Claire going to Scotland? I knew my parents suspected—especially Mamma. She is the one who suggested I go to London for a while, and perhaps it was cowardly of me, but I agreed.

"At the time, I decided the best thing I could do for my family was to end things with you. At least until the rumors died down. Amanda was on the cusp of becoming engaged. I did not want anything to jeopardize my sister's future happiness.

"In London, I escorted her to parties and balls, and tried to follow Mamma's advice to find another young lady to love. But I could not find her in London. For she had moved to Sidmouth."

He leaned closer. "I never stopped thinking of you or missing you. My mother has thrown countless women in my path, but I could not seriously consider any of them, for my heart already belongs to you."

Charles took her hand. "I know I hurt you, Emily, but I hope you will forgive me. Will you? Will you give me another chance?"

She heard the veranda door in the next room open and shut, yet Emily did not stir.

Her chest ached. For more than a year she had prayed Charles would admit he'd been wrong, realize he loved her, and propose. Now he seemed ready to do just that, yet she hesitated, uncertain of her answer. What was wrong with her?

Charles cradled both of her hands in his. "Will you marry me? I loved you then and love you still. Let us forget the past and start anew."

Emily tried to smile, but her lips seemed frozen. She suddenly felt dizzy and nauseated.

These were the words she had longed for. Here was Charles, holding her hands, his handsome face near, looking at her with all the admiration and affection of old. Why was she not bursting with happiness?

Through the window, she saw Mr. Gwilt out on the veranda shaking crumbs from a tablecloth, humming as he did so.

Beside her, Charles remained silent as he awaited her reply.

Some of what he'd told her was not very flattering—neither to himself nor to her family—yet he had told her the truth, trusted her with the good and the bad. She should be grateful. His proposal was not the starry-eyed, romantic scene of her daydreams. She'd heard no harp music, and her knees had not weakened. Perhaps those had all been foolish imaginings. Perhaps real love was not like that.

But she wanted it to be.

From the parlour came the sounds of Georgie and Hannah laughing over a game.

Emily swallowed another hard lump. "May I think about it?"

Disappointment dulled his eyes, and he opened his mouth to object.

Georgie appeared in the doorway. "Emily, we need another player. Oh! Sorry, Charles. I did not know you were here."

Their private tête-à-tête had become too noisy and too public.

316

He rose. "Why do I not return when things are . . . quieter. Tomorrow?" he suggested, then frowned. "No, I have already agreed to take Mamma to call on a friend after church. Will Monday afternoon suit?"

She mutely nodded.

"I will speak to your mother first when I return, which might be appropriate under the circumstances."

Emily suddenly wished to speak to Mamma as well. To ask her advice. To beg her to explain why she felt as she did. Why, when Emily's dearest wish had been offered to her, she did not immediately snatch it up in both hands.

23

Marinate for two or three days with thyme.
—Antonin Carême,
recipe for Hare Prepared in the Royal Manner

Mamma had gone to bed early with a headache by
the time Charles left, so Emily decided to wait until
the next day to seek her advice. In the meantime,
she ruminated over her conversation with him into the wee
hours, turning one way in bed, then the other, like a chicken
on a spit.

She stewed in his words throughout Sunday's church service—at least until the parish clerk read a verse of Scripture
that caught her ear. "'If any of you lack wisdom, let him ask
of God, that giveth to all. . . .'"

Latching on to this hope, Emily prayed, *Yes, God, please
give me wisdom. Help me decide what to do.*

James Thomson did not attend church with them that morning. He'd told Sarah he was interested in attending a dissenting
church service while in Devon, and planned to join the Congregationalists at Marsh Chapel, so named for its location near
the river.

He had not told her.

Emily was as aware of his absence in their pew as she was of Charles sitting across the aisle, now and again glancing in her direction.

One thing Charles had said kept returning to her. At the time she had tried to brush it off, knowing Charles had always been particularly fastidious—but now it gave her pause. He'd said, *"You may judge me harshly, but if you think I am the only gentleman who would abhor such scandal, then you would be mistaken. . . . Many gentlemen would not even consider connecting themselves with a family who had been thus disgraced."*

Was James Thomson such a gentleman? Would he be repulsed if he learned of her eldest sister's fall? On one hand, he did not seem as exacting as Charles. Then again, James held a royal appointment, perhaps even aspired to a career in politics. Scandal would not aid such aspirations.

She asked herself why she cared about Mr. Thomson's opinion. He had already made it clear there was no future for the two of them. All too soon, he would leave Sidmouth and move far away.

Emily already felt the distance between them.

That afternoon, Emily found her mother alone in her room, at her writing desk.

She knocked on the open door. "Do you have a few minutes?"

"Of course, my dear." Mamma turned on the chair to face her and gestured to a nearby armchair.

Emily shut the door behind her before sitting down.

"I would like to talk over something with you."

Studying Emily's no doubt troubled countenance, her mother said, "Please tell me this has nothing to do with . . . Scotland."

Emily looked up in surprise. "No."

"Good."

Emily did want to talk about Scotland, or at least her sister in exile there, but decided this was not the time.

"Before I tell you, please don't get excited. I have not said yes."

"Yes to what?"

Emily took a deep breath and announced words she had once feared she would never have the chance to say. "Charles has asked me to marry him."

Her mother's eyes widened. "After all this time? I must say I am surprised."

"So am I."

Mamma again studied her face. "You do not seem pleased. I would have thought you'd be dancing around the house, shouting the news to one and all. Not shut up in here looking very grave indeed."

"I know." Emily looked down at her clasped hands. Would a ring ever grace her finger?

"What is it?" Mamma asked gently. "What troubles you?"

Emily hesitated, thoughts failing to settle into coherent reason.

Mamma ventured, "Are you finding it difficult to forgive him? We all thought he was about to propose before . . . before our family troubles began. I know you were devastated when he broke things off."

"I believe I can forgive him. He is sincerely sorry. For inviting Lord Bertram to May Hill—"

"Do not speak that name."

"—and for going to London when Papa was ill. He said he thought distancing himself was for the best, especially for his sister's sake. At least until any rumors died down. I think he anticipated the news would spread quickly and far more widely than it has."

Mamma nodded. "We all dreaded that."

"And he did not want to be associated with us if it did," Emily said, the words distasteful on her tongue.

Mamma sighed. "It is only natural. You know he was brought up to do everything properly, and to expect everyone else to do the same. It is part of who he is, so I suppose we must not judge him too harshly. Many people would be far crueler—ostracize us forever and spread our shame with gossipy abandon. Certainly not come and apologize. Like it or not, society can be merciless when a woman is caught in impropriety—even the appearance of it."

"So I am learning."

Lines of regret marred Mamma's lovely face. "I tried so hard to instill caution and modesty in all my daughters. Clearly I failed."

"No, Mamma. You did not. None of this is your fault."

"Well. I shan't argue the point, as you did not come in here to talk about my past decisions, but rather your pressing one. How can I help?"

Emily groaned. "By telling me what to do!"

"That, my dear, I cannot do," Mamma gently replied. Then she added, "As a woman with several daughters not yet married, a part of me would love to see you well settled. Charles is a gentleman, financially secure, and well-known to us. A good-hearted boy, I always thought, although I don't pretend to know him well as a man. His family and ours were once on good terms and likely could be again. Louise might not be the ideal mother-in-law, but that would be nothing if you and Charles truly loved one another and thought you could be happy together."

Emily looked away. "I know."

She was aware of Mamma's gaze on her profile. "Is there someone else?"

James Thomson's face appeared in her mind's eye until Emily blinked away the image. Yes, she liked James. Found him attractive. Enjoyed his company. But he was leaving. And she barely knew him, at least compared to her long relationship with, her long love of, Charles.

Emily said, "I admire Mr. Thomson, I admit. But I should not make a monumental decision like this based on whether I have another suitor standing by. Which is not the case anyway, as he has made it clear he is not in a position to marry."

Mamma tapped her lip in contemplation. "Even so, do you think you would hesitate to accept Charles had Mr. Thomson never come here?"

"What a question!" Emily exclaimed, yet she quickly realized it was oddly stilling as well as thought-provoking. "Honestly, I am not certain. Very insightful, Mamma. If uncomfortable. In any case, I had better decide soon, because Charles plans to return for my answer Monday afternoon."

"Do not be pressured into making a decision until you are ready."

"The Parkers are due to leave in a few days."

"They can wait. This is a decision that will affect the rest of your life, Emily. Don't make the wrong one on account of a few days."

Emily nodded thoughtfully.

"Besides," Mamma said on a lighter note, "are you really ready to leave Sidmouth? I thought you'd grown rather fond of the place."

"Leave Sidmouth? Why would I . . . ?" Emily stopped abruptly and flushed. "I mean, naturally I'd have to leave when, if, we married, but I could still live here during our betrothal, could I not? There is no hurry."

"Of course you could. Though something tells me that, after all this waiting, Charles would not want a long engagement."

"I see your point." Emily rose. "Thank you, Mamma."

"I am sorry I could not be of more help."

"Not at all. You have given me much to think about."

At the door, Emily turned back. "By the way, he plans to seek you out first when he returns."

"Me?" Panic crossed Mamma's face.

"In lieu of Papa, yes."

"Good heavens. What shall I say?"

"How can I tell you what to say when I don't know what to say myself?" Emily blew Mamma a kiss and left the room.

She walked down the passage and wandered across the hall. She paused once again below the large painting of Finderlay, their former home.

How Emily had resented being torn from all she had known, the house she loved, the village where she had grown up, and all her neighbors and friends—Charles Parker most of all. For months, all Emily had wanted was to return home. And she'd known the only way that would happen was if Charles realized his mistake and came to Sidmouth to rescue her. To marry her and take her back to May Hill.

The house was lost to them forever—passed to their father's heir. But the village would have been close enough.

If she married Charles, they would probably live in May Park, his family's estate, which Charles would one day inherit. She could stand at its windows and gaze upon the lovely tree-topped hill that had given the village its name. She could pay calls on old friends and neighbors. Sit in the Parkers' family box at the parish church. Share Charles's life and bed. Bear his children. All she'd ever wanted. All except to remain in close contact with her mother and sisters, which would be difficult from such a distance, although not impossible. After all, she was an excellent letter writer.

Oh, Lord, she prayed again. *Please give me wisdom.*

After that, Emily decided she needed to talk to someone who knew her better than anyone else on earth did. Someone who loved her despite her many foibles and would tell her the truth.

Pulling on a hooded mantle, Emily hurried over to Westmount to talk to Viola.

As soon as the two were seated near the fire, Emily confided her dilemma.

In reply, Viola began, "First of all, I am astonished and honestly impressed that you did not accept him immediately, after so many years spent besotted with him. That shows a new maturity. I hope that does not sound critical—we are still young, after all."

"Don't you like Charles?" Emily asked. "Please. Tell me honestly."

"I never said I did not like him. I do. Nor did I say he would not be a good match. He would be—for someone. But, Emily, I know you. You would chafe under his rigid propriety, as well as his mother's."

"You never mentioned this in the past."

"You would not have listened! You never expressed any doubts before. I think this time apart has given us all new perspective."

Emily nodded. "So much has changed."

"And much of it for the better, in my view. Do you still wish you could leave Sidmouth and go home?"

Emily sighed. "I am not certain. Is May Hill really home any longer?"

Viola held her gaze. "Not for me."

"I admit I am no longer as eager to leave here as I once was. But to marry Charles Parker? There was a time I would have done anything to make that happen. I cannot believe I am hesitating!"

"Will he support your writing?"

The question caught Emily off guard. "I . . . I gather he would not be eager for me to publish under my own name, but he would not forbid me."

"Neither would he encourage you, would he?"

"I don't know."

"And here is another question for you to consider. What would happen if Claire returned one day and rejoined our family, as we both sincerely hope she will? How would Charles react?"

Emily's stomach dropped. "I don't know. Did you tell Jack about Claire before you wed?"

Her sister nodded. "I told him everything, and it did not impede him in the least. Then again, Jack cares nothing for the opinion of society. Whereas Charles . . ."

At the thought, Emily bent and held her head in her hands.

"I am sorry," Vi said. "Did I overstep?"

"No," Emily groaned. "I came here because I knew you would tell me the truth. If only hearing it were not so painful."

A few minutes later, Emily returned home and retreated into her bedchamber, relieved to find it empty. As she tossed her gloves into the chest in the corner, she spied her old diary. She pulled it out and sat on the bed with it. Opening the cover, she extracted Charles's handkerchief and briefly skimmed the lovelorn words she had written as a girl of seventeen. *I will love Charles Parker until the day I die! . . . I will marry him one day, if it is the last thing I do.*

She closed the book and ran a gentle finger over the monogrammed initials on fine linen while she thought and remembered and thought some more. Then, making a decision, she placed the handkerchief into her pocket.

Mr. Thomson did not return to Sea View until late afternoon. Emily was sitting alone reading in the parlour when he entered the room, his face drawn with concern.

Emily poured him a cup of tea and handed it to him without being asked. He certainly looked like he could use one.

"What's wrong now?" she asked.

He grimaced, sipped the tea, then said, "I am worried about His Royal Highness. He is nearly delirious with fever and suffers from chest pain as well as vomiting. Dr. Wilson bled him again, which is supposed to reduce fever, but the duke seems only to worsen. Wilson has also applied blisters, and today plans to attempt cupping."

Emily cringed at the thought of the painful procedure. Cupping involved making cuts on the skin and drawing blood from them using heated glass suction cups. They had once tried it on her father before his death, to no avail.

"Poor man," Emily breathed. "And his poor wife, how she must share his suffering."

"She does indeed," he replied, "yet is tireless in nursing him. Dr. Wilson urges her to rest, but she will only leave his side to spend a few minutes with her daughter. She administers every dose of medicine to him personally."

"That's devotion."

He nodded. "Devotion coupled with fear."

Mr. Thomson rubbed a weary hand over his face. "I have been praying for him, but otherwise I feel so dashed useless."

Emily felt convicted. She had not been praying for him as much as she ought and inwardly vowed to begin doing so. She said weakly, "I am sure they appreciate your prayers."

She recalled her earlier musings over how prayer worked and longed to ask his views. He seemed like a man who would have given the subject deep thought. Perhaps now was not the best time for a theological discussion, yet she found herself saying, "I have been wondering about that lately. Why some prayers are answered and some are not."

Again he nodded. "I have wondered as well."

"What do you think?"

He paused to consider. "I am no expert, but I'd say there are several reasons God might choose not to grant our requests, or at least not immediately. Perhaps our motives are selfish, or we ask for things that would not be good for us or are outside God's will."

Emily scrunched up her nose. "So I should only pray for things I know to be God's will?"

He shook his head. "We can't always know. We do know God wants us to seek Him in prayer and through Scripture. So I think it's all right to pray about whatever is in our hearts and then leave the outcome to Him."

He paused, then added, "I also believe there are specific prayers we can know He will answer. Biblical promises like, If we confess our sins, he is faithful and just to forgive us. Or, If we ask God for wisdom, He will give it generously."

Emily looked up in surprise. "I heard a verse like that in church this morning. In fact, I have been praying for wisdom."

She half expected him to ask what she needed wisdom for, but he did not.

The two sat for several moments, the silence broken only by the steady comfort of the mantel clock ticking away the time.

Then she asked, "Have you eaten? I would be happy to bring you something."

"Thank you, but I am not hungry. I appreciate the tea, though."

A few more minutes passed, then Emily spoke again. "Might I ask you something else . . . in confidence?"

"More secret writing projects?"

She shook her head. "Not this time. A more significant secret. Perhaps even shocking."

He set down his cup and gripped the chair arms, clearly steeling himself. "Very well. Tell me."

She looked down and considered how best to proceed. "Would you refuse to associate with a woman and her family— say, a family like mine—if you learned that one of her sisters had made a mistake? Had trusted the wrong man and now lived with the dread of that private scandal becoming generally known?"

His nostrils flared. "If Parker did anything to dishonor or—"

"No! Not Charles. This is not about me. Truly." She swallowed. "But it is about . . . another of my sisters."

"The one in Scotland?"

She supposed it was obvious, and since he'd guessed, she nodded. "Please don't repeat it."

"I shan't. You have my word."

"I don't know Claire's side of the story," Emily said. "But she eloped with a lord, believing he would marry her. He may even have intended to, until he learned her dowry was far less than he'd believed. Each of us has only three thousand pounds." She watched his face, searching for disappointment.

His expression remained serious. Inscrutable. "Go on."

"I won't blame you if you are shocked. I know I was when I learned of it. Apparently, he abandoned her somewhere on the way to Gretna Green. Instead of coming home in disgrace she sought refuge with our great-aunt in Edinburgh, who is known to be something of a dragon, so probably an uncomfortable refuge indeed. This was more than a year and a half ago, and still Claire remains with her, serving as a companion. And *that* was the only story my parents passed around. Dutiful

Claire, gone to assist our elderly, infirm relative. But within the family, we barely speak of her. Especially Mamma and Sarah. Father forbade them, declared she was dead to him."

"How awful for you all."

"Yes. It was. Is."

He nodded slowly. "I cannot pretend it does not sadden me. And I understand why your father might have wanted to protect the rest of you from being harmed by the scandal. I imagine he thought the less said of her, the less chance of the truth coming out, and the better for all of you."

"I don't know that his motives were that selfless. Then again, I don't know that they were not. He was certainly angry and frustrated, although at the time I did not understand why, as they kept the truth from me, Viola, and Georgie. Only Sarah and Mamma knew. Then Papa had his first apoplexy. After that, it was difficult for him to speak, and hard to understand him when he tried. He died two months later.

"It's Mamma I feel the worst for. I know she must miss Claire, but she is holding fast to Papa's edict, not to speak of her eldest daughter or even to write to her."

"And would you welcome her back, should she wish to return?"

"In a heartbeat."

Again he nodded. "I do not blame you."

She tilted her head to better regard his face. "And would you condescend to be introduced to a fallen woman, if she came here?"

His serious expression softened and his dark eyes warmed. "My dear Miss Emily. Have we not all fallen short in some way?"

"Very noble. But I am not asking James Thomson, the man devoted to Christian charity. I am asking James Thomson, esquire, private secretary to the Duke of Kent, who might need to be careful about whom he associates with. A man with a future to plan and to protect."

He chuckled wryly. "You do know my employer lived with his mistress for nearly thirty years and would likely still be living with her without benefit of marriage had the Princess Charlotte not died, compelling him to marry and produce a legitimate heir to the throne? And don't even get me started about the behavior of the Prince Regent. No, Miss Summers, I am not shocked. Nor do I fear such an association might injure my career. Of course I do not condone immorality, but nor do I judge your sister. Who, I must say, seems to be the victim of a scoundrel."

"I agree she was, yet we both know society holds young ladies to a much higher standard than they do men."

"I do know. I also know that is unfair."

He looked down at his hands, fiddling with his cuffs. "I must admit I would be grieved indeed had such a thing befallen you. But I would not hold your sister's mistakes against you, as I hope you would not hold my brother's against me. Though I can see that your sister's plight and absence wound you."

She nodded, eyes heating at his sympathetic words.

"I'm sorry. I pray she rejoins you one day soon."

They sat quietly for a few moments longer, then he slapped his thighs and rose. "If you will excuse me, I think I will go to my room for a short Sabbath rest."

She nodded in acknowledgment and watched him leave the parlour, still thinking over his answer.

Sarah sat in the quiet workroom with a cup of tea, looking through cookery books and idly sketching out some new menu ideas to run by Mamma and Mrs. Besley.

Antoine Bernardi found her there and announced, "Yesterday, I cooked for the poor house. Tonight, I should like to cook for you. Remember, I promised to do so when we visited the market?"

"I remember."

"What shall it be? *Perche à la hollandaise*, as was served at the Royal Pavilion? Or perhaps the dish served to Tsar Alexander when he came to Paris: oysters, *consommé a l'allemande*, and roast of veal served with *artichauts à la lyonnaise*?"

"That all sounds grand," Sarah replied. "But if I'm honest, I would rather taste one of your mother's dishes you mentioned to me. Something with—how did you describe it?—simple, fresh, ingredients of the best quality? Something with garlic?"

His hazel eyes gleamed. "That would be my pleasure."

They did not serve a meal to their guests on Sunday nights, so Sarah did not have to worry about Antoine Bernardi getting in Mrs. Besley's way—or vice versa. She left him and went upstairs. He could have free rein to prepare one of his mother's favorite recipes. Hopefully it would not involve frog legs. And hopefully the smell of garlic would not make its way upstairs.

It did.

Later that evening, following the enticing, savory smells, Sarah went belowstairs. Reaching the workroom, she paused at the threshold and murmured, "What in the world . . . ?"

When Mr. Bernardi had offered to cook a grand meal for her, she had thought he'd been exaggerating. She'd chosen one of his mother's "simple" dishes, imagining a single pot simmering on the stove, and him offering her a small dish of her own before whisking the remainder off to Woolbrook or Fortfield Terrace.

Instead, the scene within stunned her. She looked around the room, taking it all in. The scrubbed worktable was covered in white linen with a chair pulled up to one end. A branch of candles illuminated the scene, adorned with a spray of silk flowers. China, silver, and glasses were arranged with the elegance of a lord's dining room. Had he done all this or had Mr. During helped?

"Good heavens," she breathed.

The chef stood at the workroom stove, stirring something in a sauce pot. He glanced up. "Ah, Miss Summers. You are just in time."

Mr. During appeared from the larder and laid a swan made of butter on the table, next to a rustic loaf of bread. He glanced from Mr. Bernardi to Sarah with a boyish grin and raised both hands. "Now I am leaving, I promise." He scurried away, looking pleased. It was good to see him smile.

Sarah stepped out of the way to let him pass.

Mr. Bernardi beckoned her over. "Come, taste this. Mamma's famous sauce. I was forced to substitute dried herbs for fresh, but still, the smell is of home."

She walked closer. He lifted the wooden spoon, cupped his other hand beneath it, and held it toward her.

Tentatively, she leaned forward and put her lips to the spoon, taking a small taste. She felt self-conscious. The simple act seemed strangely sensual.

Flavor burst inside her mouth. Rich tomatoes, savory herbs—sweet basil, thyme, marjoram, and the promised garlic—and other ingredients she could not name. She closed her eyes to savor.

When she opened her eyes again, he tasted from the same spoon. Seeing his lips where hers had been filled her with strange warmth and a tingle of unease.

"Oh my."

Satisfaction lit his face. He then turned and pulled out the single chair placed at the table. "Please, be seated. This needs a few minutes yet."

She did so, suddenly wishing she had taken the time to change her frock or do something with her hair.

He laid a small saucer of oil before her and sprinkled it with salt and pepper. "Olive oil, for dipping the bread. Or there is Selwyn's butter swan, if you prefer."

"Are you not joining me?"

"Tonight I serve you, as you so often serve others."

Sarah did her best to hide her self-consciousness behind a bite of warm bread dipped in salty olive oil. *Delightful.*

He said, "I had to make alterations to the menu, of course, due to available ingredients, and the size of the party." He winked at her, then brought her a bowl of soup. "*Semolina soupe à la Palermo.*"

Sarah tasted a spoonful of small noodles in a rich broth. Then another. Simple yet delicious.

The soup was followed by a fish dish.

"Fillet of cod, *à l'italienne.* I prefer turbot, but alas found none for sale. Served in a brown sauce, with anchovy and capers."

"Good heavens."

"*Buon mangiata.*"

Sarah was not certain she liked anchovies and did not even know what a caper was but gave the dish an experimental taste anyway. She decided she liked both very much indeed.

"This is astonishingly good. Thank you."

He flashed a smile. "We are not done yet."

Sarah said, "Please do sit down and eat something, I implore you."

"I shall join you for dessert."

She wanted to insist, but the allure of the delicious food before her kept her from wasting time in argument.

Between bites, she asked him about his family, his childhood,

and his time as a student with the renowned French chef Antonin Carême.

"I own his book, *Le Pâtissier Royal Parisien*. Someday I
shall write my own."

"You should."

"Do you know, his parents abandoned him on the street
when he was only, oh, eight or nine years old."

"How sad. Why?"

"They were desperately poor and had many other children
to feed. To survive, he worked as a kitchen boy, later for a
fashionable pastry shop, and voilà. After years of hard work,
he cooks for kings and tsars."

"You might one day as well, if you liked."

"We shall see."

He next set before her a plate filled with a generous serving of chicken.

"Chicken, *à la milanaise*."

Near her plate, he also laid two serving dishes of vegetables.

"There's more?" She chuckled in disbelief.

"Oh yes. Artichokes with Mamma's sauce and mushrooms
au gratin."

She tasted first a bite of the tender chicken, then the artichokes in their savory sauce.

"Mm. These are wonderful as well. My compliments to
you and to your mother."

He looked down, then glanced up at her through dark
lashes. "Perhaps one day you shall meet her."

"Oh. Um. That would be . . . pleasant."

An awkward moment stretched between them, and Sarah's
self-consciousness returned. The room suddenly seemed too
quiet, and the private dinner too intimate. The possible inap-
propriateness of dining alone with a man, even in her own
home, began to settle over her.

She forced herself to take another bite, hoping to dispel the tension. He stood there, looking down at her, watching as she chewed, a gratified look on his face.

Hearing rapid footsteps, she looked over in time to see Georgiana dash into the room in a flutter of printed cotton, hair in characteristic disarray.

"What is that heavenly smell?" she called, heading for the stove. "I had to come and investigate. It smells nothing like Mrs. Besley's cooking, that's for sure." Her gaze shifted from the pans on the stove, to the table set in finery, to Sarah sitting there in candlelight, the chef hovering nearby.

"Oh. Sorry. Am I intruding?"

"Not at all," Sarah hurried to assure her, relieved at the interruption. "You are just in time to help me eat this feast. Mr. Bernardi was introducing me to some of the flavors of his childhood."

Georgie hesitated, glancing uncertainly at the chef.

He smiled with obvious effort and retrieved an extra plate as Georgie dragged in another chair. His displeasure soon fled, however, as Georgiana praised each dish even more effusively than Sarah had.

When it was time for the dessert course, he removed their plates and replaced their forks.

He set before them a layered sponge cake with cream filling and cherries. "*Genoise à la maraschino*, a favorite with the Prince Regent. We would say '*Genoese*' in Italian. And Milanese flan, which is not as sweet as you might expect."

Sarah said, "Remember, you said you would join me for dessert."

He nodded, poured three small cups of strong coffee, and pulled up a stool.

"Taste the flan first."

They did so. As he had said, it was not sweet, but rather

rich and buttery. Almost cheesy. It reminded her of a moist, dense Yorkshire pudding, although she kept that to herself and said only, "Delicious."

Then she took a bite of the sweet, buttery cake, which melted in her mouth in a cherry-flavored puddle of heaven.

"This is amazing," Georgiana declared. "No wonder the Prince Regent likes this. I do too."

When the meal was complete, Sarah and Georgiana insisted on helping with the washing up.

"Thank you for letting me join you," Georgie said.

"Yes, thank you, Mr. Bernardi," Sarah echoed. "I will probably never visit France or Italy, but now I almost feel as though I have."

His gaze lingered on her face, and his lips parted as though to speak, but with a glance at her sister, he remained silent and made do with a bow.

24

The duke was bled and cupped day after day.
—Christopher Hibbert,
Queen Victoria, A Personal History

On Monday, the Summers sisters gathered at the east office window as an official-looking traveling chaise accompanied by outriders came up Glen Lane. Then they hurried across the hall to the parlour to look out the north window in time to see the new arrivals disappear up Woolbrook's drive.

"Who is it, do you think?" Georgie asked.

Emily replied, "Mr. Thomson told me the duchess sent a messenger requesting a royal physician to attend the duke."

Mr. Hornbeam, sitting on a sofa nearby, asked, "Did he mention a name?"

"I don't recall."

"Perhaps Sir David Dundas?"

"Yes, that was it! How did you guess?"

Mr. Hornbeam replied, "He is reputed to be a capable, experienced physician, one of the medical men treating King George. I believe Dundas has known Prince Edward since childhood."

337

"Good. Surely he'll know what to do," Emily said, and prayed for the duke as she'd vowed to do earlier.

Sometime later Mr. Thomson returned from Woolbrook and joined them in the parlour, once again looking as though he carried a heavy burden on his broad shoulders.

"What did the royal physician say?" Emily asked.

He slumped onto the sofa beside Mr. Hornbeam. "A doctor from London arrived, but not the one we wanted. The duchess is upset. King George appears to be dying, so Sir David could not leave him. Instead they sent William Maton, who was Queen Charlotte's physician before her death."

"Does Her Royal Highness not esteem him?"

James shrugged. "His German and French are both very poor. The duchess is confused and anguished by his plan to bleed her husband yet again, yet she finds it difficult to communicate. She said, 'It cannot be good for the patient to lose so much blood when he is already so weak.' I translated as best I could, but Maton insists the duke has not been bled sufficiently."

Emily's heart went out to the poor woman. "Let's hope the new doctor is right and will be able to help him."

"If bleeding has not helped the duke so far, I don't know why it would now. Nor does the duchess. But what can we do? I know of no other course to suggest, and even if I did, no one would listen. I feel so blasted helpless."

Mr. Hornbeam reached out until he found James's shoulder and gave it a comforting squeeze. "You have done what you can, son. The rest is in God's hands."

James slowly shook his head. "It is not God's hands I'm worried about."

After that, Emily busied herself around the house, dusting and straightening and trying to order her thoughts. Now and again she slipped a hand into her apron pocket to reassure herself the folded handkerchief was still there.

When Charles arrived later that day, Emily's courage at first failed her.

"Oh, um, Charles. I did not expect you so soon. I am not . . . yet . . . prepared."

"Then I will speak to your mother first," he said. "Give you time to collect yourself."

Her unease only worsened. "I don't think you need to speak with her first, not unless you specifically wish to. I have apprised her of your . . . of our discussion, and she has left things in my hands."

"I see. If you are certain she will not feel slighted?"

"Quite certain."

Rousing her flagging courage, she led him into the library-office, which would be more private than the parlour.

She sat first and he sat nearby.

He smiled at her, but after looking into her face, the smile quickly wobbled away. "Have you decided?"

Emily gulped, then began evenly, "I have a few questions for you."

"Of course. Ask anything."

She drew a quavering breath. "First of all, about Claire . . ."

"We've talked about this," he said. "Soon, two years will have passed. Few remember, or at least talk of it—men like Craven aside, and no one pays him any heed. It need not cast a pall on your family forever. Claire lives far from here, and I gather your mother has no intention of inviting her to return. It has blown over."

Emily shook her head, sorrow washing over her. "Oh, Charles . . . If you think for one minute that I want Claire to stay hidden away in Scotland, you are very much mistaken. I love her, despite what happened, and would happily welcome her home."

He hesitated. "Even if her return sparked gossip that could ruin the marriage prospects of the rest of you?"

Emily lifted her chin. "I would not fret about our prospects. May I remind you that Viola has recently married an excellent man. And Sarah has had more than one gentleman pursuing her over the last year."

"And you?"

"This situation already ruined my prospects once."

He took her hand. "That was in the past. Can you not forgive me? Can we not start again?"

"And if Claire returned tomorrow? What then? If her return would cause you to change your mind about renewing our relationship, then you ought to turn around and leave without delay."

He stared at her, unblinking. "Might she return?"

"At present, we have little reason to hope and have had next to no contact with her. But if there is ever a chance to see her again, I will grasp it, whether you approve or not."

"Emily, please. You are obviously still angry with me. I suppose you think me heartless for being concerned about the reputation of the family I marry into. What about your Mr. Thomson, who has clearly developed a tendre for you. Does he know about your sister's fall from grace? Would he shrug it off as immaterial?"

"We are not talking about Mr. Thomson. We are talking about you."

Before he could respond, she raised a related subject. "Your mother has made it clear she expects you to make a good match, as Amanda did. To marry someone 'of impeccable character and family.' She may like me, but she does not approve of me."

"I won't pretend she is delighted about the prospect of our union. However, she admits you have a great deal of potential and could become a lady of distinction with very little guidance."

Emily knew she was far from perfect. Even so, she bristled at the notion of Mrs. Parker being the one to guide her.

He went on, "And I think, should Claire remain in Scotland, my parents will lay aside their misgivings and give their blessing to the match."

She stared at him, betrayal twisting deep in her gut. "So. To be clear. Any happiness between you and me depends on Claire staying away. When I want nothing more than to see her again, to see her reconciled with our family and restored to us."

She slowly shook her head. "I cannot embrace your vision of happiness, Charles. For I would never choose you over Claire. Not for all the marriage proposals in the world."

For several ticks of the mantel clock, he looked down at his hands. When he raised his head, his golden-brown eyes glistened with tears.

Seeing them was almost her undoing. She felt pity for him. Real pity. Yes, a part of her still loved Charles—the boy next door, the prince of her dreams—and always would. But she could not marry him.

Regardless, she did not like causing him pain. "I am sorry to disappoint you. Truly."

"And that is your reply?" he asked in a small, astonished voice.

She looked away from his tear-filled eyes and handed him the handkerchief. "I have kept it all this time. You should have it back."

He accepted it with barely a glance, his stunned gaze quickly returning to her face. "Is this really good-bye?"

Emily bit her lip. Was she making a mistake? Would she regret this for the rest of her life? *God, please, show me.*

An image of her oldest sister appeared in her mind—beloved and much missed.

She inhaled deeply and said with calm resolve, "Again, I am sorry. But I will not forget Claire. In fact, I am going to write to her this very night."

Charles flinched, then nodded. He stood, retrieved his hat, and turned to go. At the door he turned back. "Please tell her how sorry I am . . . for everything."

After Charles left, Emily sat in a stupor, feeling numb and shaky.

A short while later, there was a tap on the door. She assumed it was Mamma, come to see if Charles still wished to speak to her. She was not ready to talk to Mamma. She was not ready to talk to anyone, except perhaps—

"Emily?" The door creaked open and Viola herself appeared. "May I come in?"

"Oh, Vi." Tears filled her eyes. "How did you know?"

"I spied on you, I'm afraid. Watched from our house until Charles left, then came over straightaway."

"I'm glad you did." Emily patted the chair beside her, the one Charles had recently vacated.

Once Viola was seated, Emily told her everything, then leaned into her arms and wept.

"Was I wrong not to accept him?"

Viola held her and stroked her hair. "Oh, Em. I hate to see you so upset. I hope I did not give you poor advice. If you think you were wrong to refuse him, you could tell him you changed your mind."

Emily shook her head and spoke over a hot lump in her throat. "It's too late. Oh, Vi. It was so much harder than I expected. I've cut Charles from my life and given up my long-cherished hope for the future. It was a part of me—almost like a third twin." Emily sat up and pressed a hand to her chest. "It hurts. And I hate that I've hurt him too."

"Did he truly not relent? When you told him you would not marry him if that meant never seeing Claire again, did he not suggest a compromise? Perhaps agreeing to visit her elsewhere but not invite her to May Park, something like that?"

Emily looked at her in surprise, the notion never having crossed her mind. "No."

"Then, my dear, I don't think you have made a mistake."

Emily swiped the heels of her hands across her eyes. "I pray you're right. But Claire may never return, and I will have lost them both, forever."

When Viola left, Emily went to Mamma's room, determined to remain calm. Through the open door, she saw her mother, neatly dressed and sitting at her writing desk. When she turned toward the door, Emily also saw that she looked nervous.

She glanced past Emily. "Is Charles not here yet?"

"Here and gone. I told him he need not speak to you first. I hope you don't mind?"

"I don't mind at all, but—"

"Oh, Mamma . . ." Despite her intentions, Emily's chin quivered and tears swamped her eyes.

"My dear!" Mamma rose quickly and embraced her. "What has happened?"

"I told him I could not marry him. Are you very disappointed in me?"

"No, of course not." She handed Emily a handkerchief, and the two sat down beside each other. "Why are you so upset? Did he demand a reason? A larger dowry . . . ?"

Emily shook her head. "I certainly gave him a reason. Several."

Mamma straightened, expression wary. "What reasons?"

Emily wiped her eyes and took a steadying breath. "Because of . . . Claire. Sorry. I know you don't like her spoken of, but she is part of the reason. I can't abide that Charles blames her and severed ties with our entire family while . . . *that man* . . . goes on his merry way." Indignation surged, briefly surmounting her sadness.

"Emily, please." Mamma held a hand to her head, face contorted in pain. "Your father made me promise on his deathbed. . . ."

"It's not fair."

"I agree. But as I've told you girls time and again, society holds young ladies to higher standards. We may not like that, yet we ignore it to our peril. Many lives and whole families have been destroyed by less, as we've had a taste of."

"What about *her* life? Charles said his parents would only give their blessing if she remains in Scotland."

Mamma's eyes narrowed. "Charles told me he'd said nothing to his parents about what happened."

"Even so, they apparently have their suspicions."

Mamma closed her eyes and groaned. Then she looked up and said flatly, "Please understand, I have no intention of asking anyone to return. Tell me that is not the only reason you refused him."

"It's not. His mother does not approve of the match. She has never really approved of me, even before what happened. She told Charles I *could* become a lady of distinction with very little guidance. Hers."

Mamma's eyes flashed. "Louise has always had too high of an opinion of herself."

Emily mentioned another reason, although a lesser one. "Charles is not keen on my writing books either. At least, not publishing them, or being paid for them, and certainly not having my name on them."

344

"That does not surprise me. Novel writing is another thing society frowns upon, and the Parkers have always cared a great deal about the opinion of others."

Emily nodded. "Charles is genuinely sorry, though. About everything. And he cried, Mamma, when I said no." Emily's voice broke. "I feel terrible. I may not like everything he's become—so determined to toe the mark, to satisfy the demands of society and his parents. But Charles himself, the boy from May Park . . ." Again Emily's eyes filled. "I suppose I shall always love him."

Mamma reached over and held her hand. "Yet you cannot marry him?"

Emily pressed her eyes closed for a long moment and then opened them again. "No."

"In that case, my dear, I am sorry for you both. However, if you have this many misgivings, you were probably right to refuse, even though it is painful."

"Thank you, Mamma." Emily held her mother's gaze, then said gently, "One more thing. Please understand that I made no such promise to Papa. I have given up Charles, and I would give up novel writing before I would give up Claire."

Emily had not seen Mr. Thomson for several hours, which was a relief, considering the tumultuous events of the day. At dinner, Mr. Bernardi mentioned that he had gone to spend the evening with General Wetherall at Fortfield Terrace.

That night, Emily sat down to write to Claire but struggled to compose more than a salutation. Exhausted in mind and body, she craved nothing more than the sanctuary of sleep.

Emily was crossing the hall, intent on an early bedtime, when Mr. Thomson returned, removing his hat as he entered.

He paused when he saw her, his whole body tensing. He took a deep breath and faced her as if preparing for a blow.

"Miss Emily. Good evening. I passed Charles earlier, on his way here to see you. He told me the . . . good news." James swallowed hard. "May I be among the first to wish you happy?"

"I don't know why you would."

Confusion puckered his brow. "He said he had proposed, and—"

"I did not accept him."

"Oh." He blinked rapidly. "May I ask why?"

"Several reasons. But I don't wish to go through it all again. Not now."

"I understand. Are you . . . all right?"

"I hardly know."

He reached out as though to comfort her but quickly retracted his hands, tucking them both behind his back.

Emily amended, "Mostly, I am tired." She gestured toward the stairs. "I was just on my way to bed."

"Forgive me. I shall not delay you any longer." He stepped aside. "But please let me know if there is anything I can do."

25

⁓⁓⁓⋄⁓⁓⁓

Entrepreneurs who opened beach-side circulating
libraries vied with each other. In Sidmouth, Mr. John
Wallis and Mr. John Marsh both published guide
books in which their own library was highly praised.

—Ian Maxted, *Etched on Devon's Memory*

Over the next few days, Emily spent a great deal of time
in the office finishing her draft of the new Sidmouth
guide for Mr. Marsh. She hoped to put Charles from
her mind, and to overcome the grief and misgivings that still
assailed her.

Miss Stirling came over for tea, and Emily wondered if
her visits would become far less frequent after she married.
Engagements were not often celebrated, yet even so, Mamma
presented her with a gift wrapped in tissue, saying, "With our
heartfelt appreciation for all your support and friendship over
the years."

Miss Stirling pulled back the tissue to reveal a beautiful
lace cap from Mrs. Nicholls's shop.

"You shall need a new cap, now that you are to be a married
woman," Mamma explained.

Fran shook her head. "It's far too beautiful to wear."

"Nonsense. It is as lovely as you are."

"Thank you. Thank you all."

Mamma continued to be supportive of Emily's decision not to marry Charles. Sarah was supportive as well. In fact, only after Emily confided that she had rejected him did Sarah admit she'd long had reservations about someone who could abandon a woman he supposedly loved during her family's time of need.

"I wanted to give him the benefit of the doubt. And if he had come to apologize sooner, I would have believed him sincere. But we moved away well over a year ago, and he has just decided to come here and admit he might have been wrong? To try to pick up where you left off? All that to say, I think you made the right decision."

Only Georgie vocalized disappointment. She had wanted Charles for a brother-in-law, the older brother she'd never had. "I can't believe you, Emily. You have moped around since we moved here, pining for Charles. And now to refuse him? If that's what comes from reading so many novels, I'll keep to sports."

Emily did her best to console her and kept working on the guidebook.

Whenever Mr. Thomson returned from Woolbrook, she would step into the hall to hear the latest report. The news he carried grew more and more worrisome by the day.

Apparently, the recently arrived Dr. Maton continued to perform more painful cupping and blistering on Prince Edward. Yet despite all this torment, or perhaps exacerbated by it, his fever, headache, and chest pain persisted.

On Thursday Mr. Thomson returned, shoulders slumped, eyes weary, his expression almost desolate.

Seeing his state, Emily put a hand on his back and ushered

him into the parlour and into a comfortable chair near the fireplace.

"Sit." A few moments later she returned with a steaming cup of tea with sugar and milk. Good for shock.

"Drink."

He obeyed her.

She pulled a second armchair closer to his and faced him. "Now tell me."

"I should not. It was awful."

"Whatever it is, it's clearly weighing on you. I would share the burden if I could."

He slowly nodded, gaze lowering to his cup. "After yesterday, there was very little of the duke's body, even his head, not inflicted with cuts. I stayed with the duchess to translate between her and Dr. Maton, but I could hardly bear to watch.

"Sir Thomas Acland and his wife came to call, but the duke was not equal to visitors. I was asked to speak to them instead. It was a welcome reprieve, I admit.

"Then today, Dr. Maton announced that yet more bleeding was needed. The duke himself wept. Actually wept. Oh, Emily. To see such a strong man brought so low. And his devastated wife. Over and over she laments, 'My poor Edward,' and there is nothing I can do for either of them."

Tears shone in his eyes, and Emily's filled in sympathy. She took his hand. "It was good of you to try to help."

"What little help I can offer."

He swiped his free hand across his eyes. "Considering the severity of the situation, we decided it would be wise to send messages to the duchess's brother, Prince Leopold, and to the Prince Regent, informing them of the duke's dangerous illness. Composing letters, at least, was something I could do."

"And I am sure she appreciated it."

He nodded. "She did. I wish I could do more."

A foreign thought crossed her mind, and Emily suggested, "Should we . . . maybe . . . pray together?"

He squeezed her hand. "Good idea."

Knees almost touching, they each prayed briefly and then sat in silence for a few moments. Emily raised her head and found Mr. Thomson watching her intently.

He blinked and rose stiffly. "I suppose I should turn in. Tomorrow is going to be another long day."

The next afternoon, Emily dressed warmly and walked the length of the esplanade to Marsh's Library and Public Rooms, portfolio containing the completed guidebook pages tucked under her arm.

Seeing her enter, John Marsh rose from his desk and swiftly crossed the room to her, gaze latched on to the portfolio.

"Is that it?" he asked, all but snatching it from her.

She nodded. "It's only a draft. I know it could be improved, but a fair start, I hope."

"And in record time."

"You said you wanted it as soon as possible."

"Indeed I did. Well done. I look forward to reviewing it. I trust you understand that I will edit the draft as I see fit?"

"Yes, of course. You are both editor and publisher."

"Good, good. Just so we understand one another." He returned to his desk, opened the cover, and began to read.

Emily followed, stood before the desk, and forced herself to ask, "When shall I bring in Mr. Gwilt's manuscript?"

"Hm?" he murmured, still concentrating on the page.

"The adventure story for children? You said you would read it once I'd completed the guide, and then consider publishing it."

He looked up in confusion, then realization dawned. "Ah,

the uncle's story, right. Let me read and edit this first. I am eager to get it to the printer."

"Oh. I see," Emily said, although doubts gnawed at her. "I will be happy to make any revisions or additions you'd like, or to correct proof pages when the time comes."

"No need. I will see to it." He waved a hand, dismissing both her and her offer.

Emily gazed down once more at her carefully written manuscript, and found it strangely difficult to move away. To go home without it felt like leaving a favorite child or pet to the mercy of a stranger. Would he guard it well? Give it all the devoted attention it required?

"Very well." Feeling rebuffed, Emily forced her leaden legs to turn and retreat to the door.

As Emily stepped from Marsh's establishment, she saw Mr. Wallis exiting the York Hotel. Her heart lurched.

He walked toward her, his expression revealing surprise and hurt. "Miss Summers." He bowed. "We have not had the pleasure of a visit from you in some time." He glanced at the building she had just left. "And perhaps now I understand why."

"Mr. Wallis, I . . . It is good to see you. We have just been so busy with, well, our guests, and the happenings at Woolbrook, and so on." Guilt coursed in her stomach. Compounding her betrayal with deception was probably making them both feel worse.

She ended with a lame "Sadly little time for pleasure reading lately."

He regarded her, his expression all too knowing. "Sad indeed."

Face flaming, Emily turned away. She went up Fore Street to avoid extending the awkward encounter, which would happen if she walked back in the same direction as Mr. Wallis.

She decided to visit the post office before returning home.

As she crossed the marketplace on her way there, Emily glanced toward Broadbridge's Boarding House, thinking of Miss Stirling. The front door opened, and a man emerged. Mr. Bernardi. He walked swiftly away in the opposite direction, whistling, while Fran Stirling stood in the doorway, her hand lifted in farewell.

Strange, Emily thought, wondering what business had taken one of their guests to another lodging establishment.

Noticing Emily, Fran waved to her.

Emily hurried over, curiosity piqued. "What did he want?"

Fran waited until she was closer before replying. "He heard I might be selling and came to inquire."

"Did he? How unexpected."

Fran nodded. "And he is the second person to inquire in as many days."

"Really? I hope that means you shall get a good price. A little competition never hurt anybody!" Emily grinned as she said the words.

Then, thinking again of Mr. Wallis, her smile quickly faded.

On Saturday night, James returned to Sea View looking calmer and more composed.

"Did the duchess's brother arrive?" Emily asked.

"He did and I am relieved. Prince Leopold speaks excellent English, and naturally, he and his sister share the same native tongue. The duchess now has someone close to her to support her and speak on her behalf."

"Good. I am sure he shall be a comfort to her."

James nodded solemnly. "And she shall need a great deal of comfort soon, I fear, for the end is near."

"Oh no."

"Yes. General Wetherall was most anxious that the duke's new will should be signed—leaving everything to his wife and entrusting her with the care of their daughter. With some effort, His Royal Highness was roused to listen to the new will being read. He then managed to sign it legibly before falling back on his pillows, exhausted."

"Merciful heavens," Emily breathed.

She thought, then said, "Hopefully enough people witnessed his signature that the will's legality won't be called into question."

"Several people were there," he assured her. "His wife, of course. Prince Leopold. The doctors. General Wetherall. I was there, at the back of the room, just in case I was needed."

"And Captain Conroy, I assume?"

Frown lines scored his brow. "Actually, now you mention it, he was not there." James took a deep breath. "At all events, after resting, the duke woke once more. He said, 'May the Almighty protect my wife and child and forgive all the sins I have committed.' Then he begged his wife, 'Do not forget me.'"

Emily impulsively took James's hand.

He clasped her fingers in reply. "I had not realized how close I felt to him until that moment. How much I appreciated him taking me on when men like Conroy advised him against it. Whatever others say about Prince Edward, he has always been good to me, and a loving husband and father to his wife and daughter. My heart breaks for them both." His voice thickened. "When I think of that little girl growing up without her doting papa . . ."

"Oh, James. I am so sorry." Not knowing what else to do, Emily leaned close and laid her head upon his shoulder.

26

I am hopelessly lost without dearest Edward, who
always shielded me. He was my adored partner in life.
Whatever shall I do without his strong support?
—The Duchess of Kent, translated letter

The next morning, James Thomson did not attend
church with them, but instead returned to Woolbrook
to join those sitting vigil at the duke's bedside.

Later, when the family returned to Sea View after divine
services, they found Mr. Thomson there before them, waiting
in the hall. He stood there, still wearing his coat, hat in hand,
complexion pale.

Emily knew as soon as she saw his face. "Is he . . . ? Is he
gone?"

He nodded. "Just as the clocks struck ten. The duchess was
kneeling beside the bed, holding his hand."

"Oh no."

He nodded. "She refused to leave his bedside till the last.
She has barely slept in days."

"That poor woman," Mamma said, tears glistening in her
eyes, perhaps remembering her days sitting at Papa's bedside
before he died.

Shaking her head in disbelief, Emily said, "A strong man like him, who had never before been ill in his life, and now to die of a cold?"

Sarah nodded. "It's shocking. His daughter is too young to understand her loss, but how his wife must be suffering."

"Yes. She loved her husband deeply," Mr. Thomson said. "Any man would be blessed by such devotion."

Emily saw the longing on his face, and her chest ached at the sight.

The day after the duke's death, normally quiet Glen Lane was busier than ever, with a stream of people and carriages going to-and-fro on important, morbid business: surgeons, embalmers, undertakers, and royal officials. A postmortem had to be carried out, measurements taken for a fine coffin to accommodate the large man, and arrangements made for the duke's lying in state.

The duchess was eager to finalize arrangements. Apparently, her brother, Prince Leopold, was urging her to leave this site of her deepest grief as soon as possible.

Sarah watched all the activity with melancholy interest and offered to sew black armbands for the three members of staff staying with them.

Mr. Thomson spent a great deal of time at Woolbrook over the next few days, composing death notices, answering inquiries, and greeting officials as they arrived. Mr. Bernardi was assigned to Fortfield Terrace to prepare food for the staff and visitors there rather than in the house of mourning. Sarah did not see much of Mr. During in that time, so she did not know where he was . . . or what he was up to.

When another day went by with barely a glimpse of Mr. During, curiosity and worry got the best of Sarah and she knocked on his door. She wanted to talk with the man, to assure herself that nothing untoward was going on. More than a week had passed since General Wetherall asked to inventory the plate chest. Since then, Mr. During had often been absent, and strangely silent.

She knocked again.

No answer.

Sarah hesitated, then brought out her key. It would not be the first time she had let herself into a guest's room during his or her absence—usually to tidy up or collect the rubbish. But in this instance, she felt like a sneak as she unlocked the door.

Inside the room, she glanced around quickly, her pulse racing. The plate chest sat closed on the floor, as it had before, while Mr. During's valise lay open on the dressing chest. She walked over and peeked in, finding it partly filled with rumpled shirts, stockings, and cravats. Was he already packing to leave?

On the bed, she saw a haphazard jumble of supplies: linen table napkins, ornamental serviette rings, silk flowers, blank name cards, and several pen-and-ink table diagrams showing where each serving dish and decoration would be set, and even the man's trusty ruler for aligning plates and silver. The tools of his trade lay in an untidy heap, as though he had dumped out his large table-decker's case onto the counterpane. She did not see the case itself, however. She bent to look under the bed. Nothing. The handled leather case was missing. Why?

Had he gone to set a table for a dinner at Fortfield Terrace? Possible, although if he had, would he not have taken his supplies?

Sarah turned toward the plate chest with a sickly premonition. From this angle, she saw that the padlock was lying on the floor beside the chest. *Oh no.* He must have forgotten to lock it.

Nerves jangling, she knelt before the plate chest—the precious chest that only Mr. During was allowed to open.

For a moment, she stilled, ears alert for the sound of approaching footsteps.

Only silence met her.

With trembling fingers, she reached for the latch hook and lifted it. The lid opened easily. She looked inside, instantly relieved not to find it empty. There lay the decorative gold box Mr. During had mentioned, along with a few medals and the tall silver candlesticks.

Realization prickled over her. There were only two here. She looked over her shoulder around the room but saw no sign of more. Where were the others? He had said there were four, and she had seen them on the banquet table during the duke's evening party.

Footsteps sounded in the passage, and Sarah's heart banged against her ribs. She quickly shut the lid and leapt to her feet as a knock shook the door.

She stood there, hand pressed to throbbing chest.

The door creaked open. . . .

Her brain scrambled for words of explanation or excuse, but nothing materialized.

She was caught.

The door opened farther. Sarah took an unsteady breath and faced it, expecting Selwyn During.

Instead her sister appeared, eyes wide and expression anxious.

"Emily!" The name came out in a whoosh. "You scared me."

"And you scared me. I saw the door ajar and heard someone shuffling about in here. What were you doing?"

"Spying, actually. I know I should not, but something isn't

right. Mr. During is preparing to leave, by the looks of it." She gestured toward the open valise.

"Perhaps not terribly surprising now that his employer has died," Emily replied. "Has he said anything to you about resigning?"

"No. But there's more. See there—he has dumped out all his table-decking things. And worse, the plate chest was left unlocked. I looked inside. Unless I am mistaken, a pair of silver candlesticks is missing. There are only two inside."

"Oh no. I hope we shan't be blamed for the missing ones."

"Ugh. I pray not."

"Maybe he took them to Woolbrook," Emily suggested. "They used them there the night of the party, remember?"

"Yes, perhaps you're right. I should not leap to conclusions."

Unbidden, she recalled what Mr. Cordey had told her. Mr. During had asked known smugglers how to sell something "quiet-like." She prayed her suspicions were wrong.

They left the room together. Sarah paused to lock the door and followed Emily down the back stairs.

As they reached the bottom, the front door knocker banged hard, and they both jumped.

A few moments later, a harried-looking Jessie met them in the back passage, her eyes lighting upon them with relief.

"There you are, miss. That Captain Conroy is at the door, demanding to see Mr. During. But he's not here. I saw him leave."

"Did he say where he was going?"

"No, miss. Just saw him from the window, heading that way." She pointed south, toward the sea.

"Was he carrying anything?"

Jessie shrugged. "Not sure. Might have been. Now, please. Come and speak with the man—he frightens me."

"Me too," Sarah murmured.

She and Emily shared a look, then continued through the main floor corridor and into the hall.

Captain Conroy stood just inside the door, gloves in one hand, slapping them impatiently again his leg and looking as if he'd like to slap someone else. He turned at their approach. A fierce frown scored the skin between his brows. His furry whiskers and pugnacious expression put her in mind of a peevish bulldog.

"Captain Conroy," Sarah began. "How may we be of assistance?"

"I came to find Mr. During and was unhappy to be told he is not available. Does he refuse to see me?"

"No. He has gone out. I am certain he shall return soon." Sarah wasn't certain he would return, but the fact that his partially packed valise was still there seemed to justify the words.

"Do you know where he went? Or even which direction?" the captain asked. "I could send someone to fetch him."

"I don't know where he is," Sarah replied, ignoring Emily's sharp look. "In the meantime, may we help somehow?"

"I came for some items in the plate chest."

Sarah's stomach twisted. "Oh?"

"Yes. Her Royal Highness wishes the room to be draped in black and lit by candles when the duke lies in state. The chest contains tall silver candlesticks that would suit the purpose perfectly. She requested them specifically."

Sarah's mind searched for a way to forestall him. "I believe Mr. During always takes his key with him. Do you . . . have another?"

He lifted one shoulder. "The duke probably had a spare somewhere, but things are rather chaotic in the house at present, with all the preparations."

"Understandably so. I will send Mr. During to Woolbrook with the candlesticks as soon as may be."

359

His black brows lowered ominously. "And keep the duchess waiting?" He shook his head. "Take me to his room. At once!"

"T-to what purpose? If only Mr. During can open the chest?"

"We shall see about that." He charged up the stairs. Sarah and Emily exchanged worried glances, and then Sarah hurried after him, wishing she had thought to secure the padlock before leaving Mr. During's room. Emily followed more slowly.

As soon as Sarah unlocked the door, the captain pushed past her.

He swooped down on the chest like a buzzard to prey. "Unlocked! I'll throttle the toad." He threw back the lid, and Sarah held her breath.

Instead of the volley of curses she expected, Captain Conroy lifted out two large silver candlesticks, face alight with satisfaction.

"I shall take these to the duchess directly. Tell During to see me immediately about the unlocked chest. There will be consequences for this oversight."

"I . . . I will," Sarah stammered, confusion washing over her. Did the captain not know there should be two more candlesticks? Apparently not. Despite this reprieve, Sarah knew it would not be long until the others were discovered missing, and During would certainly be blamed then.

When the captain left, Sarah expelled a sigh of relief. If the situation was as desperate as she feared, at least they had a little time to right it, if Mr. During was willing. First she had to find him.

She became aware of Emily studying her.

"Jessie told us which direction Mr. During went," she began. "Why did you not mention it? And why did you say nothing about the missing candlesticks?"

Sarah decided not to repeat what Mr. Cordey had told her—that Mr. During had asked around about how to sell something quietly. "I don't want to say anything until I know more. I'd hate to cast doubt on Mr. During's character without just cause."

"Surely you can tell me what you suspect. Do you think he stole them? Intends to sell them?"

"It's possible. Yet I still hope I am wrong. Did he ever confide in you about the letters he received? They certainly seemed to upset him."

"Only that he'd received news from home."

Sarah shook her head. "Something has made him desperate and foolish."

"Do you truly believe he's a thief? He is not my favorite person, but he seems like a decent man deep down. And he is clearly devoted to his family."

"I agree."

With an attempt at humor, Emily added, "And anyone who loves his sisters cannot be all bad."

Sarah did not respond. Staring vaguely across the room, she said, "I think I will go belowstairs and ask if anyone spoke to Mr. During before he left. I may walk down to the esplanade as well. See if I can spot him. Can you watch over things in the office for a while?"

"Of course I can. Will you be gone long?"

"No. I should be back soon."

Emily went into the office and tried to busy herself. There was a letter from a potential future guest to answer, as well as her languishing novel, which was not going to write itself. She wondered if Mr. Marsh would really consider publishing her manuscript when he seemed halfhearted about Mr. Gwilt's. Either way, she owed it to herself to finish the draft.

Taking up her quill pen, she bent to the task.

When she looked up again from her writing, it was almost

time for luncheon. She had expected Sarah to return by now. Perhaps she had come in through the back door and was busy elsewhere in the house, helping with meal preparations or tidying one of the common rooms. Emily put the quill in its holder and rose to look for her.

She passed first through the empty drawing room and into the dining room, where Georgiana and Mamma were just sitting down. "Ah, there you are, Emily. I was about to send Georgiana to fetch you. I know you lose track of time when you are writing. And where is Sarah? It is not like her to be late."

"I was just wondering that as well. Have you not seen her?"

"Not since breakfast."

Emily frowned. "She went to find Mr. During. Said she might walk to the esplanade to look for him. I expected her back before now."

"Well, there is sure to be some simple explanation," Mamma said. "Come and sit down before the soup gets cold."

"Do you mind if I don't join you today? I am not hungry."

Concern shadowed Mamma's face. "Are you feeling all right?"

"Yes, yes. You go on with your meal."

From there, Emily went into the parlour and found Mr. Thomson seated at the table, penning a letter.

"Pardon me, have you seen Sarah?"

Mr. Thomson glanced up from his page. "No." Rising from his chair, he studied her face, then frowned. "Why? Is something wrong?"

"Probably not. I simply expected her back before now. She went in search of Mr. During."

Emily wished she had pressed Sarah for more details about where she planned to look.

Mr. Gwilt came in with a tea tray for the guests. "Good afternoon, Miss Emily. Mr. Thomson."

"Mr. Gwilt, have you seen Sarah?"

"Aye, though some time ago. Asked if I'd seen Mr. During. When I said I had not, she said she would keep looking. It seems he is wanted at Woolbrook."

"Did she say where she planned to go?"

"Not to me, but Bibi was here finishing her work. Miss Sarah asked if her father was out fishing or at home. Bibi didn't know but reckoned at least one of her brothers would be there, tending nets."

Emily nodded her understanding. Perhaps Sarah was still talking with the Cordeys and would return any moment. Where else would she be?

The chef came in, adding a platter of small iced cakes to the tea table.

Mr. Thomson asked him, "You don't know where Selwyn is, or what he might have got up to, do you, Antoine?"

Mr. Bernardi looked up and held the other man's gaze. "With that one, who can tell?"

27

Having armed myself with a knife, I declared that
I would kill the first man who came near me, and
that I would not be taken from the spot alive.

—John Rattenbury, *Memoirs of a Smuggler*

Warm hooded mantle wrapped around her, Sarah walked east along the esplanade for a time but saw no sign of Mr. During. Then she made her way down to the beach. With the sun shining and little wind, the day was far milder than they'd experienced in weeks.

Nearing the Cordeys' small cottage, she saw Punch Cordey leaning against the door, chatting and flirting with a pretty young woman she didn't know.

"Excuse me, Punch," Sarah began with a wave of her hand. "I am looking for one of our guests. A Mr. During. Did you see a man pass this way?"

"Incomer?"

"Yes."

He screwed up his face. "Skinny scarecrow-lookin' fellow with straw fer hair?"

"Well . . . yes." Sarah would not have described him that way, although she supposed it was rather accurate.

Punch nodded. "He went by, a-carryin' somethin'. Asked fer directions."

"Directions to where?"

"Said he were lookin' fer the cave near Lade Foot. I told him to follow the beach." Punch pointed to the west, where the beach disappeared around a jutting headland.

Sarah's last hope for some other explanation was rapidly dwindling. She asked, "How will I recognize the place?"

"There's a rock offshore looks like a boot. Can't miss it."

"Is there a path the whole way, even at the base of the cliffs?"

"Aye, when the tide is out. We go by boat to fish Lade Foot Cove, but if 'ee go now, you can make it on foot."

"Thank you."

He looked at her, a slight frown on his face. "Miss . . ." He seemed about to say more until the pretty girl nudged his arm and whispered something in his ear. Punch smiled down at her, Sarah clearly forgotten.

She started walking west along the pebbled shore, glad for her sturdy half boots.

She followed the beach as it shrank to a narrow strip of damp sand, exposed now that the tide was out, but likely to be submerged at high tide. She rounded the headland, walking in the shadow of the lime kiln on the cliff above.

Reaching the western beach, she trudged on, relieved no men were bathing there, or at least no men bathing without clothes, as they were known to do on this more secluded stretch.

As she continued westward, she kept an eye on the water and hoped she could make it there and back before the tide came in.

When she reached the cave, would she find Mr. During?

Would he be alone? She prayed she might find him before any potential meeting with a buyer could take place.

In the parlour with Mr. Thomson and Mr. Bernardi, Emily began to worry in earnest.

She rose and announced, "I am going to find Sarah."

Mr. Thomson nodded. "I will go with you."

"What's going on?" Mr. Bernardi asked, eyes narrowed.

Emily explained the situation: Selwyn During's suspicious behavior, the missing candlesticks, the possibility he planned to sell them to someone, and Sarah gone searching, hoping to avert catastrophe.

"I should never have let her go alone," Emily lamented. "I should have insisted on going with her."

"We shall go together now," Mr. Thomson said.

Mr. Bernardi nodded. "And I will go with you. But first . . . I need something from the kitchen." He looked pointedly at James. "A buyer of stolen goods, whoever he is, could be dangerous, so this might be a good time to bring one of those swords of yours. And I don't mean a practice foil."

A short while later, the three donned coats and left the house together: Mr. Thomson, sword at his side, Mr. Bernardi armed with his favorite pestle, and Emily armed with her wits and basic knowledge of local terrain.

When they reached the beach, Emily saw Punch Cordey sitting outside the family cottage, puffing on a white clay pipe, and then bending over in a coughing fit.

"Since when do you smoke?" she asked.

"Since about five minutes ago."

"That's long enough, I'd say."

Having seen them from the cottage window, Bibi came out to join them, wrapping a wool shawl around herself as she came.

"Have you seen Sarah?" Emily asked Punch. "Has she come this way?"

"Oh aye. She were lookin' fer that skinny fellow a-stayin' at Sea View."

"Mr. During, yes. Did he come this way as well?"

Punch nodded. "Asked how to get to Lade Foot."

"And you gave Sarah directions too?"

"I did."

Worry lines puckered Bibi's face. "If they'm goin' there, no good can come of it."

"What do you mean?" Emily asked.

"There's a sea cave near Lade Foot, 'tween here and Ladram Bay, where smugglers hide contraband." Bibi scowled at her brother, then cuffed his arm. "I can't believe 'ee told her how to get there without warnin' her!"

"I were, uh, thinkin' on . . . other things."

"Molly Tucker, no doubt."

He dipped his head, cheeks stained red.

"Was Mr. During meetin' someone?" Bibi asked her brother. "Did he say?"

"No, but I ain't seen no one else pass this way."

"That's something, I suppose," Emily said. "Let's go and find them before whoever he's meeting gets there."

Punch gave them directions, then asked, "Want me to go along?"

"No need. I am sure we'll be all right." In truth, Emily was not so sure. Even so, anxiety for Sarah propelled her westward along the beach as Mr. Thomson and Mr. Bernardi followed.

"Be careful!" Bibi called after them.

Waves lapped against the shore close to her feet, but Emily resisted the urge to retreat. For the second time in her life, concern for one of her sisters overpowered her fear of the sea.

After crossing the sand-and-pebble western beach, Sarah continued onto another narrow shoulder of shoreline that curved around a cliff base. As she picked her way along the rocky path, she slipped on a patch of slick green seaweed. Her arms shot out for balance, and she flailed, one of her half boots squelching into a puddle of sea water. She lifted the sodden boot with a sigh and went on.

Rounding the sandstone outcropping, she sidestepped a few fallen boulders and looked up. In the distance, she saw a formation in the water she thought might be Lade Rock. She kept going, all the while keeping a wary eye on the tide level.

On her right, a red sandstone cliff rose high above her, the bottom few yards covered in weeping seaweed, still wet from the last high tide. A miniature waterfall trickled in a frothy stream down its face.

Scanning the area ahead, Sarah saw no sign of life. Heard nothing but the cry of a distant gull. Had she mistaken the way? Or might Mr. During have changed his mind? If so, perhaps he had taken the cliffside path from the western beach to the lime kiln and made his way back to Sea View from there? Probably wishful thinking. Either way, she wanted to be certain.

She continued, drawing nearer to Lade Foot. As she did, she noticed a narrow recess in the cliff face. Gingerly walking closer, she kept to the margin of wet sand, risking both of her half boots to avoid crunching over pebbles, which would announce her presence before she was ready to do so.

While she did not relish the coming confrontation, she was not afraid of Mr. During. She was afraid, however, of interrupting a transaction with a smuggler who had successfully fought off armed soldiers with only a knife.

Was that man the potential buyer? Was his boat even now moored in Lade Foot Cove, out of sight behind the rocks? She craned her neck to look but saw no sign of a boat, nor of a rope tethering one to shore.

Or worse, had the buyer been there and gone? Perhaps even left Selwyn During for dead? *Don't be dramatic*, she scolded herself, her imagination suddenly as vivid as Emily's.

Too vivid.

Perhaps she ought to have brought her sister along. Or even Punch Cordey. But Sarah still held out hope that she could privately convince Mr. During to return the candlesticks. Whatever he needed money for, it was not worth endangering his career over, let alone his life.

Nearing the mouth of the sea cave, she gingerly glanced around the edge with an anticipatory wince, fearing what she might find. The wedge-shaped cave narrowed toward the back. It was only a few yards deep, but large enough and shadowed enough to conceal a stack of brandy barrels or a few men.

Only one stood there.

Selwyn During, his leather case on a rock nearby.

Sarah released a relieved breath and hurried forward, heedless now of the sound of her boots.

"Mr. During. Thank heaven I caught you in time. Please don't do it. It's not worth it. There must be another way."

"Miss Summers, you should not be here." He searched over her shoulder, expression tense. "Leave as quickly as you can. I cannot guarantee your safety."

"Yet you risk your own for a pair of candlesticks!"

His fair eyebrows rose. "You know?"

She nodded.

He hung his head with a groan. "You don't understand."

"Then explain it to me."

"I have no choice. My beloved mother and sisters have been sent to debtors' prison. The Marshalsea. That pit of vermin and vice and sickness."

Sarah's stomach clenched at the news. "Oh no." It was worse than she'd imagined.

He nodded. "It's my father's fault. He loves drink and gambling more than his wife and daughters. I am the only one who can help them. I would have sent them more of my wages, but we have not been paid in some time. Still, I did not realize things had become so dire until I received Mamma's letters—the news going from bad to worse. My mother is not strong. And my youngest sister has never enjoyed good health—always the first to catch every fever that goes around. You don't know what those places are. I must rescue them at any cost."

"Would your mother want you to steal to accomplish it? There must be another way."

"What way? Even if I could pry my unpaid wages from Conroy's grasp it would not be enough."

"We will think of something. I will help you." She extended her hand to him.

"It's too late. You figured out what I did. In no time others will too."

"Not necessarily. Captain Conroy came to retrieve the candlesticks but left satisfied with only two."

"Did he?"

Sarah nodded. "Apparently he does not know there should be more."

A faint glimmer of hope shone in his round, boyish eyes, then quickly faded. "The duchess knows. So does the general."

"Then return them quickly. There is still time to make this right."

He hesitated, seeming to hover on the edge of decision. Again she extended her hand toward him, hoping he would either give her his own hand or the case itself.

While she stood there, silently pleading with him, water

lapped over her feet. She sucked in a breath. Just a wave, or was the tide rising?

For a moment longer he studied her face, perhaps searching for deceit. Finding none, he lifted the bag with one arm and reached for her hand.

"Well, well, well," a voice said. "Ain't this a sweet scene? Right touching."

They both whirled. The roar of the sea had concealed the approaching boot steps. The man who stood there was a bull-ish, broad-shouldered man in his forties with a thick head of hair, a deep crease between bushy brows, and a prominent nose. In his beefy hand, he held a knife.

This must be the man Mr. Mutter worked for, Sarah real-ized, dread filling her.

"Surprised I was to hear voices, as you was told to come alone. I beached my boat a ways up shore, in case it were a trap. Thought you'd been stupid enough to bring an excise man. Reckoned this one must be young indeed, with a voice not yet changed." He pointed his knife toward Sarah. "Who's this, then? Yer sweetheart?"

"No. She . . ."

"He did come alone as instructed," Sarah said in a rush. "I was worried about him, so I came to find him." Thinking quickly, she added, "The Duke of Kent's men are looking for him too, and you don't want to be here when they come. Captain Conroy will be armed."

"As am I." The man lifted his knife. "Tut-tut. Such threats. And here I thought we was to have a quiet and civil business dealing, Mr. *Dearing*."

"We were, but I . . . I have changed my mind."

"After I come all this way? Ain't keen on leavin' empty-handed. Let's see what 'ee brought."

Mr. During hesitated, then glanced anxiously at Sarah.

She said, "Unfortunately, we must leave directly. The candlesticks are needed at Woolbrook Cottage. The Duke of Kent has died and is soon to lie in state. The entire village is invited to pay their respects."

He laughed. "Won't see me there. Ain't a sentimental sort, nor beholden to royalty. I'd rather have what's in that bag to remember 'im by."

He stepped closer, each footfall crashing onto the pebbles while another wave slapped the shore, water splashing up the shanks of his boots.

His eyes narrowed menacingly. "Show me."

With a visible swallow, Mr. During set the heavy bag back on the rock and leaned down. Opening the clasp, he extracted the two large candlesticks.

A shaft of sunlight pierced the cave's shadowy interior and glinted on the gleaming silver. The smuggler's small eyes gleamed in reply.

"Well, well, well. A pair o' pretties, I must say. Like to fetch a pretty price too. Although I may 'ave to sail to Normandy to sell 'em safe-like." He stuck out a demanding hand, knife still poised in the other. "Let's 'ave 'em."

Sarah gulped down a lump of fear. "As mentioned, he has changed his mind about selling those."

"Too late, maid'n. I'm 'ere now and I'll 'ave what I come fer." He smirked at her. "Or I could kill 'im and take the bag and you in the bargain."

Sarah felt the blood drain from her face.

"Y-you have not shown us the money yet," Mr. During faltered, clearly trying to forestall the man.

"Ain't 'ee precious. I ain't paying up front fer something that ain't yers and may take a great deal of time and effort to sell. I do the work, I get the pay. Now, if 'ee promised more such bounty I might be persuaded to strike a deal."

"I already made a deal with your associate, Mr. Mutter. He said you'd give me a fair price."

"Oh, Mutter is much more generous than I am. Always 'as been."

Snatching the candlesticks from During's impotent hands, the man shoved them into the case, then turned and sauntered away with it.

What should they do? What *could* they do?

During hung his head. "I was prepared to hang to save my family. After this I'll still hang, and for nothing. My poor mamma."

"Wait!" Sarah called after the retreating figure, desperate to stop the man, although uncertain what to say. "If you take those, we'll have no choice but to report you to the authorities. It won't take them long to track you down."

The man paused and turned his head as if considering her words.

Emboldened, she added, "If you leave without them, we shan't tell a soul you were ever here."

He turned all the way around to face them. Then began walking back to the cave.

Sarah's momentary relief faded with each step that brought the man nearer, and she saw more clearly the look on his face.

The murderous look.

"How good of 'ee to think of me," he said, lip curled. "And yer right; can't have 'ee blabbing to the authorities. Not till I've a chance to unload these lovelies." He stepped inside the cave and set the bag at his feet.

Before Sarah could guess what the man intended, he gripped her wrist and twisted her arm behind her.

Mr. During made to lunge forward, but the brute stopped him with a fierce command. "Stop or I'll slit 'er throat."

Sarah felt cold steel against her neck.

Mr. During raised both hands in surrender and stepped back.

"Good. Yer cleverer than 'ee look."

The smuggler then wrenched Sarah's other hand behind her back and began tying them together with a length of thin, coarse rope. "Never reckoned there'd be a lady present, so only brought enough for one. Good job there's a hook here, driven into the stone, see? Handy for securing a boat fer unloading, or a sunken line o' barrels, or a loose-lipped female."

Securing the rope, he said to During, "Don't like killing ladies if I can help it. But if she stays here long enough, the tide'll do the deed fer me."

Terror jolting her, Sarah shouted, "Go, Selwyn, run! Get help."

He blinked, expression tormented, then his pale face cleared with resolve. "I shan't leave you alone with him."

"Ain't we gallant all of a sudden-like?" the smuggler scoffed. "Truth is, she ain't getting free and neither are 'ee." He lifted his knife, then paused. "First let's move this foine bag out o' the way, so it don't get stained with blood." He bent and picked up the case again, moving it just outside the mouth of the cave.

Then he turned back and raised his knife.

Bile burned the back of Sarah's mouth. *Lord, have mercy.* This was the end unless God chose to intervene. Her family would grieve her loss, but they would manage without her, despite the self-importance she'd worn like a medal of valor since Papa's death. *God, forgive me. Please accept my soul for Jesus's sake. . . .*

She saw the fatalistic fear on Mr. During's face and closed her eyes to block out the harrowing look of pain about to replace it.

A tumult whipped the air. Running feet. A shove, and a grunt.

Eyes flying open, Sarah was stunned to see a whirling figure, and before she could fathom how he managed it, James Thomson had shoved the smuggler aside, taking advantage of his step out of the cave to leap inside, inserting himself between them and the man. He now stood facing their attacker, sword drawn.

Mr. Thomson's face was beaded with sweat, his expression rigid with determination. Even so, Sarah glimpsed fear in his eyes. And who could blame him?

She braved a look at the smuggler, expecting vile curses or a warrior's charge at this new opponent.

Instead, the man howled with laughter.

"Now, this is rich, I'm blowed! Let me guess . . . Yer dandyship were fencing champion of yer hoity-toity gentlemen's club."

"Second place, actually."

As though a lightning strike, Mr. Thomson lunged forward, his sword whizzing down and knocking the knife from the smuggler's hand.

Then the man did curse. "You devil! You cut me hand!" He reached into his pocket and withdrew a pistol.

Mr. Thomson blanched.

"Aha! Never saw that coming, did 'ee?" The man's lips stretched in a self-satisfied leer.

"If 'ee will stand right there in front of *Dearing*, one bullet might do fer 'ee both." He cocked the gun.

Sarah glimpsed movement from behind the smuggler. Another man crept toward the mouth of the cave. Friend or foe? He raised his arm and brought down some weapon onto the smuggler's head with a thwack.

He crumpled to the ground.

With the bulky man no longer blocking her view, Sarah saw his unexpected assailant was none other than Antoine Bernardi.

Mr. Thomson looked at him in relief. "Good timing."

The chef raised the large, club-like pestle in his hand. "And here you told me a kitchen tool would be useless."

"I was wrong. Thank you, Antoine."

"Yes, thank you both," Selwyn said, voice shaky. He did not, however, meet either man's eyes. Instead he looked down at his wet shoes, shame coloring his face.

The chef picked up the knife that had fallen from the smuggler's hand, and with it, cut Sarah free as easily as cutting twine from a trussed hen.

"Th-thank you," Sarah whispered, rubbing the tender flesh of her wrists until something pulled her attention away.

Another man appeared from the opposite side of the cave, and Sarah tensed, hoping it wasn't Mr. Mutter or some other accomplice.

Relief whooshed out of her. Mr. Cordey. His gaze darted wildly around the cave—from her, to the men, to the smuggler limp on the sand. Apparently assured of no imminent threat, he bent over, hands on his knees, breathing hard.

"All right, maid'n?" he asked between pants.

Sarah opened her mouth to answer but found it difficult to speak between chattering teeth. The rest of her began to shake as well. Mr. Bernardi held her elbow in support.

"Y-yes."

Mr. Thomson asked him, "Did you run all the way from Sidmouth?"

He shook his head. "Came by boat, soon as Bibi told me where 'ee went. Hoped to get 'ere sooner but an ill wind slowed us down."

Punch and Tom Cordey appeared from the west as well, red-faced and tense, fish-gutting knives in their hands. *Goodness.* They were clearly familiar with the smuggler's reputation.

Mr. Cordey nodded to Thomson and Bernardi. "You lot

got the jump on 'im, I see. Well done." Mr. Cordey knelt at the fallen man's side and felt for a pulse at his neck. "He'll live." He turned to his sons. "Help me carry 'im to his boat afore he comes to."

Next Emily tentatively crept to the mouth of the cave, her frightened gaze traveling over the scene. Seeing the fallen man, her eyes widened. She ran forward, taking her sister's hands.

"Oh, Sarah! I was so worried. Are you all right?"

"What are you doing here?"

"It's due to Miss Emily we're here at all," Mr. Thomson said. "She's the one who told us what was going on and decided to come after you."

"Did you?" Sarah embraced her. "You should not have put yourself in danger."

"Mr. Thomson insisted I wait up the beach, out of harm's way. If things went badly, I was to return to town for help."

"Things did go badly," Mr. During muttered.

"They could have gone far worse," Sarah reminded him. "True."

Sarah turned back to Mr. Cordey as his sons secured the smuggler's wrists with the rope in case he should awaken and put up a fight. Thankfully fishermen were skilled in knot tying.

"What are you going to do with him, Mr. Cordey?"

"Don't 'ee worry, maid'n. I'll not take his life. He has a missus and little'uns. I'll set 'im adrift without oars or sail. The current will return 'im to shore, but he'll have time to repent of his ways till then. At least, I hope so."

"You won't take him to the authorities?"

"Not on yer life, maid'n. These three'll leave soon," he said, nodding to the visitors. "But we live here. This rascal's got powerful friends and many accomplices. If we had 'im arrested, he'd get off anyway, and might come lookin' fer revenge. I don't want to put yer kin, nor mine, in that kind of danger."

Sarah's throat tightened at the thought. She said, "I understand. Thank you for coming to our aid. I know it was a risk to do so."

He nodded, then said, "Couldn't let anythin' happen to me best customer, could I?" Yet his teasing bravado did not erase the anxious lines from his face.

When the Cordeys left, Sarah turned to the others. "Get the case and let's go."

After retrieving it, the group hurried away, Emily linking arms with Sarah to lend her strength for the walk back.

28

The room was made quite dark, except for candles placed on
very high candlesticks. . . . In the middle were two coffins—
one of which held the body and the other THE HEART.
—Charlotte Cornish, letter from Sidmouth

When they returned to Sea View, the five of them—
Emily, the three men, and a bedraggled-looking
Sarah—gathered in the office with the door
closed to discuss what to do next.

"How should I proceed?" Mr. During asked, pacing in agitated strides across the room.

Emily sent Sarah a questioning look. Emily supposed they
ought to advise him to confess, much as she and Georgiana
had urged Billy Hook to confess after shooting Woolbrook's
window. In this case, however, Mr. During's life was in real
danger. If his intention to steal royal property was discovered,
he might be hanged or at the very least transported, and what
would happen to his mother and sisters then?

He covered his face with his hands. "I deserve whatever is
coming to me."

"But you decided not to go through with it, remember?" Sarah prompted.

"Only because you talked me out of it."

"And you let me. I think you had already realized it was a mistake and were ready to return the candlesticks."

He sighed. "I was."

She glanced at the others, then back to Selwyn. "May I tell them why you did it?"

He nodded, shame again coloring his face and neck.

She turned to Emily and the men. "Mr. During learned his mother and young sisters have been sent to debtors' prison. He has not been able to send his wages in some time and was desperate to help them somehow."

"Ah." Mr. Thomson lifted his chin in understanding.

"Sorry, Selwyn," Bernardi said. "That is dreadful."

Sarah laid a hand on the man's sleeve. "I said I would help you, and I shall certainly try. We will think of a plausible explanation."

He shook his head. "I am no good at fabrication. If someone is going to come up with a story it won't be me."

Mr. Thomson turned to Emily. "This is a challenge for our resident author."

Emily met his gaze. "Very well. It seems simple to me. Mr. During had taken the candlesticks out to polish them, readying them for the day's solemn use. A local criminal sneaked into the house, held Mr. During at gunpoint—or knifepoint, take your pick—and made off with them. His colleagues joined forces and pursued the man. You two caught up with him in a sea cave, overpowered him with a sword—"

"A kitchen pestle, actually."

"We shall not mention that detail. Stretches credulity."

"And where is this criminal now, supposedly?" Mr. During asked.

"He got away in his boat, of course. We never learned his name, so authorities shan't be able to find him or question him. A pity, to be sure, but at least the royal treasure is secure."

"You *are* good at this," Mr. Thomson said, looking at her with admiration.

Sarah said, "I don't think we need to go into all that. Captain Conroy is angry about the unlocked chest, but he might not yet know about the missing candlesticks. We simply have to plausibly explain their absence." She looked down at Selwyn's feet. "And perhaps his ruined shoes."

"Good point." Emily tapped her chin. "Something closer to the truth, then. You were . . . polishing a pair of candlesticks in our workroom when a letter came for you. When you learned about your family's dire predicament, you were shocked and upset. You left the candlesticks there and went for a walk on the beach to clear your head and think how best to help them."

Bernardi nodded. "Maybe then he'll pay your wages."

During shook his head. "The captain will still be furious that I left the plate chest unlocked."

Sarah said gently, "You could admit to a brief lapse of judgment. And perhaps this would be a good time to resign from that position—to avoid such temptation in the future."

"You're right, of course."

Mr. Thomson said, "We will go with you to confront Conroy and the general and demand your back wages. Once you explain your family's situation and we all lend our voices, there is every chance they will comply."

"We *all*? Does that mean Mr. Bernardi will accompany us?" Selwyn looked hopefully at the chef.

Antoine Bernardi shrugged. "Why not? In for a penny, in for a pound."

Mr. Thomson asked, "Will you go with us as well, ladies? Another witness or two might help our case."

Emily looked at her sister, her hair fallen from its pins, skirt hem damp and stained green with seaweed, her usually straight posture slumped with fatigue. "I think Sarah has faced enough frightening men for one day. But I will go with you, if you think it will help."

Privately, Emily was not keen to face an angry Captain Conroy again, but at least she would do so with James Thomson by her side.

When they reached Woolbrook Cottage a short while later, James quietly let them into the house, holding the door wide for Mr. During, who carried the plate chest.

As they entered the vestibule, Captain Conroy's angry voice rang out. "I don't know where he is, but find him!"

"Aye, sir."

A man in uniform exited the morning room—an officer she did not recognize. On his heels came Captain Conroy.

Seeing them there, both men stopped abruptly.

"Speak of the devil." Conroy's eyes narrowed. "Her Royal Highness told me there should be four silver candlesticks. I was about to send out a search party."

"No need, sir." Though visibly straining under its weight, During lifted the chest higher. "They are right here."

Conroy dismissed the officer and gestured them inside.

A moment later, Emily found herself once more in the Woolbrook Cottage morning room, which Captain Conroy evidently used as his personal office. She again felt called to account, even as she reminded herself that she had done nothing wrong. The captain glowered at her, perhaps at her presumption in being there at all, and then turned to Mr. During.

"Well, what have you got to say for yourself?"

"I am sorry I left the chest unlocked and two items not

where they should have been when you called. I deeply regret my lapse in duty."

The captain gestured toward the chest in During's arms. "The other two candlesticks are in there?"

"Yes, sir. Miss Summers told me the duchess requested them. I believe you will find the pair well polished and in excellent condition."

"I should hope so. Let's see them."

Selwyn During set the chest on the desk, unlocked it, and opened the lid. With gloved hands he lifted out the gleaming candlesticks, setting them almost reverently on the desk.

Conroy rose and bent close to inspect them.

"Is that sand in the well here?"

"Sand? Where?" During lunged forward, yanking his polishing cloth from his coat pocket.

Mr. Bernardi improvised. "Probably only a bit of residue from the polish, I imagine."

"Hmm. So where were you?" Conroy straightened. "I trust you have a good reason for leaving the chest unlocked and unattended?" The man's black eyes bore into his.

Selwyn quailed. "I . . . um . . ." He swallowed and looked to the others.

Emily spoke up. "As you can see he is still shaken. The truth is, Mr. During received alarming news about his family. Is that not right?"

"Y-yes. I . . ." During faltered, then cleared his throat and began again with resolve. "I am ashamed to say my mother and sisters have been sent to debtors' prison. I had been helping them, sending them what I could of my wages, but as you know we have not been paid in some time."

Emily said, "When he learned of this, he was justifiably distraught. He left the candlesticks he'd been polishing and walked down to the beach, trying to think of what to do."

"A moment of madness, that's what it was," Mr. During said. "I was that desperate and not thinking clearly. I was ever so relieved when my two colleagues and Miss Summers came to find me and bring me back . . . to my senses."

Conroy glared at Bernardi and Thomson. "This true?"

After the slightest hesitation, James nodded. "He has been distraught, yes. Certainly you can understand, given the circumstances."

"No, I *don't* understand. I would never abandon my post or neglect my duty for any reason."

"Even if your wife and children were in danger?"

The man's eyes hardened. "Even then."

Mr. Bernardi offered, "I am sure Mr. During will never do the like again. Will you, Selwyn?"

"No. No, I won't."

Clearly skeptical, Conroy harrumphed.

"Actually, sir," During blurted, "I duly resign my place as keeper of the plate. I must return to London as soon as may be and help my family."

Captain Conroy frowned. "Your resignation is not accepted. At least not yet. Stay for the next few days, as we will be receiving many high-ranking officers and other visitors and will need all the help we can get."

Mr. During blinked in surprise. "I . . . will stay for a few days, if I am needed, but after that I must return to London."

Mr. Thomson asserted, "To that end, Captain, I respectfully insist that Mr. During be paid all the wages owed to him, as the delay in payment has contributed to his family's financial ruin."

"You insist, do you?"

Mr. Thomson lifted his chin and met his superior's gaze. "Yes, sir."

Conroy shook his head. "You talk of money at such a time?

When your master lies dead in the next room and his widow grieves, finding comfort only in her infant daughter?"

"Yes. At precisely this time," Mr. Thomson replied. "For Mrs. During is grieving as well, and justifiably worried for the future of her daughters, and we are all equal in God's sight."

"Are we indeed? That's the sort of radical thinking that led to the French Revolution."

"I don't want revolution, Captain—merely for During to receive the wages he's due, so he may help his family."

Again Conroy harrumphed, suspicious eyes raking over one face and then the next.

"Something is off here. I smell a rat." He swiveled to Emily. "And why are you here, Miss Summers? Standing before me to defend the cause of another misbehaving lad. The last one was guilty, but you got him off by playing on the duke's sympathy. Do you think to try your wiles on me?"

Mr. Thomson stepped forward and faced the captain squarely, eyes glinting with suppressed anger. "Captain, may I remind you that Miss Summers is a lady and has done nothing to deserve your biting sarcasm. If you wish to cut down someone, let it be one of us. Miss Summers is not under your command for you to treat in such an ungentlemanlike manner."

"You forget yourself, Thomson."

James's jaw clenched. "Not I, sir."

Emily thought quickly, eager to alleviate the tension. "Come, everyone. This is a sad, difficult time and emotions are running high. Let us not quarrel. As you reminded us, Captain, the duchess awaits these candlesticks, no doubt eager to see arrangements completed for her husband to lie in state."

Conroy scowled at her and for a moment longer his black eyes shot daggers at all four of them. Then the door opened, and the duchess herself appeared, eyes red from weeping, her eight-month-old daughter in her arms.

"Captain . . . ?"

The men bowed and Emily immediately curtsied, but Her Royal Highness's red-rimmed eyes latched on to the gleaming candlesticks. "Ah, *gut.*"

As his gaze shifted to the duchess, Conroy's glower evaporated, and his demeanor became obsequious and almost . . . caring. "Yes, they are here. Now we may finish readying the room."

He grasped a tall candlestick in each hand and followed the duchess out.

The others took advantage of the interruption and quickly retreated.

Plans for the duke's removal from Sidmouth and funeral were changed by yet more grievous news. His father, King George III, died less than a week after his son. His Majesty's death and funeral taking precedence, Prince Edward's was therefore postponed.

It was a strange, somber time. King George had been ill for years. He was eighty-one years old. His death should not have been a shock or even a surprise.

Yet it was.

He had been king for almost sixty years. Most people alive had never known another monarch. Yes, his eldest son had reigned as Prince Regent since his father had been declared mentally unfit to rule, yet even so the king remained a fixture in people's hearts.

God save the king.

Affectionately called "Farmer George" because of his simple

tastes and interest in farming, King George had long been their absentee leader, their benevolent grandfather, their comfort and anchor during dark times. And he was gone.

Of course there were a few scoffers—mostly young people—who muttered "Good riddance" or "Down with the monarchy," but most people were regretful, nostalgic, and respectful. They viewed the king as a man of sincere Christian faith and moral piety who took his title "Defender of the Faith" far more seriously than the Prince Regent was ever likely to do.

Remembering the fortune-teller's prophecy that this year two members of the royal family would die, Emily felt she had been struck an even more personal blow, forced to consider the woman's words once more. *"You shall break your heart. Lose it . . . utterly."*

Two members of the royal family had died. And Emily had broken her heart over her first love—had lost him once and for all, even if by her own choice.

Another thought struck her. Was she destined to break her heart all over again when James Thomson left? Because of the duke's death, his wife and entire retinue would be leaving soon, not staying through the rest of the winter as originally planned. And who knew where James's next assignment might take him?

A small voice whispered in her mind, *God knows.*

The simple words bolstered her and reminded Emily that the old woman did not hold her life in her hands. God did.

You, heavenly Father, are the only one who knows my future. Help me to trust you with it.

On the last day of January, Prince Edward, the Duke of Kent, lay in state in Woolbrook Cottage. The public would be allowed to come and pay their respects. Most of the citizens of Sidmouth and its environs were expected to attend.

That morning, a long and somber line of people gathered along Glen Lane, waiting to file past the coffin.

The Summers and Hutton families dressed in black gowns or black arm bands and joined the queue. Emily was touched to see the major's friend from India, Armaan Sagar, waiting to pay his respects as well. Fran Stirling was there, walking arm in arm with Mr. Farrant, as well as many other friends and neighbors.

Emily also saw Mr. Marsh, who stepped close to her and said, "Good news, Miss Summers. A project dear to us both is at the printer! And not a moment too soon."

She glanced around to see if anyone had heard and answered in a lower voice. "I am glad. I hope that means it required only light editing?"

A strange gleam shone in his eyes. "Yes, yes. Very light. I found only a few sections lacking—nothing a few strokes of blue ink could not address."

"Oh no. I am sorry you found it lacking."

"Don't be. Your work surpassed my expectations. But you know I had to add my own flourishes!"

He grinned at her and then joined the queue.

As they waited, huddling close against the chilly air, Emily recalled Prince Edward's cheerful round face, his kindness to her, and his affection for his baby girl, and she felt warm tears gather and run down her cold cheeks.

The line moved slowly forward, and eventually Emily and her family reached the door and shuffled inside, which was a welcome relief from the cold. James Thomson stood across the entry hall, talking quietly to a uniformed guard. Noticing them, he excused himself and joined the Summers ladies, walking with them through the house.

The room where the duke lay was quite dark, hung with heavy black cloth that excluded the light of day, and lit by wax tapers on familiar silver candlesticks.

In the middle of the room, raised on trestles, was a coffin more than seven feet long and three feet wide, covered with a crimson velvet pall. Brass plates on each side were engraved with the duke's name and titles. A splendid plume of ostrich feathers adorned the head of the coffin, while three smaller plumes graced each side.

As Emily's eyes adjusted to the dim light, she realized there was a second coffin as well, which she assumed held the duke's heart. Having one's heart buried separately was not all that uncommon among royalty and the aristocracy. Even poets sometimes requested that their hearts be buried in a place they had enjoyed during life. Still, seeing two coffins was strangely unsettling. She wondered if his heart would be sent to wherever his former mistress lived, or perhaps to his wife's beloved Coburg.

Whatever the case, the sight also made Emily ponder. Not that she would ever request such a thing, but theoretically, where would she want her heart buried?

Not long ago, she would have known the answer to that question. Her heart should be returned to May Hill.

But now? Her heart, broken or not, no longer belonged there. She was not yet certain where it did belong.

As Emily passed the coffin, she made no effort to hold back her tears. Over a lump in her throat, she whispered, "You shall be missed."

Beside her in the darkness, James Thomson took her hand.

29

Set it on a clear fire, but be careful it does
not blubber and boil. When you perceive it
rise, it must be stopped immediately.
—Joseph Bell,
A Treatise On Confectionary

The next day, while Sarah was in the kitchen helping
Jessie and Mrs. Besley tidy up after breakfast, Mr.
Bernardi came and found her belowstairs.

"Miss Summers, might I have a private word?"

Glancing up and seeing his intent expression, nerves prickled through her. *Oh dear.* She noticed Jessie and Mrs. Besley share knowing looks.

Not trusting her voice, Sarah managed a nod. He gestured her into the nearby workroom and followed her inside.

Once there, he tucked his hands behind his back and glanced around.

"You and I have spent a good deal of time together in this room, have we not? Much of it inspired by our shared love of pastry."

Again Sarah nodded. She was struck by how clean-shaven

he was. His side-whiskers and eyebrows were unusually well-groomed. Even his ears and nose hairs had been trimmed.

He fastened his gaze on her and cleared his throat. "You may remember I told you I sometimes long to open an establishment of my own, to settle down in one place?"

"Yes . . . ?"

"We spoke of it at the market, near Broadbridge's."

"I remember."

"And now your friend has decided to marry and sell the boarding house. Is that not amazing timing? Might that not seem like . . . fate?"

"I will be sorry to see her go."

"Yes, yes, but she is not going far. She mentioned her intended lives less than two miles away."

Sarah nodded weakly, knowing her response had been little more than an evasion. Blood roared in her ears, making his voice seem as though coming from a great distance. Her palms perspired and dread—yes, dread—churned in her stomach. Why had she allowed things to progress to this point? Had she given him reason to believe she was interested in him romantically?

"I have been thinking," he went on. "And I have a proposal for you. I thought I might buy the place and become *chef de maison* of my own establishment. I could not do it alone, however. I know how to cook for large parties, but I have no experience with the lodging side of things. You do. Together, we would make an excellent team, do you not think?"

Sarah blinked, thoughts whirling then shuddering to a halt. Was this not a marriage proposal, then, but a business arrangement?

She swallowed. "I already have my hands full with Sea View. My mother and sisters help, of course, yet I still manage much of the day-to-day."

"Well I know it. Yet you also find time to bake, and go to market, and do other tasks I could perform. And you would not be far away, if your mother and sisters needed you for some reason. After a year or two, we might take the profits, go somewhere more fashionable like Bath or Brighton, and open a bigger place."

Sarah stared at him. "What exactly are you proposing? Are you asking me to be your business partner?"

"Well, yes. And more, if you are willing. I realize we have not known one another long, so I would not push for . . . that . . . yet. I admire you, as I think you know. You have many excellent qualities, and I think, or at least hope, that you like me, a little."

Sarah drew a long, shaky breath. "Thank you, Mr. Bernardi. I am aware of the compliment you pay me. But I could not accept your offer. For one thing, as you say, we are not long acquainted, and while we . . . like each other, that is not enough."

"In time, I—"

She held up her hand to forestall his rebuttal. "There is also the fact that I will be needed here for the foreseeable future. The Duke of Kent's death might cast a pall over Sidmouth. Visitors could drop off. My family may need my help more than ever."

He ducked his head, then looked up at her from beneath his dark fringe. "That is not the real reason you object."

"Well, I . . ."

"Do you view a pastry chef as beneath your station in life? I would not have thought it, when you have opened your own home to guests and even work in the kitchen."

Sarah thought about making more excuses or asking for time to think it over. The proposal was unexpected, after all. But that, she knew, would be cowardly, and would only postpone what would be a difficult answer to give at any time. Delaying would allow him to hope, which would be cruel or, at least, unfair.

For a moment, she lifted her eyes, forcing herself to hold his gaze. She saw a trace of nervousness in his expression, and perhaps the anticipation of rejection, but not, she thought, deeper emotions. He did not even pretend to love her, so she guessed he would recover from this disappointment rather quickly.

She said, "The life of a boarding-house keeper has never been something I aspired to. We have merely done what we've had to do to keep our family together. Nor can I deny that my mother would be somewhat disappointed by such an alliance. Yet that is not why I cannot accept your offer. As I mentioned, I was once engaged, and would be married now, had my intended not died. I don't claim it was an earth-shattering passion, but we loved one another without a doubt. I like you. I admire your skill and loyalty to your friends and family. But if I ever marry, it will be for love."

He screwed up his mouth. "If I had said I was in love with you . . . If I had asserted that, instead of being more honest, might you have agreed?"

Sarah managed a tremulous smile. "You are not so accomplished an actor."

He looked away with a wince.

She said, "I am glad you were honest with me, for it made it easier to be honest in my answer. You have not lost your heart here in Sidmouth, but there is every chance you may do so where next you go. For there are other practical, hardworking women in the world, and other establishments for sale. Perhaps you may find one closer to your parents one day."

He shot her a look. "You are telling me not to buy Broadbridge's."

"I don't presume to tell you what to do, but in all honesty, I cannot see you being happy there. Your talent for grand cuisine and masterful sugar work would be wasted. I cannot believe you would be content to poach kippers and fry eggs, even for a year or two, with the highlight of the week being a Sunday roast with boiled potatoes, and perhaps a humble rice pudding for dessert, which is what the patrons of Broadbridge's would expect."

He frowned, a shudder passing over his frame. "You are trying to lessen the sting of your rejection."

"True. But let me tell you where I can see you. I can picture you in that small hotel you mentioned, perhaps in Mayfair, with a fashionable restaurant that serves fine French and Italian cuisine."

Again, he looked off into the distance, and this time his eyes shone. He nodded slowly. "Yes. I can see that too."

With the duke's removal from Sidmouth postponed, the staff members at Sea View had time on their hands. As a distraction from grief and idleness, James gave Georgiana another fencing lesson. Emily went up to the nursery to watch and cheer on her sister, whose skill was rapidly improving. Even so, her gaze returned most often to Mr. Thomson, his masterful wielding of a foil reminding her yet again of his heroic rescue in the cave.

When the practice bout ended, Georgiana let out a loud exhale and announced, "I'm going down for the biggest glass of lemonade I can find. Anyone else?"

"You go ahead," Emily said. "You've earned it."

When she had gone, Emily regarded Mr. Thomson anew. "I meant to say something earlier. But with everything else going on, I have not. Doing what you did—standing up to that dangerous man and rescuing Sarah and Mr. During—that was very brave."

James shrugged. "In truth, I did it for you. I knew how much it would devastate you if anything happened to one of your sisters."

Warmth rushed through her. "You are right. And I am deeply grateful."

"I was also terrified, to be honest," he added. "Yet in the moment, instinct and training took over, thank God."

"You were amazing. You put yourself between them and a smuggler brandishing a knife."

"I may be somewhat out of practice with the sword, but I felt I might be able to fight off a man with only a knife. But when he drew a pistol . . ." James puffed his cheeks and blew out a breath. "I was never so relieved as when Bernardi struck him from behind. He is the one who truly saved the day."

Emily shook her head. "He would never have got close enough had you not taken on the smuggler first. Sarah said you struck the knife from his hand."

"That the maneuver worked surprised even me."

"You are too modest, James Thomson."

"I suppose that is what comes of being a younger so—"

"Don't say it!" Emily interjected, palm raised. "You must stop limiting yourself by your birth order. You are far more than a younger son. You are a strong, humble man willing to risk his own comfort and safety to help others. Those are rare, valuable qualities. Do you not know it?"

His voice lowered. "I begin to, when you say it."

She met his gaze and gave him a slow smile. "Then I will keep saying it until you fully believe it for yourself."

He returned her smile, eyes glimmering with pleasure as he gazed into hers. Then he took a step closer, his focus lowering to her mouth. Emily's chest tightened, and she suddenly felt light-headed.

"Emily," he breathed, looking intently into her face.

Her heart tingled at his use of her Christian name.

"Y-yes?"

He moved closer yet, his forehead near hers, his nose even nearer. She was tempted to angle her face and lean up.

In a husky voice, he began, "How I wish . . ."

When he did not finish, she prompted softly, "What do you wish?"

For a moment longer, he wavered near, his eyes moving from her mouth to her eyes and back again. Then he drew a ragged breath and retreated a step. "I wish we were free."

"I am," Emily quickly replied.

He looked at her in surprise. "Are you? Are you truly over Charles?"

Emily nodded. "And no one is more astonished than I am. I loved him for years, but I realize now it was a schoolgirl sort of love. And I am not sure he ever fully loved me. He certainly did not approve of me, even before Claire's misstep. I laughed too loudly and spoke my opinions too freely. Nor did he care a whit about my ambitions or talents, such as they are."

She managed a small grin, but he remained serious.

"Perhaps I should have said, I wish we were *both* free."

She blinked up at him. "Are you not?" Emily's stomach clenched tight. "Are you still thinking of Miss Moulton? Or is there another woman?"

He pressed his lips together and said dryly, "There is only one other woman. The Duchess of Kent, who relies on me. Though less so, since her brother's arrival. Regardless, I am not free. I am bound to earn my own living. I am expected to leave here soon and go where the duchess goes—or wherever my next position takes me."

"I knew that, yet I thought . . . maybe things had changed now the duke is gone?"

He shook his head. "If I were the firstborn, perhaps."

She opened her mouth to again protest, but he laid a gentle finger on her lips. "I say it *only* because then I would have the freedom to marry and the means to support a wife. I would not be beholden to an employer. Nor required to move far away from here, and far away from you."

Tears stung Emily's eyes, and she swallowed a sour draught of self-pity. She could not marry Charles and she could not marry James. Was she destined to be alone?

Something Prince Edward said to her echoed through her mind. *"You will discover that you shall have more than one chance at love in this life."*

Emily fervently hoped he was right.

30

The Poor's Friend Society has sustained an irrepa-
rable loss in the death of his late Royal Highness
the Duke of Kent, who had most cheerfully sub-
scribed, and consented to become its patron.
—*The Beauties of Sidmouth Displayed*

Over the next few days, Sarah and her sisters watched
as an impressive contingent of troops assembled in
Sidmouth, preparing to carry the duke to his final
resting place.

With the royal party's departure imminent, Sarah began to
worry in earnest. They still had not been paid for the men's
stay at Sea View—a stay of a month and a half. Her family
had accumulated bills they could not pay for all the meat and
groceries purchased for meals, additional fuel expenses, and
other outlays.

Sarah discussed the problem with Mamma, who advised
gently broaching the subject with Mr. Thomson. Sarah did
so, feeling uncomfortable all the while.

"I hate to raise the subject of money at such a time," she
said, "and I realize everyone is preparing to leave, but I don't
wish our bill to be overlooked in all the busyness."

"Nor I," Mr. Thomson agreed. "I will talk to General We-therall before he departs. Unfortunately, Captain Conroy is insisting the duchess will need all her husband's remaining funds. He says we'll send payments later, but I fear *later* could be *never* due to current financial difficulties."

"Our financial situation is difficult as well," Sarah admitted, embarrassment heating her face.

He nodded gravely. "I understand and will do my best."

Unlike the rest of the duke's retinue, Mr. Thomson had been asked to stay on a few days longer to see to any remaining visitors or late-arriving correspondence, and then to close up Woolbrook securely and return the keys to the property agent.

Emily was clearly relieved at this development and no doubt wished he could put off his departure far longer. Aware of the bond that had developed between the two, Sarah could not blame her.

Mr. Bernardi, however, would be leaving with the other members of staff. He'd begun packing up his tools in the kitchen and workroom, and Sarah went in to ask if she could be of any assistance—and to surreptitiously make sure he did not mistakenly take anything that belonged to Sea View, like their remaining store of sugar.

"Need any help?" she offered.

In the act of packing his wooden pestle, he lifted it and mimed delivering another blow.

Sarah shied away.

"Sorry. Too soon? I suppose I should not joke about such a thing." He packed a few other utensils into his handled bag, then looked up at her once more. "I have been thinking. Cooking for those old folks at the poor house . . . That was satisfying indeed."

"I am glad to hear you say so."

"How about one final feast before we all leave? There are still plenty of ingredients."

"Really?" The offer surprised her. "That would be splendid."

"You will assist me? One last time?"

She smiled indulgently, pleased he would ask after she'd declined his other offer. "Of course I will. Happily."

"Excellent." Mr. Bernardi stopped what he was doing and set about planning a menu that would be delicious *and* make good use of the remaining stores of food at Fortfield Terrace and Woolbrook Cottage. There was no sense in letting it go to waste.

Sarah assisted where she could, fetching utensils and cooking pots for him. She also made a trip to the grocer in the eastern town for a few ingredients they did not have on hand, although it meant another charge on their account.

On her way back, she stopped at Mrs. Novak's home to invite the recovering cook to join them for the meal.

Mrs. Novak quickly accepted and said she would contribute something as well. Sarah was worried Mr. Bernardi might scoff at the woman's offering, which was likely to be rather humble.

"How kind of you. But there is no need. Mr. Bernardi is taking care of everything."

"I insist. I must bring my famous soup."

"Are you equal to all that chopping and stirring?"

"My granddaughter will help. She can stand at the stove for me. Only my ankle pains me. Hands work tolerably well. In fact, I hope to be back to cooking for the dear souls soon. For now, I can at least manage some soup."

Sarah bit back further protests. "Very well. I am sure we shall all enjoy it."

Later, Sarah let her family know that they were to have a final feast at the poor house. She insisted Mamma join them and invited the major and Viola as well.

Mr. During was packing to leave for London when she stopped by his room. "What do you say, Mr. During? Would you like to set one more table before you go?"

He consulted his watch. "Sadly, I must decline. I must finish my packing here, and then I promised the captain I would polish all the silver we used at Woolbrook to ensure we leave everything in as pristine condition as we found it. Could take several hours, and my coach leaves first thing in the morning. But if you give me a few minutes, I might yet contribute to the cause."

Mr. During folded linen serviettes into rose shapes and handed her a low arrangement of silk flowers he had made with his own time and funds.

"Thank you, Mr. During. I will return them before you go."

"Oh, and take my advice and bring extra candles. Nothing like candlelight to add a festive air."

"I shall. You will say good-bye before you leave tomorrow?"

"If you are up that early."

"I think all of Sidmouth shall be up early to witness the procession."

Later, at the poor house, they added a second table to make room for the extra guests and spread one long cloth over them both.

Emily laid the table with help from Georgiana, setting out extra candles as well as Mr. During's rose-folded serviettes and the silk centerpiece.

When the residents gathered, they again exclaimed over the table. "Beautiful!"

Viola came in, pushing Mrs. Novak in a rented Bath chair to keep her off her injured ankle, while the major carried a pot of her famous soup.

Mr. Bernardi eyed the pot dubiously.

"Be nice," Sarah warned under her breath.

Sarah directed the major to put the pot on the stove to keep warm. Mrs. Novak asked Viola to take her into the kitchen as well.

Clearly expecting the worst, Mr. Bernardi lifted the lid and studied the soup warily. The broth had a rich red color, similar to claret. He leaned down and took an experimental whiff.

"What do you call this?"

"I call it soup. You might call it Polish soup or even borscht."

"What gives it this unusual color? Cochineal?"

"Beetroot, of course. Fermented juice of beetroot, along with grated beets."

He made a face. "I am afraid I do not like the taste of beet-root."

She sent him a saucy grin. "You have not tasted it when *I* prepare it!" Reaching over, she handed him a spoon with a challenging lift of her wiry grey eyebrows.

He accepted the spoon, dipped a modest portion, and raised it to his lips, sipping cautiously. His eyes widened.

"But this . . . this tastes . . . good. So many flavors. What am I tasting? Clove and thyme and sweet basil?"

"As well as bacon and chicken and pork sausages."

He took a more generous spoonful, mounded with onions and celery. "But the vegetables, they have something else. . . ."

"Fried in butter before added to the pot."

"Ah. Delicious. I must have your recipe."

"I just told you. It's not written down, if that's what you mean."

"Pity." Mr. Bernardi ladled himself a bowl of the soup.

Mrs. Novak watched him with satisfaction. "It's even better served with eggs with horseradish, dipped in breadcrumbs and fried."

After another spoonful, he closed his eyes to savor and pronounced, "You, madame, should be cooking for kings and queens."

Mouth quirking, she gestured through the door to the table where the poor-house residents gathered. "I am. And today, so are you."

Together they enjoyed the meal, the residents praising the food and everyone talking and laughing and eating some more.

Sarah noticed Viola looking around the gathering with pleasure, keeping the conversation going, asking if everyone had all they needed, and now and again sharing gratified smiles with her husband. She looked very much like Mamma at the moment, reigning graciously over the table like a long-accomplished hostess.

Early the next morning, while the rest of Sidmouth was preparing to view the royal funeral procession, those at Sea View were preparing for another somber leave-taking.

The Summers family and their guests lined up in the hall to bid farewell to Selwyn During.

He bowed first before Sarah. "Again, Miss Summers, I am utterly ashamed of myself. I never in a hundred years intended to endanger you."

"I know, Mr. During."

"Danger? How were you in danger?" Georgiana asked, eyes wide.

"Never mind. I shall explain later." Though how she would, Sarah didn't know.

Sarah handed him a paper-wrapped parcel. "Here are a few baked goods for your journey. Nothing as fine as Mr. Bernardi could have made, but—"

"Not at all. I am grateful."

She had guessed the man would not want to spend money his family desperately needed to purchase meals at inns along the road.

In return he handed her the arrangement of silk flowers they had borrowed the day before, made with his own money. "I will leave these with you."

Sarah looked up at him in surprise. "Might you not wish to give the flowers to your mother?"

"I should like you to have them. A small memento of my gratitude."

"Very well. Thank you. We shall put them to good use."

Selwyn During proceeded down the line.

"Godspeed, Mr. During," Mamma said. "I will be praying for your family. May the Lord protect them until you can."

"Thank you, ma'am. That means more than you know."

Emily handed him a small book of verse. "Something to pass the time on the journey."

"Thank you, Miss Emily."

Mr. Thomson shook his hand, then handed him an envelope. "I managed to pry my back pay from the captain as well as yours."

"James, I . . . I can't accept this."

"Of course you can. If my family were in dire straits, I know you would do the same. And one more thing." Thomson handed him a folded letter. "I've taken the liberty of writing you a character reference. I hope you understand that I did not mention your time as plate keeper. But I would not wish your excellent performance as the royal family's table-decker to go unrecognized."

"I understand perfectly. And I am obliged to you."

Next Mr. Bernardi stepped forward. Had he prepared some food for his departing colleague as Sarah had? Instead, he handed over an assortment of notes and coins. "And here are my wages as well. Minus what I owe Miss Summers for sugar. I hope it will help you gain your family's release."

"Good heavens. I don't know what to say." Selwyn During's voice thickened, and tears brightened his eyes. "I am humbled and unworthy and exceedingly grateful."

Sarah felt her own eyes fill in reply.

The scene reminded her of God's amazing compassion. In His immeasurable mercy, He not only forgave His children but blessed them in ways beyond anything they could imagine or begin to deserve.

Hand pressed to his heart, Mr. During gave them a final bow, and then hurried away to catch his coach.

A short while later, Mr. Bernardi gathered his bag and va-lise, ready to join the other staff leaving Sidmouth that day.

On his way out, he stopped and gripped Sarah's hand. "Good-bye, Miss Summers. While I am sorry to be taking my leave of you, I am also grateful to you. My brief time here has made me a better man. If I open that French and Italian restaurant, you shall be the first person I invite."

"I would be most honored," Sarah replied. "All the best, Mr. Bernardi. God bless you."

After he left, she joined Emily, Georgiana, and Mr. Thomson at the hall windows to watch the many participants gather for the procession.

As the troops in their various uniforms took their places, Mr. Thomson identified them.

There were forty dragoons from Exeter, fifty yeomanry, and fifty of the king's troops. They wore black scarfs, and their caps were covered in crepe.

Next, the town band assembled, a group of local amateur musicians. The hearse and mourning coach were positioned behind them, followed by coaches to carry the duke's family and attendants.

Then the entire Sea View household, including Mr. Hornbeam, Mr. Gwilt, and the other servants, put on their coats and walked to the end of the drive to watch the royal procession from there.

Emily stood close to Mr. Thomson, wanting to draw out every possible moment by his side.

At about nine o'clock on that damp February morning, the procession began to move—first the yeomanry two by two. Then came four riders all in black, with their horses covered in black as well. Then came the town band playing the "Dead March" on bugles and trumpets, which sounded very fine indeed. Then came the mourning coach, carrying the coffin containing the heart. Then came the hearse with the Duke of Kent's arms emblazoned in gold on the side. The hearse was drawn by eight horses covered in black velvet with black plumes on their heads.

A trio of family carriages followed, the first carrying the nurse and infant princess, who gazed at the crowds with an oblivious, cheerful countenance, her little hand against the glass. The Duchess of Kent and Prince Leopold were in the second carriage, followed by John Conroy and a few others in the third.

Then came two more mourning coaches pulled by six horses each, which carried the duke's attendants. A file of soldiers marched alongside, and officers brought up the rear.

The procession came to an abrupt halt not far from Sea View. A group of men lined up to form a cordon across Glen Lane, preventing the cortège from moving forward.

"What are they doing?" Georgiana exclaimed.

Mr. Thomson muttered, "I warned Conroy something like this might happen. He said they would not dare."

"What is happening?" Mr. Hornbeam asked, eyebrows high behind his dark glasses.

Emily said, "Some men are blocking the road."

"I recognize most of them," Sarah said. "The barber, Mr. Turner. The poultryman, butcher, and greengrocer. Even Mr. Farrant."

Mr. Thomson nodded. "Tradesmen and shopkeepers who supplied the party's needs and have not been paid."

Captain Conroy leapt from the third carriage, pistol drawn.

"No!" James sprang forward and sprinted up the lane, moving quickly to put himself between the captain and the line of people who were simply demanding what they were owed.

"James, no . . ." Emily protested, hands to her mouth. He was not even armed.

The captain growled, "Out of my way, Thomson!"

Nearby, the soldiers stiffened to attention.

At that moment, General Wetherall, the comptroller, alighted from the attendants' carriage. He shouted Conroy's name and raised a staying hand. Then, with humble solicitude, he apologized and thanked the tradesmen for their forbearance. He handed James a ledger and leather pouch and assured the men Mr. Thomson would pay them what they were due.

Georgiana quietly narrated the events to Mr. Hornbeam while those watching—especially Emily—sighed in collective relief.

James waited until the captain returned to his carriage and then began paying the tradesmen. The soldiers, horses, and coaches began to move again.

A short while later, James rejoined the others, handing Sarah an envelope. "What we owe Sea View."

"Thank you."

The procession continued toward the beach and then through

the town, where the streets were lined by silent, grieving folk there to witness the melancholy parade.

After departing Sidmouth, and after three overnight stops on the way, the cortège would continue to St. George's Chapel, Windsor, where Prince Edward would be laid to rest.

When the procession had disappeared from view, everyone returned to the house. Georgiana's friend Hannah joined them, and the two younger girls went up to Georgie's room. Mamma went to her own room, Mr. Hornbeam to his, and Sarah went belowstairs with the servants to prepare a belated breakfast.

Finding herself alone in the parlour with Mr. Thomson, Emily said, "Captain Conroy is certainly ill-tempered."

"Yes. He is also unfailingly attentive to the duchess. And the truth is, the duke left her with little more than debts, and she has yet to receive permission to return to Kensington Palace. She will need a great deal of help. For all his faults, Conroy is a skilled administrator."

"It was brave of you to stand up to him again today."

"I learned from you."

"Ha ha. No, I am serious. It was good of you. And when I think of you giving Mr. During your wages!"

He shrugged. "Bernardi did as well."

"Yes, and I was impressed with you both. But mostly you, truth be told. As I said before, you, James Thomson, Esquire, are a gentleman in the best sense of that word. You are strong and honorable, gentle and brave. And that is enough for me."

His eyes kindled, and he stepped closer. Voice low, he said, "Is it?"

She nodded, heart rate accelerating. "That, and you are well-read."

His lips quirked and his gaze swept over her face—her eyes,

her cheeks, her mouth. The admiration in his deep brown eyes was evident even as his expression remained serious. He slowly leaned in, bringing his face close to hers. He glanced into her eyes again to gauge her reaction, and whatever he saw there emboldened him to lean nearer yet, his lips a hairsbreadth away.

In a throaty whisper, she teased, "I would also add *handsome*, but I don't wish for you to become vain."

He chuckled and pressed his lips to hers. All thoughts of teasing fled. The sweet pressure filled her with longing, and she returned it, kissing him back. He wrapped an arm around her, holding her close, while warmth and pleasure flooded her every inch.

Her first kiss.

She had read so many novels and poems that described a heroine rendered breathless and weak-kneed by the hero's kiss, and she had been skeptical. Emily now knew those descriptions had not been exaggerated in the least.

James finally pulled back just enough to rest his forehead against hers.

"Emily, you don't know how much . . ."

"I do know."

"I should not have kissed you. I will be here for a few more days, and then I am supposed to follow the others. I don't want to be another man who raises your hopes and then disappoints you."

Emily did not want that either. Her chest ached at the thought, her beleaguered heart beginning to crack.

31

It must have been a source of great satisfaction
to Wallis that Marsh was declared bankrupt.
—Ian Maxted in *Six Centuries
of the Provincial Book Trade in Britain*

Emily entered Marsh's Library and Public Rooms carrying the pages of Mr. Gwilt's story in a plain paper
folder. Mr. Marsh had not told her he was ready to read
it, but Emily did not want him to forget his promise now that
he was done editing the new Sidmouth guide.

When she pushed through the door, the first thing she noticed was how quiet it was. She supposed that after the recent
royal deaths, few people were interested in new novels to read.
Although she would have thought his selection of newspapers
from around the country would be much in demand at such
a time.

Stepping inside, she saw Mr. Marsh at his desk, staring off
into space, a strange look on his face.

"Good day, Mr. Marsh."

He startled at the sound of her voice.

Had he been concentrating on something so deeply that

he'd not heard her enter? On the desk before him lay a low pile of folded, printed sheets.

"That's not the new guide, is it?" she asked.

"An early proof copy. I've just approved it."

"Already?" She had thought he would allow her to review the proof first. "That was fast."

He nodded. "Paid extra to rush Denner along. I am in a hurry to start selling copies."

Emily gazed hungrily at the proof pages, eager to see her words set in type.

"May I see them?"

"Hm? Oh, why not." He pushed them across the desk. "Take them with you."

"Thank you. By the way, I brought Mr. Gwilt's story. Now that you are finished with the guide, I hoped you might have time to read it."

He sighed. "Can it not wait? I have much on my mind presently. Let us delay until the guide is printed and selling. Being a sole proprietor is taxing on so many levels."

"Oh. I see. If you need a bit more time, then of course. I will take these proof pages home to read and let you get back to work. How soon do you need them returned?"

He waved a hand. "No rush."

Emily seemed to fly home, her feet barely touching the promenade. Yes, she was disappointed not to have a chance to proofread the pages, but she was still eager to see her words in type-set form. She wondered how far along Mr. Denner was in printing the actual books. Perhaps if she found a glaring error, she could run to the print shop and request a correction before it was too late.

Reaching Sea View, she hurried into the library-office and sat at the desk, shrugging off her cloak onto the back of the chair.

She lifted the cover sheet and began to read.

There was the long, frilly title Mr. Marsh had insisted upon, now even lengthier with a few more phrases added:

> THE SIDMOUTH GUIDE
> *And a View of the Place*
> *with an accurate description of the situation, picturesque*
> *beauties, and salubrious climature of that much-admired wa-*
> *tering place and the circumjacent country within fifteen miles.*

And there, the attribution: *Printed for John Marsh at his library and public rooms.*

She had known her name would not be included, yet she still felt a bit depressed at seeing the title page in its final form.

Emily turned to the next page and saw he had added a dedication:

> To the Nobility and Gentry
> whose temporary or permanent
> residence at Sidmouth
> has contributed so greatly to its
> attractions and improvements,
> This work is most respcetfully dedicated
> by their devoted servant
> John Marsh

He had spelled *respectfully* wrong, or perhaps the printer had set it that way. She wished again he'd allowed her to proof-read it.

But as she read on, she realized with sinking heart that this was not the most jarring change or addition he had made.

After reading through the entire proof copy, sickly remorse filled Emily, and she agonized over it for hours. Mr. Wallis would not be pleased.

Emily recalled telling Sarah and Mamma about the project, explaining her name would not appear in the publication, so hopefully Mr. Wallis wouldn't discover her involvement. And Sarah had replied, *"Few things remain secret in a small town."*

Now, more than ever, Emily very much feared Sarah was right.

She tried to convince herself that she had done nothing wrong, that she had not known Mr. Marsh would make those changes. But her conscience would not be assuaged.

With a heavy sigh, she decided she must warn Mr. Wallis and try to explain before he heard it from someone else or read the guide himself.

Emily dragged her feet to the Marine Library and timidly entered the establishment for the first time in well over a month. His clerk stood assisting two gentlemen at one end of the library, while Mr. Wallis sat at his desk on the other side, bent over some work, as he often did.

Pulse tripping, she walked toward his desk.

He looked up as she approached, his customary welcoming smile absent.

"Miss Summers. I was just thinking about you."

That could be good or bad, she realized. "Oh?"

She looked at him expectantly. When he did not explain, she glanced down at the pages on his desk, hoping to forestall her confession a bit longer.

"W-what are you working on?"

"I am reading an early copy of a new book. Not officially published yet."

Heart twisting, Emily recognized the title on the unbound pages. *Oh no.*

"How did you get that?"

"The printer is a friend of mine. I send a lot of business his way. More than . . . my competitors."

"Mr. Wallis, I came here to tell you something. I hoped to tell you before you read it, but it appears I am too late." She licked dry lips. "I am afraid I helped Mr. Marsh write that."

For a moment he stared at her, expression inscrutable, while she held her breath.

Then he nodded curtly. "I thought so, but thank you for telling me."

She tucked her chin in surprise. "How did you know? Did Mr. Marsh give it away?"

"No. You did."

Surprise flashed through her once more. "I did?"

He nodded. "Or rather your words did." He turned a few pages and read, "'Bicton Church has a most pleasing and solemn appearance. The elegy of Gray must occur immediately to the mind of the spectator on contemplating its solitary and shadowy churchyard, thrown into twilight even at noonday by the masses of impeding foliage.' This is followed by a stanza of Gray's poem."

He looked up. "You cannot expect me to believe an uncultivated mercenary like Marsh wrote that."

Emily ducked her head, feeling embarrassed, chastised, and flattered in equal measures.

"I'm curious," he asked. "Why did you quote this particular stanza, when Thomas Gray himself cut it from later editions?"

Emily lifted one shoulder. "I did not wish it to be lost."

Mr. Wallis slowly nodded, a ghost of a smile on his lips. Then the smile quickly faded.

He regarded her over the top of his small spectacles. "I confess I was far less pleased with the comparisons between Marsh's library and my own. I thought you liked my humble establishment."

"I did. I do!"

"Evidence to the contrary." He flipped a few more pages and read, "'The views from the Marine Library are good, but rather inferior to those from the library of Mr. Marsh. And Wallis's shop furnishes a few books and newspapers; but labours under the disadvantages of confined space and accommodations. These considerations induced Mr. John Marsh to build a new most beautiful structure, combining the advantages of an uninterrupted view of the sea with an extensive library, furnished with every appropriate article of utility and fancy.'"

Her stomach knotted. "I did not write that. That is, some of those are my words but others have been changed. I did describe the pleasant situations and views of each library as well as their offerings, but Mr. Marsh edited the manuscript and made changes to flatter himself. I was as surprised and unhappy to read those revised sections as you no doubt were."

He studied her expression as though for sincerity and nodded once again. "My just deserts for urging Mr. Butcher to praise my library to such a marked degree in his book. I suppose it is only natural Marsh would do the same. Turnabout is fair play and all that. I must say I am relieved to learn it was not the *writer's* intention to malign me, though perhaps a bit of revenge for my failure to aid in her own publishing aspirations?"

Emily shook her head. "Revenge never crossed my mind, I assure you. Though I admit I had never even entered Mr. Marsh's establishment until after you rejected Mr. Gwilt's story. I had been trying to find the courage to ask if I might edit or proofread for you, but I had no intention of asking you to read my novel, which isn't even finished yet. When you made it clear you were not interested in my work, I lost my nerve. So I went to Mr. Marsh instead."

His brows rose in surprise. "If it was proofreading work or editing experience you wanted, I wish you would have asked me. I am weary of finding mistakes in my publications."

"Really? I have noticed a few, but I doubted you'd want me to point them out."

A corner of his mouth tipped up. "I would much prefer you to find mistakes *before* we print a thousand copies rather than after, when there is precious little I can do about it."

He hesitated, as if weighing what to say next, then began, "By the way, I would not expect to receive much work from John Marsh in future, nor a publishing offer. I have it on good authority that he is on the verge of bankruptcy."

Emily gaped. "What? Oh no."

Satisfaction glimmered in the man's eyes. "Oh yes."

Emily hurried to Marsh's establishment, anxious and queasy with concern for the man. Despite his liberties with the guidebook, she was sincerely sorry to hear his business was failing.

She found him in his library and public rooms, alone, the place emptier and more echoing than before.

"Oh, Mr. Marsh! I just heard."

"Bad news travels fast, ey?"

"Is this why you were in such a hurry to get the guidebook printed?"

He nodded. "Much good it will do me now."

"Will the sales not help you?"

"Not enough. It will be a case of too little, too late."

"Oh no. What will you do?"

He shrugged.

"I am sorry. For your sake and for the town's sake."

He sent her a knowing look. "Not for yours?"

"Yes, for my sake too. And Mr. Gwilt's."

He winced. "About that. I said I would help you, and despite everything I am not without honor." He reached into a desk drawer and withdrew a calling card. "Here is a card of a colleague of mine. I have written to him about your uncle's book. I think it will be right in his line. I will let you know when he replies."

She accepted the card. "Thank you, Mr. Marsh. I will let Mr. Gwilt know."

His usually bright eyes were dull. "I realize I have let you down. But I do have contacts. I will do all I can to help you find a publisher for your novel as well."

"That is very kind." Now if only she could, would, finally complete it!

As if reading her doubtful thoughts, he said, "Don't wait too long. Remember, nothing ventured, nothing gained." He exhaled a deep breath and stared bleakly across his prized library. "Or lost."

32

Who can be in doubt of what followed?
—Jane Austen, *Persuasion*

Emily slumped into one of the armchairs in the library-office with a weary sigh. *So much for that.* Now that Mr. Marsh was facing bankruptcy, Emily feared her publishing aspirations were at an end. They had certainly suffered a major setback. Mr. Wallis had seemed amenable to the idea of her editing or proofreading for him, but he was still not interested in publishing Mr. Gwilt's book or her own.

Yet that disappointment seemed minor in comparison with her dejection over James Thomson, who was due to leave the next day. She had seen little of him in the last few days and imagined he was busy closing up Woolbrook. She hoped he would at least say good-bye before he left.

Emily pressed a hand over her heart, trying to massage it through bone and flesh. It physically ached. Unbidden, the fortune-teller's words returned to her once more. *"You shall break your heart. Lose it . . . utterly."*

At the time, Emily had thought the words must be about Charles. Now she knew she'd been wrong, for she had utterly lost her heart to James Thomson, and that heart was indeed breaking.

She reminded herself she did not believe in such things and willed the words from her memory. The woman's prophecy was not real. Though the pain in her chest most assuredly was.

James himself came in just then, an odd expression on his face.

Emily rose and steeled herself. "Have you come to say good-bye?"

He slowly shook his head. "I am not leaving."

Her pulse leapt. "No? But I thought you were supposed to return to Kensington Palace and await reassignment."

"I was. I am resigning my post."

"W-what about your career?" she faltered. "And the duchess?"

"She will manage perfectly well with her brother and her German lady-in-waiting."

James crossed the room to stand before her. "If I learned anything from watching the duchess and her husband, it is this: When you find the love of your life, don't waste a single moment."

He lowered himself to one knee.

Emily's heart thumped hard and again she laid her hand over the spot. "Heavens . . ."

He took her other hand in his. "Emily Summers, will you marry me?"

Emily swallowed. "I . . . would like nothing more, but you told me you were in no position to marry."

"That was true, but that has since changed."

"Really? Tell me everything. But first, do have mercy on your kneecap." She tugged his hand and helped him rise.

Once on his feet, he asked, "Are you familiar with Sir Thomas Acland?"

"Vaguely. I remember you spoke with him at Their Royal Highnesses' evening party."

"Yes, and again when he and his wife called at Woolbrook during Prince Edward's illness. Sir Thomas was MP for Devon for six years and plans to stand for reelection. He is also a generous philanthropist. When we met initially, he hinted he might have a situation for me. At the time, I was not sure how serious he was, or if I was willing to leave the duke for a career in politics. But now? I went to see Sir Thomas this morning, asked if he still had a situation available, and when he said he did, I accepted."

"Would you have to work in London?"

James shook his head. "I already told him I am not interested in living in London. His country estate, Killerton House, is only thirteen miles away. A reasonable ride from Sea View. I would be based there."

"So your . . . wife would not have to leave Sidmouth?"

"Not unless she wanted to."

"And she could still write?"

"Of course. She is very talented. I plan to encourage her all I can. Who knows, perhaps the two of us might one day start a publishing company of our own."

"Oh! I like the way you think."

"And I love everything about you."

He framed her face in his hands, looked into her eyes, then leaned down and kissed her.

Ah . . . heavenly. His lips moved against hers in soft, slow, lingering caresses. Heady and sweet, and filled with promise.

He lifted his face and met her gaze once more. Low voice rumbling, he said, "You have not given me an answer."

Emily wrapped her arms around his neck, drew him toward her, and pressed her mouth to his.

At this encouragement, he angled his head to deepen the kiss.

Finally, he pulled back breathlessly once more. "Should I take that as a yes?"

"Please do. Now do please hush and kiss me again. I have waited a long time for this."

He grinned and warmly obliged her.

And Emily decided then that kissing the man you loved wasn't like poetry.

It was better.

A short while later, Emily and James went to share the news with Mamma. They found her reading a book in her room.

"Oh, Mamma! You will never guess. Mr. Thomson is staying on. He has taken a situation with Sir Thomas Acland and will soon take a wife as well."

Mamma's brow furrowed; she was clearly perplexed by the unexpected development. Then her gaze dropped to their joined hands and her brow cleared.

"Pray forgive me, Mrs. Summers," James said. "I should have sought your blessing first."

Mamma rose. "Never mind. I heartily bestow it."

"That means a great deal, ma'am. Especially as I have grown fond of you and your entire family while I've been here."

"The feeling is mutual." She reached out and pressed first his hand, then Emily's.

"You have the advantage of me there," Emily said. "As I have yet to meet your family."

Mamma asked, "They will come for the wedding, I trust?"

Tension tightened his mouth. "My mother will make every effort to be there, I know. I am less certain about my father and brothers."

Emily knew James longed to be on better terms with them and decided then and there to help him.

When they left Mamma's room, Emily took both of his hands in hers. "Let's do all we can to mend the breach."

"We can try. But don't raise your hopes too high."

Together they went into the office, where he sat and began a conciliatory letter, announcing his engagement and inviting his parents to Sidmouth to meet his bride-to-be. James asked Emily to read the draft, and she did so, offering a few suggestions, helping him as he had so often helped her.

After he had sealed it, he said, "Now we wait."

She laid a hand on his shoulder. "And pray."

He rose and said, "I will go and post this. I am sure you are eager to share the news with your sisters."

Awash with giddy happiness, Emily smiled at him. "You read my mind."

As soon as James left, Emily went to find Sarah, only to recall she'd gone to the market. Georgiana too was out. She would tell them later.

Emily was about to put on her cloak and hurry over to Westmount when Viola let herself into Sea View.

"Oh! I am so glad to see you," Emily exclaimed. "I am bursting with news."

"Tell me."

Emily grasped her hand and pulled her into the office. There, she turned and announced, "Mr. Thomson has asked me to marry him, and I have accepted."

"How wonderful!" Viola exclaimed. Then hesitation puckered her face. "Except . . . tell me you are not moving to London?"

Emily shook her head, cheeks aching from grinning so much. She told Viola about the situation with Sir Thomas Acland, adding, "So we might stay here for a time, if our guest house can spare a room. Otherwise, I suppose we could find somewhere to live between Sidmouth and Killerton—perhaps in Exeter."

"Oh, do stay here," Viola urged. "When I married, I moved only yards away. I could not bear it if you went too far."

"We shall have to see what Sarah and Mamma have to say about us living here."

"Will you marry in Sidmouth or wherever he is from?"

"Here, if Mamma has her way, although we hope his family will be able to make the trip."

Viola nodded, then said, "Speaking of weddings, you will never guess. My dear husband has finally offered to take me on a belated wedding trip."

"Oh good! I am happy for you. How soon will you go?"

"Probably in late spring or early summer."

"And where will you go? The Continent? Or somewhere closer to home?"

Viola glanced through the doorway as though to reassure herself no one was near, then said, "Actually, I was thinking of Scotland."

Emily stared at her, surprise and excitement winging through her veins. "To see Claire?"

"Well, we could not travel all the way to Edinburgh without calling on our relatives, could we? Aunt Mercer cannot object to that."

"Oh, I'd wager she can." Emily smirked, then lowered her voice. "What about Mamma? What will she say? I mean, she cannot very well forbid you—a grown woman and her husband!"

"No. Even so, I'd hate to injure her feelings."

"So what will you do?"

"I think you mean, what will *we* do. You and I and Sarah, and maybe even Georgie, will have to work together. The major and I won't travel for months yet. We have until then to convince her to change her mind."

33

He clasped me in his arms, and we kissed each other again
and again! His beauty, his sweetness and gentleness—
really how can I ever be thankful enough to have such
a husband! Oh! This was the happiest day of my life!

—Queen Victoria, diary

Mrs. Thomson quickly wrote back to accept the invitation, saying she hoped her husband would join her, but either way, she would happily visit, and looked forward to meeting her son's intended.

A week later, both of James's parents arrived at Sea View. As they alighted from their chaise, Emily and James stood side by side in the hall, ready to greet them. Emily held James's hand, knowing he was nervous about seeing his father again.

Mrs. Thomson entered first and embraced each of them with warmth and friendliness. Mr. Thomson was more aloof. He bowed to Emily and shook his son's hand rather woodenly.

After Mr. Gwilt had taken their cloaks, Emily introduced the couple to her family, and soon they all sat down to a meal together. Within hours, Emily and James's mother had formed a fond, fast bond.

Mrs. Thomson got on well with Mamma and Emily's sisters as well, chatting pleasantly over tea and wedding plans.

Emily enjoyed the visit, although she remained aware of the tension between James and his father and wished there was something she could do about it.

The night before they left, Mr. Thomson gestured James away from the others and into the library. James sent her an uncertain glance before disappearing within, the door shutting behind them.

Emily tried not to be anxious but could not help it. Was his father expressing disapproval of her or her family? Or of James's new career? Or had Edward, his eldest brother, decided to blame James for yet another of *his* misdeeds?

While the two men were absent, Mrs. Thomson promised to return for the wedding, although she sheepishly admitted she could not speak for the other members of her family.

When James and his father emerged some twenty minutes later, Emily held her breath. She was relieved to see the two men talking politely, Mr. Thomson still reserved, while his son's posture seemed less tense.

Later that evening, James took her aside and confided their conversation.

"I can hardly believe it. Father apologized. For blaming me for Arthur's accident and more. He always took Edward's side, believed his word over mine. Evidently when I was not there to serve as scapegoat these last few years, he began to grow wise to Edward's ways. I feel sorry for him, really. Yet it's also an immense relief to be exonerated at last, to have hope that our relationship might finally improve."

"I am so happy for you both. Happy for all of us."

Emily clasped his hand tight, only resisting the urge to

throw her arms around him and kiss him because their families were nearby. There would be plenty of time for kissing soon enough.

⌒

On a bright spring morning, Miss Emily Summers and James Thomson, Esquire, walked into the Sidmouth parish church in eager anticipation of their wedding.

The pews were filled with local friends and a few from May Hill, although the Parkers had sent their regrets. Major Hutton, his father, brother, and friend Armaan were there, family to the Summerses by marriage. Other guests included Mr. Hornbeam and Miss Reed, Mrs. Denby, Mr. Wallis, Fran and her new husband, and many others—even Mr. Marsh.

Emily would have loved for Claire to be there as well, but the letter she had sent inviting her to attend had gone unanswered.

There was as yet no sign of James's family. Emily hoped they were simply running late and would still come, especially now that tensions between James and his father had lessened.

Having a few minutes to spare before the service, Emily slipped into the Lady Chapel to pray.

She thought fleetingly of the three things she had once wished for: to return to May Hill and marry Charles, to be reunited with Claire, and to see her novel published. None of these things had happened, yet Emily was no longer discouraged. Instead she was filled with gratitude, and looked forward to a happy future.

James soon joined her in the side chapel. From there, he scanned the crowd, no doubt searching for his family. Emily's heart went out to him.

A few minutes before the hour, the parish clerk closed the

double doors. The wedding would soon begin without them. Emily took James's hand and gave it an apologetic squeeze.

Then the doors opened once more and James's parents entered, although neither of his brothers. There was time only to acknowledge them with nods across the nave before the first chords of organ music sounded through the church.

Emily tightened her grip on his hand and whispered, "At least your parents are here."

James nodded, exhaling in relief.

Then Viola and Fran were beside her, handing her a bouquet of flowers, straightening the silver cross around her neck, and adjusting Emily's veil.

It was time.

After the service, the new-married couple rode back to Sea View in the Huttons' carriage, which the sisters had festooned with colorful bunting.

The guests followed in carriages of their own, or by chair, or on foot, to attend the wedding breakfast.

Reaching Sea View, Taggart halted the horses, and Chown hopped down to help them alight.

A second carriage arrived after them, carrying Mrs. Besley, Lowen, Jessie, and Mr. Gwilt. Emily had insisted that their dear retainers be included in the wedding before having to hurry back to Sea View to finish laying out the banquet.

Only Antoine Bernardi, who had returned for their nuptials at James's invitation, had decided to stay behind and prepare several fine dishes for the wedding breakfast.

The new Mr. and Mrs. Thomson were the first to enter the house, and there they paused to share a deep, lingering kiss.

Realizing they were standing beneath the painting of Finderlay, Emily glanced up at her former home and found she did not feel wistful in the least.

James noticed her looking at the painting and met her gaze with a flicker of concern in his eyes.

She gave him a reassuring smile and another kiss.

James's parents soon arrived. Mrs. Thomson hurried to them with enthusiastic congratulations and embraces for them both. Mr. Thomson approached more slowly, yet he surprised them all by affectionately clapping his son's shoulder and kissing Emily's cheek.

Mrs. Thomson apologized for their tardiness and for their absent sons. She explained they had decided it would be too difficult for Arthur, an invalid, to make the journey. "And I have no idea where Edward might be," she added, with an obvious effort to sound casual. "You know how he is."

Her husband frowned and muttered, "Probably off on another gambling spree."

Mrs. Thomson's expression remained determinedly bright. "Let's not worry about that now. Today is a happy day. A celebration."

Beside her, her husband merely grunted.

The wedding breakfast was soon underway, the dining room, drawing room, and parlour filled with loved ones, delicious food, many embraces, and sincere well-wishes.

Emily surveyed the gathering with satisfaction, heartened to see so many friends and family members together. There was Fran looking pretty in a new gown and Mr. Farrant looking trussed and uncomfortable in a fine suit and tight cravat. And there were Georgie and her friend Hannah eating and laughing with Colin Hutton and his father. Nearby, Mrs. Denby chatted amiably with Mr. Hornbeam and Miss Reed.

Mr. Gwilt fluttered about, serving and smiling—a smile that widened when Mr. Wallis stopped him to ask about Parry. Sarah too remained busy as usual, refilling cups and clearing plates, until Viola took her hand and pulled her down onto the sofa to join her, the major, and Armaan, insisting she relax and enjoy herself for a while.

Then Mr. Cordey plopped down next to James's father, balancing a heaping plate of food on his knees. He pointed to the fish on Mr. Thomson's plate. "Good, ey? Caught 'im meself this mornin'."

Emily chuckled.

And through it all, Mamma presided capably over the festivities looking pleased and proud. She paused to link arms with James's mother, confiding with a girlish grin, "I am so happy. Two daughters married!"

Emily wondered which of her sisters might be next.

Later, when there was a lull in the party, James took Emily's hand and led his bride from the drawing room into the quieter hall to steal a kiss.

Finding herself standing near the painting of Finderlay once more, Emily recalled the question she'd pondered before. Where did her heart belong? Right where it was. With her family, and her husband.

Author's Note

Thank you for returning with me to the lovely town of Sidmouth on the south coast of England for book two of On Devonshire Shores. I hope you enjoyed it. I have one more full-length novel planned for the series, as well as a Christmas novella.

When I learned during my research that the Duke and Duchess of Kent and their baby daughter, the future Queen Victoria, visited Sidmouth the winter of 1819–1820 and stayed in Woolbrook Cottage (on the same lane as Westmount and fictional Sea View), I knew I wanted to include them in the novel. They arrived with too many attendants to accommodate at Woolbrook, so some of the staff were indeed lodged elsewhere. I thought it would be interesting to send a few staff members to Sea View. Much of what I've depicted is true: an extremely cold and snowy winter, the fortune-teller, the Duke of Kent's illness and ultimate death (probably caused by a chest infection complicated by extreme bloodletting), the royal funeral procession through Sidmouth, et cetera.

However, I did fictionalize and take liberties with several details. For example, the duchess, the princess, Prince Leopold, and some others actually left Sidmouth earlier in a modest procession of their own, but I decided to depict only one procession to improve pacing. Also, the tradesmen blocking the cortège until they were paid was described in *Sidmouth's Royal Connections* as "a local story, which may or not be true." I couldn't resist including it.

If you would like to read more about the factual events of the royal party's visit, I recommend any of the books about Queen Victoria's life quoted in the epigraphs of this novel, especially *The Young Victoria* by Deirdre Murphy and *Sidmouth's Royal Connections* by Nigel Hyman. It was through Nigel's book that I read Sidmouth resident Charlotte Cornish's eyewitness account of visiting Woolbrook Cottage while the duke was lying in state, and her description of the funeral procession on its way, ultimately, to Windsor. I found these details especially interesting to read after the death of Queen Elizabeth II and all the solemn observances surrounding her funeral. I was touched to be in Britain when she passed away.

You may recognize Nigel Hyman's name from my previous author's note, where I thanked him for all his help in researching book one when I could not travel to Sidmouth in person. I am glad to say I have since been able to visit (August of 2022) and was delighted to meet him, Ann Tanner, Ann Jones, and the other Sidmouth Museum volunteers who have been, and continue to be, extremely helpful.

While in Sidmouth, my husband and I stayed at the Royal Glen Hotel, formerly known as Woolbrook Cottage. We slept in the room the Duke of Kent used and saw the nursery window the local lad shot through, now marked with a colored pane of glass. We enjoyed our time there.

Antoine Bernardi is a fictional character, yet he and his recipes were inspired by two actual chefs: Antonin Carême and Charles Francatelli.

Publishing rivals John Wallis and John Marsh are historical figures, as are Edmund Butcher, Emanuel Lousada, Abraham Mutter, Charlotte Cornish, Sir John and Lady Kennaway, Sir Thomas Acland, Dr. Wilson, Dr. Maton, John Conroy, General Wetherall, and of course the Duke and Duchess of Kent and Strathearn, but they appear in the novel in fictionalized form. Other characters are not meant to represent real people.

The passages from the guidebook Emily writes for Mr. Marsh were taken from the actual *The Sidmouth Guide* printed for John Marsh, with a few modifications.

The fencing lessons described in the book were drawn from various sources, especially a nineteenth-century article, "Nellie Bly Takes a Hand at Foils and Likes the Exercise." Any errors are mine.

As always, I am thankful for the helpful input I received from first reader Cari Weber, as well as Anna Shay and author Michelle Griep. Warm gratitude also goes to my agent, Wendy Lawton, my editors, Karen Schurrer, Rochelle Gloege, and Hannah Ahlfield, cover designer Jennifer Parker, and my entire team at Bethany House Publishers.

Finally, thank you again for reading my books. I appreciate each and every one of you! For more information about me and my other novels, please follow me on Facebook or Instagram, and sign up for my email list via my website, www.julie klassen.com.

Discussion Questions

1. In the nineteenth century, many people visited the seaside and even went sea-bathing during the winter—not only in summertime. Does this surprise you? If you read book one (which took place in spring and summer), in what ways was it a different experience to "visit" Sidmouth in the winter?

2. Which character(s) from *The Sisters of Sea View* did you most enjoy revisiting and why? Did you miss anyone from book one? Do you have a favorite new character? Least favorite?

3. This novel incorporates a fictionalized account of the wintertime retreat of (the future) Queen Victoria, her parents, and their staff in Sidmouth. What, if anything, most interested you about these historical figures and their time in Sidmouth (e.g., the local youth shooting through the nursery window, the fortune-teller's prediction, the Duke of Kent's death, et cetera)?

4. Mrs. Denby reminds Emily and Viola that the "Scriptures warn us to have nothing to do with divination

or soothsayers [fortune-tellers]." In what way is her warning timely even in today's world? How does Emily go from being devastated by the woman's prophecy about her own future to remembering that God is the one who holds our lives in His hands?

5. Which do you prefer: cooking or baking? Did you enjoy reading the descriptions of the dishes prepared by Mr. Bernardi? Any you'd like to try to make yourself?

6. What did you think about Sarah and Mr. Bernardi's relationship? What did they learn from each other? Do you think Sarah made the right decision about Mr. Bernardi in the end?

7. Emily has long pined for her first love. In what ways does his reappearance impact her? Did you care for him? Would you have forgiven him for his past actions?

8. When this former neighbor shares fond memories of Emily's father, Emily realizes that "she'd too often allowed the difficult months after his apoplexy to blot out the happier years before it." Have you ever experienced similar emotions or challenges when a loved one mistreated you or changed toward you? If you feel comfortable sharing, what have you learned from that?

9. At the beginning of the book (and series) Emily resented having to leave her former home (and first love) to move to Sidmouth. How does her attitude toward her new home and situation change by the end of this book? To what would you credit the change?

10. What do you hope will happen in book three in the ON DEVONSHIRE SHORES series?

Julie Klassen loves all things Jane—*Jane Eyre* and Jane Austen. Her books have sold over a million copies, and she is a three-time recipient of the Christy Award for Historical Romance. *The Secret of Pembrooke Park* was honored with the Minnesota Book Award for Genre Fiction. Julie has also won the Midwest Book Award and Christian Retailing's BEST Award, and has been a finalist in the RITA and Carol Awards. A graduate of the University of Illinois, Julie worked in publishing for sixteen years and now writes full-time. Julie and her husband have two sons and live in a suburb of St. Paul, Minnesota. For more information, you can follow her on Facebook or visit www.julieklassen.com.

Will an unexpected reunion bring
longed-for reconciliation . . .
or widen the divide?

Return to Sidmouth for more romance,
second chances, and sweet sisterhood
in book three of

ON DEVONSHIRE SHORES

*A Seaside
Homecoming*

Coming December 2024

Sign Up for Julie's Newsletter

Keep up to date with Julie's latest news on book releases and events by signing up for her email list at the link below.

JulieKlassen.com

FOLLOW JULIE ON SOCIAL MEDIA

Author Julie Klassen   @julie.k.klassen   @Julie_Klassen

More from Julie Klassen

When their father's death leaves them impoverished, the Summers sisters open their home to guests to provide for their ailing mother. But instead of the elderly invalids they expect, they find themselves hosting eligible gentlemen. Sarah must confront her growing attraction to a mysterious widower, and Viola learns to heal her deeply hidden scars.

The Sisters of Sea View
On Devonshire Shores #1

In pursuit of an author who could help get her brother published, Rebecca Lane stays at Swanford Abbey, a grand hotel rumored to be haunted. It is there she encounters Sir Frederick—the man who broke her heart. When a mysterious death occurs, Rebecca is one of the suspects, and Frederick is torn between his feelings for her and his search for the truth.

Shadows of Swanford Abbey

Laura Callaway daily walks the windswept Cornwall coast, known for many shipwrecks but few survivors. And when a man with curious wounds and an odd accent is washed ashore, she cares for him while the mystery surrounding him grows. Can their budding attraction survive, and can he be returned to his rightful home when danger pursues them from every side?

A Castaway in Cornwall

BETHANYHOUSE

You Are Invited!

Join like-minded fans in the
Inspirational Regency Readers
group on Facebook.

From book news from popular
Regency authors like Kristi Ann Hunter,
Michelle Griep, Erica Vetsch, Julie Klassen,
and many others, to games and giveaways,
to discussions of favorite Regency reads and
adaptations new and old, to places we long
to travel, you will find plenty of fun and
friendship within this growing community.

Free and easy to join, simply search for
"Inspirational Regency Readers" on
Facebook.

We look forward to seeing you there!

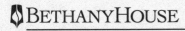